NEVER
ENOUGH

FORGE BOOKS BY HAROLD ROBBINS

Never Enough
Never Leave Me
The Predators
The Secret

NEVER ENOUGH

HAROLD ROBBINS

A TOM DOHERTY ASSOCIATES BOOK
NEW YORK

NEVER ENOUGH

Copyright © 2001 by Jann Robbins

All rights reserved, including the right to reproduce this book, or portions thereof, in any form.

This book is printed on acid-free paper.

A Forge Book
Published by Tom Doherty Associates, LLC
175 Fifth Avenue
New York, NY 10010

www.tor.com

Forge® is a registered trademark of Tom Doherty Associates, LLC.

ISBN 0-765-30000-1

First Edition: October 2001

Printed in the United States of America

0 9 8 7 6 5 4 3 2 1

Harold Robbins left behind a rich heritage of novel ideas and works in progress when he passed away in 1997. Harold Robbins's estate and his editor worked with a carefully selected writer to organize and complete Harold Robbins's ideas to create this novel, inspired by his storytelling brilliance, in a manner faithful to the Robbins style.

NEVER ENOUGH

PROLOGUE

JANUARY 15, 2000

David Shea took the last sip of his Dom Pérignon from the crystal flute. He watched as Marilyn Henry, a tall blond with an athletic body that showed she worked out at the gym every day, and Carrie Blake, equally as tall and with an equally well-toned body, jet-black hair, and a cherub face, cleared the table. Both were models. He looked out across his balcony. His apartment on the eighteenth floor looked out over the East River. The twinkling lights of the city painted a spectacular view of Manhattan.

He turned as Marilyn filled the flute with more champagne. He looked across the table at Ron Bryant, his attorney. He appeared deep in thought. Only his graying temples betrayed his handsome, youthful face. He had chosen Ron Bryant after Cole had refused to represent him any longer. He made his choice because Ron was a self-made man. He had served as a colonel in the air force before going to law school at Oklahoma University, and he represented Chase Manhattan after the fall of the oil business in Oklahoma during the eighties.

"Okay, Counselor, what's on your mind? You have been distracted since you walked in the door."

Ron looked over toward the two girls in the kitchen. He got up and started toward the balcony. "Let's go outside."

He and Dave both pulled out cigars. Ron lit his Cuban. Dave, who had never smoked in his life until a few months ago, lit up his cigarillo. He took a deep drag.

They both stared out at the view. "Giuliani is after you," Bryant said finally.

"It's not the first time someone has been after me." Dave shrugged.

"I know, but you're a great target for a man who is considering running for the Senate. Wall Street is a safe target. You saw what he did to Milken and Boesky. He was relentless. The good guys get the bad guys. A politician's dream and the voters love it."

"I am a good guy. I've made millions for people. I am the 'American Dream.' I came from nothing, I made my own opportunities. I was born with my assets, looks and charm and determination. I didn't have a trust fund or a pedigree," Dave said in his own defense.

"You've stepped on a lot of people along the way. You're exposed."

"They have nothing. Anybody who could give them any information is in just as deep as I am, and none of them would want to be exposed. People in high places keep their mouths shut."

Dave turned and faced into the apartment. Marilyn and Carrie had settled on the sofa. Marilyn was rubbing Carrie's leg.

"There's a better view right here." Dave smiled as he took another drag from the cigarillo.

Ron turned to look into the living room. Marilyn's hand had traveled up under Carrie's skirt. Carrie lifted her skirt, revealing her black lace-top hosiery. She wore no underwear other than the hosiery. Carrie reached out and began to play with Marilyn's hardening nipples under her tight cotton T-shirt.

"Are you familiar with Tabatha Morgan?" Ron questioned.

"ADA. She called Janelle in once and questioned her about me. But I resolved that problem."

"Maybe not, her name came up," Ron said distantly.

Marilyn took off her T-shirt and began to moan as Carrie gently grazed her nipple with her teeth.

Dave thought for a moment. "Let's see what we can get on this 'would-be' senator."

They walked inside and joined the two ladies.

ONE

SATURDAY EVENING, APRIL 20, 1974

Four of them were together that Saturday evening: Dave Shea, Cole Jennings, Bill Morris, and Tony DeFelice. These four had minor reputations as more than troublemakers.

Dave Shea was a handsome young man, tall and muscular, a football player. He was very charismatic. Every girl's dream was to date Dave Shea. He had been his school's quarterback for two years, during which his team lost only one game. In his senior year the team went undefeated. Besides that, he was an outstanding scholar. He was inducted into the National Honor Society in his junior year. His special subjects were mathematics, chemistry, and physics. As of April he had accepted a football scholarship at Rutgers University. Without the scholarship he would have been unable to go to college. But he had the scholarship and his future seemed assured.

But he had a dark side. It wasn't alcohol. The fact was that Dave was a *cheat*. He did it on the football field, where he had an exceptional talent for knowing when officials weren't looking and then clipping, face-mask violations, even for punching an opposing player in the nose. In close contact with a defensive lineman, he started his "trash talk." Calling people names until he would get them to react. A trick that could get a star defense man ejected from the game, while Dave stood gaping and shaking his head, wondering what had caused the foul. In the chemistry lab he knew

11

what results were expected from a problem in qualitative analysis and pretended to have achieved that result, when he really hadn't. He was in fact a good player and a good student, but he had his little tricks to make himself look even better.

"You're good enough, Shea," Cole said one day. "Why not play it straight . . . ?"

"Look, Jennings. Your family will send you to college, no matter what. You're smart, too, but you don't need a scholarship. I *do*. I have to cover myself . . . be better than good . . ."

"Gotcha. But you *are* good enough!"

"Yeah? Well, I'm looking for a little insurance on it. The son of a wholesale grocery salesman who drives around the county begging for little orders . . . Hey! They add up their nickels every month, hopin' there's enough to make the payment on the car. I don't want to live like that, Jennings!"

He didn't want to live without sex either. He first shoved his big penis into a girl when he was thirteen years old.

She was seventeen.

"Jesus Christ! The guys said you're . . . Hey, I can't take all that, Shea."

"Bet ya can," he said, with a hard-on that ached for release.

He began to enter her slowly until he was buried deep inside her.

"God almighty! Hey! I wouldn't have believed it!"

Eventually, Amy, who also declared she couldn't possibly, did. And complained it hurt. But he couldn't get enough, and after the first time neither could she.

Cole Jennings played basketball and was good at it. He was tall, six feet six, and had an indefinable agility on the polished floor that brought him recognition as a valuable player. His blond hair fell over his forehead as he dribbled toward the basket, dodging this way and that, avoiding the players trying to guard him, until at the last moment he passed the ball to a teammate close to the goal and charged in to take the rebound if the shot missed. He made most of his points by capturing rebounds and jamming the ball through the basket.

He, too, was an excellent student. One of them, Dave or Cole, would be valedictorian of their high school class.

As Dave had suggested, Cole did not need a scholarship, athletic or academic, to go to college. His father was senior partner in a major realty firm. His family could and would pay his tuition at any school he wanted to attend.

From the time he was old enough to drive, Cole had his own car. That night he was driving his graduation present, already given him though graduation was seven weeks away. It was a black Pontiac TransAm. His parents had always indulged their son. His graduation was no exception.

Cole was a responsible, thoughtful young man, and even if he could burn rubber he didn't. Conservative, compared to Dave.

Dave envied Cole when he saw the beautiful black TransAm. Someday, he thought . . . someday . . . but he never even got to drive his father's old Chevy. That car was too important to making a living for his father to allow his son to drive it.

Bill Morris played both football and basketball, though he was not the star that Dave and Cole were. He spent most of his time on the bench. Even so, he "went out" for sports and was considered a jock. All of these four were. He was not the scholar his two friends were, either; and his parents had been squirreling away money for years, in anticipation of his college tuition. Bill would not win a scholarship.

He was a solid young man, not heavy enough for football and not tall enough for basketball. On the basketball floor he wore plastic-rimmed eyeglasses held in place by a rubber strap behind his head. On the football field he wore no glasses and relied on a slightly blurry vision of the developing play. Since he was a guard and all but invariably was blocked after he did or did not block *his* man, it made little difference. He was dark-haired, and oddly was already showing, on his forehead, the initial evidence of baldness.

Of the four, many would have called Tony DeFelice the one most likely to succeed. They were all jocks, but Tony was a jock in a very different sense. He was a Golden Gloves boxer with a promising future.

He was a welterweight, knife-thin, with muscles as hard as the steel of a knife. Many were afraid of him, but he had been trained to restrain himself and never use his boxing skills outside the ring. His ambition was to go to the Olympics and then to turn professional.

He was an extremely intense young man, with hard eyes. People who knew him well were aware that he had a ready sense of humor and found amusement in all manner of things and people.

His family owned a score of packer trucks and collected trash and garbage over a wide area of Bergen County. They were said to be "connected." They were a family of shrewd, hardworking Italian immigrants, who had hauled first in a single mule-drawn wagon and had gradually worked their way up to the considerable business they now owned.

On this humid April Saturday night it was the same old thing: nothing to do. They were silent as they listened to Bruce Springsteen sing his latest hit. The four boys had bought six-packs of beer and drunk twenty bottles between them. The remaining four bottles were on the floor of the backseat of Cole's car. A little after ten Cole drove into the parking lot of Pizza Palace on the edge of Wyckoff.

The Palace might more realistically have been called the shack. It had only four small tables. Customers were expected to take delivery of their pizzas and drive them home. The boys ordered two pizzas and returned to the car to wait the twenty minutes until their pizzas would be ready. They opened their last four bottles of beer and talked about whether or not they should drive off during the twenty minutes and buy another six-pack or two.

They had sat there, drinking their last beers and talking aimlessly when Jim Amos came alongside the car.

"Well, if it ain't Slaw," he said in a beer-slurred voice. Slaw was a nickname sometimes fastened on Cole. He didn't like it, but he didn't make an issue of it. "New wheels, Slaw?" Amos goaded.

Amos was twenty-four years old and had served four years in

the United States Navy. He was known in the town and area as a drunk and a bully. He would walk up to a smaller and younger boy on the street and ask him what was the finest service in the United States Armed Forces. The boy might not know that Amos had been in the navy and might say United States Marines or something else. If he didn't say navy, Amos might deck him.

Or he might say, "You're wrong, and I'll let you buy me a few drinks to make up for it."

In any case, Jim Amos was a bully. He'd been beaten up two or three times, for having taken a swing at the wrong man; but that had not discouraged him, and he remained a two-bit punk, looking for someone to intimidate.

Tonight he was feeling aggressive.

"Slaw and his Three Muskeeters. Mommy and Daddy get this for baby boy?" he said as he hopped up on the fender and sat.

Dave came out of the passenger side, fast, and rushed around the car. "Get your ass down from there, Amos," he yelled.

"Y' gonna make me?"

"I'm gonna make you."

Cole was out of the car now, followed by Bill and Tony from the backseat.

"Oh. All four of you. Fine. Suits me. Who's first?"

Dave grabbed Amos by the legs and threw him off the fender, onto the gravel of the parking lot. Amos was drunk, but he was quick and strong. He scrambled up and charged Dave, throwing a shoulder against his chest and knocking him back against the car, where he was vulnerable to the punch to the chin that Amos threw. Dave was dazed for a second.

Amos set himself to throw more punches to Dave's face and down one of his opponents. But Cole grabbed him from behind and wrestled him away. He punched him hard on the kidneys.

Amos broke out of Cole's grip, turned, and punched him in the stomach. Cole doubled over and vomited beer.

Bill stunned Amos with a hard punch to the ear.

Dave had gained his sense with a fury. As Amos was momentarily disoriented, Dave shot a hard fist against his nose, which collapsed in a spray of blood. Amos shook his head and moaned. His knees began to buckle. He was finished.

But Dave's anger was not assuaged. He stepped up to the staggering Amos and put every ounce of his weight and strength into a crushing blow to Amos's jaw. Amos dropped backward to the gravel. His head hit with a sickening crunch.

The police arrived a moment later. One of the officers knelt beside Amos and examined him.

"This man is dead."

The families gathered at the Bergen County Jail.

The Sheas were frightened. Dave's mother was weeping, and his father's lips trembled. "That poor boy! That *poor* boy!" Mrs. Shea kept murmuring through her tears. She meant Jim Amos.

The Jennings family was grimly composed. Stuart Jennings was prepared to confront trouble and had summoned his lawyer.

The Morrises seemed not to comprehend what was going on. Their faces were blank, as though they were in shock, which in fact they were.

Anthony DeFelice glowered. When his father arrived he told him to keep his mouth shut and slapped him on the side of the head.

Witnesses from Pizza Palace assembled to give statements. None of the witnesses was quite sure what had happened, except that all agreed Tony DeFelice had not hit Amos.

From that point, all was confusion.

"Those three there, they all hit him. I seen 'em," an old man with a three-day stubble of white whiskers declared.

"It was self-defense," Dave asserted angrily.

"Three of you? Self-defense against *one feller?*"

A fat girl spoke. "Jim Amos was a drunken bully. He was always starting fights."

"We know that," said the chief of police. He was a muscular, middle-aged man in a tan uniform. "On the other hand . . . well—"

"He's dead," said the old man. "An' three of 'em were beatin' up on 'im."

"Which one of you swung the punch that broke his neck?" asked the chief of police.

"Uh . . . just a moment," said a white-haired man with a flushed face. "I'm going to advise these boys not to answer that question, or any others, until they've had a chance to consult with counsel."

The white-haired man was Lloyd Paul Strecker. He was attorney for the Jenningses and had arrived at the police station before they did. He had a formidable reputation in Bergen County, not just for being a tough lawyer but for his political connections.

An assistant district attorney arrived. Her name was Lela Goldish, and she was about thirty years old, an attractive young woman, with broad hips and a prominent ass. She was also hyper, moved in jerks and spoke in clipped sentences.

"What've we got here?" she asked.

The chief of police gave her a brief statement.

"Manslaughter," she said. "Maybe involuntary manslaughter. Sure as hell not murder."

"Okay," said Strecker. "I think these boys should be given a chance to confer among themselves. They are all involved. They should sing from the same sheet."

No one disagreed. Dave, Cole, Bill, and Tony went into a little conference room to talk.

Dave put his elbows on the table and his face in his hands. "Shit . . ." he said. "It's the end for me. Manslaughter charge. There goes my scholarship. There goes my fuckin' life. Even if I don't go to the slammer, Rutgers won't want me. It's the end!" He looked grim.

"You didn't have to hit him that last time," said Cole. "We had him. He was finished."

"I was . . . pissed," Dave said. "The *son of a bitch* . . ."

"We're the witnesses," said Tony calmly. "Whatever we say happened, happened. Self-defense."

"They won't buy that," Dave muttered. "Four of us . . ."

"Only the guy that shot the last punch," said Bill Morris. "He was out. The guy that—"

"Yeah, sure, Morris," said Dave. "I killed him."

"Jesus, man," said Cole. "I guess it's gonna go tough for you. I don't think you'll get a big sentence, but—"

"What the fuck does it matter!" Dave glared. "I'll wind up like my old man. A nobody."

"We oughta talk to the lawyer," said Tony.

They asked Strecker to come in.

"Here's where it stands," he told them immediately. "We can make it involuntary manslaughter. The man who threw the last punch can plead guilty to that. He'll get probation."

"But he'll have a felony record," said Dave despondently.

"Well . . . actually, that can be expunged from the records in a few years. It won't prevent a man from getting into law school, for example—because the record won't exist."

"But right now—" Dave muttered disconsolately.

"For a while it will be an impediment," said Strecker.

"An impediment that—"

"Can ruin his whole life," said Cole sadly.

"I see where this is going," said the lawyer. "I'm going to leave you boys to talk together."

With the lawyer out of the room, the four boys sat silent for a full minute. Then—

"I'm the one with the most to lose," said Dave. "You guys are going to college because your families can pay for it. Mine can't. My scholarship is the only way I'm going to get a college education. The only goddamned way."

"What you're saying," said Tony, "is that one of *us* should confess he shot the last punch."

Dave closed his eyes and nodded. "I'm the only one whose life is on the line."

"I'll go this far," said Tony coldly. "If one of these guys wants to take it, I won't screw it up. I won't tell the truth."

Dave looked at Cole. "You've got the *least* to lose. You're going to whatever university you choose, because your family will pay for it. You've got a first-class lawyer. Your family and your lawyer have got political connections. You can come out of this smelling like roses. *I* come out piled in shit."

Cole drew a deep breath. "Except for you, Tony, we all hit him. All of us. Dave couldn't have—Well, he couldn't have if Bill and I hadn't done what we did. I mean, I figure we *share* the responsibility. And—Dave's right. He's got the most to lose. I've got the least." He stood and opened the door. "Mr. Strecker—"

The lawyer listened gravely to what Cole told him. He shook his head. "All right. I don't buy it, but if that's what you want to do. I know what you have in mind."

The newspapers were angry.

TEENS BEAT NAVY VET TO DEATH!

Rampaging Wyckoff teenagers, drunk on beer, beat a navy veteran to death in the parking lot of Pizza Palace Saturday night.

What began as a Saturday-night rumble, arising from the fact that the veteran sat on the fender of a car belonging to Cole Jennings, 18, resulted, after a savage beating, in the death of James Amos, 24, a veteran of four years' service in the United States Navy.

Cole Jennings has entered a guilty plea to involuntary manslaughter. His companions, David Shea, William Morris, and Anthony DeFelice, have not been charged.

James Amos, Senior, father of the slain young man, says that his son had an exemplary record in the navy and had never been in any kind of trouble at home.

"Half the town believes that," said Bill Morris.

"And the other half knows what a prick Amos was," said Dave.

"Anyway . . . it's all settled," said Cole. "Three years probation, after which the record will be erased. I'm accepted at Princeton. And—" He turned to Dave. "Your scholarship is intact, and you'll be going to Rutgers."

Dave nodded. "I won't forget this, Cole."

Cole looked at him. "Yeah sure." He knew in his heart that Dave would never look back.

TWO

I

A SUNDAY AFTERNOON IN OCTOBER, 1976

"I don't like this. I don't feel right about it, Dave."

"Hey! C'mon, babe. You're *beautiful!*"

She knew she was beautiful. It was the governing fact of her life. It had attracted boys who had mistreated her and made her wary of all of them, Dave Shea not the least.

Her name was Sally McMillan.

Now twenty-one, she had been homecoming queen at Ramapo High School three years ago. Now she was a hospital receptionist and was taking courses on her slow way to what she hoped would be a college degree. She was a natural blond, with creamy skin and a spectacular figure that—together with her winsome personality—had won her election as homecoming queen: an honor she continued to cherish.

"I just don't feel right about it," she said again.

They were on a secluded wooded hillside, in an abandoned eighteenth-century burying ground. Dave had convinced her that posing nude among the ancient, tilted, flaking, greenish headstones would have a special artistic quality—especially now when a low sun cast long shadows, when leaves were yellow and red.

"Look at this place," he said. "What a setting!"

She had removed all her clothes except her panties and bra but

21

now hesitated to go further. "C'mon, now. What is it you're gonna do with these pictures?"

"Like I told you. Put 'em in an album."

"Just for you."

"Just for me."

"I imagine you've got other girls in that album."

Dave shook his head. "I don't tell tales."

She stiffened. "Promise me *nobody else* will see them."

"Nobody else will see them," he assured her. "You look great, babe. A real *Playboy* foldout."

Sally turned down the corners of her mouth and nodded. "I think I'm doing something stupid," she said. "I think I'm letting you talk me into being a dummy. You're not gonna want to—? This would be a perfect setting for that, too, wouldn't it?"

"Your body makes me crazy," he said. "Sure, I'd like to. But it's entirely up to you. I won't argue we should. I'm not gonna try to seduce you, babe. Anyway, I took some damned hard shots to the body in that game yesterday afternoon, and I'm not sure I can do it right now."

"Well . . ."

With what was maybe—or maybe was not—an exertion of will, Sally reached behind her back and unhooked her bra. Her breasts were large but solid; they did not hang down but stood on her chest like two half cantaloupes. Shiny pink areolae covered all the forward part of each breast, and her nipples were dark and wrinkled and prominent.

"*Jesus!*" muttered Dave.

"Wha'd you expect?"

She slipped out of her panties. That she was a blond was apparent. Her pubic hair was sparse, and her fleshy parts under it were not obscured.

Dave had a Nikon camera. He had borrowed it from Bill Morris, to whom he had promised a set of whatever pictures he took with it. He was shooting black-and-white film that he and Bill could process in the Morris family home darkroom. Sally supposed he was shooting color film that would show the autumn colors.

She dodged behind a lichen-covered headstone that read:

GEORGE MORRIS
1751–1809
LIEUTENANT, PENNSYLVANIA LINE

Behind the headstone, Sally's breasts were exposed, but her belly and hips were hidden. Dave shot several pictures.

"Okay, babe. Great so far. But you gotta come out from behind the stone."

She sighed. "Okay. But, hey, man, shoot a couple of my butt while I get used to this."

He shot one picture of her from behind, then suggested she bend over and pretend she was putting flowers on the grave. She did, maybe aware, maybe not aware, that this displayed her most private parts from behind.

"Moment of truth, honey babe."

Sally nodded. She turned and presented herself full-face.

"Y' know . . . I don't have to tell you how gorgeous you are. You see that every time you look in a mirror. It's a real damned privilege for me to see."

"C'mon, Shea. Take your pictures."

She posed in front of the tombstone, and he shot a dozen pictures. They moved around the old cemetery, and he photographed her standing at the collapsing wrought-iron fence that was supposed to enclose the place. He encouraged her to lie down and roll in the grass.

"Hey, Shea," she said after a while. "What you want me to do is *spread*. I mean, hey, c'mon, the *pink* parts! Shit!"

"I'm not asking," he said guiltily.

"Well, *there they are*, kiddo," she said, spreading her legs wide. "Take a picture of that!"

The photo shoot had aroused Sally, and she lay back on the

grass and let Dave enter her. He was bruised and sore, but the girl was okay; she had made him horny as all hell; and he performed better than he had supposed he could.

II

He sold forty-three sets of the nudes of the Ramapo High School homecoming queen at ten dollars for a set of five prints. He sold separately the picture of her with her legs spread wide—five dollars for a five-by-seven glossy black-and-white print—and nineteen boys bought those, too. After he'd paid Bill Morris for the film, paper, and chemicals, and given him his share, he had a profit of about) $275. It would buy his pizza and beer for quite a while.

That was how it was. He always needed money, and he always had to hustle for it. The university provided tuition, lab fees, books, and room and board. His fraternity waived dues in order to have a star jock on its roster. His father sent him twenty dollars a month.

When Dave met Julian Musgrave for dinner two weeks after he took his burying-ground pictures and was still peddling them, he came to the restaurant with a sense that maybe something important was about to happen for him.

Musgrave owned four automobile agencies in metropolitan New Jersey. He was a flamboyant character who featured himself in his television commercials. ("Hey! Check 'em out! Check 'em *all* out! If one of my trained salesmen doesn't make you a better deal, come right in and talk to *me* face-to-face. If I can't do better for you than anybody else in this area, I want to know why. If you've got a deal I can't match—and better—*buy* from the other guy! But I know I can beat 'em! So, c'mon in! What you got to lose?"

He was loud but not charismatic. A man of maybe fifty years, he was wiry and bald. He wore a Stetson to hide his baldness and his piercing dark eyes, which belied the bounciness that was his trademark.

He had arranged to meet Dave in a fine Italian restaurant in Patterson, where he was known and had been given the back booth he had asked for, where almost no one would see him talking with the star football player.

Musgrave was wearing a yellow-and-tan checked jacket, a white dress shirt, no tie, and did not have his hat on. Dave, not knowing what to expect, wore a blue blazer, white shirt, and striped tie.

Commenting that an athlete didn't drink hard liquor, Musgrave had told the waiter to bring a bottle of good, dry Chianti in a basket. When they had toasted, he raised a subject—

"Dave . . . has anyone ever suggested to you that you throw a game?"

Dave drew a deep breath. "No, sir," he said emphatically.

"What if someone did and offered a lot of money?"

"Maybe I shouldn't have met with you." He moved in the booth, ready to exit.

Musgrave grinned. "Relax. You're answering the way I wanted to hear. You say you wouldn't do it, huh? Good! Believe me, I'm not gonna suggest any such thing. I wanted to hear you tell me you wouldn't do it."

"I wouldn't do it," Dave said glumly.

"Well, you're the kind of young guy I want to talk to. Look. I'm an alum. And I'm a great booster of our university's football team. I don't suppose we'll ever win a national championship, but wouldn't that be *glorious*. I mean, hell, we beat Temple, we beat West Virginia . . . Great! How 'bout an undefeated season? How 'bout *that*?"

"That would be great," said Dave.

"I gotta wonder, though," said Musgrave. "You're out there on the field. Your thoughts one hundred percent on the game?"

"What else?"

"On money. I know something about your circumstances. I take the trouble to look into these things."

"I have to hustle," Dave admitted.

"I'll give you a hundred bucks for a set of those pictures."

"You know—?"

"My *son* bought a set—incomplete, I'm sure. I'll want 'em all. But that's small potatoes. Let's talk, Dave. We can work out something."

Over veal parmigiana their talk abandoned the subject Musgrave
had raised and ranged over other subjects: the likely outcome of
Saturday's game, Dave's course of study, his family, the automobile
business, the comparative merits of Buicks and Toyotas, Musgrave's
television commercials, the sexual activities of New Jersey girls and
whether they were different from those of girls anywhere, Sally
McMillan's tits, Dave's plans and hopes for the future . . .

Then Musgrave returned to what he had in mind. "I'd like to help
you, Dave. I'd like for you to be able to focus on the game alone."

"I can't take money, Mr. Musgrave."

"So they say. That's the rule. But who has to know and what's
the harm if from time to time I slip you a little cash?"

"If it's found out—"

"Why should it be found out? I've helped out a lot of players
before. Hell . . . nobody ever found out. Let's start with this. Suppose one of my guys goes to see your dad and says, 'Hey, man, I
can put you in a brand-new car for—' Whatever. A goddamned
good deal."

Dave smiled and shook his head. "I'm not sure my dad would
have the smarts to understand it."

"My guy says, 'We wanta do this for you because your son is
such a credit to Rutgers.' "

"I don't know . . ."

"What's your dad's car payment now?"

"About eighty dollars a month, I think."

"Suppose I said to him I can put him in a new Buick for *fifty*
dollars a month."

"Jesus—"

"You can't turn it down, Dave."

Dave nodded. "I can't turn it down."

"Okay! Now. For you. When we leave here tonight you'll be
wearing *my* hat. You live in the jocks' dorm, right? When you get
there, check the inside hatband. There's something there for you.
I'll see you again. There'll always be something for you. And all
you have to do is go out there and play your heart out for our
school."

"Well, I—"

"And let me tell you something else. When you graduate, if you've got nothing else waiting, you got a job with me. Man! A football guy like you! You start off as a salesman. Two, three years you'll be . . . Who knows?"

Dave left the restaurant wearing Musgrave's hat and feeling foolish under it. In his room in the dorm he looked inside the hatband and found four hundred dollars in twenty-dollar bills. An athlete was not supposed to take money. It was a serious offense. He unloaded the money into his foot locker and put the hat on a shelf in his closet.

"Hey, Shea! You got a phone call."

"Yeah?"

"Some guy named Bill Morris. Wants you to call him. Says it's urgent."

With a stack of quarters at hand, Dave dialed Bill's number on the pay phone.

"Hey, Shea! For Christ's sake! You heard about Sally?"

"What about Sally?"

"She jumped off the roof of the hospital. She's dead!"

During the following week he received in the mail envelopes containing four sets of the Sally photographs.

"Damnit, it's not our fault," he said to Bill Morris.

"Christ, everybody loved the way she looked!" Dave said with no expression. "She had a future."

SUNDAY AFTERNOON, APRIL 10, 1977

"The Buick is the finest car I ever owned," said Dave's father. "Mr. Musgrave is an honest dealer. I believe you know him."

"I've met him," said Dave.

"All these years driving Chevys and Plymouths . . . All I could afford. Now this. My! What a turn of good fortune."

"I hope you don't talk it around," said Dave.

"Oh, no. Mr. Musgrave said I shouldn't talk it around. Everybody would want the same deal. But, you know, it even makes my work easier. People are impressed when I come to see them in a beautiful new Buick."

"That's great."

They sat around a table scarred with cigarette burns, in the kitchen of their family home. Dave's parents smoked heavily, as did his brother. As a grocery salesman handling cigarettes, the elder Shea was able to lift several cartons of cigarettes a week, nobody wiser. They smoked whatever he could get: free samples, odd cartons from broken cases, and so on—often Marlboros, their favorites, but also Kools, L & Ms, Camels, Luckys, Chesterfields . . . Dave did not smoke and thought the house reeked.

"You'll be seeing Amy this afternoon?" said his mother.

Dave nodded.

"You treat that girl with respect, Dave," his father said. "She comes from a fine family."

"I treat all girls with respect."

"That's the ticket. I never knew a successful man who didn't treat women with respect."

"Key to success . . . ?"

"One of the keys."

"It doesn't hurt to play a decent game of football," his brother said sarcastically.

"Dave plays football well because he *devotes* himself to it. You should take note of that."

The brother grinned at Dave. "Oh, I do, I do."

Amy Sclafani's family had two cars. Dave was welcome to drive the older, which was a Chevy station wagon. He almost never drove his father's car. That car was his father's living. The station wagon—an olive-green car without wooden sides, dented and with fading paint—was Amy's mother's, and Amy's.

Dave and Amy liked to drive west, into the high country and among the lakes of northwestern New Jersey. People who thought of the state as metropolitan New Jersey didn't always realize there was a rustic New Jersey. Sometimes Dave and Amy drove as far as Kittatinny Mountain, but more often they stopped somewhere short of that and spread a picnic on the ground near a lake.

They had developed a habit. Dave sat behind the wheel. Amy sat naked from the waist down on the passenger side of the seat. He could glance over and see her exposed crotch. What is more, she always wore a sweatshirt or sweater she could pull up and bare her breasts. If another car came close to them, she could snatch down the sweatshirt and skirt in a second.

That afternoon they were driving on country roads they had come to know—never the main highways—toward one of the lakes.

"My father says I should treat you with respect."

"Oh, you do, Dave. You do."

She was a girl framed for sex and for motherhood. He fucked her often. She loved it. She took The Pill and threw herself into their lovemaking without reservation. She was proud of her body and was glad to show it. To him. She was . . . reluctant about anyone else.

"If it wasn't you, honey . . . I wouldn't. I love you, Dave," she said.

God! She was slippery. She was always well lubricated. He could have wished she were a little less. But he could easily plunge his hard cock into her, every last inch. And she loved it! After the first time or two, when she moaned and said he hurt her, she never again complained.

They reached the lake. He pulled the station wagon to a spot where they could sit and talk, where they could sit on the grass and munch the snacks she had brought, drink the Bloody Marys he had mixed and poured into a Thermos. No other cars were parked within fifty yards, but still they would not have the privacy to fuck, either in the car or outside. He kneaded her breasts and nipples. She lifted her shoulders and arched her back to shove her breasts forward, but her arousal was not enough to prevent conversation—

"You still acing everything?" she asked. She meant was he still an all-A student.

"I'm on my way to make Phi Beta Kappa by my senior year," he said.

"You son of a bitch," she said, shaking her head.

Amy was a student at Ramapo College and did not live on campus. She drove the station wagon to and from her classes. She was a year younger than Dave and was a sophomore.

"We can't make out here, baby," Dave said, nodding toward cars parked too close for them to put down the rear seats of the station wagon and lie down in the open space.

"I know, and I know what you want," she said.

She unbuckled his belt, and unzipped his pants, and pulled out his stiffly engorged penis. She glanced around to satisfy herself that no one could see, then lowered her head to his lap. The trouble with doing it in these circumstances was that she could not easily lick his scrotum, but he would accept what she gave, no matter. She worked on him. She sucked him into her mouth and massaged him with her tongue. When he came, she swallowed. That had been at first a little difficult, but she had grown to love the taste of him.

She did it on his repeated solemn assurance that no other girl had ever done it for him. That was not true, but she had no way to know otherwise.

THREE

I

FALL, 1977

Cole entered the hospital room hesitantly. He expected to see and hear nothing good.

"Hi, Shea."

"Hi, Jennings."

They still followed the teenage habit of calling each other by their last names.

"Can't tell you how sorry I am."

"Can't tell you how sorry *I* am."

In the West Virginia game Dave had suffered a broken leg. No matter how it healed, his football career was over. It would have been anyway at the close of the season, but—But there had been talk that he might be drafted as a pro. That was over now. Never a top candidate for the draft, he now had a reputation for being "brittle."

"Well . . . you're going to graduate with an awesome academic record."

Dave shrugged. "Which gets me what?"

"A hell of a lot, damnit. It's your entrée into just about anything you might want to do."

"Mr. Musgrave wants me to sell cars."

"I think the less said about him the better."

"What do you know about Musgrave?"

"More than I want to know. And let's forget it."

"What do you know about Musgrave?"

"It was gonna come out. You're not the first athlete he—"

"It's gonna come out? It's gonna . . . ?"

Cole shook his head. "No. Not to worry. But Julian Musgrave is a crook. Whatever you do in this world, don't go to work for him."

"Sure. Easy to say. So, what *am* I supposed to do?"

"With your education . . . your personality, you could sell ice cubes to Eskimos, My father invests with a broker. Think about the world of finance. Man, you could do worse."

Dave sighed loudly. "Better than selling groceries wholesale."

II

FALL, 1978

His first year at Harvard Law was the most challenging year Cole Jennings ever experienced. He didn't know it, but it was the same even at second-rate law schools all over the country. Because of the expenditure of resources, medical schools accepted only the best and graduated most of them. Law schools tended to give a lot of people a chance, then flunk out a majority of those who enrolled. The course was not terribly challenging, intellectually, but there was a vast amount of material that had to be read and understood.

In June he married Emily. They leased an apartment in Cambridge.

"I hope you don't mind that I ordered in a pizza again," she said. "I was at the library longer than I expected."

While Cole was in law school, Emily was taking graduate courses in French literature. She spoke fluent French, also some German.

Emily was a tall, slender blond: a natural blond who used nothing on her hair. The only defect of her face was dental: her teeth were prominent. She had small breasts, soft and pear-shaped. Her pubic hair was scanty and hid little, and she had accepted Cole's suggestion that she shave it off, which she let him do a few days after their wedding. Because her inner labia were conspicuous, like fleshy, shiny pink petals, she was reluctant to display them and usually wore panties if she wore nothing else.

That was what she wore now, as they sat down to dinner: the pizza she had ordered. Her breasts were bare. She let him see them whenever they were at home alone.

"Why should I care," Cole asked, "if a guy goes into a store in the 1920s and buys a radio because the storekeeper promises him that radio will pick up Vatican radio and he can listen to the pope—and the radio won't?"

"So? It's got to have something to do with—"

"Contract law," Cole said.

"So? You're going to be a lawyer, you've got to know contract law."

They sipped the red wine she had bought to go with their pizza.

"Cole . . . ?"

"What, hon?"

"You want to get me pregnant?"

"Yeah. I sure do. But don't you think we ought to graduate first?"

"Right. Well, yes, right. I guess . . . I guess if I get your cock in me every night I can't complain."

"I do the best I can."

"What do you hear from Dave?"

"Well . . . Something you had to figure. Amy's pregnant. They're getting married."

Emily shook her head. "She shouldn't marry that son of a bitch. He's going to wind up in the penitentiary."

"Not Dave."

"Why not?"

"He's too fucking smart. He knows all the angles."

III

Dave sat in a booth with Julian Musgrave, in an Italian restaurant in Patterson.

"Look at it this way," he said. "I took your money. And don't think I'm not grateful. And . . . I lived up to my share in the bargain and played my ass off on the football field, until I got my leg broken."

Musgrave, now not as ebullient as he characteristically was, nodded solemnly. "I thought of you as a son, kind of," he said. "Christ, man, with your reputation and personality, you could have sold cars for me. You'd have made a goddamned *fortune!*"

"Yeah, maybe. And don't think I scorn that. But, Julian—"

Musgrave winced at hearing his first name used.

"—as good as your offer was, it was limiting. I chose to go into a business where I can—"

"You can make *ten* fortunes, if you can make it work."

"Well . . . It's a *chance.* You're the last guy in the world who wouldn't take a chance."

Musgrave turned his fork in his pasta and lifted it to his mouth. "Football doesn't cut any ice on this deal."

"Football is history," said Dave. "I played because I couldn't go to college without it. You helped me a lot, and I am grateful."

"I don't . . . You tell me this stock is gonna be okay."

"I'm not suggesting you put everything in it. I believe it deserves a major commitment. God knows if I had the money, I'd put a hell of a lot in it. But I'm just getting started. I do the research, Julian. I don't fiddle around. I work hard. I look into companies. You know me. You know I don't give less than a hundred percent to whatever I do."

"So you want me to put . . . a hundred thousand into this. Two?"

"Whatever you can do comfortably."

"And your commission on the sale won't hurt you."

"Understood. But let something else be understood. If I steer just one or two clients wrong, I'll be washed up in this business. It's not a forgiving line of work."

At home the hugely pregnant Amy knelt on the floor and gave Dave oral sex. Dave was bored, he was thinking about business, even though his cock was hard.

"Well, is he gonna do it?" Amy asked later.

"To the tune of a hundred fifty thousand."

"And our commission?"

"It'll pay the rent," Dave said, and smiled.

Dave was with a firm named Barnaby, Jenkins & Associates. Jenkins was the active partner.

"Good enough, Shea," he said to Dave. "A hundred and a half. To tell you the truth, I'm not that confident of Littleton. But I gather you are."

"Yes, sir. I've done the research."

Robert Jenkins was a somewhat flamboyant character, given to double-breasted suits and colorful bow ties. He presided at a massive desk in a corner office in a building in Jersey City, from where he had a view of Manhattan—which was Dave's goal; he didn't intend to remain long in New Jersey. Over there was where it was *big*, and that was where he meant to go.

Jenkins was observant. He noticed Dave staring at the towers of lower Manhattan. "When you've got a corner office over there, you'll look across the water and see me. I'll still be here."

"I'll be damned lucky if I do as well as you do, sir."

"Cut the bullshit, Shea. It'll never do you any good. And quit calling me 'sir.' I'm Bob."

"Bob . . ."

"Never call a customer 'sir.' Never. You can call him 'Mister Somebody' for a while, but get on a first-name basis as soon as you can. That sets up the relationship between you. No lawyer ever calls his client 'sir.' No doctor calls his patient 'sir.' And you don't either. You're a *professional*, Dave. Act like one."

"Thanks, Bob."

IV

FALL, 1979

"There's a limit," Emily said to Cole. "Your family and mine have—have . . ."

"Okay. Okay. But—"

"Tell me for sure," she said. "What exactly is your objection?"

"My wife posing nude, that's my objection."

"Your wife can make twenty dollars an hour. Doing not much. It won't interfere with your classes or mine. Five hours a week, I've got us a hundred bucks."

"Emily, you—"

"I know. I don't like to show my cunt. But we've asked our families as much as—"

"They're not complaining."

"I am. Cole . . . we're talking about legitimate art classes. I wouldn't . . . We're building a *future*! Let me contribute."

V

JANUARY, 1980

On January 3, 1980, Amy gave birth to a son that she and Dave named David Louis Shea. Amy nursed the child for several months.

"Hey, honey baby. Go on. The little fellow is *hungry*. Jack has seen tits before. Hell, his wife has a couple, I suppose. Go on."

Jack Silver was a junior vice president of Stuyvesant Banking & Trust, where he was known as a young man in a hurry. He was a little older than Dave and had a flushed face, tense with enthusiasm. He was becoming prematurely gray.

Amy gave the little boy a breast. Jack didn't pretend not to watch.

"I suppose we can talk—" said Jack.

"In front of Amy? Whatever we say, I'll tell her later. She's my *partner*."

Amy smiled. She held the baby to her breast and let it suckle. Her blouse fell open and exposed her other breast. She didn't cover it.

"Anyway . . . there's a chance here to make a killing," said Jack Silver. "I've put friends into it. But there's a limit. If the word gets around that—"

"You're into it too heavy—" said Dave.

"I'm in deep shit."

"But I, being a broker, can—"

"You got it. We have a week."

"Okay."

They sat at the dining table in the Sheas' modest apartment. They'd eaten pork chops with mashed potatoes and broccoli. Jack Silver had come directly from his office and wore a dark brown suit. Dave had been at home awhile before Jack arrived and wore blue jeans and a sweatshirt. Amy, too, wore blue jeans with the white open blouse where her baby nursed.

"It's simple enough," Jack said. "On Tuesday, AGD Corporation will announce FDA approval of something it calls Bioxin. Clinical tests have demonstrated that the little pill, taken daily, sharply reduces the risk of heart attack. Now . . . the market is going to be skeptical. But when the FDA confirms its action—Do I have to tell you?"

"It's selling at . . . ?"

"Forty-three and three-quarters. In two weeks . . . who knows?"

"My role is?"

"To put it out to people who couldn't possibly know anything about AGD and Bioxin. So the SEC can't possibly trace it back to me."

"Insider information," said Amy.

"It's called that," Jack agreed.

"I buy some for myself," said Dave.

"Sure. Hell, I'll lend you enough to buy a thousand shares."

"Where do *you* come out?"

"Two or three fake investors, trading under assumed names," said Jack. "I'm one of them, but I've got other guys. I'll pick up my profit, don't worry."

Dave looked at Amy. She was quietly nursing her baby, showing no concern. "It's how money is made, hon," he said to her.

"I never figured it any other way," she replied with a shrug.

Jack picked up his glass and sipped wine. "I'm glad we all understand each other." He grinned. "You've got great tits, Amy," he said.

She nodded. "I know. Why do you think this guy married me."

VI

JUNE, 1981

Cole graduated second in his class. In February he had been initiated into the Order of the Coif, an honor for law students. He interviewed with Hale & Dorr in Boston and with Davis Polk & Wardwell in New York but in the end decided not to affiliate with these prestigious firms but with a smaller firm named Harris & Pickens, which had offices in the Empire State Building.

He and Emily rented a tiny apartment in Midtown; and although H&P paid him forty-one thousand dollars a year as a starting salary, she continued modeling at the Art Students League.

Until she became pregnant.

"You can do it until—"

"Until it shows," she said. "Actually, after that. There's one hell of a fine sculptor who asks for pregnant models. He does beautiful bronzes of girls with big bellies and sells them for premium prices."

"C'mon, Emily!"

"All right. As soon as I begins to show, I'll quit."

Cole embraced her. "You can't imagine how much I love you."

"I love you, too, Cole."

A joke in the big New York firms was that a new young lawyer spent his first year finding out where the men's rooms in the courthouses were, then a year carrying briefcases for senior lawyers. That was why Cole had joined Harris & Pickens: because he would have real responsibilities much earlier.

"Mr. Jennings, review this file. Then come and tell me what you think we should do about it."

The file represented a lawsuit filed by a multitude of plaintiffs in a

class-action case. They contended that ARZO Corporation manufactured unsafe toys: plastic items that children could swallow.

"Is our client liable for the fact that kids stick things in their
mouths?" he said to his senior partner a few days later. "Hell, can't
you manufacture golf balls, tees, Ping-Pong balls . . . ? I'd tell them
to go to the devil. Besides, that firm does this all the time. It's a
thing with them. In my judgment, it's high time they got their ass
beat."

H&P eventually sent him to try the case. A more senior lawyer
was with him in the courtroom, but Cole argued the case to the
jury—

"What are we to say? That you can't manufacture nails, screws,
or bolts because they are so small that some child somewhere might
choose to put one in his mouth and swallow it? Paper clips, ladies
and gentlemen? Thumb tacks? Is there a limit? Marbles. Kids love
to play with marbles. But some child puts one in his mouth and
swallows it. Are we going to eliminate the game of marbles? Jacks?
What else?"

The jury found for the defendant.

FOUR

1982

Dave could not play music, not on any instrument. He never even cared much about music until he decided he was in love with a young woman who was an accomplished pianist.

Her name was Greta Sorensen, she was nineteen years old, and she was a gorgeous beauty with shoulder-length blond hair. Though she was a talented pianist, recognized as the winner of important competitions, people who knew her well described her as predatory. Her talent and her career meant everything to her, and she had no scruples about using people who could help her attain her ends.

Dave and Amy had been given tickets to Greta's concert by one of Dave's clients. After the concert, Dave excused himself as he and Amy waited for the crowd to leave. Dave went backstage and introduced himself to Greta. He gave her his card and asked her to dinner the next evening.

Amy was pregnant again. She had begun a slow process of losing her youth and her figure. She was loyal to Dave. She knew he was involved in illegal trading, but he knew he could be confident that she would never reveal anything.

Greta lived in a tiny, inexpensive apartment in Ridgefield, where she had a Steinway piano worth as much as the building. Dave loved sexy lingerie and kept her well supplied with it. When she sat and played the piano for him, she would be dressed in black bra, black panties, a black garter belt, and black stockings. The truth was, after a while he was easily bored with her music, but he enjoyed seeing her erotically dressed and seated at the piano.

"You know it can't come to pass, Greta," he said to her one evening when she had played for him and was still sitting on the piano stool. "I'm married, and my wife is pregnant with my second child."

"I know," she said. "I knew from the day I met you that we had no future together. We've only got *now!* I never asked for anything more."

"And the first chance you get, you'll—"

"Sure. You figured any other way?"

Dave grinned. "Jesus!"

"Jesus has got nothing to do with it, love. You have the biggest cock I ever saw, and you know how to use it. And . . ." she said playfully, "I can always use a couple bucks."

II

"Damnit, Dave, it's undercapitalized." said Cole.

"I know that. You know that. But the fuckin' world doesn't know it. And by the time the world finds out, B&G may have made ten fuckin' million."

"Or may have *lost* ten fuckin' million—in which case we'd be in deep shit."

"Look over there," said Dave. He pointed to the towers of Manhattan. "That's where *I'm* going. That's where it is, man. Not here in New Jersey. I'm gonna have an office in one of those buildings. And you don't get there, or anywhere, if you're afraid to take *chances.*"

"Yeah? Well, I'll tell you what you do, Dave. You drive up to Danbury, Connecticut, and take a look at the federal slammer. That's where your office may be. Plenty of guys have 'offices' up there—with locked doors."

"Somebody figured them out. You have to be smarter. You have to cover your ass."

"How you expect to cover? You're gonna sell shares in B&G; and hell, man, B&G doesn't have enough capital to go into the business it has in mind."

"It will when the shares are sold," said Dave.

"And what if you can't sell enough shares? The people who do buy are going to be left out on the limb."

"I'll cover them."

"With what?"

"There'll be something. There'll always be something. I'll give them another opportunity."

"Dave . . . what you're gonna do is *lie*. And that's what gets you an office in Danbury."

"I'll make you a little bet," said Dave. "I'll *never* see the inside of Danbury or any other slammer. I'll bet you a hundred thousand dollars that ten years from now I won't have been prosecuted, won't have risked the slammer, and will have a bank account of . . . well—say, ten million."

"Sucker bet. If you're inside Danbury, you won't be able to pay a nickel."

Dave grinned. "You're too damned smart, my friend. So, are you in or out?"

"In. Because *you're* too damned smart."

III

Tony DeFelice sat with Cole and Emily, and with his wife Margot, over a Chinese dinner in a restaurant on Lexington Avenue. Tony and Cole had remained friends. Cole had been best man at Tony's wedding to Margot Donofrio. Tony had won gold at the Olympics and had won some significant bouts as a welterweight boxer but in the end had wound up with nothing to show for it but a misshapen nose. And a gold medallion displayed prominently in his house. He had gone into the DeFelice family business, which now operated forty packer trucks in Bergen County. In the six years since the death of Jim Amos, Tony had become a prosperous young businessman. He was taking night classes in business administration at

Ramapo College and was valued by his family as the son who might turn their business into a business empire. The gold medal he won opened plenty doors.

The DeFelice family remained not "connected," only their relatives were. The Donofrios—Margot's family—definitely were, though the relationship was vague. It was convenient. But no more. The Donofrios handled labor relations for the DeFelices, as a family accommodation. They did not claim or take a percentage, though the DeFelices were careful not to let their assistance go unrewarded.

"I don't know how to look at it," Tony said to Cole. "That guy has got his nerve, doesn't he?"

"He's a hustler, Tony. He always was."

"Right. You took the fall for what he did to Amos."

"Amos had it coming," said Cole. "Anyway . . . it would probably have ruined Dave's life. It didn't ruin mine."

"Jim Amos was on his way to destruction," said Margot grimly.

She was a beautiful young woman, in a distinctively Italian way. Her dark eyes were deep and wise. Her black hair hung smoothly beneath her ears. She was fleshy. Her breasts were huge, affording her a deep, shadowy décolletage. They were on show tonight, swelling above a modest neckline on her black dress.

When Margot said Amos had been on his way to destruction, the statement could have had a gruesome connotation—or might have been only a casual comment.

"What's Dave want now?" Emily asked.

Emily had emerged comfortably from pregnancy and the birth of the daughter they named Emily. She was again slender and graceful, wearing an emerald-green dress with a miniskirt.

"Dave's selling a stock he says is going to make a killing," Tony explained. "It's called B&G, and he says it's going to make big money for its initial investors."

"I wouldn't believe that son of a bitch if he told me the sun will come up tomorrow morning," said Emily.

"Well . . . I'm looking for advice," said Tony.

"Tony . . ." said Cole quietly. "I wouldn't invest with Dave. Anyway, I wouldn't put in any money I couldn't afford to lose."

"He's damned persuasive," said Tony. "Maybe a few thousand . . ."

IV

As Cole had hoped would be the case, his affiliation with Harris & Pickens involved him in a variety of matters. He was not compelled to become a specialist.

In autumn of 1982 he was handed a file that was all but unique.

Sara Belle Lucas was a worker in a Bronx bakery. She was a woman of thirty-three, a little heavier than was stylish, and had coarse features.

Her duty at the bakery was to pour ingredients into a large mixer, where they became dough. One day in the spring she leaned over the mixer to clear flour off the sides of the tub, and the blades caught her blouse and drew her, screaming in terror, into the machine. By the time coworkers could shut down the mixer, Sara Belle had lost her left breast.

Workers' compensation and the bakery's insurance company paid her medical expenses. But they emphatically refused to pay her a pension, arguing that the want of a breast did not affect her employability. A woman with one breast could work as she had worked before, mixing dough—or, for that matter, selling threads and buttons, or whatever.

She sat down across Cole's desk.

"They won't acknowledge what I lost," she wept. "I mean . . . in the first place, what guy wants to marry a girl with one tit?"

"Unfortunately," he told her, "Workers' compensation has to do only with the ability to make a living. Disfiguration doesn't come into it. If you were an actress and suffered irreparable scars—"

"So they've said. But let me tell you something. Look at me. I'm no goddamned ravin' beauty, but I made half my income by dancing naked in cheap clubs."

"Then—?"

"Oh, no. That's not a legitimate way of making a living. Income I lose by not being able to do that anymore doesn't count."

She opened her blouse and showed him her ugly scar.

Cole argued her case in court, before the jury.

"I repectfully cite to the Court the Ohio case of *Grumble v. Workmen's Compensation Commission*. In that case, a striptease dancer stumbled over the footlight fixtures in a barely lighted theater and fell into the orchestra pit, breaking her leg. The Commission refused her compensation, saying that strip dancing was not legitimate employment. The Supreme Court of Ohio overruled unanimously, noting that what she was doing was not illegal, only that it did not meet approval with a large segment of society."

The judges frowned hard at Cole Jennings, but they did not interrupt his argument.

"Suppose my client were a blackjack dealer in a casino," he went on. "And suppose somehow, in the course of her employment, she injured her hand and could no longer deal blackjack. The legislature could have enacted a law saying that only certain specified occupations came under the benefits of the Workers' Compensation Law. Or it could have enacted a law excluding some occupations—in which case we might have before us a constitutional argument. But it didn't.

"As a result of an industrial accident, my client was deprived of her ability to earn a significant part of her income from a not-unlawful activity."

The court ruled in favor of Sara Belle Lucas and ordered she be paid annual benefits.

It was not the first or last time when a client asked to supplement payment of her fees and offered an alternative—

"I can't pay you much, Mr. Jennings," she said. "You know I gotta support other people. But what I ain't able to pay . . . I'll be glad to . . . to pay off in blow jobs, I mean . . . you know . . . it might take a long while at, say, twenty dollars apiece. I got a friend who is paying her lawyer that way. He gives her sometimes to other guys. Uh . . . clients. Guys he wants to make happy. Anyway—"

"No, Sara," Cole said gently. "It's okay. Don't think about it. Don't worry about it. I'm not going to—It might be great. But you don't need to do that."

"Is she the only client who ever offered you sex?"

"Specifically. It's been hinted. You remember the Miss Houdini case?"

"She was the hooker who figured out how to slip out of hand-cuffs," said Emily.

"Well . . . she was so young, so pretty, so upset to be arrested. She'd cry, and she'd convince the cops they had her cuffed too tight and it hurt. They'd loosen them and leave her alone in the car or in a van while they went off to chase down another girl, and she'd slip out of the cuffs and scram. She got away with it four times. I couldn't do anything for her. She's doing six months. She suggested if I could get her out she'd make me glad I did."

"You're seeing a cross section of mankind, aren't you?"

"Better than seeing a cross section of some little area of tax or securities law."

"We're going to have another baby, Cole."

Cole was surprised. "But, I thought, you didn't . . . Honey, that's wonderful."

"Let's hope it's a boy this time," she said, and smiled.

"Let's just hope it's healthy and everything's okay."

V

Greta sat beside Dave on her couch, facing a TV tray and a large pizza, with cans of beer. She wore black patent-leather shoes, sheer black stockings supported by a black garter belt—and nothing besides.

"You know I'm playing in that concert at SUNY Purchase," she said.

"I do know. That's real progress for your career."

"Well . . . I need a dress."

"Which will cost—?"

"I might be able to get something decent for, say, three hundred."

"Jesus, Greta!"

"You want me to look right."

"Yeah, but . . . three hundred dollars!"

She shrugged. Shrugging bare-breasted made her boobs bounce provocatively—which she well knew. "I thought I was seeing a guy who is making ten fuckin' fortunes. Three hundred lousy bucks?"

"You got it, hon. You got it. Of course. But I don't have the ten fuckin' fortunes yet. I took a real hit on that B&G deal."

She shrugged again. "You still want me to shave my pussy?" she asked.

"Yeah."

"Well, that's what you get for your three hundred. Only . . . *you* shave it."

"I'll want some pictures," he said.

"Well . . . of *it*. Shaved. Not me, just it. Up to my belly button, no farther. I'll spread for you, too. But it's got to be Polaroids, and I've got to see them. A girl who's a concert artist can't have pictures of her around—You know. Pictures of my pussy, okay. But not my face included."

VI

Cole and Emily, Tony and Margot, sat over dinner once again, this time in a Czech restaurant that was an adventure for all of them. The wine was the darkest red any of them had ever seen. Cole guessed the name was the Czech word for blood.

"You were half right," Tony said to Cole. "His B&G stock was a bust. I put in ten thousand and got out at fifteen hundred. The damned company never had enough capital to do what it was supposed to do."

"I was afraid of that," said Cole.

"So what happened?" Tony went on. "Dave came to me and said he had a deal that would recover my loss and more, easy. I said thanks but no thanks. At that point he reached in his pocket and handed me his personal check for eighty-five hundred."

"It cleared?" Emily asked, sardonically.

Tony nodded. "It cleared. And I'll tell you something else. If I'd bought into the deal he offered me—for, say, another ten thousand—I'd have come out of it more than okay. The son of a bitch said he had to protect his reputation. I imagine he bought out a number of investors. Then he turned around and made a huge profit on another deal."

Cole shook his head. "Using insider information, I'm afraid."

"Could be. The guy's a hustler. He always was, but he's got his own code of ethics. He's going to wind up buying and selling all of us out of pocket change." Cole interrupted. "Or he's going to wind up in a federal reformatory."

"He'll find somebody to take the fall for him," Emily said bitterly.

"He's vulnerable somewhere," said Margot with bland knowledgeability. "That's the way it is. I know. That's the world. Nobody's Teflon."

VII

Dave went to Greta's concert at SUNY Purchase, the Westchester County branch of the State University of New York. She played in a pops concert. He was unable to appreciate her virtuosity. His attention was focused on her dress, for which he had paid six hundred dollars. Also on the diamond pendant hanging in her shallow décolletage, for which he had paid twice as much.

She played a concert piece he should have known but did not: Gershwin's *Rhapsody in Blue*, which required power on the piano that he could not appreciate.

The *Times* reviewed her concert in the morning:

> The young pianist Greta Sorensen, winner of the Arthur Rubenstein International Master Competition and other competitions, appeared last night on the concert stage

at SUNY Purchase and established a legitimate claim to be a major concert artist for the next decades. Under-taking a work that has been performed by such virtuosos as Gershwin himself and Oscar Levant, she demon-strated the power and virtuosity of a commanding new talent. Even when the visiting orchestra, from Indian-apolis, was off its timing, which unfortunately it some-times was, she hit her notes hard and forced the orchestra to follow her.

"That's marvelous!" Dave said to her the next evening.

"Lot of hard work," she said. "For many years. I used to get up at six in the morning so I could practice two hours before I went to school. Lifelong habit. I get up and start my day's practice at six. That's what it takes."

Dave grinned. "Well . . . how about getting some of those extra clothes off?"

"That's all you care about, really," she said. "That's really all you care about: staring at my bod. Well . . . when do I get to stare at *you*? How about this time you strip down? This time we'll eat din-ner with *you* naked and me not."

"Greta!"

"I mean it, lover. I want to see that cock and those balls swing-ing between your legs. C'mon! You want any tonight—"

He did it. He stripped.

"Okay. Parade around the room the way you make me do. Flip your hips and make that equipment bounce around the way you like to see my tits do."

"Greta . . ."

"Hey! You're on your way. You're gonna make twenty fortunes. Well, I'm gonna cash in on *my* hard work. You're good at what you do. I'm good at what *I* do. I'm as good as you, baby. C'mon. I'll get that cock hard 'cause it's beautiful."

FIVE

I

"This is not wise," his mother said to Dave. "You are spending far too much money. What are you now, Rockerfellow?"

"How can you say I am spending too much when you don't know how much I have?"

"Anybody who pays two hundred fifty thousand for a house is paying like Rockerfellow."

They sat in the kitchen of the house where Dave grew up, over beers and a package of chips. His mother, who had always worn housedresses, had made a concession to the decade: She was wearing a white T-shirt and blue jeans. It was incongruous, somehow, on a woman approaching sixty. His father had come in from his sales rounds and had doffed his brown tweed jacket and loosened his tie.

They sat at the table that had been in the kitchen all Dave's life: an odd, round table with sturdy white legs supporting a top covered with some kind of red vinyl plastic that resisted every accident and was scarred with cigarette ash burns. The kitchen floor was covered with linoleum—which Dave had called "mino-leum" until he was twelve years old. The linoleum was worn at four places under the table, where shoes had scuffed it for twenty-five years.

Dave could not help but subside into a euphoric, reminiscent

51

state when he sat in this kitchen. It was where he came from. It was who he was.

"You got something put away, in savings?" his father asked, innocently concerned.

"Well . . . to start with, the house is worth every nickel I'm paying for it. It's going to be an *asset*. It's an *investment*. I didn't do this without studying the market for real estate in northern New Jersey. Two years from now it will be worth three hundred thousand. Trust me. I know it will."

"I guess you know something about investment," his father conceded.

Dave blew a loud sigh. "Something, yeah."

"You made a lot of money the last year or so. I hear . . ."

"Uh-huh. And it puts Amy and the kids in a nice house on a nice wooded property. Plus . . . it makes me look good."

"Which is important," said his mother. "In *your* business."

Dave sighed again. "Sometimes I don't think you approve of my business—no matter if I make money or not."

"I can't understand it," his mother said. "In *his* business, your father sells things you can put your hands on and feel and weigh. In *your* business, you sell things nobody can touch . . . or understand, or value. If I buy what you sell, what do I have? A piece of paper that may be worth something or may be worth nothing. How can I tell?"

"You can tell," said Dave. "I can't give you a crash course in the securities market."

"Well . . . it somehow seems less than honest, just to juggle paper around and take money from it. In the end, what can you say you *create*? Anything?"

"Capital. Wealth. That people invest. Which creates, among other things, *jobs*. We don't live like people used to do, when you sold cows and horses, shoes, hats, nails . . . We—"

"Or groceries," his father said.

"Or groceries. It's a new world, a new economy."

"How much you make last year, you don't mind my asking?"

"I really don't know. I've got accountants working on it, so I'll pay my taxes."

His mother frowned at him. "You also got a girlfriend, haven't you? We heard—"

"I *did* have. But that's over. She played a recital last month in Alice Tully Hall. She doesn't need me anymore."

"Alice Tully . . . ?" his mother asked. "This is—?"

"She's a concert artist. And she's making it big. She doesn't need to sleep with a stockbroker."

"That's frank," said his father. "That's honest."

"I helped her," said Dave. "Maybe I contributed a little something to her success. If so, I'm proud to have done it."

His mother frowned hard. "Now this girl is out of your life, maybe you'll concentrate on Amy. She's a fine young woman. A wonderful wife for you."

II

Amy tried to be. She knew what he liked and wanted, and she tried to satisfy him. She went around their new house, after the children were in bed, in sexy lingerie because she knew he liked it. She read books on how to make herself more exciting.

Amy was desperate. She knew he didn't love her anymore—or if he loved her, it was not exclusively. She felt herself losing him. She couldn't help it if her belly had not entirely flattened after pregnancies. The enlargement of her ass was maybe something else.

"I don't entirely understand the apartment," she said.

"Well, if you think it's a love nest for Greta, forget it. That's history. I just need a little place where the action is, where I can be at work from dawn if need be. I've got two phone lines and, believe it or not, a computer. It's an *office*. You're welcome there anytime. And you don't have to call me in advance."

They were talking about a tiny apartment he had leased in SoHo—meaning south of Houston Street, which New Yorkers pronounced *How*-ston—lower Manhattan.

"What does Mr. Jenkins think of it?"

"He doesn't know about it. I'm not long with Barnaby, Jenkins—which he well knows. Jenkins is satisfied with what he is and where he is. Not me. I'm going somewhere else."

"Take me with you, Dave."

Dave looked at her. "You're my partner, babe," he said and laughed. What else could he say, she looked pitiful.

III

He spent less and less time at the tree-shaded home in New Jersey. He immersed himself in his work and stayed in the little apartment. He was right in telling Amy she could come anytime without advance notice. He gave her a key.

His business had changed.

"I've been looking for a young man like you."

"I've been looking for a man like you," Dave responded.

They sat in the luxurious East Seventy-second Street apartment of Bob Leeman. The apartment occupied two floors of a building with a view of the East River from its windows. Essentially, Leeman lived on the eighth floor and kept his office on the ninth. The apartment featured hardwood floors and a few oriental rugs here and there. Leeman owned some distinguished art, including a Pollock.

It also featured two naked teenaged girls, neither of them more than seventeen years old. Leeman was known for this: for taking in girls and making them his, for his pleasure or others. He had made it clear that one of them, Janelle Griffith by name, was assigned to David Shea and would do whatever Leeman's money might buy from her.

Janelle was more mature than her years. She was comfortable with her role. She had supple breasts—one with a tiny black mole on it—and almost no pubic hair, but she was glad to let the two men see her nude. In fact, she conspicuously gloried in it. She smiled and drank only a little champagne and kept herself close to the man she was being paid to please.

"We can talk in front of them," said Leeman. "They're too damned dumb to have any idea what it means."

Dave heard that judgment skeptically, but Leeman was calling the shots. He was a corporate raider. His business was acquiring corporations, looting them by selling off their best assets, and leaving the minority stockholders with a bankrupt shell.

Bob Leeman was a teetotaler. He also ate sparingly. All his considerable energy was focused on his business, and he regarded alcohol and the digestion of rich food as unnecessary diversions of strength. His sole indulgence was little girls.

He was short, no more than five feet four. He was bald. What little hair he had, he shaved off. His face was broad and open. His smile was infectious. He was capable of transferring his enthusiasms to others.

"You know my business," he said to Dave. "You know what I do. You're smart enough. You've researched *me*."

"Yes, sir."

"Don't call me sir. Jesus Christ, don't call me sir. I'm Bob, Dave, and let's go on from there."

Dave nodded.

"You know my base corporation is Minnesota Copper. Hell, we don't produce a *ton* of copper a year. Did in the past, but . . . Anyway, I acquired it and have ever since used it as a corporate base. The son of a bitch was cash-rich, once. I used that cash to buy . . . Well, you know. One company, then another company. It owned a corporate jet. Boy, did I use it! And, believe it or not, a yacht on Lake Superior. That was damned good for taking my little girls out on cruises. I mean . . . you know the story."

"The SEC raised hell," said Dave.

Leeman nodded. "In a year when MC lost thirty-two million, I took a salary and perks worth four million. Oh, yeah. The government raised hell. But they couldn't establish anything illegal. I gave up the jet and the yacht, and they were happy and went away."

"Well . . . what's up now, Bob?"

"I want to take over McLeod. They know it, and they'll fight me. If I acquire five percent or more of their stock, I have to file a 13-D, disclosing my position. What I'm looking for is investors who can buy three or four percent—whose names won't be identified with me. When we've got enough we can swoop in and take McLeod."

"What's so good about McLeod?"

"Cash, to start with. Besides, it owns half a dozen subsidiaries in different lines of business. I can liquidate some of those and merge others into my companies."

"A hostile takeover," said Dave.

Leeman grinned. "*I'm* not hostile. The McLeod management is."

"You think I've got clients who can invest enough?"

"They can when they understand *I'm* putting up the money. Look. There'll be no risk for these investors. If they put in their own money, I'll guarantee they can't lose. McLeod is selling at 30⅞. Suppose it drops to 25¼. I'll make them whole for the difference. Or . . . I'll advance the money, and they won't have anything at risk. All I demand is that they vote as I require."

Dave pulled in a deep breath. "Without of course disclosing—"

"Of course. Our secret. I figure the stock will go up a minimum of ten points immediately after I acquire McLeod. They unload at that point and take their profits. They unload in any case. I don't want them for stockholders. I'll buy their shares."

Dave glanced at the two naked girls. He wondered how Leeman could have such confidence that they didn't understand and wouldn't talk. "I don't have to tell you how illegal it is," he said. "The SEC will go into hysterics."

"*If* the SEC finds out. And we're going to make it our business to be sure they don't find out. And that depends largely on you identifying the right investors. We need guys who are greedy enough to do something illegal. Of course . . . if one of them rats on us, he is in as big trouble as I would be."

Dave ran his hand along Janelle's thigh. "This brings up something, Bob. You know I do research. You've got—what?—twenty-four corporations? For most of them you're not even holding annual stockholders meetings. Some of them don't even have boards of directors. And that's fine. But I think you need to go through the motions."

"You going to tell me how to run my businesses?"

"At the risk of losing you as a potential client, yes. You're also late in filing 13-Ds. Your audits are . . . pitiful. You're steering toward a disaster. You run your business like a fief. Why wave a red flag at the SEC bull?"

"Go on."

"Hell, you run these companies. You've got guys who will do what you tell them. Hold meetings and go through the motions of being corporations. And get your goddamned accountants to make *real* audits, even if you have to transfer money from one company to another temporarily."

Leeman grinned again. "What you figure I'm going to pay you for handling this deal?"

"I'm afraid to ask."

"Okay. You make it work, Dave, and you're gonna come out a million richer—*on this deal.*"

"Can I ask how?"

"I'll pay you, say, a quarter of a mill. But I'll give you a market tip. I don't know what it is yet, but it'll be a good one. You'll come out with a million, at least."

"Insider information."

Leeman shrugged. "Always good, if nobody knows where it came from."

Janelle snuggled up to Dave, and he guessed from the look in her wise young eyes that she had understood every word of the conversation. In the wildest stretch of his imagination he could not have divined that she would one day, years later, be his third wife.

IV

Julian Musgrave favored Italian food, so he and Dave sat over dinner in a booth in Jersey City, swallowing Chianti and eating veal and pasta.

"So why you come to *me* with this deal, Dave?"

" 'Cause we know something about each other, Julian. Nixon said he was not a crook. But he was. And so am I. And so are you. What I'm offering you is a chance to make a piss pot full of money. At no risk. All you have to do is take the deal and keep your mouth shut about it."

"Illegal?"

"It was illegal to finance a football player at Rutgers. But you did it, for reasons of your own. And I'm not the only one, not by a long shot. My dad, incidentally, still drives that Buick you sold him cheap. I don't owe you any favors, Julian. And you don't owe me any. I'm looking for guys who are just greedy enough and just cunning enough to take advantage of an opportunity that's just a wee bit shady."

"Who's behind it?"

"Don't ask. A guy who could buy you and me out of pocket change. He's behind this deal, and he guarantees you can't lose."

"A big promise."

"You can invest *his* money. He'll transfer it to you."

"And I can make?"

"Who knows? But you can't lose."

"You didn't steer me wrong before."

"After this deal, there could very well be others."

"Okay. I'll put in some. And let your guy put in some more."

V

Amy did come over to Manhattan and spend an occasional night in his little apartment. She was so anxious to please him and to hold him, she would do just about anything he suggested. Tonight he had taken a shower, and he was lying on the bed receiving a sensuous tongue bath—starting on his forehead and working down, sometimes starting on his feet and working up. She would always leave his hardening cock until last. She liked seeing him respond to her.

She had just reached his nipples when the telephone rang.

"Jesus!" he said.

The caller was Leeman. Dave had long since learned that Bob Leeman had no sense of hours or of privacy but might call at three o'clock in the morning.

"Hey, kid! We've made it. Nobody had to file a 13-D, but I've got enough stock, in the hands of a few of my guys, more of yours, to vote me in. Which, by God, I'm gonna do. Hey! Now our problem is how to market the goddamned stocks in the subsidiaries. I guess I can count on you for that."

"Right."

"None of our guys are gonna lose anything. McLeod closed today at 35¼. I can keep it there until all the loose ends are taken care of. Then tell them to bail out and take their profit. The ones who owe me money can pay from their proceeds. But time is of the essence, as the lawyers say."

"First thing in the morning," said Dave.

"*First thing.* After I'm named as taking over, that stock is gonna go south."

"Gotcha."

Amy had gone into the bathroom to refresh her mouth with Lavoris.

"Do something for me, Bob."

"Apart from your making a million?"

"Yes. Janelle. Make sure she goes to college and gets an education. I'll pay for it."

"Hell . . . I've done the same for a lot of my girls. *I'll* pay for it. A girl is only seventeen once. She's got to have a life after . . . They understand I'll take care of them, Dave . . . You'd be surprised if I told you the women who did their thing for me and then went on, because I sponsored them, to great things. There's a magazine publisher . . . Well, never mind."

"Okay."

"I told you that when this deal is successful there'd be a million in it for you. Well . . . all we gotta do now is figure how we're gonna transfer that to you. You pop up to my place, say, Wednesday evening, and we'll settle that. And, uh, Janelle will be there. You didn't take full advantage of her before. Maybe you'll think about that again."

"Okay. Thanks for calling, Bob."

Amy returned from the bathroom and took up where she'd left off. "What was *that* all about?" she asked.

"It was a guy calling to tell me that a deal we'd tried to swing didn't work out."

"You lose a lot of money?"

"Just what I'd hoped to make. I didn't have anything committed."

Amy ran her tongue up his penis. "Can't win 'em all," she murmured.

Dave stared at the ceiling.

SIX

I

1984

Cole and Emily had lived in an apartment in the East Sixties. With the toddler, Emily, crawling around and an infant, Cole, in a bassinet, their tiny apartment had been inadequate. This one had two bedrooms, a living-dining room, and a kitchen.

Emily's pregnancies had not made her lumpy. She didn't even have stretch marks. The only change in her was that her beautifully pear-shaped breasts had grown a bit. She kept her pussy shaved and had lost her reticence about letting Cole see her pink, fleshy inner labia. She was on The Pill. They had decided that two children were all they wanted, at least for now. She had resumed modeling at the Art Students League but only did it one evening a week. She was one of the favorite models, and they asked her to do more. She said she had obligations at home.

Cole worked long hours, and they were taxing hours. When he came home, the first thing he wanted was a drink, to relax him.

The first thing, actually, was to play with his favorite little girl, Emily, and to cuddle Cole, but when Emily put the children to bed, Cole wanted to drink. He wanted to ease the tensions of being a trial lawyer.

"I think you're going a little heavy on that, honey," Emily said

61

to him several times. He had developed a taste for martinis, which he drank on the rocks, with twists of lemon.

Cole blew a loud sigh. "There's a saying about trial lawyers," he told her. "They say we have significantly lower life expectancies than other people, other lawyers."

"Well, you're not going to increase it by drinking too much."

"You got a point," he said. But he finished his third martini.

"What's on your plate now?" she asked.

"Well . . . you know the last thing any lawyer wants to do is handle divorce cases. And our firm doesn't. But when you have a good client for other reasons, you can't very well turn him down when he asks you to handle his divorce. So, I'm stuck with what's going to turn out to be a notorious case. I mean, the tabloids are going to go ape."

"Whose case?"

"You've heard of Jack Singer."

"The real estate guy?"

"That's him. He's fifty-two. He married a chick. She's twenty-seven. She caught him in flagrante delicto, as lawyers are supposed to say. And she's decided, if he's to be believed, to take him to the cleaners. She wants half of everything he owns."

"Nasty case."

Cole nodded. "Ugly. All full of emotion."

"What are you going to do?"

"I hate to admit it, but I've hired a private investigator."

II

Five months later the case came to trial before a judge—no juries on divorce cases.

Mrs. Singer testified on her own behalf, describing how she had come home one night, unexpectedly early, to find her husband in bed with a black prostitute.

Cole Jennings cross-examined.

"Mrs. Singer, is this the only time you ever observed your husband in such circumstances?"

She was a stunning classic blond, demure in a black knit dress.

She crossed her legs at the ankles and did not allow her skirt to creep up. "Once is enough, don't you think, Mr. Jennings?"

"But it *was* the only time?"

"I figure he did it all the time. This was just the only time I caught him."

Cole smiled at the judge. "I'll ask the court to disregard the speculation."

The judge nodded. "Confine your testimony to what you have observed and know, Mrs. Singer."

"Now . . ." said Cole. "May we assume that *you* never strayed outside your marriage?"

"Absolutely never. I've been married to Jack for seven years and have never—Well, you know what I've never."

"No. Tell us. What is it you've never?"

"I have never been intimate with another man," she said, giving Cole a dirty look.

"Has another man ever stayed overnight with you, when Mr. Singer was absent on a business trip?"

"*Never,*" she said vehemently.

"I believe you have an apartment in the East Thirties and a home in Scarsdale."

"Yes."

"Thank you, Mrs. Singer."

When Cole mounted the case for the defense, he called for a witness, the sixty-year-old night-desk man from the apartment house where the Singers lived.

"May I assume you have a general knowledge of which tenants are present in the building and which are away?"

"In a general way, yes."

"Would you know when Mr. Singer was away?"

"Yes, sir."

"How would you know?"

"When he comes down carrying a suitcase, I figure he's going somewhere."

"And when he comes back carrying the suitcase, you would know he is at home."

"Yes, sir."

"Have you ever observed . . . *gentlemen* visiting the Singer apartment when Mr. Singer was away?"

"Yes, sir."

"Did these gentlemen stay all night?"

The witness nodded. "They had to sign in. Which they did before I came on duty. I saw them leave in the morning, early."

"Are we talking about *one* gentleman?"

"No, sir. I think about three."

The lawyer for Mrs. Singer rose. "Your Honor, this testimony is at least as speculative as was my client's when she said she believed the defendant—"

"If the court please," Cole interrupted. "We have subpoenaed and will submit the sign-in books for several months. We can prove—and will prove if we must—that these 'gentlemen' signed in under false names. Mrs. Singer may be able to identify them."

Cole detested private detectives. But, when the time came, he offered testimony—

"Under my instructions, you kept the Singer house in Scarsdale under surveillance for a week, at night."

"And until daylight, sir."

"I believe you took some photographs, did you not?"

"I did, sir."

"We will submit those photographs in evidence, Your Honor. Is it your testimony that these pictures are true representations and have not been doctored in any way?"

"It is, sir. They were shot with infrared flashbulbs, on infrared film. The subjects didn't know their pictures were being taken."

In one picture Mrs. Singer appeared in a sheer shorty nightgown, standing tippy-toe to reach and kiss a man. In another she appeared entirely nude, again kissing, in the doorway of the Scarsdale house. The private detective testified that he had taken these photographs just at dawn, when he was hidden in a hedge.

"I call to the attention of the court that these pictures are not of the same man."

III

"I don't know. I don't know," Cole said to Emily as he sipped his martini. "There's no honor in scrutinizing personal lives. If they had accepted the settlement I suggested before they went to trial, he would have paid her a hundred thousand dollars a year for the rest of her life and no one had to know the details. As it is—As it is, both of them hate me because of what I had to do in court."

"And what does her lawyer get?"

"*Nada.* It's a dumb lawyer who takes his client's word. Hell, Singer lied to me, and she lied to her lawyer, people always do in divorces. I knew he was lying. I have to wonder if her lawyer knew she was lying."

He lifted his martini and drained it.

"You've got to get out of this line of business, honey," Emily said. "It's going to kill you, like you said. Think of going back over to New Jersey. You're admitted to the bar there. Let's find a little town where we can live in peace, and you can open an office of your own. We don't want to bring up our kids in Manhattan."

"It's where the world is, Emily."

"What world, if you kill yourself in it?"

IV

In October Cole and Emily left the Manhattan apartment and moved into a small house in Wyckoff. He opened an office in a building on Franklin Avenue and—as lawyers say—hung out his shingle. To his surprise, Harris & Pickens asked him not to disaffiliate with the firm but to designate himself on his letterhead as "of counsel" to Harris & Pickens. The partners said they would send him some business and might occasionally call him back to Manhattan to work on a case.

The idea of a New York City lawyer coming home and opening a local office in a small town intrigued many, and it didn't take long for him to build a thriving practice, drawing clients from all over northern Bergen County.

Amy Shea was not one of his clients exactly, but she came to see him, to consult. They sat in his office, where windows overlooked the street from the second floor. His desk was a big table. Behind him, serving as a sort of credenza, sat a handsome old cherry rolltop desk. Amy wondered if Cole had not consciously arranged the office to look something like the Abraham Lincoln office in Springfield, Illinois. He was very old-fashioned, not like Dave at all.

"He's involved himself with a man called Leeman. Have you heard the name?"

"Definitely."

"I suspect he's a crook."

"Well, Amy . . ." Cole said cautiously, "Bob Leeman is a voracious corporate raider. He acquires companies, appropriates their best assets, and leaves them unprofitable shells. He skates along the fine edge of the law."

"And ethics," she suggested.

"Yes."

"Then so is Dave. What I'm afraid of is that this Leeman will make Dave take the fall for something he does, the way Dave did to you in the Amos case."

"Dave's too smart for that."

Amy paused and looked around the room. On one wall he had hung a framed print. It was a portrait of Lincoln, with a quote from Lincoln as a caption—

A LAWYER'S TIME AND ADVICE
ARE HIS STOCK IN TRADE

"I'm going to ask for your legal advice," she said solemnly. "This may shock you, but I'm wondering if I could divorce Dave and if I did what could I get out of him?"

"What would be your grounds, Amy?"

"He had a girlfriend. He told me."

He had heard about Dave's girlfriend.

"What can I say?" Amy had tears in her eyes.

"I think he'd fight you. Very hard. Suppose you won. You'd get custody of the kids—but with liberal visitation rights. You'd get child support. Alimony . . . probably. You'd get the house. What do you think he's worth?"

"God knows. He used to tell me everything. He doesn't anymore, I mean about business. That's another point. I was once his partner, so to speak. I'm not now."

"You married him because you loved him. Do I understand you don't anymore?"

"I don't know . . . I don't think *he* loves *me*—I mean, like he used to. Anyway he's the father of my children. I go the whole nine yards to please him, meaning with sex. But—it kills me to think he's got somebody on the side."

"You say 'the whole nine yards.' Are his demands sadistic or . . . ? I'm not asking you to be graphic."

"Why not?" She paused. "The only thing you might call cruel is that he's decided it's fun to tie me up. Of course . . . he's only home two or three nights a week."

"If you don't like it, have you asked him to stop?"

"I want to please him, how can I?" she said.

"Scanty grounds for divorce," said Cole. "Of course, if a divorce humiliated him—"

"It would humiliate me, too. And the kids would hear about it sooner or later."

"I can't recommend you try it."

"I'm not seriously thinking about it."

V

When Tony DeFelice's father died, Tony became executor of the will, and he asked Cole to handle the legal matters. Probate fees are fixed by rule of court, so there could be no question as to what Cole would charge. The estate was appraised at more than a million dollars, so Cole received a nice fee.

The practice in Bergen County was not as challenging as his Manhattan practice had been, but it wasn't as demanding either.

Except that he found himself drawn into community activities that occupied many of his evenings. He was invited to join the Rotary Club. He was *expected* to be active in the Junior Chamber of Commerce. He was assigned to collect contributions for the United Way, from a motley collection of professionals: accountants, architects, and veterinarians.

"Fair-share giving is not an option," the chairman explained to him. "We know how much they make and therefore how much they owe. And we can make it tough for a man who doesn't give his fair share."

Cole sometimes wondered why he had left New York.

Dave invited him to lunch. They met in a Chinese restaurant with bowing and bobbing waiters who incessantly inquired if everything was all right or if they needed anything more. They both drank saki. A feature of the place was a huge aquarium in which large and colorful fish glided back and forth among the bubbles of the filtration system.

"I'm told," said Dave, "that in China you go in a restaurant, point at a fish in a tank, and say you want that one on your dinner plate. Of course, they're not *that* kind of fish."

"Those don't look very palatable," Cole said.

"You surprise me, Cole. Here I am, struggling to get over to the City, and you were established there and moved back."

"Maybe when you get over there, *you'll* move back."

"No. No way."

"From all I hear, you are doing very well."

"I've put together some good deals," Dave said modestly.

"That's what I hear."

"I was wondering, Cole, if you would be interested in investing some of the cash in the DeFelice estate."

"In what?"

Dave grinned. "Junk bonds. No, listen. There's a lot of money to be made there."

"Well . . . In the first place, Tony is the executor. That's a fiduciary position, and the law is very clear. He can invest the estate's funds only in some very secure things, like federal notes."

"Hell, he'll never make any money that way."

"His duty is to preserve the assets of the estate. I'm surprised you didn't know this, Dave. Tony could not put estate funds into junk bonds, even if he wanted to. There are very few things he can invest estate assets in."

"How about you? Would you like to take a flyer, say for a small amount?"

Cole shook his head. He knew Dave was playing his angle. He knew the estate couldn't make an investment. "I just made an expensive move, Dave. I came home, bought a house, and started a business. I can't take a flyer in anything."

"Understood. So how're Emily and the kids?"

"Great. And how's Amy?"

"Well . . . she's not very happy. I don't know what the hell she wants. She's gotten a little lumpy, you may have noticed, if you've seen her. The kids are okay."

"Got a little something going on the side, Dave?"

Dave grinned again. "You know, that's a funny thing. No, I don't. I've had opportunities, but . . . no. You?"

"No."

"Monogamous through thick and thin, hmm?"

"By choice."

"Someday some babe will come along. They always do."

"I'm not in a glamorous business like you're in. Small-town law-yer. By choice."

"Is there anything I can do for you, Cole? I owe you. I can steer some business to you maybe. And when you're ready to invest, I can put you onto some real deals."

"I'll keep it in mind."

SEVEN

I

AUGUST, 1986

Dave was fond of thick, rare steaks and loved to eat at Sparks, the famous Manhattan steak house. It was the site where Paul Castellano was gunned down on the street as he was emerging from his limousine to come in for a dinner meeting with other mob figures. Dave liked the way the wine was served at Sparks: in eight-ounce glasses. The waiters were brusque but attentive. Many thought it was a man's restaurant, though many women came there.

Bob Leeman had suggested this place for a meeting. He didn't eat steaks and would content himself by nibbling on a Caesar salad and sipping wine sparingly, but Leeman was well known at Sparks; he brought guests there for lunch and dinner, often.

"Don't order yet," he said to Dave. "There'll be three of us."

"Really? You didn't mention—"

"You'll be very happy to meet our dinner companion. Besides being a looker, she's damned smart."

"She?"

"In our line of business, sooner or later—let us hope later—we are going to need good public relations. Alexandra Fairchild is the best. She came out of obscurity and founded an aggressive p-r firm—Fairchild, Douglas & Jones. She's so well thought of that she worked on the Reagan campaigns, both times. Her specialty is *attack!* She never defends. She goes for the throat. If you want to go

71

after a client of hers, you better be clean as hell. She'll change the whole focus, from what her client may have done wrong to what his accusers did wrong."

Alexandra Fairchild arrived. My God! She was a striking woman—brilliant shoulder-length red hair, a flawless face characterized by a wide mouth and full lips, a spectacular body, though it was in no sense on display. She appeared in a white sequined sweater, with a rose-colored dinner skirt.

"I've heard your name, Mr. Shea."

"I'm flattered."

"And until just now you never heard mine."

"Well . . . it didn't come up."

"I've explained to Dave what you can do for us," Leeman said.

"Don't forget the old cliché," she said. " 'An ounce of prevention is better than a pound of cure.' "

"Meaning, in our case?" Dave asked.

"Getting down to business quicker than I expected, it wouldn't hurt you guys to establish yourselves as sterling citizens, contributors to the community." She signaled a waiter and ordered a double Glenlivet on the rocks, then turned to Dave and said, "Better for your plumbing than that gin you're drinking."

"An authority on liquor, too," Dave said, half smiling.

Alexandra shrugged. *"Chacun à son gout,"* she said.

Leeman frowned. Apparently he didn't know what she had said.

"What do you suggest we do to make ourselves sterling citizens?" Dave asked.

"Sponsor something," she said. "A basketball team for inner-city kids. A Little League team. You provide the uniforms and equipment. It won't cost you all that much. You buy and present trophies. Just a suggestion. There's a thousand things you can do."

"You're anticipating something," said Dave.

"Which is?"

"That we might someday have to appear before a jury."

"It can happen. You guys are in a dicey business. Dennis Levine has been indicted for insider trading. Ivan Boesky is in trouble. There's a fine line—"

"We know where it is," said Leeman.

Alexandra shrugged again. "Forewarned is forearmed," she said.

Dave chuckled. "You seem to have a cliché for everything."

"That's the p-r business," she said. "You talk to people in terms they can understand. Speak a language they understand. You remember the old commercial for some deodorant or other. The woman smeared it on her forehead. A little later she said, 'My faar-id is dry.' She wasn't wrong, but ninety-five percent of Americans call it a forehead—and were turned off. Tricks of the trade."

"So tell me a little about yourself, Miss Fairchild. It's none of my business, but—"

She smiled. "I'm thirty-two years old, married once, divorced once, and I have no progeny. I was born in Kiev and was brought to this country by my parents when I was eleven. I'm naturalized. I've spent twenty-one years trying to learn English, and I guess I speak it reasonably well, though you may catch me once in a while in some odd, unidiomatic expression. That used to amuse Ron Reagan, who would double over laughing when I said something awkward. I graduated from Columbia. My politics were, and are, very right-wing, coming as I do as a sort of refugee from the Soviet Union. Reagan was intrigued with the idea of having a Soviet citizen working on his campaign. He liked me. He helped me get started in my business. In the first campaign I was a hewer of wood and a drawer of water—another cliché. The second time I wrote speeches and designed ads. I still have connections with that crowd. I expect to work on the Bush campaign."

"Damned interesting," Dave said.

"Now you, sir. Give me your curriculum vitae."

"Not nearly as interesting. I'm from Bergen County, New Jersey. My father sold groceries wholesale for a living. I went to Rutgers on a football scholarship. Otherwise I couldn't have gone to college. I'm married. I've got two kids. My wife and the kids live in New Jersey. I live mostly in an apartment in Manhattan."

"Too modest," said Leeman. "This guy knows how to make *deals*. And he's taught me something about being careful. I figure he's got a hell of a future ahead of him. In a few years he's learned more about how Wall Street works than I've learned in a great many more years."

Alexandra leaned back and regarded Dave with a curious eye. "Are you satisfied with your life so far, Mr. Shea?"

"I'll be better satisfied if you'd call me Dave."

She nodded. "Dave . . . So, Alexandra."

"If I may ask, what was your name in Kiev?"

"Alexandra Petrovna Krylov. It means Alexandra, daughter of Peter Krylov. I haven't legally changed it."

"I could call you Alex, couldn't I?"

"I'd as soon you didn't. I've been called worse."

"I don't know . . . Somehow it appeals to me."

"Uhh . . . you guys could do worse than get together, if you don't mind my saying so," said Leeman. "Alexandra . . . He's got a wife, but it's not one hell of a marriage."

"Give him one of your little girls, Bob?"

"Yeah . . . and *nothing*."

"Got to stop that, Bob. Get publicity on that, and your public relations is shot to shit."

Dave smiled at Alexandra. "You like your steaks thick and rare?" he asked.

"Is there any other way?"

II

NOVEMBER, 1986

On November 3, Dave flew to Nassau, Bahamas. He stayed only three days, long enough to go to the Nassau branch of Pictet & Compagnie and establish a Swiss bank account, in which he deposited fifty thousand dollars, under the name Joseph Windsor. He retained a Bahamian lawyer and formed a Bahamian corporation, which he called Windsor Nassau Associates. The lawyer found some Bahamian citizens to serve as directors and officers of the corporation.

Now Dave could trade in securities, and it would be virtually impossible to trace the trading to him. Windsor Nassau bought the securities with funds transferred to it from Pictet. The corporation would buy and sell securities through various brokers.

On the evening of November 18, Jack Silver came to Dave's apartment. He was casually dressed in a gray turtleneck sweater. He sat down, and Dave mixed martinis for them.

"So you're going big-time, hey?" said Jack.

"I've set up the vehicle."

"I suggest you sever your connection with Barnaby, Jenkins. They're strictly small-time. They don't make for a good introduction."

Dave nodded. "I've got résumés out. I have quite a track record—thanks in part to you—and have some nibbles. One of them is pretty promising. I may go with Harcourt Barnham."

"Investment bankers? Not a brokerage?"

"Like Willie Sutton said, banks are where the money is."

"Well . . . we can do each other a lot of good," said Jack.

"You've done *me* a lot of good. I'll return the favor."

"We can't have it known that we communicate. We'll have to set up some codes. For example, if you're at Harcourt and I call you, I'll say that Mr. Harrelson is calling."

"Harrelson."

"Right. And Harrelson will say something that you'll be able to interpret."

"Okay. When I call you, I'll say it's Kimble."

"Kimble."

"Right."

"When we meet," said Jack, "I think it ought to be here. I can come in and out of this building without taking any chance of running into anybody who knows me."

"Yeah. Banker types don't live in places like this. I'm gonna get a better place, but I'll keep this one."

"Fine. Now tell me something, Dave. Why did you and Leeman hire Alexandra Fairchild?"

"Is it so well known?"

"The word's around."

"Okay. Alexandra convinced Bob Leeman we needed to look like sterling citizens."

Jack nodded. "In case you ever have to face a jury. Which brings up something else. You're going to have to break off with Leeman. You'll have a perfect excuse. Harcourt Barnham will insist on it. I mean Harcourt will *really* insist on it. Bob Leeman is the only bad mark on your résumé. Harcourt won't tolerate any identification with him."

"He's made me a lot of money."

"You've made as much for him."

"I suppose," Dave conceded.

Jack went to the window and looked down on Mercer Street. "I imagine Harcourt Barnham will suggest you break off with Alexandra Fairchild, too."

"That's not gonna happen, Jack," Dave said grimly.

Jack turned. "Don't tell me!"

"The business relationship, sure. But not the personal relationship."

"You and—You and Alexandra are a pair?"

Dave nodded.

"Jesus H. Christ!"

III

DECEMBER, 1986

Dave and Alexandra still favored Sparks, but this evening they had decided to be adventuresome and had crossed the Williamsburg Bridge to Peter Luger's Steak House in Brooklyn. It was set up like a German *bierstube*; and following the canon of the house they sat over huge steins of *real beer*, not American slop but German beer with real beer flavor.

"Well, it's set," Dave said to Alexandra. "First of January, I'm with Harcourt Barnham."

She raised her stein. "Congratulations, Dave. That's a good move."

"There are conditions," he said solemnly. "One of them is that I break all connection with Bob Leeman."

"Understandable," she said.

"There was another condition, and I didn't accept it."

"Which was?"

"That I break all connection with *you*. I refused to do it, Alexandra. I told them you would no longer be my public-relations representative, but—"

"You won't need one," she said.

"But I told them that you and I had a personal friendship and that I was unwilling to abandon it."

"What did they say to that?"

"They said they were perfectly willing that you and I have a personal relationship . . . provided that you, too, break off with Leeman."

She frowned hard. "What's so—?"

He reached for her hand. "I told them it was not impossible that you and I might be married. They said fine. But not to a woman through whom information might be fed to Bob Leeman."

She looked at him for a long moment. "You haven't spoken of marriage, Dave."

"I'm not divorced," he said.

"Your childhood sweetheart . . ." she murmured.

He nodded, but he stared at her. Her copper-colored hair gleamed where it hung to her shoulders. She was wearing a cream-white cable-knit sweater that he recognized as something imported from Ireland, with tight black slacks. Also, a single strand of pearls hung around her neck.

"And you have kids."

"They hardly know me."

"And your wife?"

He shook his head. "She doesn't know me anymore, either. I know it's a cliché. I'm a guy promising marriage to one woman and promising to get free of another one. You deserve better than that, Alexandra. But I'll keep my promise."

She took his hand and they left the table.

They went to her apartment. She lived in the West Seventies, in an apartment far larger and far more luxurious than his digs on Mercer Street. Among its decorations were original posters advertising performances by the *Ballets Russes de Monte Carlo*, featuring among others Alexandra Danilova.

He picked up the phone and called his own apartment to be sure Amy wasn't there. She would answer the telephone. She didn't answer, so Dave and Alexandra spent the night together. Most of the time he left about 4:00 A.M.

Alexandra was a genuine redhead. Her pubic hair was like a burst of flame between her legs. When he first saw her breasts he wondered if she had implants. But she didn't. They were heavy and solid—and real. She would take off her clothes for him, when he asked, but she was not enthusiastic about it. Right now, she kept her panties on and was in no hurry to slip them down.

"You know something?" she asked. "You haven't told me you love me."

"I'm sorry. I should have. I do."

"You do?"

"Alexandra. I'd do anything for you. I mean, to have you for my wife."

IV

Dave invited Cole to join him for dinner at Primavera, an outstanding Italian restaurant on First Avenue. He specified it was just for the two of them; he wanted to talk to Cole privately.

"I recommend everything on the menu," he said. "Whatever you have, it'll be good."

Cole had cut down sharply on his drinking, and a bottle of wine was already before them. "What are you doing at Harcourt Barnham?"

"At the moment, I'm an analyst. But I'm going to be in mergers and acquisitions. That's understood."

A waiter came. Dave ordered veal and pasta. Cole nodded and said he'd have the same.

"Well . . . you said you wanted a private conversation."

"Yes. I want you to represent me in New Jersey. A matter of domestic relations."

Cole lifted his chin abruptly. "You want . . . ?"

"It's not called divorce anymore. It's called 'termination of marriage.' I'm thinking of it being uncontested. I'll—"

"I can't be your lawyer in that, Dave."

"Why not?"

"Amy has already consulted me on the matter."

"*She* wants out? That's great!"

"She doesn't necessarily want out. She asked me how it would work."

"Look. I'll give her the house. I can give her some securities. I'll pay child support. I'll pay her reasonable alimony, for a reasonable time."

"I can't be your lawyer," Cole insisted.

"I don't care which one of us you represent, officially. In fact, I don't know if I *need* a lawyer, if we can agree on everything. With you in the picture, we keep the matter in the family, so to speak. Why don't you talk to her and explain—"

"You mean you want me to *tell* her you want to terminate the marriage? Haven't you told her yourself?"

"I don't want any tears, Cole."

"Dave, that's goddamned cold-blooded."

"What good will it do for her to cry and beg me to stay with her?"

"Don't you have any feelings for her?"

"We've grown miles apart," Dave said realistically. "It doesn't work anymore."

"Money will talk," said Cole wryly.

"It makes things easier."

EIGHT

I

The telephone rang on Dave's desk at Harcourt Barnham. "There is a Mr. Harrelson on the line, sir."

"I'll take it." He picked up the phone. "Good morning, Mr. Harrelson. What can I do for you?"

"I'm thinking of taking a small position in Procter & Gamble. I wonder if you've got any thoughts on it."

"It's not a company I've researched."

"Well, I have a hunch about it and may take a flyer in P&G."

"Let me know how it turns out," said Dave.

He understood. Somehow, Jack had gotten some insider information on Procter & Gamble and was advising Dave to buy. During his lunch hour he carried a roll of quarters and placed a call to Windsor Nassau Associates. By this time he had used information he had learned at Harcourt Barnham to increase his account at Pictet & Compagnie from the original fifty thousand dollars to eighty-five thousand. He instructed the corporation to buy fifty thousand dollars' worth of P&G. Then he called Pictet & Compagnie, identified himself as Joseph Windsor, gave his account number, and transferred fifty thousand dollars to Windsor Nassau.

Later in the week P&G announced that it had acquired Whipple, Incorporated, a leading manufacturer of shortenings and cooking oils with an impressive set of brand names and trademarks. Whipple was a family-held company, the brothers were ready to retire and enjoy being multimillionaires for the rest of their lives, and so sold for a price most favorable to Procter & Gamble. P&G announced it would retire a few of Whipple's less profitable products and expand the manufacture of others.

On this news, the price of P&G stock rose eighteen percent. Dave held it only a few days, then ordered Windsor Nassau to sell it. His profit was not great, but it was worth his short-term risk.

He rewarded Jack Silver with information from Harcourt.

II

APRIL

"Dave, this is a harebrained scheme. It could very easily put an end to your career."

"And make half a million dollars—maybe more—if it works. Look, I've studied the risk. Very carefully. I don't think I can do it alone, though. I need a partner. The guy is a man of routine. He never varies. I've been watching him for weeks."

"But you'll have to do it more than once."

"Yes. I figure."

"And each time—"

"No subsequent time is more dangerous than the first."

Jack shook his head. "I don't know if I want to get into this, Dave."

"Well, you're either in or you're out."

"Let me have the details."

"Okay. Theodore T. Logan IV—sometimes called 'Eye-Vee'—is with Drexel Burnham Lambert, in mergers and acquisitions. He hasn't been touched by the scandals, yet. Now . . . He's a man of sixty. People who do business with him are accustomed to getting calls from him at all hours of the evening—which means he carries documents home. He leaves Drexel Burnham precisely at six every evening and takes a cab downtown to the Broadway Athletic Club. You're a member, and I'm a member. He undresses and stashes his clothes in his locker—also his briefcase. He goes in the steam bath for fifteen minutes, then goes in the pool and swims laps for an hour. He never varies that routine. I swim with him. We've gotten to be nodding acquaintances."

"Does he know what you do, who you're with?"

"I doubt it. Anyway, when members are not using their lockers, they leave them latched."

"Rule of the club," said Jack. "So nobody could stash a bomb in a locker."

"Or cocaine or whatever. Anyway . . . I've experimented with the latch on my locker. With a plastic credit card you can open a locker in two seconds. Just stick it in the gap and push, and the latch surrenders. Those lockers were never meant to be very secure."

"So you lift his briefcase, and . . . ?"

"We've got an hour and fifteen minutes. One briefcase looks pretty much like another, and I walk in earlier, carrying mine. I walk out carrying his. Nobody's going to know the difference. You know the Wakefield Hotel a couple doors up the street. We'll have a room there. I bring the briefcase to the room, and we look over what he's got in there. We find out what the hell he's doing. There's a coin-operated copy machine in the hotel. No one notices what you copy. We can copy anything we want to."

"Then you take the briefcase back—"

"No. *You* do. I can't walk out of the club and come back in half an hour or so. You go to the locker room, watch your chance, open Eye-Vee's locker, and return his briefcase. You undress and use my locker. I'll give you my key. You go swimming for a while. Then you come back, open my locker with my key, dress, and take out *my* briefcase, that'll be waiting there. You come in with a briefcase and come out with one. You come back to the hotel, where I'll have been studying the papers we've copied."

"All very smooth if there's not a hitch," said Jack.

"Simple as hell," said Dave. "If there's a hitch, improvise."

•   •   •

Dave came into the locker room from the pool, stripped off his Speedos, and took a shower. While he was in the shower, Theodore Logan came in, stripped and stashed his clothes and briefcase in his locker, and went out toward the steam room and pool.

Dave hurried to his own locker and pulled the plastic card from his jacket pocket. He defeated the latch on Logan's locker but left the door closed while he dressed.

Now a hitch *did* develop. Too many men passed in and out of the locker room. He needed a moment alone to open Logan's locker. He grew nervous with the delay.

Until he realized that none of these men knew what member had what locker. He opened Logan's locker when no one was at an angle to see the clothes hanging inside, pulled out the briefcase, and left.

In the hotel room he and Jack spread the papers over the bed and scanned them.

"Hot damn!"

"I can't believe it. Mead wants to acquire Boise Cascade!"

"Makes sense," said Jack. "Mead's a paper company. BC's a forest products and paper company. Mead diversified wildly in the past twenty years, acquiring companies involved in industries its management doesn't really know—"

"Like computers," said Dave. "LEXIS/NEXIS."

"Well, that's damned successful. They plowed a lot of money into it, but it works. We've got the system at the bank. I'll bet you've got it at Harcourt."

"I haven't used it, but I understand some people *rely* on it."

"You'd never believe the kinds of things you can find out. It's gotta be one of the world's largest databases."

"Do we really need to copy any of this?" Dave asked.

Jack shook his head. "We can see what Eye-Vee's into. Mead's going to want to get a bank to underwrite a bond issue to finance its bid. It's not going to be Stuyvesant."

"It's not going to be Harcourt."

"Let's get these papers back into the order they were in when we took them out, and you can go to the club and return the briefcase."

"We've got to keep *on* this," said Jack. "When Mead has the underwriting, they'll move. We've got to pull this stunt every day."

Jack went to the club, returned Logan's briefcase to his locker with no trouble, and took a swim.

They went through the same routine the next day, without a snag. On that day they copied half a dozen pages. The details of the Mead deal were beginning to fall into shape. And the next day. After that they varied the routine—some days Jack went in first and lifted the briefcase, and Dave returned it. Using the hotel copier, they accumulated their own file on the coming tender offer for Boise Cascade.

On the eleventh day they learned that Citicorp would underwrite Mead.

Dave hurried to the club with the briefcase. When he arrived he found the locker room too crowded to allow him to replace the briefcase in Logan's locker. He stashed it in his own locker and covered his presence by taking a swim. When he returned to the locker room there were still a couple of men there. So he took a shower. When he came out the room was vacant, so he pulled Logan's briefcase immediately from his locker and moved toward Logan's locker.

At that moment in walked Theodore T. Logan IV.

Dave all but panicked. Others might not distinguish Logan's briefcase from his own, but Logan would take one glance at it and recognize it as his.

One human foible saved the moment. Logan did not pay any attention to the briefcase, even to wondering what a naked man was doing with a briefcase. As almost any man or woman would, he stared at Dave's penis. He nodded a half-friendly greeting, then turned and walked into the shower. Shaking, Dave quickly opened Logan's locker and shoved the briefcase inside.

He didn't tell Jack of the close call.

"Well, it all fits into place," said Jack. "Mead is going to make a tender offer for Boise Cascade. Which is going to drive Boise Cascade stock up. God, what an opportunity!"

Dave frowned. "Yeah . . . well. The problem is, I've only got a hundred thousand I can put in it. I'm not going to come out so great."

"Okay. Okay, man, you've put me onto something great. I'm going to buy half a million dollars' worth. When I unload, the gain on a hundred thousand is yours."

"That's very generous of you, Jack. I . . . I assume you've got a way of covering yourself."

"And I assume you do, too."

Dave nodded. "Offshore."

"I went direct to Geneva myself. How do you communicate with your . . . well, your foreign corporation and your bank?"

"Phone booths, feeding quarters."

"Look. Go to the phone company. Surely you've got a credit card that doesn't have your real name and address on it."

Dave smiled. "I'm thinking about getting a fake passport."

Jack shook his head emphatically. "Too risky. What address do you use on your fake credit card?"

"Alexandra's."

"And the line rings into . . . ?"

"Her apartment."

"Buy a fax machine. You can send out your orders in writing. Confirmation will come back in writing. You can still be cryptic. I guess you trust this woman?"

"We're going to be married."

"Not the same as trusting her."

"I trust her. God, man, a guy's got to trust somebody. I trust you."

"And I trust you, too. We've taken a hell of a risk and have set up something that's going to make a lot of money for us. Be careful that your offshore company doesn't buy too much Boise Cascade. I'll spread my investment. If it doesn't look like any single investor made a windfall, we'll be all right. Otherwise, the SEC will be looking into the deal."

III

"Please marry me," Dave said to Alexandra. He handed her an engagement ring, simple, with one huge stone.

They sat in the living room of her apartment, under the posters of the *Ballets Russes.*

For the first time since he had met her, Alexandra showed tears. She nodded and let him slip the ring on her finger. They kissed.

"I love you," he said.

"I love *you.* Usually I don't do reckless things, and this is reckless." She threw her head back and laughed. "Otherwise, we die of boredom. And I think that's one thing I will never experience with you, Dave Shea."

"I won't be boring, Alexandra."

They went to bed and lingered there for a long time, then went out to dinner. This time, to celebrate their engagement, they went to the Russian Tea Room, late, after the tourists had left. They drank Stolichnaya, so cold that it was all but frozen and was thick, sipped with caviar. They followed this with *Borscht Ukraïnsky,* Ukrainian-style beet soup. Alexandra introduced Dave to blini—raised buckwheat pancakes with caviar. Their main course was nothing more complicated than beef Stroganoff, with deep-red wine.

Dave waited until they returned to her apartment before he raised with her a subject that was important to him but troubled him. "How do you think Bob Leeman would react to a contact from me?"

"He understands why you broke off with him. He doesn't hate you."

"I need to talk to him."

IV

Confident that no one from Harcourt Barnham would see him there, Dave arranged to meet Bob Leeman at Al Cibelli's Restaurant in Perth Amboy. Even there he asked for an obscure booth in the rear. When Leeman arrived, he had a martini in front of him. Leeman stared at that scornfully and ordered a glass of white wine.

"Y' meet your girlfriends here?" Leeman asked sarcastically. "And get drunk?"

"I've got a big deal to share with you, Bob," said Dave. "Neither one of us can take any chances on our being seen together."

"Share . . . ? Why me?"

"Two reasons. I figure I owe you. More important, you're a guy who knows how to cover a deal so nobody is going to find out."

"What you been up to?"

"Don't ask me how I know, but there's going to be a big tender offer. When it hits, a certain stock is going to go up significantly."

"Insider information," said Leeman. His faced flushed: a sign he had just heard something intriguing.

"From the very best possible source."

"How'd you get it?"

"Don't ask. The guy I got it from doesn't know he let it loose. Let's put it this way: he was careless with his documents."

"You stole his papers?"

"Borrowed them. He never knew they'd been touched."

"So, when you gonna tell me what stock?"

"When you and I've got a deal. When this tender offer comes out and the stock goes up, you can bet the SEC's going to look hard at who bought how much in the preceding two or three weeks. You've got guys who buy and sell for you, in shell accounts that are really yours. I watched you work that way. These guys invest your money and take a percentage. You can invest a big piece of money—and spread it out so no single purchase is going to arouse suspicion."

"Two reasons," said Leeman. "I see a third one. You want a piece of my action."

Dave nodded. "Thirty-five percent."

"How much you think I'm going to put into this?"

"You'll tell me after I tell you the deal."

"Let me hear it."

They paused while a waiter took their orders: Dave's for a rare steak, Leeman's for a Caesar salad.

Before he heard the answer, Leeman had another question. "How you gonna explain on your 1040 how you came into this money?"

Dave grinned. "Bob . . . for Christ's sake! How do you report your income? I've got a friend with an account in Geneva, one with an account in Belize. I won't ask where yours is. Don't ask where mine is. We've got accounts. We've got shell corporations offshore. When you write a check to me, I want six or seven checks written to Joseph Windsor."

"Certified?"

"No, for God's sake! I trust you. You're going to trust me."

"You've moved into the big time, Dave. I guess I never figured you wouldn't. Hell . . . ten years from now you'll be able to buy me and sell me out of pocket change."

"You work things right, I'll keep you in pocket change. Now, let's get something straight. There is no way anybody can trace this back to me. Absolutely. The way I got the information, *nobody* can trace it to me. *No way!* Your role is to make sure I can stash the money with no suspicion it went to me."

"My role is to make sure nobody can trace it to me, either," said Leeman.

"I'll tell you the deal. You tell me how much you want to put in. Within ten days Mead Corporation is going to make a tender offer for Boise Cascade—"

"Jesus! You're not dealing with itty-bitty corporations."

"What'll you put in it, ol' buddy? Don't forget, you can't lose. That stock is surely not going to go down."

"A mill."

"Don't be chintzy. Chances like this don't come in every day."

"Two . . . It'll hurt if it don't work."

"It'll hurt if you don't try. Make it three. If the tender offer is not made, you'll have a three-million-dollar position in a sound company."

"Okay."

"I'm going to give you another level of insurance. I want to make one more foray into my friend's papers. After all, I'm putting in more of my own funds than I can afford. So, within the week you will get a call from 'Mr. Kimble.' Kimble will say, 'You won't believe this, but Larry has proposed to Elena'—or like that. That means the deal is on. If I say, 'Elena has said no to Larry,' that means the deal is off. If it's on, go for it! Now, don't hang in too long. You know how to judge that. Sell when it peaks."

V

Dave looked into Logan's briefcase one more time. He didn't have to take it. He just scanned the documents and put it back.

He put through a call to Bob Leeman—"Larry has proposed to Elena."

With his own $100,000, Jack's $100,000, and his $1,050,000 share of Leeman's commitment, he had $1,250,000 in the deal. Boise Cascade rose thirty-one percent on news of the tender offer. He made $387,500, to be deposited in Pictet & Compagnie in the Bahamas.

The chief winner was Leeman, who made more than $600,000. Dave didn't ask how much more Jack put in and so didn't know his profit.

Dave married Alexandra Petrovna Krylov—still her official name, never changed. They decided they would live for a short time in her apartment. He already had a telephone line there, and a fax machine—under an assumed name—and he moved in a few other things. They would be comfortable until they found the place they wanted. They didn't want to leave on a wedding trip immediately, so settled down into a comfortable domesticity for about two weeks.

He already knew she was a vigorous and exciting lover. She loved sex and wanted a lot of it, but she frowned and said she would think about it when he suggested something besides the straight thing. She satisfied him, and he satisfied her.

One thing she did like to do was take his penis from his pants and hold it in her hands, kneading and stroking, while they shared their evening drinks or watched television. She would be in no hurry to bring him to ejaculation.

One evening Jack Silver came to the apartment. As they sat and talked and drank, Alexandra began to rub Dave's cock inside his pants—right in front of Jack, who stared. Dave's pants were strained as he and Jack continued to talk business. Jack continued to stare.

On June 10 they flew to the Bahamas for their wedding trip. He carried checks rolled up in his socks, and on their first day "Joseph Windsor" went to Pictet and deposited them. His balance there now approached half a million dollars.

That night in bed she asked him, "Are you going to tell me what you're doing?"

"Do you really want to know?"

"I'm not sure if I do or don't."

"Let's put it this way. In all modesty, I'm doing damned well with Harcourt Barnham."

"And a hell of a lot better on your own."

VI

In the morning over breakfast, before they went to the beach, he read the *Times*, and she scanned the *Wall Street Journal*.

"Better take a look at this one, my friend," she said, handing him the *Journal*. She pointed to a story.

MEAD, BOISE CASCADE TENDER OFFER
UNDER INVESTIGATION
By David Link
Journal Staff
Unusually heavy trading in Boise Cascade shares in the week preceding the announcement of the Mead tender

---

offer has generated speculation and an investigation on the part of the SEC and the office of the New York District Attorney.

The sharp rise in the price of the stock, occasioned by the announcement of the offer, seems to have been anticipated.

"It's not a major deal," said Ralph Eddy, spokesman for the SEC, "but there is a clear suggestion that a few investors at least were working on the basis of insider information.

"We have no reason to believe," he went on, "that either corporation or the underwriter intentionally leaked the information. We think they are entirely innocent. We think it more likely that a dishonest or careless employee tipped a few friends, who then invested through delegates and probably made a maximum of a million dollars. It's small-time stuff. Nonetheless, we are continuing to look into the situation, which we will be doing in cooperation with the office of the New York District Attorney."

The district attorney was far more sanguine. "This is déjà vu all over again, as Yogi used to say. We have been on a crusade to root out this kind of thing and protect honest investors. I intend to get to the bottom of it."

Dave shrugged his shoulders insouciantly. "Good luck to Rudy," he said.

NINE

I

For Christmas, 1987, Emily had bought Cole a painting. With the help of the art school where she had last posed as a model, she located a young woman painter and bought from her a nude study she had done with Emily as a model. The young woman was an excellent painter, a disciple of realism, and she had begun to make her living painting portraits. Her portraits hung in the lobbies of banks and the reception rooms of law offices. Her studies of children were especially appreciated.

Emily's painting was a rather chaste nude. She sat on a rumpled dark green drape, with her legs folded back under her. She looked out of the painting with a faint smile on her face. Her breasts were of course bare, and a fringe, no more, of her pubic hair showed.

Emily had meant it to hang in their bedroom, but Cole insisted it must hang in the family room behind their living and dining rooms, where casual visitors to their home would not see it but their friends would.

Emily and Cole had to explain to the kids that they were not to take their friends back to the family room to see it. The kids took their friends to their own playroom in the basement, and in fact their friends never saw much of the house at all, much less the family room.

Friends did see it and without exception admired it.

Among the friends who did see it were Dave and Alexandra. Dave brought Alexandra over to New Jersey to introduce his bride to his friends. They went to dinner, and after dinner and brandies they settled in the family room where the painting hung.

"It is *so* beautiful!" Alexandra exclaimed. "Do you think this artist would do one of me?"

"Oh, I'm sure she would," said Emily. "That's how she makes a living."

Alexandra stood before the painting and admired it. "Do you look just like this?" she asked. "Did she paint you exactly as you are?"

Emily grinned and glanced back and forth between Cole and Dave. "The likeness of the face and the likeness of the boobs are the same."

Alexandra nodded thoughtfully. "You did pose as a nude model for some time, didn't you?"

"Yes."

"Would it embarrass you terribly to—"

Emily looked at Cole.

"Well . . . I can understand that it would be embarrassing. So— I'll tell you what, Emily. You take off your top, and I'll take off mine. Then you won't be the only one—"

Emily laughed. "What the hell. Hundreds of people have seen me."

"I don't believe this," Cole muttered.

Emily lifted a pink cashmere sweater over her head and un- hooked and dropped her bra, exposing her small, pear-shaped white breasts with vivid pink areolae and darker pink nipples. Alexandra had to remove a black knit dress, then her bra, to show breasts that were three times the size of Emily's: firm and shaped like half melons, with brownish areolae and hard, wrin- kled, dark nipples.

"See?" Emily asked. "She painted my boobs with just as much accuracy as she painted my face."

"I don't believe this," Cole repeated.

Dave smiled and watched to see what would happen next.

"C'mon, honey," Emily said with a smile. "I mean, c'mon. We're grown-up." She turned to Dave. "Y' like?"

He nodded. "I like."

Alexandra turned to Cole and tipped her head.

"I like," he said.

Alexandra was sitting now in a half slip. She pulled it back, showing her legs above the tops of her dark stockings and the black garter straps that held them up. Emily pushed back her skirt. She was wearing panty hose, so showed only her legs.

II

One of the duties that fell to the more junior members of the bar was to represent indigent criminal defendants by appointment. It was in the Miranda warning: ". . . if you can't afford an attorney, one will be appointed for you." Only in exceptionally difficult cases, or cases that required appeal, did the young lawyer receive more than a hundred dollars for conducting a defense.

Most of the accused were pitiable wretches. Cole would never forget a man accused of forging a check telling him that he *couldn't* be convicted. "I didn't write the man's name on the check. I just wrote his *first* name. *She* wrote his last name. Neither one of us wrote his whole name." The man grinned through the bars of the jail. He refused to believe and asked for another lawyer when Cole told him that he and his wife would both go to prison for the forgery.

Almost none of the dozen or so criminal defenses he conducted on appointment generated any sympathy except one.

A nineteen-year-old girl named Rosaria Lopez, a seamstress who lived in lower Manhattan and worked in a sweatshop, was under indictment for burglary. If convicted she faced years in prison. Her story was that her boyfriend had taken her to a house he said was his uncle's. He told her to sit on the front porch while he went around in back and got a key from under a flowerpot, after which he would come through the house and let her in. He did come to the front door and let her in, and they gathered up and put in his car a portable television set, an electric coffeemaker, a toaster oven, and some silverware—all of which he said his uncle had told him he wanted to give him. They were stopped and arrested within a mile of the house.

Cole had heard a lot about the case, was inclined to believe the story, and suggested to the judge that he be appointed to defend Rosaria Lopez—that is, for once to be appointed to defend someone who might not be guilty.

He went to the jail, where she sat disconsolately on her cot, smoking a cigarette and talking listlessly to a fifty-year-old black woman on another cot. It was a four-cot cage, barred on three sides, one of two that constituted the women's jail.

"Miss Lopez."

She crushed her cigarette, got up, and came to the bars.

"My name is Cole Jennings. I'm a lawyer and have been appointed by the court to defend you."

"Yeah?"

She was a little pudgy but otherwise was an attractive young woman. It was summer-warm in the jail, in spite of the open windows outside the cage, and she was wearing a T-shirt and a pair of skimpy blue-denim shorts cut down from jeans. He had been told that deputies and others came in to have a look at her. Two or three had taken pictures of her.

"I'm going to try to get you out of this mess."

She gripped the bars in tight fists and nodded. "I no like it in here. I *hate* bein' locked in. And I'm scared!"

"Scared of—?"

"Bein' sent up! I don't want to go . . ."

"I've heard your story, that your boyfriend lied to you."

"*He did!* An' you know where he's gonna be tonight?"

"Where?"

"Drinkin' beer someplace. Drivin' around. Prob'ly seein' some other girl. He's out on bail. An' I'm locked up in here, like a animal! His family could put up the bail for me, too. But—" She shook her head. "But they wouldn'."

"You've been in jail . . . three months?"

"Three months an' some."

"Okay. The deal is probably going to go something like this . . . Rosaria. The district attorney is going to want your testimony against your boyfriend Darryl."

"If I testify, does that get me outta bein' sent up? Does it get me outta here?"

"I can't promise. I'll work on it."

"Mr. Jennings . . . I got a little sister by my mama's second marriage. She kept askin' where Rosaria was. Finally they had to tell her I was in jail. She cried! She sends me little pictures she draws with her crayons on poster paper. Some of them are me, behind bars, with big tears on my face."

She stepped over to her cot and reached under it, retrieved a picture childishly drawn with red and brown crayons on yellow paper.

Real tears swelled out of the girl's eyes. "I didn' do nothin' wrong," she wept. "I didn' do nothin' wrong. I just *believed* that son of a bitch! *An' here I am!* Here I am. I wanta go home!"

When Cole met with the district attorney a problem arose.

"I can't just drop this case in return for her testimony, Cole. You believe her. I don't. I think she knew perfectly well what she was doing. She's a pretty worldly girl. So far as her value as a witness is concerned, her testimony isn't going to add much to anything. We know they were in the house. We know they stole what they stole. Her little story that he lied to her doesn't do much."

The district attorney smoked a cigar as they talked. His desk was covered with a sheet of heavy glass, under which he had pushed a dozen photographs. Framed, autographed pictures on his walls were of prominent politicians, including—to Cole's surprise—a personally autographed picture of Hubert Humphrey.

"You're saying her testimony—her cooperation—isn't worth anything?"

"Not a hell of a lot. She can testify they were inside the house. We have fingerprint evidence of that. She can testify they stole a TV set. We know that; they had it in their possession when they were arrested."

"What if she's telling the truth?" Cole asked. "It'd be a tragedy if the kid goes to prison for a long term."

The district attorney studied the ash on his cigar for a moment. "The reformatory is full of Hispanic girls. She'll be at home there. But tell you what I'll do," he said. "In return for her testimony I'll let her plead guilty to breaking and entering."

Cole frowned. "She'll have a felony record."

"If she keeps her nose clean, that won't make much difference. She's not going to apply for a job in a bank or as a schoolteacher."

"And what kind of a sentence?"

"Six months. She's already done ninety-eight days, more than half of it. Of course, she might win a jury's sympathy and get acquitted. Chance she can take."

Cole tried to explain it to Rosaria. "If you plead guilty to breaking and entering, which is a reduced charge, you'll have to spend eighty-two more days in jail. But you won't, as you put it, get 'sent up.' "

Her lips trembled, and she sobbed. *"Eighty-two more days!"*

"You'll be out in October."

She leaned on the bars as though she could somehow squeeze through them. Her breasts hung out over the cross brace.

"Let me explain this," he said. "You can plead not guilty to burglary and get maybe five years if a jury finds you guilty. Or you could be found not guilty."

"You don't think I got a good chance for that."

"I'm afraid I have to say I don't."

She gripped and tugged as if she could shake the unyielding steel bars. "Eighty-two more days! I'll miss my little sister's birthday."

"One more thing. With a guilty plea, you'll have a criminal record. It'll be with you the rest of your life."

"Meaning what?"

"Meaning you could never get a job in, say, nursing or teaching school."

She sneered. "Who's gonna?"

"Well . . . the decision is up to you."

She began to cry. "All I want is to *go home!* It ain't much—jus' a crowded apartment on Eighteenth Street—but it's home. I don't like it in here! All I want is to go home. Eighty-two more days! *Jesus!*"

On the day when she entered her plea, Cole met her in the jury room to rehearse what she was to do and say in the courtroom. She was wearing a very plain white blouse and a dark blue skirt. Only when the time came to go into the courtroom did the matron take off her handcuffs.

"Miss Lopez," the judge said in as kindly a manner as he could, "you have been represented by able counsel. I know he has explained your rights. But you must understand that a plea of guilty is final. You cannot appeal. Do you understand?"

She glanced around the courtroom. For her it was undoubtedly more frightening a place than the jail. The judge wore a stern black robe. The big room was paneled with dark wood. People stared at her.

"Do you understand, Miss Lopez?"

She nodded, mouth open.

"Then, how do you plead to the charge of breaking and entering: guilty or not guilty? And you must say it, Miss Lopez. I cannot accept a nod."

"Guilty, I guess," she whispered hoarsely.

The judge smiled tolerantly. "I'm sorry. It can't be 'I guess.' Do you plead guilty or not guilty."

"Guilty," she croaked, then began to sob.

"On your plea of guilty, the court sentences you to imprisonment in the county jail for a term of six months. The hundred and seven days you have already been confined will count against your sentence. In view of the fact that you seem to be without means, the court will not fine you and will waive the costs."

The matron stepped up, handcuffed the sobbing girl, and led her out of the courtroom.

III

Cole sat with Emily over martinis and sticks of celery and carrot. He was despondent.

"I have just taken part in sending a nineteen-year-old girl to jail—*back* to jail, actually—saddled with a felony record, when she was not guilty."

"You're sure she's not guilty?"

He shrugged. "Judges charging juries on the definition of 'reasonable doubt' say, 'Everything in human affairs is subject to doubt.' But I'd make book on this one."

"What were your options?" Emily asked.

"That's the system. If she'd gone to trial, I have to say I think she would have been convicted by a jury—because she would have been the only witness for her defense. Her boyfriend Darryl could have testified that he lied to her, but you couldn't trust him to do that. He'd have figured that made *him* look worse."

"If she took her chances—why couldn't she have pleaded not guilty to breaking and entering?"

Cole shook his head. "Not an option. The DA offered the reduction of charge in return for a guilty plea. Anyway, if she'd pleaded not guilty to breaking and entering and had been convicted, she'd have got a year at least, instead of her six months."

"Why? Why a bigger sentence?"

"Every judge I ever heard of will do it. They say confession is good for the soul, a step toward rehabilitation, I suppose. Well, it's good for the sentence, too. Judges like to talk about 'owning up to it.' If you 'own up'—plead guilty—you do less time than you do if you insist on your right to a jury trial."

"In other words, there's a penalty for asserting your rights."

"Exactly. That's the way it is."

"What about Darryl?"

"He pleaded guilty, too, but to burglary. He's going to do five years. But there's something damned wrong with a system that sends Rosaria Lopez to jail for six months for a crime I'm just sure she didn't commit."

"What about a lie-detector test?" Emily asked.

"There is no such thing as a lie detector," Cole said firmly. "It's a myth. They say a lie detector can be manipulated. That's why the so-called evidence it produces is not admissible in court. No. Rosaria got snared in the system. It's nobody's fault, I suppose, but she's going to miss her little sister's birthday party. She'll still be in jail, until October."

IV

Emily had become a little leery about the social relationship that had developed between her and Cole and Dave and his new wife. She had bared her breasts in their family room that evening, in the presence of the painting, but now it seemed that Dave or Alexandra would suggest they do the same whenever they were together. For Alexandra it was a completely casual thing to do. Emily, who had after all posed many, many hours as a nude model, was not prudish about it but wasn't entirely easy, either.

Cole accepted the idea with restrained enthusiasm. Obviously he enjoyed the sight of Alexandra's big boobs and saw no reason why Emily should not let Dave see hers.

Alexandra hired the artist who did Emily's nude to do one of her. It hung prominently in the living room of the apartment she and Dave still shared. It was very different. She stood facing out of the painting, her hands interlaced behind her head, her hips tilted slightly. She faced the viewer with an open, amused smile. The picture had been painted in the apartment. Alexandra's behind touched the marble top of an antique Russian sideboard, and one of her ballet posters hung on the wall behind her—all meticulously painted and clearly fixing the place where the painting had been done.

The two paintings could not have contrasted more. Alexandra's was flagrantly erotic.

They had come to the apartment after dinner at the Russian Tea Room, where Emily had been introduced to a culinary experience she had never known before.

When the two wives stripped to the waist and the two couples were sipping champagne, Dave said, "Y' know, Cole, the world is filled with marvelous opportunities, and I have to think you're missing out on most of them. I can understand your going home to Wyckoff after establishing yourself in a Manhattan firm. What I don't understand is why you don't look out for ways to make big money."

"How would I make big money?" Cole asked. He knew what Dave had in mind, but he asked anyway.

"Well . . . I could give you some market tips. That's my business, you know: to research investments."

"Strictly straight?" Emily asked.

"Let me put it this way," Dave said. "I have a stock in mind. Every shred of information I have about it came off of NEXIS, the computer search system. You can get SEC filings. But you can also get news stories. You put two and two together. Every bit of information I have on the stock I'm about to mention is public. Anybody can get it. You just have to know what you're looking for and how to find it."

"Okay. What company do you have in mind?"

"Ever hear of Mountain Gas? Put a few dollars into it, Cole. I'll call and tell you when to buy. I swear you won't be sorry."

"Mountain Gas . . ."

"And be ready to sell when I call you."

V

Cole put a thousand dollars into the stock. It was selling at 13¼. Two weeks later it was selling at 22⅝, and Dave called and advised him to sell. Net of commissions, Cole made almost seven hundred dollars on the transaction.

What happened was that Mountain Gas announced the opening of a major new field. The stock rose. Independent geologists came in and took a look and pronounced the field minor. The stock fell back to 12⅞.

They sat down again in the Manhattan apartment.

"They drilled in a well," Dave explained. "I knew they were drilling. That was public information. The well made gas. They got enthusiastic about what they'd found. Their announcement sent the stock up unrealistically. I was skeptical. That's why I told you to be ready to sell. In and out at the right time . . ."

"Do you mind if I ask you a question?"

Dave was distracted. Alexandra was stroking his penis.

"Question?"

"How much did *you* put in it?"

"I can't have a trading account," said Dave, his voice strained by what Alexandra was doing. "I can help my friends."

He didn't say that Windsor Nassau Associates had put a hundred thousand dollars into the deal and come out with seventy thousand dollars profit.

Alexandra looked curiously at Emily. "Don't you play with Cole?" she asked innocently, cupping Dave's scrotum in one hand and raising it, straining his slacks.

Emily frowned quizzically at Cole. "Usually in private."

"I wouldn't mind," he said.

Emily put her hand in his crotch and began to stroke his engorged penis.

"I can put you onto lots of deals," said Dave. "Like I said, you ought to be making some big money. What you're doing brings you alot of satisfaction, but you aren't going to get rich at it."

Cole looked at Emily. "You want to be rich, honey?"

"I can think of worse things," she said.

Conversation about stocks was not really possible with two wives sitting bare-breasted and two husbands with their penises pulled out of their pants. They drank champagne. Alexandra used the clicker and switched on the eleven o'clock television news.

"You guys ought to stay overnight," Dave said when the news was over. "Your baby-sitter . . . ?"

"Was told we might stay. We can call her."

"Well, then," said Alexandra. "Let's bring them, Emily. We can do it again while we look at Johnny Carson."

She handed Emily a wad of Kleenexes and clutched another wad in her left hand. She began to masturbate Dave vigorously, and in a minute he ejaculated. Emily did the same, and shortly after Dave did, Cole came hard.

Emily called home. She told the baby-sitter to call her parents and say that Mr. and Mrs. Jennings were staying in New York overnight. It was all right. The girl was eighteen and sometimes stayed overnight with her charges.

They finished the bottle of champagne. Without asking what anyone wanted, Alexandra went to the freezer and poured the icy Stolichnaya into glasses also from the freezer. She brought this into the living room with a tray of crackers and a bowl of black caviar.

The vodka was cold enough to cause the head to ache. It had to be sipped slowly. When they had finished their glasses, she brought others.

Emily knew she was getting drunk. In fact, they were all getting drunk.

Midnight came. Carson's guest was Jonathan Winters. They always laughed at him, but this time they laughed louder and longer.

"Tell y' what," Alexandra said to Emily, slurring her words. "Why don't I jack off Cole and you jack off Dave?"

Emily didn't want to, but she no longer had the will to refuse.

The two men accepted the idea.

They switched seats. Emily found herself with Dave's oversized cock in her hands. She accepted Kleenexes and set to work on him. It didn't take long. He moaned as he squirted into the tissues. Alexandra brought Cole a moment later.

Dave didn't try to touch Emily's breasts or to kiss her. He stood and returned to his seat beside his wife.

"Maybe we can switch sometime," Alexandra whispered into Dave's ear. "Would you like to watch me and Cole?"

Dave smiled and kissed her.

TEN

APRIL, 1989

"What's it come to?" Emily asked as she watched Cole tote up the numbers on a yellow legal pad.

"It comes to $58,315.25, after brokers' commissions," he said.

She shook her head. "It troubles me."

"You think he's feeding me tips based on insider information?"

"He's too damned uncannily right," she said. "Besides that, he's got to be making ten times as much for his own account—even though he says he doesn't have one."

"That's easy enough to figure," said Cole. "He's got an offshore account somewhere. And what's more, he doesn't pay taxes."

"I'm uneasy about knowing those people," she said. "It's only a matter of time before they suggest we trade off—I mean, *really* trade off."

Cole shrugged. "We won't do it. That's all there is to that. We won't do it."

"We've gone a long way already," she said. "If you'd asked me six months ago, I'd have said I'd dissolve into utter hysterics if anyone suggested we do what we've done. And now . . . God! It seems like it's commonplace."

"I don't see how we can stop seeing them." He tapped his finger on the numbers on the yellow legal pad. "But we can say no if—"

"Right," said Emily dryly. "Just say no. We seem unable to say no to anything they suggest."

II

Alexandra Petrovna Krylov Shea wanted to return to Kiev, to see the city of her birth.

"We can fly to Kiev and from there to Leningrad," she said.

"Moscow?" he asked.

She shrugged. "If you want. But I'm not much interested in Moscow. I want to see the old St. Petersburg. I want to see the Winter Palace and the Hermitage."

"Well . . ."

Alexandra was no fool, and when he said he wanted to spend a couple of days in Zurich on the way, she didn't even ask why. She knew why.

They checked into the Dolder Grand Hotel, and Alexandra went out to explore Zurich while Dave kept an appointment previously arranged by telephone from New York.

The offices of Trust Management AG—that is, Trust Management *Aktiengesellschaft*, meaning joint stock company—were peculiar. Though situated in a modern, high-rise, steel-and-glass office building, they had the look of something from the nineteenth century. Maroon plush drapes covered the glass outer walls, as if they covered only windows. Oriental carpets lay on the parquet floors. No fluorescent lights glared. Bulbs in milk-glass globes, plus bankers' lamps, lighted the offices.

Executive offices had fireplaces. Dave wondered where, in a building of this type, the smoke went.

As Dave would learn, the status of people in the offices could be known at a glance by those who knew the dress code. Men wore three-piece suits with white shirts. The highest ranking men wore dark blue pin-striped suits. They alone wore colorful bow ties. Bow ties and dark blue pin-striped suits were forbidden to juniors, who wore gray and black suits and ties with regimental stripes. Women wore skirts. Slacks were forbidden. Women's status was indicated by the length of their skirts. Secretaries and file clerks wore minis; women with some executive status wore their skirts knee length. Women with status wore jackets over white blouses. Secretaries and file clerks wore pastel-colored blouses and no jackets.

Dave was received in the office of Axel Schnyder, a senior man at TM AG. Schnyder was sixty years old or more. His face was wrinkled and jowly. His blue eyes, set in concentric wrinkles, bulged. He wore the dark blue pin-striped suit and a red and gray bow tie.

Schnyder's desk was a massive antique, made of cherry and elaborately carved. He took a flask from the rolltop desk behind him and poured brandy into snifters.

"I believe you said on the telephone that you can place a million dollars with us for management. Frankly, Mr. Shea, that is our minimum."

The man spoke flawless, British-accented English.

"I can maybe put more with you, if I sell—"

Schnyder raised a hand to interrupt him. "The million will be entirely satisfactory. We will review your situation, to see what we can recommend to you. The million, I gather, is with the Pictet bank, Nassau branch."

"Yes."

"Under a different name."

"Under the name Joseph Windsor."

"I assume you have not disclosed to Pictet that Joseph Windsor is a fiction."

Dave nodded.

"But they know," said Schnyder. "Pictet is not stupid."

"They haven't suggested that they know."

"They are also circumspect."

"As are you," Dave said with a faint smile.

"Let that not be exaggerated," said Schnyder. "We will hold completely confidential whatever financial information we receive from you, including the name you choose to put on your account. If you are sued, we will not disclose any information about your assets. There is an exception. If someone obtains a judgment in a

Swiss court, the Swiss court will order us to disclose, and we must. You should note, too, that if it sees any reason, your Internal Revenue Service will seek a judgment from a Swiss court. In any event, Mr. Shea, Trust Management AG is not in the business of helping Americans to evade their income taxes. We will assume you are complying with American law."

Axel Schnyder lifted his brandy snifter in salute and took a sip. Dave followed. The cognac was old and excellent.

He had found what he wanted. Schnyder knew perfectly well that Dave would not be paying taxes on his profits—indeed would not file the required disclosure that he had assets on deposit overseas.

"Now, then, sir," said Schnyder, "what are your investment goals?"

"I want confidentiality," said Dave. "To begin with."

"Yes. Harcourt Barnham would be most distressed to learn that you are trading on your own."

"I want to trade internationally and build an asset account sufficient to allow me to exert a major influence on mergers and acquisitions in the States—where there lies the promise of immense profits. Ours is a merger-and-acquisition economy. Little companies are being squeezed out."

"One million dollars is a modest beginning," said Schnyder.

"I can be patient. Besides, I expect to add to that amount very shortly."

Schnyder nodded thoughtfully. "Very well. I will ask you to sign a power of attorney. It will authorize us to set up bank accounts for you and to invest funds as you instruct. It will also authorize us to invest as we see fit. You have checked our record. Otherwise you wouldn't be here."

He pulled a document from his desk drawer. It was the power of attorney, with Dave's name already typed in. "Read it over."

The document was short and simple. One paragraph read:

The settlor represents to the trustee that he owes no unpaid taxes to any government and that he will file all legally required reports and pay all his several tax obligations in a complete and timely manner.

Dave pulled a Mont Blanc pen from his pocket and signed the document with a flourish.

"Now, sir," said Schnyder. "I imagine you will want to assume another name."

"If you recommend it."

Schnyder smiled wryly. "I do. And more than that, I am ready to suggest a name and nationality. If there is one nation in Europe where confidentiality is better respected than in Switzerland, that nation is Austria. Unfortunately for Austria, it went through many traumas while we here were sheltered by our neutrality. Otherwise, Austrian banks might be the world's asset managers. Anyway . . . I suggest the name Reinhard Brüning." He shrugged. "I don't know why. It comes off the top of the head, as you Americans say."

"Okay. And I'm a resident of—"

"Vienna. If you agree to the name, please sign your new name on these cards. Keep one, so you can practice the signature. I will open your account for you. Also, you will need a deposit box, which I will arrange."

"At . . . Pictet?"

"No. I have every confidence in Pictet & Compagnie, but putting everything in one bank is a mistake. I would like to set up an account for you at Deutsche Bank, where your deposit box will also be. You will have an account number, which I can use to get into your account or your box."

Dave nodded.

"Now. Communication. TM AG has a modest office in New York City. It is in the Chrysler Building. You can leave messages there for me, and they will be sent to me over our private wire. I suggest that our office call your home only and leave only the message that Mr. Lee is calling. Then you can pick up my message at our office. *You* can pick it up? No. You must never be seen anywhere near our office. Your wife . . . a trusted friend . . . somebody. Better it not always be the same person. Your messenger should say only that he or she has come to pick up the message from Mr. Lee."

"Sounds good," said Dave.

"You understand, our services are not free of charge."

"I didn't expect so."

"You may find that the way we *invest* your money is the best thing we can do for you."

"That's why I came to you."

Schnyder lifted his snifter. "To a long and mutually profitable relationship."

They drank.

"One more thing, Mr. Shea. I strongly recommend you cease to trade on insider information. It is very dangerous."

III

Alexandra enjoyed her visit to Kiev. She took Dave to see the house where she was born and where she lived until her parents took her to America. Dave knew almost nothing about Kiev and Ukraine. He knew the Nazis had overrun the area in 1941, and he expected to see a shattered city being shabbily restored with grim, square Stalinist architecture.

Well, maybe. But they stayed at the Hotel Ukraina, built in 1908, and still a hotel that would do credit to any city in the world. Great churches had survived: St. Sophia, built in the eleventh century and modeled on Hagia Sofia in Constantinople, had been dynamited during the war but had been lovingly restored; St. Andrews, built in the eighteenth century; a Roman Catholic Cathedral, called the Gothic Cathedral; the Shevchenko Opera Theatre; and so on. Alexandra explained that the culture of Ukraine was older than the Russian and different.

Alexandra did not want to look again at the huge sculptures erected in memory of the war dead, so they did not go to the memorial.

"We think the Russians barbarians," she said. "The princes of

Kiev were building great churches and beautiful homes when the Russians were still building wooden kremlins."

They took their dinners in the excellent restaurants of the hotel, where she introduced Dave to Ukrainian dishes. One evening her uncle and aunt joined them for dinner: two sixty-something people who were happy to be invited to dinner in the Hotel Ukraina. Dave could understand nothing of the conversation, except when Alexandra broke off to explain to him.

Though she did not entirely favor miniskirts, she wore one that evening, maybe to demonstrate to her family how American she had become.

"My uncle wonders what you do for a living. My Aunt thinks you're very handsome!"

Dave smiled. "Tell them the next time we visit I will try to speak their language."

Back in their room, Alexandra wanted them to take a bath together in the huge bathtub that was the focus of the bathroom. "You could float a canoe in it," Dave had said when he first saw it. They were soaking in warm, soapy water. For the first time, she put her mouth to his penis. As her warm tongue slowly circled his penis, he turned her body so his tongue could perform the same on her clitoris.

They skipped Moscow and flew to Leningrad. Their airplane was a Tupolev 104 marked, "АЗроФПоТ."

The exterior paint was worn through, the interior was drab, and the service was surly. There was no nonstop service from Kiev to Leningrad, so they sat on the airplane for an hour at Moscow's Sheremetyevo Airport before taking off again for Leningrad Pulkovo Airport.

They stayed at the Astoria Hotel and from there toured the city and the area, including of course the famous Winter Palace and the Hermitage.

Alexandra was happy as a child. Though she was from Kiev, she had never seen Leningrad. Even so, she knew what was there and what was to be seen. They spent an entire day in the Hermitage, viewing the most prestigious art collection in the world. Alexandra knew what was to be seen. She pointed out Rembrandts, Titians, El Grecos, Goyas, Manets, Monets, Van Goghs . . .

Her enthusiasm might have been infectious, but Dave's mind was focused elsewhere. He hoped he concealed his boredom and his anxiety to be back in New York.

IV

SEPTEMBER, 1989

David Shea was not a fair-haired boy at Harcourt Barnham. He was a successful analyst and had been allowed to involve the bank in several small ventures; but he was not playing in the big leagues with Harcourt, and he resented it. The fact that he had only been with the bank three years did not influence his thinking. He saw others from the class of 1978 ahead of him, and he smoldered.

The problem for the bank was that he did not seem wholly committed. They did not guess that he was trading through offshore accounts. He was distracted. His attention was fixed on those accounts, and he really had limited energy for the pedestrian work he did at Harcourt.

He was not entirely surprised when he was summoned to the office of John Thomas Miley, executive vice president and chief operating officer.

Miley was a tidy-desk man. He had been heard to voice the cliché, "A tidy desk is a tidy mind." On his desktop he had a pen-and-pencil set, mounted on square-cut black stone, a gold clock in the middle of a ship's wheel, and a single leather folder. These items were set precisely parallel to the front of his desk.

On the credenza behind him sat an IBM AT desktop computer. It was obsolete, but probably Miley didn't care. To either side of it sat family pictures, precisely aligned.

"I've called you in because I am curious about your goals, Mr. Shea."

Dave's thought, which he did not voice, was that it was to do better than John Thomas Miley, who probably didn't take home more than half a million dollars a year. Instead, he murmured modestly that he hoped to make a success of himself.

"With us?" Miley asked bluntly.

"I hope so."

"You're not going at it very well."

Miley was fifty-five years old, a man who sunburned and did not tan on weekend cruises on his ketch, *Sally II*. He glowed red today. He was a squat man, not more than five feet seven. He was bald. His piercing little eyes seemed always to stare, never just to glance casually. His gray suit could have been better tailored, and right now it could have stood pressing.

"What am I doing wrong, Mr. Miley?" Dave asked humbly.

"It's difficult to put my finger on," said Miley. "We sense a lack of dedication. We wonder if you are really happy here."

"I am happy," Dave said crisply. "I think I am ready for heavier responsibilities."

"What *you* think in that respect is not material. You will have promotion when *we* think you are ready."

"Yes, sir."

"How could you afford to take a vacation in the Soviet Union?"

"My wife was born there. She paid for it."

"You didn't ask permission to be gone those two weeks. You just announced you were going . . . and went."

"Would permission have been withheld?"

Miley raised his chin. "I suppose not. But the *form* of the thing—the courtesies, the niceties—might have been observed. Banking, Mr. Shea, conservative banking, has many traditions. It is a culture, almost. There is no place in it for eccentrics."

"Individualists . . ." Dave suggested.

"Nonconformists," said Miley. "Your generation prizes nonconformity as a value. Fine. There are plenty of places where it is valued. The banking floor of a bank like Harcourt Barnham is not one of them."

"Are you terminating me?"

Miley shook his head. "Another tradition is that young men are given the opportunity to become a part of the culture. Regard this meeting as the occasion for a word of friendly advice."

Dave nodded. "I appreciate it."

That evening Dave described the meeting to Alexandra. "The son of a bitch treated me like some kind of schoolboy," he said.

"Maybe you should quit. You don't need him."

"That's the trouble. I do. I need a front. I need to have it look like I'm a banker. I need to file income tax returns. If I didn't report my salary and bonuses as income, the IRS would want to know what I live on. Boesky and Milken have got us all on an IRS shit list. I have to be careful."

"Let me tell you something," said Alexandra. "I've been retained by United to look out for their public relations. They're going to make a raid on Allegheny, and they're afraid they'll get a reputation as a voracious aggressor. You should be able to pick up a little change by having Windsor Nassau or TM AG lay a few quiet dollars on Allegheny."

"I'm deeply grateful to you, Alexandra, but I'm not going to take the slightest risk—"

"I thought you had things set up so there will be no risk," she said. "What else were we doing in Zurich?"

"If word of the Allegheny raid leaks," he said, "everybody who knows about it will be suspect. Including you. And you're married to an investment banker, small-time though he may be."

Alexandra shrugged and lifted her glass of single-malt Scotch.

"But I'll tell you what," said Dave, sipping Beefeater gin from a glass of ice cubes and no vermouth. "I'm going to *get* that son of a bitch! I'll teach *him* not to call me on the carpet and lecture me like a schoolboy."

V

John Thomas Miley was the conservative, tradition-bound man he said he was. He had no idea what he had bought for himself when he incurred the animosity of David Shea.

A banking lobby with tellers' cages occupied the first floor of the Harcourt building. A trading floor equipped with computers occupied the second. It was there that Dave had his desk. The executive offices of the bank were on the third floor. The fourth was used for the storage of files. The ten floors above that were leased to law firms, insurance companies, and the like.

Dave arrived at the building a little after three in the morning. He was wearing beige coveralls with a sewn-on pocket patch reading MAINTENANCE, INC.

The doors were locked, but many people had keys, since many worked as late as midnight, often going out for a deli snack in mid-evening and then returning and letting themselves in with their keys. He opened the door to the right of the revolving door that was the main entry.

Immediately inside the front doors was an elevator lobby with a reception desk. The banking lobby was behind that.

Dave paused in the elevator lobby and pulled on surgical gloves. Then he entered the stairwell and climbed stairs to the third floor.

Apart from the lights in the EXIT signs, the floor was dark. He explored a little to be sure there really was no one on the floor. No one was. At this hour the cleaning women had long since finished their work and left the building.

Miley's door was unlocked. This was another element of his banking culture: that an obsession with physical security was undignified.

His desk drawers were unlocked.

Dave sat down in Miley's chair, opened a drawer, and began to read files by the light of a flashlight he had carried for the purpose.

After half an hour he carried one file folder to the copying room and Xeroxed twenty pages of documents, making two copies of each page.

His find could not have been more perfect. Harcourt Barnham was a member of a consortium of banks being asked to underwrite a bond issue to finance a hostile takeover.

The target company was none less than Texaco. What was more, the documents disclosed that the raid on Texaco was only fronted by the company that would make the tender offer—North American Investments. Behind NAM was the dark and brooding presence of Carl "Les" Lester, a rapacious raider who had acquired and dismantled many companies, selling off what didn't suit him as to profitability and keeping control of those that did.

Texaco management knew what was coming and were dragging their wagons into a circle. One defense against a raider like Lester was to find what was called a white knight—that is, a more friendly bidder who would not dismantle a company. Texaco had been talking to DuPont, which already owned Conoco as a wholly owned subsidiary. DuPont was a major player in the petroleum and petroleum-marketing businesses, and acquisition of Texaco could strongly fortify its position.

The prospective tender offer would drive up Texaco stock. Disclosure that Lester was behind it would drive it up more—because it would be understood he would bid unrealistically high, in the expectation of making an enormous profit from dismantling the company.

Dave restored the file folder to Miley's drawer, then tucked the copies inside his coveralls. On a whim he moved the pen-and-pencil set so that it was no longer parallel to the front edge of the desktop—but only slightly so. Miley would assume a cleaning woman had nudged it while dusting his desk, but he would be at pains to realign it, would in fact take half a minute to get it just right.

Dave left the bank as he had entered, through the front door. He walked as casually as he could, feigning weariness. A police car came by, and he lifted his hand in a weak salute to the cop.

Two blocks from the bank he entered a dead-end alley. At the end, to one side of a loading dock, sat three green Dumpsters. The space behind them formed a small cranny. Dave climbed on the loading dock, then jumped down into that space. The things he had left there had not been disturbed.

One thing was a cheap vinyl briefcase, soft and without a handle, that you carried under your arm. He pulled out his copied documents and stuffed them in the case. Then he stripped off the coveralls and pulled on blue jeans and a gray sweatshirt. His surgical gloves were in a pocket of the coveralls. So was his flashlight, which he had been careful not to touch so as to leave fingerprints. He dropped the coveralls into one of the Dumpsters, then opened one of the others and pulled out stuffed plastic trash bags, which he tossed in the first Dumpster until the coveralls were buried under two or three layers of trash bags.

He walked to a subway station and caught an uptown train.

VI

On his instructions, Trust Management AG bought Texaco stock for his account. Then its New York office arranged for the copied documents to come to the attention of a reporter for the *Wall Street Journal*. The *Journal* was ethical and cautious. It verified the facts, then broke the story.

Texaco fought off the Lester bid. Its investors didn't like his reputation.

Nonetheless, Dave's account at Deutsche Bank was $200,000 richer on the timely buying and selling of Texaco stock.

That was not a lot of money. But Dave was to have greater satisfaction.

He arrived at the bank at eight o'clock on the morning after the *Journal* article appeared. Another member of the class of 1978 came immediately to his desk.

"Hey, it appears that Mr. Tidy is in deep shit."

"Really? Why?"

"Some of the information leaked to the *Journal* was stuff that only Tidy knew. If he didn't leak it himself, at very best he was careless. Lester is apoplectic. The board of directors is meeting this morning. Tidy is toast. I wouldn't be surprised if he's out of here before the day is over."

And so it proved. John Thomas Miley was terminated as an officer of the bank.

Dave sat beside Alexandra on their couch that evening. He had a martini on the rocks, and watched the financial news talk about Miley's demise.

"I said I'd have his ass."

"Don't take too much pleasure in it," she said. "There should be little satisfaction in destroying a man."

ELEVEN

I

MARCH, 1990

Little Emily spoke to Emily over the breakfast table after Cole had left for his office. "Mommy . . . uh . . . the, uh . . . *nude* painting of you is *beautiful*! I mean . . . I always just thought it was sort of funny."

" 'Mommy nekkid,' was what you used to call it," said Emily gently.

"Well . . . I'm sorry I called it that."

"Don't be sorry. I'm glad you like it," Emily said.

"I've explained to Cole that it's a work of art. I don't think he understands. He just grins, then puts his hands over his face."

"He's a little young to understand," said Emily. "You didn't, when I brought it home."

"I'm older now," the child said gravely.

"Yes, you are."

"Mommy . . . When I'm older, can I be painted like that?"

"If you want to."

"Could I be painted that way *now*?"

"Let's wait awhile, Emily. Sooner than you think, you'll be an adult, and you'll be one the rest of your life. There'll be plenty of time to do grown-up things."

•　　　•　　　•

In his office that morning, Cole received Julian Musgrave, the automobile dealer who had subsidized Dave Shea as a football player. The man was sixty-four years old now, but the years had not been unkind. Except that the fringe of hair around the edges of his bald head had turned white, he was still a bouncy, exuberant man. He still wore a checked jacket of cream-white and brown, a red golf shirt, and dark brown slacks.

"I understand you're a talented lawyer," he said bluntly.

"I hope someone knowledgeable said so."

"Someone knowledgeable did," Musgrave affirmed. "To come straight to the point, my lawyer, who has represented me for twenty years, is retiring. I need a new man. To be frank, Mr. Jennings, it appears to me that you are doing work not entirely worthy of your talents. Probating small estates. Getting people divorces. Defending criminals. Writing wills and deeds and leases. You can tell me it's none of my business, but I wonder why you left Harris & Pickens and came home to New Jersey."

"I won't say it's none of your business because I've answered the question many times. Harris & Pickens had made me a litigator. The pressure was getting to me, and I was drinking too much. So . . . I'm not getting rich, and there's no glamour in what I do; but I am comfortable. I have a nice home, a wife, two small children . . ."

Musgrave pulled a cigar from his jacket pocket, ran it under his nose, sniffed it, then apparently made a decision not to light it and returned it to his pocket. "I own six automobile agencies," he said. "I can sell you anything from a Lincoln Town Car to a Honda Civic. I don't know if you realize this, but Chester Motors is mine. So is Brunswick BMW. So is Nelson Oldsmobile-Cadillac." He glanced down at the cigar in his pocket but did not take it out. "I started out selling used cars in 1948. I'd been a buck sergeant in the army, slightly wounded in the Battle of the Bulge. I was no hero, but when I came home people wanted to do things for me. I went to Rutgers under the GI Bill. I got a veteran's loan to buy that used-car lot. I bought my first new-car agency in 1955." He paused and sighed. "I figured my sons would go in the business. But they didn't, and won't. Bill Nelson is my son-in law. I tell you this, and I'll tell you more, in the anticipation that you are going to be my lawyer."

"You must have some legal problems," said Cole.

"I do have legal problems. My taxes are handled by my account- ant. But I've got problems with corporations. I've got too many of them and wonder if I shouldn't consolidate. Suppose Musgrave Enterprises, let us call it, owned controlling interest in all the com- panies."

"Is each agency its own corporation? And if so why?"

"There was a time, not entirely gone yet, when, for example, General Motors would not franchise an agency owned by a man who also owned an agency with a Ford franchise. So . . ."

"So by forming multiple corporations you concealed it from the manufacturers."

"Something like that."

"You may have problems I can't handle."

"So you're my general counsel, and you retain whatever experts you want."

Cole looked away from Julian Musgrave, out the window and down at the street. "Did Dave Shea send you to me?" he asked.

"Nobody sends me anywhere," Musgrave said firmly. "I told Dave I was going to need a lawyer, and he told me you are damned smart."

"Who *is* your lawyer, the one who is retiring?"

"Hayward Becker."

Cole winced, and Musgrave saw it. Becker was a hack. He had charisma, and the only people who saw through his incompetence were his fellow lawyers.

"All right. I see what you think. Are you willing to take on the job of straightening out what may be my tangled affairs?"

"It may not be cheap."

"We can agree on an hourly rate. In the meantime, to cement our relationship and insure your confidentiality, I will pay you a retainer. I suggest a car."

"I—"

"What would you like? I can set you up in a Caddy, equipped with everything."

"I always wanted a Porsche."

Musgrave laughed. "Damn! You *are* smart. What color?"

"White."

"You got it. It'll take me a couple of days."

II

Two weeks later Cole sat over peanuts and cocktails with Emily.

"It's unbelievable," he said. "I knew the man was incompetent, but I never guessed *how* incompetent. I mean, required reports have not been filed, there are no corporate minute books, no stock registers. Brunswick BMW is not even a corporation. Becker just had stock certificates printed, handed them to Musgrave, and that was that. The corporation does not exist. It files tax returns as if it were a corporation, thanks to a competent accountant who never guessed no corporation was ever formed. Musgrave takes a salary from each agency. No dividends are paid on the stock. In fact, there couldn't be, because there has never been a stockholders meeting."

"Musgrave is the sole stockholder," she said.

"Even so, he is supposed to elect a board of directors. And the directors are supposed to elect officers."

"Who signs the checks?" she asked.

"He just authorizes banks to honor signature cards. Each agency has a check signer, but the man is not a treasurer."

"How does Becker get away with this?"

"Small town," said Cole. "He walks to his office every morning: a tall, distinguished-looking man with wavy white hair; and every morning he stops in a flower shop where they have a rosebud waiting for his buttonhole. He knows everyone. He has a good morning for everyone. Six months ago I represented a family who'd just built a house. I asked Becker for a release of mechanics' liens. He'd never heard of such a thing and tried to smile me off. I had to prepare the documents, and he got the contractors to sign them."

"Charismatic, I believe you said."

"Every morning at ten he goes to Duke's Coffee Shop and sits down with local businessmen, who take him at face value. Once a week he lunches with his Rotary Club. Other days he lunches in various places, where he is expected and welcomed. He works several fund-raising campaigns. He plays golf."

"Well . . . he's gone, and you'll be well paid to straighten out the mess."

"You won't believe what he had the nerve to say to me. He told me he expected to be kept on a retainer, so he could advise me on aspects of the Musgrave businesses."

"And what did you tell him?"

"I told him he'd be lucky if I didn't have Musgrave sue him for malpractice."

III

MAY, 1990

Emily's concern that the Sheas would sooner or later propose that they trade partners continued to trouble her.

When Dave and Alexandra returned from Leningrad, they brought gifts: an elaborately hand-carved-and-painted wooden animated toy for Little Cole, that he could activate by pulling a string; a set of nested dolls for Little Emily, and for Cole and Emily, a pair of sable hats. When Alexandra suggested that night that they stop being coy and simply enjoy each other's nudity, neither Emily nor Cole could say no.

Dave and Alexandra closed the apartment on the Upper West Side and moved into a larger apartment on East Seventy-second Street, where they had a view of the East River from their living room.

Harcourt Barnham had promoted Dave. He was now allowed to supervise accounts of a small number of millions of dollars. He chose investment strategies and invested pretty much as he saw fit. Occasionally he would run an idea past Axel Schnyder, asking if a particular investment would be good for his account in Zurich.

He didn't do it often. He didn't want Schnyder to suspect he was using the expertise of Trust Management AG to govern his New York investment decisions. On the other hand, sometimes he used a report from Schnyder to suggest a sound investment for the clients of Harcourt Barnham. Schnyder was investing the money in his Deutsche Bank account in European companies Dave had never heard of. Also, Schnyder was taking for Dave modest positions in currencies—and making quick profits.

Dave had opened his Zurich account with $1,000,000. Now, a year later, it was worth $1,575,000. Of that $200,000 represented the profit on the Texaco deal, and about $125,000 from suggestions to Schnyder from things Dave learned at the bank, but the rest of the increase represented what Axel Schnyder and Trust Management AG could do.

The fact that Dave was paying no taxes on his profit left the entire amount intact for further ventures.

This Saturday evening Dave, Alexandra, Emily, and Cole went to a performance of *Cats*, and when they returned to the apartment Alexandra ordered in the most elaborate display of Chinese food that could be imagined. They ate with the ivory chopsticks that Alexandra provided. They talked about the play.

"I noticed something in the *Times* this morning that you may not have caught," Cole said to Dave.

"And what was that?"

"A former vice president—you must have known him—named, uh . . . Miley, shot himself yesterday."

"*My God!*" Emily cried.

Dave frowned. "I'm sorry to hear it."

Emily had tears in her eyes.

"C'mon, hon." Cole looked at her. "You never even met him."

"He . . . was . . . a human being."

Dave shook his head. "Miley made a big mistake," he said. "He ignored personal relationships. He cared nothing about having friends. When the shit hit the fan, nobody would stand up for him. A man in his position should have been able, in time, to switch to another bank or to a brokerage. But he'd made no friends. No-where. He was a cold fish."

"He must have left a wife," Emily whispered.

"Yes, but don't worry about her," Dave said. "Financially, I mean. He had a golden parachute. Even the circumstances in which he left the bank couldn't have divested him of that. He didn't have to live on Social Security. And neither will she."

"But—"

"He brought his troubles on himself," Dave said curtly, staring Emily down.

Alexandra left the table and went over to the disc player and put on the soundtrack of *Cats*. She walked over and closed the curtains. As she stood in the middle of the room, she began to take off one piece of clothing at a time until she was completely nude.

They all watched. Each of them was aroused.

She walked over to Emily and began to unbutton her blouse. She placed Emily's hand on her naked breast. Under the soft touch of Emily's hand Alexandra's nipple thrust forward. Her breath quickened as she unsnapped Emily's bra.

The two men began to stroke themselves as they watched the two women.

Alexandra had begun to suck on Emily's nipple. Emily could feel the juices begin to flow inside her. Alexandra reached under Emily's skirt and pulled down her panties, then she led her to the sofa. As she lay back on the sofa, Alexandra opened the fleshy lips of her vagina. She began to probe inside of her. Emily began to moan. Then she spread her legs wide and with her tongue brought Emily to a shuddering orgasm.

No one said a word as Alexandra then moved to Cole and kissed him fully on the mouth allowing Emily's juices to mingle with his own. His penis was fully erect and she quickly used her hand to bring him to an orgasm.

As she came to Dave, she saw the excitement in his eyes. She reached inside herself and brought her fingers up to his lips. He sucked each finger. Then she placed her hand around his neck and mounted his throbbing penis. They both exploded simultaneously.

Cole, Amy, and Dave were completely awed by Alexandra's performance. Dave poured brandies for everyone and turned on the television. Johnny Carson was doing his monologue.

"Cole . . ." Dave said. The next morning Dave and Cole were drinking coffee. "How would you like to give me three or four days of your time? I don't mean *give*, of course. I mean at your hourly rate, plus expenses."

"What do you have in mind?"

"Ever hear of a computer called Sphere?"

Cole shook his head.

"At one time it rivaled Apple as the machine most likely to compete successfully with IBM. It still has great features—or so I'm advised by people who know something about this. But it needs development. In some ways it's obsolete. The problem is, it's cash-poor. It needs an infusion of capital. I think I can get that for it. But there's another problem. It's a closely held corporation. It belongs to a guy named Tom Malloy in Houston."

"And . . . ?"

"I'd appreciate it if you'd fly down to Houston and meet with this guy. I got an idea somebody might be interested in acquiring Sphere. The problem may be Malloy. From all I hear, he's a genius and an egomaniac."

"And a Texan," said Emily.

Dave grinned. "And a Texan. And he has big pride in this thing he built."

IV

Cole checked in at the Hyatt Regency Hotel in downtown Houston—picking up a message to call Dave before he met Malloy. The glass-enclosed elevators traveled up and down through a floor-to-ceiling lobby, giving occupants a view of the entire lobby area:

including a sunken cocktail lounge shielded from the rest of the lobby by huge potted shrubs. He took note of the glassed-in restaurant on the second floor, where he would meet Tom Malloy for dinner.

It was after six-thirty in Houston, after seven-thirty in New York, and he rang Dave and Alexandra's home number.

"What kinda town is it?" Dave asked.

"Big. Texas big. It sprawls all over hell and back. The cabdriver tried to stiff me on the drive from the airport, but the doorman shot him down. Anyway—?"

"There's another possible buyer interested in Sphere. Damndest thing you could possibly imagine! Ever hear of a chain of sexy lingerie shops called Cheeks?"

"I bought Emily a nightie in one in Manhattan, for Christmas."

"Okay. The chain is owned by a family named Cooper. The story is that they're connected, but people say that kind of thing about everybody, so I don't take it seriously. Jerry Cooper built the company from nothing, and now it's cash-rich and looking to diversify. He's a guy without much education, but he's sharp. His son, Len Cooper, has got education *and* smarts."

"And they want to take over Sphere?"

"Let me tell you how to play Malloy," said Dave. "The Sphere computer is his baby. If the Coopers take over, they'll use the Sphere name, which may be the company's chief asset; and they may very well scrap the Sphere computer. If my guys take it over, they're prepared to guarantee Malloy they'll keep his baby alive."

"You sent the wrong guy down here, Dave. I don't know anything about computers."

"You know *people*, my friend. Just don't forget that Malloy has an ego a mile wide. Play it!"

Cole wished Dave had been there to meet Tom Malloy, who was nothing like the Texan Dave seemed to have expected. He did not appear dressed like Gene Autry, but in a charcoal-gray, three-button suit with narrow lapels, a white shirt, a regimental tie. He was six feet five or so and by no means rawboned and leather-skinned as Texans were reputed to be. In fact, he carried a little extra weight, though his suit was tailored to accommodate it. He had not asked his barber to try to hide the premature baldness that was coming for a man in his early forties.

That he *was* a Texan was demonstrated by his wife, Betsy, who had been an Oilers cheerleader, as both Tom and Betsy were anxious to have him understand. She was maybe thirty-five years old, as Cole judged. She did not wear a beehive hairdo—of which he had already seen several since he arrived in Texas—but her hair was luxuriant. It had also been stripped: not bleached, stripped. Her eyebrows did not betray her as a brunette, because she had no eyebrows, almost. They were thin arched lines, colored with dark eyebrow pencil. Her lipstick, applied with a brush, he guessed, was glistening pink. Her white silk minidress was without sleeves and was held up by two gleaming strands of tiny pearls. It stretched low across breasts thrust up and forward into overstated points by nylon and rubber. The skirt rode high on sleek legs clad in black panty hose. Cole struggled to keep his eyes above the table and not below where sometimes she showed her hips, even her crotch.

Tom Malloy spoke without a trace of Texas accent. Betsy spoke as Cole had supposed all Texans did.

"Ah *love* jee-in," she said when the waiter came to take their drink orders. "Sumpin' 'bout it. Ah don' know. They say Scotch whiskey is jus' Bourbon with some iodine added."

Tom laughed at his wife's *bon mot.* "Actually," he said, "Bourbon is Scotch with maple syrup poured in it."

"Which is whaa Ah drank jee-in," said Betsy.

The restaurant was excellent. Though oysters were out of season, they had a dozen apiece, on the half-shell, with a bottle of chilled Chablis.

Eventually, Tom turned the conversation to business—

"I understand your client is interested in investing in Sphere. Can you tell me the name of your client?"

"Not at the moment," said Cole. "I'm sorry, but I'm obliged to hold that information in confidence for the moment."

"What do you know about Sphere?"

"Only that you developed an excellent computer that was once regarded as superior to IBM machines. It's a highly respected design. The problem is, it's obsolete. In order to bring it up-to-date, you will have to commit a lot of capital. My client may have a source of that kind of money."

"It's not obsolete," said Tom calmly but with cold firmness. "The problem is, it's exactly the opposite; Sphere is more advanced than the IBM computers and the IBM clones. Apple might be competitive. But Apple has the same problem we have, which is the Microsoft monopoly. We did not design Sphere to run on DOS, as Apple didn't. Apple has now compromised and will run on DOS as an alternative. We could do that. I'm afraid we have no choice but to do it."

"I know very little about computers," said Cole. "Would you allow an expert to come and examine yours?"

"Fine," said Tom. "Your guru won't be the first one. Now—we are having a little pool party tomorrow evening. Come early, and I'll show you the Sphere. Then . . . barbecue."

"I'll have to buy a swimsuit," said Cole.

"Don't think of it. We keep a lot of them, in all sizes, for men and women."

V

Cole knew nothing of the geography of Houston, but his sense of direction told him that the cab was taking him west from the city center. Shortly he was delivered to an address in a posh suburb characterized by manicured woods and three-to-four-acre lots, each house out of sight of all its neighbors. The Malloys lived in a sprawling one-floor house shaded by tall, ancient oaks—except in the rear where the land had been cleared to afford sunny space for a large swimming pool with a redwood deck.

Tom came to the door to welcome him. He was wearing Top-Sider boat shoes, tight blue jeans, and a golf shirt. Betsy greeted Cole inside the house. She was dressed in the uniform of an Oilers cheerleader: abbreviated shorts that hugged her hips well below her navel, a fringed vest fastened only just under her breasts, and white boots.

The house was furnished in what Cole took for a Texas style: rough-knit Indian blankets for throw rugs and wall hangings, couches and chairs upholstered in brown leather, and two bronze cowboy sculptures that may have been originals and worth two fortunes. The living room was dominated by a huge fieldstone fire-place.

"Glad you came informal like I said. C'mon back to my office, and I'll introduce you to my baby."

The office had a western style. A cattle skull and a pair of spreading longhorns hung from one wall. Cole took note of diplomas that may have explained why Tom did not speak like a Texan. He had graduated from Amherst, then from the University of Chicago with a degree in electrical engineering.

"Say hello to Sphere."

The computer sat on a table under the longhorns. It was unlike any desktop computer Cole had ever seen. He could make no judgment of its functionality, but it looked different, for sure. Most computers were enclosed in beige steel cases, square and functional and unimaginative. The Sphere was enclosed in dark green transparent plastic. The components—transformer, rectifier, disk drives, modem, and circuit boards—were all visible. The case was by no means a sphere, but it was gently rounded. The whole design had an elegance of appearance that set it apart from all other small computers.

"The problem, if in fact it *is* a problem, is in the operating system," said Tom. "We found DOS clunky, so we designed our own. It works great. But it won't run any off-the-shelf software, like Lotus 1-2-3, Word, WordPerfect, Quicken, and the like. You have to use our proprietary software. Unfortunately, that makes a lot of people nervous."

"Is your software as good as those others?"

"When we designed it, it was far more capable than anything

else available at that time. But in five years, the others have been totally redesigned and are far more sophisticated than they were. We haven't been able to redesign all that much."

"For want of capital," said Cole.

"You got it," said Tom.

"So you can use investors."

"I won't surrender control. I built this business, and I would rather see it fail and have to liquidate than have to give control to someone else."

"I'll convey that to my client," said Cole.

"So . . . enough business for today. You *do* swim?"

A few minutes later Tom came to the room assigned to Cole and led him out to the pool. They were wearing tight, skimpy Speedos, Cole's in a gaudy abstract pattern of dark and royal blue, maroon, and white. The Lycra stretched over his lower belly, hips, and genitalia. He tugged at the waistband to keep his pubic hair from showing and was uncomfortably aware that he could not tug the vestigial legs down enough even to begin to cover his nates. If Tom had not been wearing the same, in green and white, Cole would not have ventured outside his door.

"Odd thing," said Tom. "I swim pretty well, but I never did learn to dive. I can't even dive off the edge of the pool without flopping on my belly."

Cole would learn in a moment that Betsy neither dived nor swam. If she had dived she could have lost at least the top of her spectacularly scanty white bikini.

Other guests had arrived. Some of them were diving off the Malloys' high board.

A woman went off the low board. She hit the water with a splat and splash and swam vigorously to the edge of the pool.

"Meet Liz McAllister," Tom said to Cole. "She's vice president for technology, Gazelle, Incorporated. You asked if we'd mind an expert looking into Sphere. That's what Liz is doing."

Liz McAllister was not obese, but she was big; and she was gawky. Her dishwater-blond hair was coarse and frizzy. Her features were regular but exaggerated. Her big face was round and flushed. The bikini provided her by the Malloys did not flatter her. She extended too much around the edges.

Tom went on. "Liz, meet Cole Jennings. He's a New Jersey lawyer representing some investors who might want to buy into Sphere."

She ran her hand through her hair to dispel water. "It's very nice to meet you, Mr. Jennings," she said, all ingenuous.

Liz McAllister had, apparently, no notion at all that her bikini was too small for her—or that she was too big for it. Cole's initial judgment of her was that she was the plainest, squarest person he had ever met.

Before he could open a conversation with her, Tom introduced him to a woman maybe ten years younger: an extraordinarily attractive brunette with pale blue eyes dramatized by dark eye lining, a spectacular figure, and, like Betsy, obviously no intention of getting her hair or swimsuit wet.

"Laura Mason," Tom said. "She's an Oilers cheerleader. Betsy's an alum. Laura's active." He pushed Cole aside and spoke softly in his ear. "Assigned to you. You want it, you got it."

A gargantuan hunk of beef hung on a spit over a pit not far from the pool, dripping grease onto hot wood coals below and sending up a cloud of redolent smoke. It whetted the appetites of all the guests—some twenty by now—and they drank draft beer from oversized paper cups until they made a constant traffic to and from the bathrooms in a little building apart from both house and pool. The beef was cut and served on big paper plates, with dollops of baked beans and cole slaw. The beef was drowned in a barbecue sauce that Tom Malloy declared the specialty of the house.

Cole suspected by now that his visit was futile, but he could let that go as he enjoyed Texas hospitality, which was expansive and what he had expected of Texas.

Laura Mason stuck close to him, but he had resolved not to accept whatever favors she might be willing to extend.

After a couple of hours, Tom came to him. "Like Laura?" he asked.

"She's very beautiful."

"Let's be specific. Let me be blunt. Do you want her to come to your hotel later?"

"I . . . I don't think so, Tom. I appreciate the offer, but—"

"Understood. Not to worry."

He placed a call to Emily before he left the party. It was after ten in Houston, after midnight in Wyckoff, and she would have begun to worry.

Two other guests, a doctor and his wife, were leaving at the same time, and they drove him to the Hyatt. The wife described Tom Malloy as the "muliest" man she knew, which he understood meant stubborn.

As Cole walked through the lobby of the hotel he spotted Liz McAllister sitting alone in the sunken cocktail lounge, looking a little forlorn as he judged. He had thought about stopping there for a drink before he went to his room, so he walked down the three steps and walked over to her. She was staring into her glass and did not notice him at first.

"Get beered out?" he asked, noticing that she was drinking a martini.

She looked up and was so obviously glad to see him that he was pleased that he had decided to approach her. She was not dressed for this chic watering hole: in a white golf shirt stretched by her exorbitant knockers, and tight, faded blue jeans.

"I was beered out when I graduated from college," she said. "It was the gallons I drank then that ruined my figure. Have a seat."

"Beer can do funny things to you. When I was eighteen, three friends and I killed a man. We were beered up and—God!—I haven't spoken of that in years."

"Hit him with a car?" she asked.

"Beat him to death with our fists."

"Jesus! You go to jail?"

"No. We got away with it. Anyway, it's a bad memory . . . I'm sorry I mentioned it. I just blurted it out. I come from a small town. Everybody knows about it. I don't *have* to talk about it."

She signaled for a waiter, and Cole ordered a Beefeater martini on the rocks with a twist. She ordered a refill.

"Do you really have an investor ready to put seventeen or eighteen million into Sphere?" she asked simply.

"More than that."

"That's what it will take to redesign the Sphere operating system to make it compatible with Windows," she said.

"Is that what has to be done?"

"Minimally," she said. "And it's ironic that Tom Malloy doesn't have that much."

"He lives like he has it."

Liz shrugged. "Family money," she said. "The Malloys are into oil and cattle and are scornful of the black-sheep son and his technology business. They put up the seed money, but there won't be any more."

"And your company can—?"

"My company has cash out the gazoo. Made from selling sexy lingerie in sizes I can't wear."

When the waiter brought their drinks, he also brought a check, which she grabbed. "On me," she said. "On my expense account."

They sipped their martinis and watched the elevators going up and down.

"Cole . . ." she said tentatively. "It's going to be a long, lonely night."

It was a proposition. He didn't know how to fend her off gently, but he could not imagine spending the night with this big, ungainly woman.

"Well, I . . ."

"I know . . ." she said quietly. "I know very well—better than you can imagine. Being me, I have to be *better*. You won't forget me. You won't forget a night with me."

Since his marriage, he had never been with any woman but Emily. That was foremost in his mind when Liz put her hand on his and murmured, "Please . . ."

"All right," he conceded. "Why not? Your room or mine?"

"Your choice."

He chose his own room. As soon as the door was closed and chained, she stripped: quickly, efficiently. He had seen all but very little of her in the bikini provided her by the Malloys, but seeing her naked did arouse him.

She knelt before him and struggled to open and pull down his pants. She seized his cock in both hands and shoved it into her mouth. As he stood there, before they even sat down, much less stretched out on the bed, she licked and sucked and drew him all the way in, down into her throat, then pulled him out and shoved him in, using her lips and tongue, until she brought him to deep, violent spasms of ecstasy.

She had been right that he would never forget the night. She begged him to plunge into her and encircled him with her legs to be sure he could not slip out. She squatted over him and took him woman-on-top, introducing his cock to depths it had never felt before. But more, she worked with her mouth, even shoving her tongue up into his anus.

Toward dawn they slept a little. He woke hearing her talking to room service. She ordered four gin Bloody Marys, with bacon and eggs.

TWELVE

I

JULY, 1990

"Feng shui," said Leonard Cooper.

He was explaining to Dave the layout and decor of his office, in which the furniture was not parallel or at right angles to the walls but sat at eccentric angles. It explained too his large aquarium and the potted plants that grew in the room. Feng shui was a Chinese philosophy that held man could benefit by arranging homes and offices in harmony with nature—and parallel lines and right angles were not generally in harmony.

"Do I believe in it?" asked Leonard Cooper. "I suppose not, not really. But I will tell you, I feel more comfortable in this office than I did before."

Leonard Cooper was twenty-nine years old, a graduate of Amherst and Yale, and a lawyer. He had succeeded his father Jerry as the chief operating officer of Gazelle, Incorporated, the cash-rich corporation based on the sale of bold lingerie and a line of related sexy items—not excluding sado-masochistic devices.

It was an odd way to make money, but Dave knew it did; he had checked it out. He had to admire the way the Cooper family had turned a once-scorned enterprise into a billion-dollar empire. There could be no question of outbidding the Coopers if they wanted Sphere. The question was: Could he insert himself some way? Could he turn the relationship into a nice profit?

"I gather your problem is Tom Malloy's ego," said Dave. "I haven't met him, but I sent a man to check him out and another man to look into his technology."

"My consultants tell me his Sphere computer is a marvel," said Len Cooper. "He won't deal with anyone who won't commit to keeping that computer alive and on the market."

"I don't know computer technology," said Dave. "I hired a man who does."

"So did I—a woman."

"Are you sure you want to invest heavily in this deal?" Dave asked. "It can be arranged for other people's money to be invested."

"I have other investors," said Len Cooper. "Mr. Shea—"

"Dave."

"Sure. And Len. I have other investors. Chinese. That's where the real money is these days. We keep an office in Hong Kong. You want to see money? Try a visit to Hong Kong. I'm going out there. That's where money is."

"I can bring money from this country," said Dave. "I can get you American investors."

"I'll be glad to talk to you about it. In the meantime, I suggest you get to know Tom Malloy."

II

Cole had given Dave a full report of his visit to Houston—excluding only his night with Liz—and Dave might have carried with him a pair of swimming trunks, to avoid having to appear on the Malloys' pool deck in the kind of swim trunks that had embarrassed Cole. He didn't, though. He rather looked forward to how monumentally he would stretch a pair of Speedos.

He didn't stay in a hotel. The Malloys had invited him to stay in a guest room in their home. He had been invited to come on Friday, so they could see a rodeo on Saturday. He wondered if they would have a barbecue party on Friday night. It turned out that Tom and Betsy, and their friends—the other friend being Laura Mason—had been invited to a party at a neighbor's house.

The party was a duplicate of the one Cole had described to him. The guests, some twenty of them, gathered around the pool. A side of beef dripped into a permanent barbecue pit. From time to time their host tossed mesquite onto the fire, to give the beef a special flavor.

The host was named Melvin Johnston, and he was a vice president of Harris County National Bank. A rotund man, he was older than most of the other men present, and he wore dark blue boxer trunks, in contrast to the vividly colored strips of stretched Lycra most of the younger men wore around their hips. Dave's red Speedos were minuscule, as Cole had warned they might be; and Dave wondered if it were not a joke with Tom and Betsy to furnish their guests with such skimpy trunks. He might have thought so, except that Tom's Speedos were no more modest, and Betsy would not have dared dive or swim strenuously in her iridescent yellow bikini.

He reached a quick and uncharitable opinion: that these Houston people were essentially bored out of their minds and looked to weekly parties for relief.

"What do you think of Laura?" Tom asked Dave not long after they arrived at the Johnstons'.

"Luscious."

"She likes you, too." They had sat together in the backseat of the Malloys' car on the way to this party, and he'd had a moment, no more, to chat with her. He judged she was no more than nineteen. Betsy was an alum of the Oilers cheerleader squad. Laura was still active and would be working the games when the season began. "If you want her, she'll slip into your room during the night," said Tom.

"I'm for that."

Tom Malloy grinned. "Figured you would be."

Tom let Laura know that the deal was done, and after that she stayed close to Dave. Her white bikini was as brief as any at the pool. She did not get it wet. She was brash in conversation—

"Gawd, you're hung," she said, nodding at his Speedos, strained by his cock.

"What was it the doctor told the guy in *Deep Throat?*" he asked. " 'I can cut it down to any size you want.' "

"*Jaysus!* Don't even think about it!"

Dave swam a few laps and came out of the pool, a little diminished by the cool water.

Their host, Johnston, came over and sat down beside him. "I understand you're with Harcourt Barnham," he said.

"Yes."

"But you are not here on behalf of Harcourt Barnham."

There was no point in lying. "No."

"Ah, well. It's none of my business. I did doubt that Harcourt would be interested in putting money into Sphere, Incorporated."

"I know some people who might be," Dave said.

"What do you know about the Coopers?"

"Only a little. Potentially, they will invest heavily in Sphere. Their company is glutted with cash."

"And they'll take control, whether Tom likes it or not. You should research the Coopers, if you haven't already. They are not people to be gainsaid."

As the sun set and the beef was nearly ready, women began to shed their tops. Dave knew this had not happened at the Malloys' party. Cole would have mentioned it. When Laura dropped her bikini top and put it aside, he saw something he had never seen before. Her left nipple was pierced, and a shiny silver or platinum ring about the diameter of a quarter hung in it.

Later, when she was naked, she encouraged him to play with her nipple ring, to pull on it actually; and she didn't wince. She laughed at his fascination with it and flipped it around to show him it was loose in the hole in her nipple.

"Some of them are fastened by threads in a little ball," she told him. "A girl can take it out whenever she wants to. But not this'n. I had it soldered. Th' only way Ah could git it off would be by cuttin' it."

"Didn't that burn?" he asked. "I mean, the soldering."

She shook her head. "They used what they called a heat sink.

It was a pair of pliers lak, and the one woman held that tight on the ring while th' other one soldered. Ah didn't feel no burn at all. An', know what? Ah'm thinkin' of havin' th' other one done. What do *you* think? Would that be too much?"

She turned out to be a willing and vigorous lover—unimaginative but enthusiastic.

"Y' know. Ah don' think Ah ever seen a cock bigger'n yours. Ah *know* Ah never had that big a one in me b'fore. Let's do it agin! And t'morra nat, too, huh?"

III

They went to the rodeo the next afternoon, Dave escorting Laura on his arm. She and Betsy were dressed in the uniforms of Oilers cheerleaders, and before the rodeo began they and six others were called out into the ring to be introduced to a cheering crowd.

Momentarily alone in the stands, Tom raised a point. "My Cooper friends propose to churn tens of millions into my business. But they would change the entire nature of the enterprise."

"In what respect, Tom?"

"Their Chinese associates want to make the components for microprocessors, which we would assemble and sell in the States. You know what that means?"

"Not exactly."

Tom Malloy turned his head and glanced around, nodding and smiling at friends in the stands. "Microprocessors are little bitty computers designed to do specific jobs. Cars run on microprocessors. Sensors tell the microprocessors what the temperature of the air is, how much moisture it contains, and so on; and the microprocessor adjusts the fuel mixture and other factors to make the car run best. There's no end to the possibilities. Within a few years, your home heating system, to use just one example, will be controlled by a microprocessor."

"A great new business maybe," Dave suggested.

"Yes. And Sphere gets eaten alive. My baby is going to be run by a marketer of women's underwear! And what do they want? The *name*. The Sphere name is as good as Apple, almost as good as IBM."

"Suppose we arrange a deal. Suppose the Sphere computer component gets sloughed off as a separate, independent subsidiary. You take in the Chinese money, let the Cooper guys make microprocessors with the Sphere name, and your Sphere computer subsidiary goes its own way. If you want to, you can skim off some of the Chinese money and put it into the computer. I can arrange independent financing for Sphere, Incorporated."

Tom Malloy nodded. "Idea," he said. "Let's work on it."

Betsy and Laura returned to their seats, nodding and waving as they received applause from the rodeo fans.

Laura clasped Dave's hand. "Y' gonna lak this," she said as a gate opened and a lunging bull charged out, angrily trying to throw its rider. So far as Dave was concerned, the bravest men in the rodeo were the clowns who rushed forward to distract a bull that had thrown a man and was about to gore him.

IV

In truth, Dave did not have the kind of money he was talking to Tom Malloy about—at least, he didn't have it without committing all he had. He tried to avoid personal conversations with Axel Schnyder, but this time he flew to Zurich to meet with him.

"The point is," he told the Swiss banker after he had described the whole situation, "that whoever owns the Sphere computer may become a major player in the field of personal computers, which is a big and growing business."

"And one replete with powerful, money-rich competition," said Schnyder calmly. "I believe I detect in you a quality that can be destructive."

"Meaning?"

"Enthusiasm," said Schnyder. "Once, 'enthusiasm' was a religious term. It meant too much moved by emotion."

"You oppose the investment?"

"I oppose nothing. I neither endorse nor oppose investments. I *analyze* them. Have you analyzed this idea? Carefully?"

"I . . . I believe I have."

"What part of your assets do you want to commit?"

Dave smiled. "I was thinking of committing *other people's* assets."

"Wise. But it also means that your enthusiasm is not great enough to lead you to destruction."

"Then . . . ?"

"I will do some research and analysis. In the meanwhile, why don't we enjoy an evening, Mr. Shea? Dinner. Maybe a show. Do you fancy naked girls?"

Dave did not fancy the usual places where naked girls were on display. They would try to sit with him and beguile him into buying expensive champagne. He could afford the champagne, even at nightclub prices, but it galled him to be cheated out of it.

Axel Schnyder, as it happened, felt exactly the same way. He took Dave to a private club—in fact, a luxurious bawdy house—where they dined on fine roast beef from cattle grazed on Dutch polders, drank wine from Bordeaux, and watched a show in which shapely girls, none of them older than eighteen, did not strip but danced naked.

"You see," said Axel Schnyder, "it is well to spend money. It is better to get value for it."

V

He returned to Houston. Alexandra went with him this time.

They talked on the plane. "The more I think about the idea of separating Sphere's computer operations from what's apparently going to become a manufacturer of microprocessors, the better I like it," Dave said. "From all I can find out, the Sphere is a superior desktop computer and potentially a major player in a line of business that's got nowhere to go but up."

"I had a friend once who used a Radio Shack computer. It was a good machine apparently, but it had the same problem your Sphere has; it was based on its own operating software and couldn't run things like VisiCalc and WordStar. It's not a major player anymore."

They were in Houston on a Wednesday, and there was no barbecue party. They were guests at the Malloys' house and spent late afternoon on the pool deck, where Tom poured drinks, not beer, and where a black cook set up a buffet of fried chicken, potato salad, and sliced red tomatoes. Alexandra would have dived, but the little blue bikini provided for her would not have withstood it.

Laura was not there and was not mentioned.

"The Coopers are not pleased with your idea of splitting the company," said Tom.

"What are they buying?" Dave asked. "In the long run, what is it they want?"

"They want to put the Sphere name on their microprocessors."

"They're buying the name—and may ruin it," said Dave.

"It wouldn't be the first name that's been bought and put on something the proprietor of the name never intended," said Alexandra.

"They assure me they'll fund Sphere IV, which is what we'll call it. It will combine the design elegance of Sphere with the practicality of, say, IBM."

"The decision is yours, I suppose," said Dave.

"At the moment, you have the role of white knight for me," said Tom. "With the kind of funding you tell me you can raise, I can fend off these raiders and keep my business and my baby."

"Let that be our goal," said Dave.

VI

The report from Axel Schnyder was explicit:

I have to suggest to you that a major commitment to Sphere, Incorporated, may entail unacceptable risks.

To begin with, the company carries a heavy load of debt, incurred by Mr. Malloy as his sales diminished. Mr. Malloy depends on family money of which no more seems to be available.

I must also advise that putting one's self in opposition to the Cooper family may not be the most judicious posture one could take. To begin with, their somewhat eccentric line of business has proved extremely profitable, and they have cash resources sufficient to outbid nearly anyone who might be interested in Sphere. More than that, they are possessed of a faintly unsavory reputation, involving friendships with men who are associated with what in America is called the Mob, the Mafia, Cosa Nostra, etc.

In brief, I cannot advise your proceeding with this idea. Money can be much better placed.

VII

Summoned—there was no word but summoned—to the office of Leonard Cooper, where he found himself facing, not Len, the son, but Jerry Cooper, the father. Dave sat watching the gaudy tropical fish swimming in the big aquarium, while Cooper completed a telephone call.

"So . . ." Cooper said when he put down the phone. He was a man in his late sixties, wearing black slacks and a white golf shirt. He was brusque. "You propose to separate Sphere's desktop computer business from the rest of it, using financing you will get from other sources."

"The idea appeals to Tom Malloy."

"Dave . . . just what is it you want out of this?"

"The same thing you want, out of anything you undertake. I want to make money."

"The difficulty, Dave, is that this is *our* deal. As we might say, my company has dibs. We found it first."

"There's enough for everybody."

"Is there? What you're saying, Dave, is that you want a share of what my son and I found and have big plans for. Why should we give you a share?"

145

"Because Tom Malloy may not go for anything if you don't. He's in love with his computer."

"We've assured him that we will help him redesign and sell his computer."

"To be brutally frank with you, Mr. Cooper, he is not entirely confident that you really will."

"And you, of course, have not discouraged him from thinking that way."

"I can't believe you are interested in redesigning a computer. I may have investors who are."

"Still, the whole deal is to make an opening for you to be a player in *our* plans."

"You can't do anything without Tom," said Dave. "Debt or no debt, he still owns a controlling interest in the company."

Jerry Cooper smiled and glanced around the room, at his son's swimming fish, his potted shrubs. "You impress me as a smart young fellow. I could like you. I could do business with you sometime, maybe. But don't try to muscle into a deal we've already got primed."

"How do you plan to cut me out?" Dave asked aggressively.

"Suppose I tell you," Jerry Cooper said, "that I am in a position to cut your fuckin' throat."

"Really?"

"Really. Your New Jersey lawyer went down to Houston and wound up in bed with our vice president for technology. You went down to Houston and wound up in bed with Laura, who incidentally works for me. Liz talked too much, but she didn't tell you anything, really. You were too smart to tell Laura anything. You like her pierced nipple? Anyway—"

"What are you gonna do?" Dave asked. "Tell my wife I fucked your girl?"

"No. No, no, no, no, no. Your wife is too smart to be influenced by that. I don't know who you could fuck that would turn her off on you, but it's not for sure our little Oilers cheerleader. You should appreciate your wife."

"So you're gonna cut my fuckin' throat."

Jerry Cooper rubbed his hands, one against the other. "Well," he said, "you are an investment banker with Harcourt Barnham. Do I understand that Harcourt is going to underwrite the financing to redesign the Sphere and market it?"

Dave drew a deep breath. "There are others," he said.

"Yes, I suppose so. But does Harcourt know about them? Is it not a fact, Dave, that you are working independently of your bank? And is it not a fact that you are functioning entirely outside the rules long established by banks like yours? Tell me something, Dave. Do you or do you not have an overseas securities account? Do you report your transactions in that account—*those accounts*, maybe—to the Internal Revenue Service? Far be it from me to snitch. But bug out of my business, Dave. Just bug out, sonny. When I want you, I'll let you know."

VIII

". . . like a fuckin' *schoolboy!*"

"Well. You can't do to him what you did to Miley," said Alexandra calmly. "You've come up against your equal, Dave. Worse than your equal—"

"My goddamned *superior!*"

She pushed his martini across the table toward him. "It had to happen. You can't win 'em all."

"But—"

"Dave . . . The fact that the guy who did it to you is, in your judgment, beneath your dignity counts for nothing. Emotion defeats you in business."

"But I—"

"*Forget Sphere!* Forget Malloy. You shouldn't have gotten involved in it in the first place. Listen to Axel Schnyder. He's what you want to be. And don't forget, Dave . . . You're vulnerable."

"Vulnerable . . ."

"Cheer up, hon. What the hell? You're doing okay. You got shot down in flames on this one, but there'll be other deals."

"I have to acknowledge to Cole that I—"

"I can't think of anybody who could be more sympathetic. Anyway, he got an expense-paid trip to Texas out of it. And he got fucked, you now tell me, with a heavyweight broad. I couldn't believe he'd do that to Emily."

"He—"

"Let's don't kid ourselves, honey babe. You'd do it to *me*. I never imagined you wouldn't."

"Alexandra . . ."

"How'd you like a consolation prize?" she asked. "You asked me about getting a nipple pierced and a ring put in. I don't know where you got that idea, but it doesn't turn me off. I asked around. I know a doctor who will do it. *Both* nipples! But only if you buy platinum rings, with maybe diamonds, maybe emeralds. And . . . hey, listen! Rings can be put in a girl's . . . *private parts*, too. And they hang weights on them to stretch their—"

"I wouldn't want you stretched, Alexandra. You're goddamned perfect the way you are."

THIRTEEN

I

JANUARY, 1991

Cole asked once about the Sphere deal and got a look from Dave that told him not to raise the subject again. He had learned more about the Coopers and their Gazelle Corporation, and he realized Dave had been playing with fire. The Coopers had a strange assortment of friends, and the elder Cooper, Jerry, was rumored to be capable of violence.

Two weeks after Christmas Cole and Emily had dinner with the Sheas in their Manhattan apartment. They sat over drinks in the living room and stared out at the East River. This time Alexandra suggested that they not take off their clothes, as they often did, but that the two women just strip to the waist. Emily, who alone had been hesitant about this kind of thing, was hesitant no longer.

She and Cole had talked after the evening of *Cats*. It was an erotic thrill for both of them. It had not damaged their relationship and Emily had always been curious about what it would be like to be with a woman. And they also knew that they couldn't or wouldn't say no.

So, she bared her little, creamy-skin, pear-shaped breasts and relished Dave's compliment, prosaic though it was—

"I don't know when I've ever seen a nicer pair of boobs—except of course Alexandra's."

But Alexandra had a surprise for her, and for Cole. She was, as usual, wearing no bra, and when she pulled her pink cashmere sweater over her head, she exposed pierced nipples with gleaming rings hanging from them. They were platinum rings, Dave explained. He didn't say how much he had paid for them, but the implication was that they had been expensive. Each one had a dazzling emerald set in it. She was conspicuously proud of her rings and thrust her breasts forward to flaunt them.

"We didn't have this kind of thing in Kiev," she said.

"We didn't have things like that in Wyckoff, New Jersey," said Cole dryly.

"And still don't," Emily added.

"Maybe we can remedy that," said Dave.

He pushed a gift-wrapped box across the coffee table. It was for Emily, and she opened it. Inside, in a satin lining, lay a pair of white-gold nipple rings—these with screw-adjustable clamps so they could be attached without piercing.

"Training bra, that pair," said Alexandra. "On and off whenever you want."

"Yours . . . ?" asked Emily timidly.

"Welded together with epoxy cement. The joints are just behind the emeralds and so out of sight. But I can't take them off—that is, without cutting them."

She pulled on her rings, gently, so that she stretched her nipples a little. She grinned.

To fasten the clamp rings on Emily, Cole did as Alexandra instructed—that is, he kneaded each nipple between his fingers until it was erect, and then he opened the clamps and closed them on each turgid bud. Emily flinched as he tightened each clamp enough so that the ring would not fall off.

"I didn't like the clamp ones much myself," said Alexandra. "They pinch. There's a little pain when the anesthetic wears off after the piercing, but in a few days that goes away and you forget all about it. Now, they're perfectly comfortable. It's something like learning to wear contact lenses. At first they irritate your eyes, but pretty soon you don't even know they're in."

"You think *I* should—?"

"Up to you. But, uh, hey, Cole. You find them sexy? The truth now. Don't they give you a hard-on?"

II

MARCH, 1991

Amy supposed Dave might come to New Jersey to visit his son on the occasion of his twelfth birthday, but she was not surprised when he didn't. He sent a gift: a collection of fifty toy soldiers from England, gaudy in the uniforms of the Household Brigade, mounted on horses and carrying lances. The little boy was overjoyed and pretended at least that he did not notice that his father had not appeared and had not so much as sent a note along with the soldiers, which were impersonally delivered by UPS from FAO Schwarz.

His checks came regularly, from a New York law firm that was the only return address on the envelopes. She could have contacted him maybe but not without effort.

She sat with Cole Jennings over lunch. Unsympathetic as Cole was—and Emily would be—toward David Shea for his treatment of his first wife and his two children, Cole could not help but see the contrast between Amy Sclafani Shea and Alexandra Krylov Shea. Alexandra was *fun*. Amy didn't know how to be. She was fleshy. She was bland. The marriage had been a mistake.

"It doesn't make any difference," she said to Cole. "It's over. There's nothing left between us."

"He's worth a lot of money, Amy. A *lot* of money."

"Nothing surprising in that."

"Uh . . . I've represented him in a business matter and collected a nice fee. I can't represent you anymore. I'll give you a word of advice, off the record. You should go after his ass. When we settled, it was on the basis of what he was then worth."

"I can't reopen—"

"Maybe you can. If I were you, I'd talk to another lawyer and see what can be done."

Five weeks later a New York lawyer named Robert Bailey sat in Dave's office at Harcourt Barnham.

"I see no reason to be anything but straightforward about this," he said to Dave.

The lawyer was boldly unimpressed by the bank and Dave's office in it. Though not at all sold on feng shui, Dave had arranged his office with some reference to the office of the men who had beaten him on the Sphere deal. He had never liked desks anyway. He sat at a big round table, facing Bailey at some distance. Two screens sat at convenient distances: one with the latest market numbers running across, the other the monitor for a Hewlett-Packard computer.

Bailey was a big, tall man of maybe forty or forty-five years, squinting from behind oval brown spectacles and wearing a very well-tailored suit.

"The fact we have to address, Mr. Shea, is that you obtained your divorce—"

"Termination of marriage," Dave interrupted.

"Very well. Termination of marriage. You obtained it without disclosing to Mrs. Shea the extent of your assets."

"I don't think so," said Dave coldly. "In any event, I don't think you could prove any such thing."

"I wouldn't be entirely confident of that, if I were you. Do you recall that you used to call Mrs. Shea your partner, to whom you entrusted everything?"

Dave shrugged.

"Do you remember Jack Silver? Do you remember that you and he were so close that you encouraged Mrs. Shea to nurse your son in his presence? And do you recall what you discussed as Mrs. Shea sat and listened?"

"What is she thinking of doing, blackmailing me?"

"Oh, come, Dave. We don't want to use words like that."

That this lawyer now began to call him Dave was ominous. "What does she want?" he asked.

Bailey drew and released a deep breath. "How long has it been since you've seen Mr. Silver?"

"Some years, I guess."

"Do you know where he is?"

"I guess I don't."

"Well . . . he is in the federal prison at Danbury, Connecticut, where he is going to be for another five or six years." The lawyer shrugged. "Which is immaterial."

"Jack . . . ?"

"Jack. Securities fraud. Now. Let's talk about Mrs. Shea's alimony and child support."

"What's she want?"

"Only what's fair. Nothing more."

"Which is . . . how much?" The telephone rang. Dave picked it up. "I'll have to get back to him. In half an hour, tell him. *** What? All right then. *** Don? What's up? *** The hell you say! *** No, we won't buy any more, for God's sake! *** No, and we can't sell either, right now. Just hang in there, Don. I'll be in touch." He put down the phone and spoke to Bailey. "General Rommel is supposed to have said, when he heard of the Normandy landings, '*Wie dumb von mir!*' Well . . . it's not easy to make a living in this business. Now . . . What are we talking about?"

"What do you offer?" asked the lawyer coldly.

"An ironclad agreement," said Dave, equally coldly. "She's never to come back on me again."

"For which you will pay?"

"Half a million dollars."

"No. One million."

"Jesus Christ, man!"

"I don't think you would like to sit down in a courtroom and have to testify about your assets," Bailey suggested. "How much they are, where they are . . ."

"It's blackmail!"

"You can't be blackmailed if you've nothing to hide," he said, looking over his glasses. "Anyway, I guarantee you that if you transfer one million dollars to her, it will be her last demand."

"You personally guarantee it?"

Bailey smiled and shrugged. "I'm a lawyer. I'm representing my client. When she's satisfied, I'm satisfied. Let's do justice by Mrs. Shea. She is an honest woman."

III

"It's the second goddamned time I've been blackmailed," Dave groused. "I didn't realize I was so fuckin' *vulnerable!*"

"Have you considered the possibility that you're *not* vulnerable?" Alexandra asked. "Cooper was just guessing. That's all: just guessing. And Bailey—"

"Knew too much," Dave finished her sentence. "Amy knows about Windsor Nassau."

They sat in their living room, over crackers, a wedge of brie, and drinks: a martini for him, single-malt Scotch for her. Alexandra was wearing black panty hose, spike-heeled black shoes, and nothing more. She so much admired her rings that she kept her breasts bare most of the time when they were at home alone.

"*Think . . .*" she said. "Is your first wife going to snitch on you about Windsor Nassau? Or anything else? She may want a million, or whatever, but she's not going to get it if she shoots you down. *Think!* If she damages you, where's her million going to come from? Where's her child support going to come from? She's on *our* side! She has to be. Dear little Amy—and I'd sure like to meet her— has no options."

"Still . . . the million. It's a hell of a setback. Goddamn it. I'm going to need a *coup!*"

Alexandra shook her head. "Not a coup. We're not broke. We just need to pour some money in the till."

"Harcourt will finish its accounting and pay the bonuses soon. Mine won't be peanuts."

"I am still a partner in Fairchild, Douglas & Jones. And I hear things. You've refused to risk using my information. Now let's see."

"It can be traced," he said.

"You think I'm stupid? You worked it out so you could copy documents from Eye-Vee's briefcase. You rifled Miley's desk. You don't lack guts or smarts, my husband. So why don't we cut the pity party and get to work?"

"I suppose you have something in mind."

"Let's start by liquidating Windsor Nassau. It was a peanuts deal to start with. Amy knows about it. Now Bailey knows about it. Axel Schnyder will know a way to close it and make it disappear."

"And transfer everything into—? All eggs in one basket, in Deutsche Bank?"

"Not necessarily," she said. "Pictet is a useful ally. Axel Schnyder will agree on a way to establish a new account. Your Austrian name is, as I recall, Reinhard Brüning. Of Vienna. Brüning can establish an account with Pictet et Compagnie in Vienna. Let Amy or Bailey find that one. Let Cooper. And while we're at it, let's see where the Coopers keep their money—and if they pay taxes. Everybody can play this game."

Dave bent forward, slipped one of her rings between his lips, and gently tugged on it. Alexandra moaned. She loved it.

"I wish you had been my first wife," he said.

"I do, too."

IV

AUGUST, 1991

"It is a very great pleasure to meet you, Mrs. Shea," said Axel Schnyder. "I knew your name before you married Dave."

"You did?"

He smiled placidly. "It is my business to know as much as I can about everybody. Your firm does public-relations work for some important American companies. By virtue of which you have access to important information."

Dave grinned. "I believe you recommended I not deal in insider information," he said.

The Swiss asset manager was smooth. "That altogether depends on the source of the information, its value, and how it is used."

"We begin to understand each other better," said Dave.

"You are a more experienced young man than you were when I met you."

"I've been shit on."

Schnyder shrugged. "Shit happens. Isn't that how you Americans say it?"

"I'd like to put that goddamned Jerry Cooper down."

"What did I tell you about enthusiasm?"

"Emotion," said Alexandra.

"Anyway . . . we know a lot more about the Coopers and their corporation," said Dave.

"I've looked into them myself, since I had your report. I would call them virtually invulnerable. They'll be taking some heavy risks in the Far East. They may experience a comeuppance there."

"Jerry has married his late wife's sister," said Dave. "She was a German collaborator during the Second World War, had her head shaved, was paraded naked through the streets."

"I know," said Schnyder.

"All of which," said Alexandra, showing some impatience, "has nothing to do with finding a new deal. I've got something in mind, Mr. Schnyder. Dave knows about it. I'd like to run it by you."

"I should be happy to hear it."

"I hardly need tell you how I come by my information," she said. "United Forests has retained my group to open a major p-r campaign for the company. They've hired Dan Wilson away from NBC to become a spokesman for them. What they want is to establish themselves with a reputation for being something other than clear-cutting ravishers of forest lands—which is what they really are. They've been censured by the Sierra Club, to name just one."

Axel Schnyder poured modest sips of brandy into three snifters, nodded, saluted with his snifter, and resumed the solemn attitude of studious listener.

"Oh, we're coming up with some great stuff for them. 'United Forests—the company that brings you the warmth of wood. If you build your new home of wood, likely you can trace the origin of that wood back to UF. United Forests. The company that brings beauty and comfort to American homes.'"

"And such a campaign is going to influence the price of UF stock?"

Alexandra grinned. She was on a roll and went on. " 'Plastic? Cold, environmentally destructive. Just look at the emissions from those plastic factories. The small branches, twigs, and leaves from harvested trees are burned in power plants, where the natural emissions of wood smoke are carefully controlled. When you switch on your lights in Maine, the electricity may have been generated by the waste-not folks at United Forests.' And so on and so on. All in the mellifluous voice of Dan Wilson, on Sunday mornings."

"Dan Wilson is a whore," said Dave.

"If he is, so am I," said Alexandra acerbically. "He reads for money the lies I write for money."

"I still ask," said Axel Schnyder, "what impact this is going to have on the price of United Forest stock."

"None," said Alexandra. She sipped brandy, appreciatively. "It is *why* they want a better image that is going to impact on the value of a stock."

"Explain, please."

"They are trying to build a better reputation because they are going after another forest-products company. Potlatch."

"Potlatch?"

"Potlatch Corporation owns a million and a half acres of timberland in Idaho, Arkansas, and Minnesota and has a reputation for effective timberland management. United wants to clear-cut those forests. They are a little afraid of an antitrust suit, but they think they own enough western senators and congressmen to forestall that. Their problem is that when they make the offer, there'll be a storm. Environmentalists from all over will raise hell. So . . . the campaign to portray UF as the company that supplies warm and beautiful wood for new homes. Environmentalists have something of a reputation for being kooks, anyway. How dare they attack a wonderful company like United Forests?"

"Such a public-relations campaign will take time," said Schnyder. "A year or more."

"So we start a rumor," said Alexandra. "United Forests is said to be considering an assault on Potlatch. It's premature. UF will go nuts. But the market will take note, and Potlatch stock will rise. Maybe only a little, but if Reinhard Brüning buys some through Pictet in Vienna . . . and *you* buy some, then sell of course, the profit should be significant."

"Dave cannot be Reinhard Brüning with Pictet in Vienna. He will have to use a different name there. Friederich Burger will suit. A citizen of Luxembourg."

"We know how to launch the rumor," said Alexandra. "How soon should we move?"

"Let us take two weeks to make the necessary arrangements with Pictet," said Axel Schnyder.

"Good."

"Incidentally . . . I am glad you disestablished Windsor Nassau. I have always been afraid it could be traced."

V

SEPTEMBER, 1991

Dave launched the rumor. He used the reputation of Harcourt Barnham—something he ordinarily avoided. It only took a confidential word dropped here and there—

"What the hell's going on? There's some odd movement in Potlatch Corporation."

Of course there was. His European affiliates had already taken minor positions in Potlatch—enough to show analysts and brokers that something was going on.

Alexandra reinforced it. She was careful not to use her known relationship with United Forests. It came up at cocktail parties—

"What is this I hear, that UF wants to initiate a raid on Potlatch? I do some work for United Forests, and they've never said a word to me about an unfriendly acquisition. I think it's a planted rumor."

When the people she talked to checked their market computers, they found that indeed there was some inexplicable movement in

Potlatch shares. Some of them bought modest positions, driving the stock up a little more and giving credence to the rumor.

"You do know," Dave said to her one evening, "that we could go to the slammer for manipulating the market this way."

"How could that happen?" she asked. "Nobody *we* know has bought any Potlatch."

"That's why I haven't suggested it to Cole as a way to make a little profit."

"Good!" she said. "And for God's sake, don't tell him. Don't tell anybody we know. We aren't going to make a Rockefeller-type fortune on this, but the risk is hellish."

"No risk if we keep our mouths shut."

"I like this way of doing business," she said.

"We can't run it *many* times, baby."

They didn't make the million back that he had paid to Amy. Deducting Axel Schnyder's fees and expenses they made $437,000.

VI

OCTOBER, 1991

Dave was not a forgiving man. He forgot nothing, and he forgave nothing. He was truthful when he said he was sorry what he had done to John Thomas Miley had driven the man to suicide, but he did not dwell on it.

He did not imagine he could drive Jerry Cooper to suicide, but he wondered if there were not some way to harm him.

Axel Schnyder had been right when he said the Coopers were all but invulnerable. From all Dave could find out, their business was in order: cash-rich, sound, tax returns filed, and taxes paid.

There were scandals in the family. Jerry's second wife had been a collaborationist, but that meant nothing anymore, particularly in the States. Len's first had been an aggressive lesbian, but she was his *first* wife. Len's second wife was both a Luchese and a Castellano: "connected" if ever anyone was. It would be a mistake to go after the Coopers on that account.

They were, though, vulnerable on one count that he could identify. Some of their merchandise was made in sweatshops, in violation of law.

Cole had told him about the case of Rosaria Lopez, the girl who'd done six months in jail for a crime she probably didn't commit. Dave wondered if Rosaria could have worked for the Coopers.

He put a man to work on it, and within a few days the man came up with Rosaria.

A few days later, Rosaria Lopez sat down in Cole Jennings's office in Wyckoff.

"I thought you might remembering me, Mr. Jennings," she said. "Remember? I was *in jail*. You worked out a deal for me."

"I remember you, Rosaria," he said. "You got a rotten deal. It was the best I could do for you, but it was a rotten deal."

"I need a lawyer," she said. "I am remembering you."

She said nothing about how she came to New Jersey to look for the lawyer who had gotten her out of jail, eventually. Especially, she didn't say that she had traveled to Wyckoff at the expense of a New York banker who had sworn her to secrecy.

"What's your problem, Rosaria?"

"I work for man who no pay minimum wage, in place without toilets, in *slave* conditions. Better than jail. But not much. All of us work like this. No laws about this? Yes. Laws, I do believe."

She worked for a man called Charlie Han. Dave had taken the trouble to find out that Charlie Han was one of the Coopers' chief suppliers. Cole discovered the connection and wondered if Dave was not somehow behind Rosaria's complaint. It made little difference to him. The girl had been given a rotten deal before. He decided she would not get the same now. He filed complaints with the New York city and state authorities on working conditions, also one with the United States Department of Labor.

"Cole . . . Can we settle this?"

Liz McAllister asked the question. That she asked it confirmed Cole's suspicion that Dave was somewhere behind Rosaria's complaint. On the other hand, he had checked. The girl's complaint was factual. She did work in a sweatshop. She sewed erotic undies for Cheeks shops.

"How do you propose to settle it?" he asked.

Liz smiled weakly. Obviously, she was uncomfortable with the role she had been assigned to play.

"A nice settlement for the client. Case dropped. Something fun for the lawyer. Like—"

"I'll never forget it, Liz. But it happened, and it's history."

Charlie Han was driven out of business in New York. The cost of manufacturing Cheeks merchandise in the garment district became all but prohibitive. The Coopers sent Han to Hong Kong, where he would manage their businesses in a more forgiving environment.

VII

NOVEMBER, 1991

For the first time, Little Emily was allowed to spend some time with the Sheas. When Dave and Alexandra came to Wyckoff they came early enough that the little girl could be with them during their cocktail hour.

Alexandra brought a Russian doll for the girl, also a Russian board game that would not be too challenging for the little boy. Little Emily was glad to receive a gift and old enough also to understand what Russian was. Little Cole was not entirely glad to see these odd New York friends in the house. He went to his own room as soon as he could. The children did not have a nanny, but a teenaged baby-sitter was sophisticated enough to know when her charges were to be kept upstairs and not allowed to come down. Emily paid her enough to be certain of that.

"Okay . . ." Emily said when Little Emily had gone to bed. "You made a believer of me."

She opened her blouse and showed her rings.

They were not platinum as Alexandra's were but gleaming silver installed by a nondoctor operator in New Jersey who had used a spray local anesthetic and pierced her nipples, one on one day, the other a month later.

Her breasts remained small, after two children had nursed. She took modest pride in her rings.

"Like you said. They don't pinch. It hurt a little when she did it, and they were sore for a day or three. But—Well . . . Damn! They feel good now. And they're . . ."

"Beautiful," said Dave. "And distinctive."

Emily lifted her left ring and flipped it with her finger. "I think we'll hang something on one of them one of these days. My engagement ring . . ."

"You can buy all kinds of ornaments," Alexandra said.

Dave grinned. "Well, Alexandra, I guess it's time to show what *we've* got."

Alexandra was wearing a black microskirt and flesh-colored panty hose. She pulled down the skirt and then the hose.

"Jesus!" said Emily.

They were used to the fact that Alexandra did not shave her crotch, as Emily did, and was bushy with sandy-red hair almost as vivid as the hair on her head. Dave had said he was proud of her luxuriant pubic hair and would not want her to cut it off as Emily had always done.

Now her cunt was bare. The pallid flesh to either side of her slit was stark naked, showing not even a stubble of the hair that had been shaved off.

But—

Hanging from inside her cleft were two oval rings, much larger than the ones in her nipples. They hung from holes in her inner labia—from the thin, wrinkled, fleshy reddish petals inside her most private part. Attached to each ring was a small cone-shaped weight. They were stretching her labia, pulling them down and making them more visible.

"Each one weighs about half a pound," said Dave.

"Kee-rist!" said Cole.

"You like?" asked Alexandra with a wicked smile.

She walked around the room. The weights swung, clicking against each other and slapping her inner thighs.

"I know I'm not the only woman in town with rings in her nipples, but—" Emily said, almost blushing.

"They feel *good*," said Alexandra. "Every day, all day, I feel them tugging at me. And when they swing . . . *my God!*"

"They feel good to me, too," said Dave.

"So—"

"For me, I don't think so," said Emily.

FOURTEEN

I

Hermann Reitsch sat across the table from Dave Shea in his office at Harcourt Barnham. He was a less-than-impressive man: maybe thirty years old, blond but thinning, with light blue eyes that swam behind thick eyeglasses.

"It's of course a matter of money," he said. "It's always that, isn't it?"

"Especially when you don't have it," Dave said in a tone that verged on sarcastic.

Reitsch was not fazed. His reaction suggested that he had heard the same tone before, and likely often.

"I understand that other banks have turned you down," said Dave.

"Without giving me the time of day."

"You have to understand that Harcourt Barnham is a conservative bank. We don't underwrite risky ventures. Some banks do. We don't."

"May I ask you to do me a personal favor, Mr. Shea?"

"To recommend we approve your application?"

"No. I ask you to come and see what I am trying to fund. Other banks have turned me down without seeing what I have. I don't suggest you owe me anything, but I do suggest that somebody should do me the justice of seeing what I am trying to build."

"When and where would I see this, Mr. Reitsch?"

"At your convenience. My shop is in New Rochelle. I will show you something that is worth money."

"New Rochelle . . . ?"

"It is a quick and easy train ride from Grand Central."

Dave nodded. His mind was working. This earnest young man might have something worthwhile. A man did not succeed in business by ignoring his kind.

"It will have to be in the evening."

"That will be fine. My wife will cook dinner."

"In which case, maybe my wife will come, too."

II

What Reitsch called his shop was, in fact, a laboratory, occupying the entire living room of an apartment in an old brick building between the railroad tracks and Long Island Sound. The night was frigid, and Dave and Alexandra had to take a cab from the railroad station to the building. Inside, they went up in a creaky elevator and found their way to the apartment.

"My wife, Sara," said Reitsch, introducing a woman as nondescript in appearance as he was: chubby, round-faced, wearing a blue dress Dave surmised she had bought at JCPenney. "We are honored to have you here."

"We did not know what you might like to drink," said Sara Reitsch. "Ourselves, we drink only wine, but it is not to everyone's taste. Not knowing, we bought Scotch. Most people do like that, I believe."

"We do like that," said Alexandra, glancing hard at Dave who would have preferred gin.

"Your clothes are most beautiful," said Sara.

Alexandra was wearing a black wool pantsuit, adorned with a single strand of pearls. She had selected carefully. Dave had advised her that they might be visiting people in straitened circumstances and should not come too expensively dressed, nor yet so inexpensively as to seem condescending.

The living room was dominated by Reitsch's equipment. Whatever he was going to present, it was obviously computer-based. His computer was surrounded by three large television screens. While Sara was pouring Scotch and water, he switched on his equipment.

"Do you, by any chance, fly, Mr. Shea? I mean, have you a pilot's license?"

"I'm afraid not."

"Then I will show you something that is maybe a little easier to understand—saving the air show for a little later. Will you be so good as to sit down here."

Dave sat facing one big color screen, with the two others at angles to his right and left. Abruptly a color image of an expanse of water appeared on the screens. He recognized the shoreline of Staten Island on the left screen, the Brooklyn waterfront on his right, and the Verrazano Narrows dead ahead. The images on the screens changed very slowly, suggesting the view from a ship moving toward the Narrows.

"You are a harbor pilot guiding a huge supertanker toward a berth in Bayonne," said Reitsch. "You steer with the computer mouse and control the speed of your engines with the arrows, up and down. The stripe across the bottom of the center screen gives your speed and course, the water depth, the speed and direction of the current, the velocity and direction of the wind. Fancifully, I call this tanker the Exxon Reitsch. All right? You want to go under the Verrazano Narrows Bridge a little right of center. So. Steer."

Dave moved the mouse a little to the right. A line on the screen showed the angle of the rudder of his imaginary ship.

The Exxon Reitsch responded only sluggishly, and Dave increased the angle of the rudder. His imaginary bow shifted right. Shortly the Brooklyn shoreline loomed ahead, coming ever closer. He turned the rudder sharply to the left.

"You are going to run aground, Mr. Shea."

Dave used the down-pointing arrows to reverse engines, but the supertanker moved inexorably toward the Brooklyn docks, until the screen went blank.

"You have run aground," said Reitsch. "Well . . . You were maneuvering a ship displacing half a million tons. It is more than nine hundred feet long and more than a hundred fifty feet wide. This is not a game, Mr. Shea. I have programmed into the system the actual data. When you tried to turn the ship to the right, its huge inertia resisted being turned. So you added more rudder. Then the Exxon Reitsch turned right. When you discovered you had turned too much, you reversed the rudder and the engines. But once again the inertia of so huge a mass of steel and oil kept the ship moving on the course you had given it—and you crashed into the Brooklyn waterfront."

Alexandra had been watching from behind. "Impressive," she said. "A disaster!"

"Thank you," said Reitsch. "Now . . . How do we train pilots to guide huge ships into ports that were never designed for them? Or, to put it another way, how do we design ships that can cope with the navigation requirements of the world's seaports? Or . . . how do we train pilots to bring the ships in and out?"

"I see. By letting them maneuver your electronic ships," said Alexandra.

"There is a great deal more to this than what you've seen," said Reitsch. "Currents. Winds. Traffic. And there are scores of ports with differing conditions. Would you like to try again, Mr. Shea?"

"At the risk of creating a monumental oil spill," said Dave. "Well . . . at the risk of making a fool of myself."

"You have already learned a little, just a little, about maneuvering a half-million-ton supertanker on one course into New York," said Reitsch. "Shall we try it again?"

Dave tried again. This time a small ship crossed his course, and he rammed it.

"But with time you could handle it," said Hermann Reitsch. "You can't *practice* with a real supertanker. But—"

"With enough experience on your system," said Alexandra, "you could maneuver safely."

"Exactly. Now let me show you something more. Let me sit down at the controls, Mr. Shea, if you please."

This time the screens showed an airport runway. The system provided sound for this—

"Bonanza seven-five-zero, cleared for a Gamma departure from runway Two-niner. Be aware of Piper twin on approach to Three-six."

"Rolling," said Reitsch. "Piper in sight."

On the screens, an airplane hurtled down a runway and lifted off. The Piper appeared on one of the side screens. The Bonanza took to the air, retracted its landing gear—as shown on the stripe at the bottom of the screen—and climbed away from the airport.

"Contact New York Departure."

"Roger, and thank you, sir. Good day."

Reitsch looked up at Dave and Alexandra. "The market for *that* would be immensely greater. We can program departures and arrivals—bad-weather arrivals far more difficult—for any kind of aircraft, for any airport in the world. That one happens to be Teterboro."

"Flight training without flying," said Dave.

"Exactly. Immeasurably less expensive. And without danger. Of course, the equipment can easily be made more realistic. We can use *five* screens instead of three, in effect surrounding the pilot with a picture of his environment. Shall we move to the dining table?"

The round dining table set in the end of the room farthest from the equipment was covered with a white cloth. Candles burned in two candelabra. Place settings of white china and heavy silverware faced each chair. The whole was modest, yet elegant.

"Forgive," said Sara when they were seated. She lowered her head and said a brief prayer in Hebrew. "We keep a kosher home," she explained.

"With us, this is necessary," said Reitsch. "We could never abandon the traditions."

"Hermann's grandfather died at Auschwitz," said Sara quietly. "His grandmother died at Ravensbrück. She was mauled to death by a Doberman pinscher, goaded to do it by a female guard."

"And cousins and others . . ." said Reitsch. "My parents escaped in 1938. From Austria: Salzburg. There was an organization that rescued children. They were taken to England first, then to Canada, finally to Long Island. I was born in Levittown. My parents had done well. They funded my education at MIT. But that is neither here nor there."

"My family came to New York almost three hundred years ago," said Sara. "I was horrified by the stories of the Holocaust, but I knew no one who suffered in it, until I met Hermann."

She served the food. It was a kosher dinner: beef and potatoes and a salad. Sara had been right in suggesting the Sheas would not much like the wine, which was sweetish. They accepted second and third rounds of Scotch and soda.

"I have begged and borrowed the money—a not inconsiderable sum—to design and build what you have seen," said Reitsch.

Dave glanced at Alexandra and saw her interest. "Mr. Reitsch," he said, "can we speak in confidence?"

"Yes, of course."

"Well . . . frankly, you are not going about it right. A bank like Harcourt Barnham is not going to lend you money. It is not going to underwrite a stock offering. Bankers don't have that kind of . . . imagination. What you need is private investors—individuals who are willing to take a risk on you."

"Yes! Yes!"

"Here is where it becomes confidential," said Dave, speaking to Alexandra and watching for her reaction.

She nodded.

"Let us suppose," said Dave, "that you find the money—make that *we* find the money—and your enterprise is a hugely profitable success. In that event, my bank will be very upset with me. You came to me with a marvelous business opportunity, and I did not seize it for the bank."

"It is what you call a conflict of interests," said Sara.

"It is what has been called catch-22," said Dave. "If I recommend to the bank that we invest in you, and they do, and you fail, then I have led the bank into a big loss. If I recommend that we don't, and you succeed, then I have lost an opportunity. I come out on the short end of the stick either way."

"And the solution to this?" asked Sara.

"This is what is confidential," said Alexandra. "We may have resources. We may know where you can get the money. But if we do, Harcourt Barnham must never discover what we did."

"You are *both* involved in this?" Sara asked.

Alexandra smiled tolerantly. "So. Aren't you involved in *his* business?"

"I am," said Sara,

"All right," said Dave. "I don't think any financial institution is going to back this program. On the other hand, there may be individual investors with enough imagination to back it. My business will be to find those investors. I can't promise that I'll be able to do it, but I am willing to try—on the condition once more that this is to remain absolutely confidential."

"*Entre nous,*" said Sara.

"*Entre nous,*" Alexandra agreed. "How much money do you think you will need?"

"Well . . ." Reitsch ventured. "I suppose we go for the airport system first. It has many more potential customers."

"It has that," said Dave, "but it also has immensely greater problems. How many airports would you have to program into the system? Would a hundred be enough? Then I heard your controller speak about a Gamma departure. That means, I should think, there must be Alpha and Beta departures and probably several more. Then there are approaches. I know almost nothing about instrument flying, but I understand there are plural approaches to plural runways. You would have to take cameras to every one of those airports and make the videotapes to feed your screens. And you would have to do it for daylight and night, in varying weather conditions. Finally, you have to sell many, many flying schools."

"Many problems," Reitsch agreed.

"On the other hand, how many seaports would you need to cover? Wouldn't a dozen make a beginning? And if you could sell a dozen shipping companies . . . How much money would make it possible to cover ten or twelve of the world's busiest seaports?"

Reitsch shook his head. "Several millions," he said.

"Let's say ten million. We might be able to work a deal."

III

"You have a deal in mind," said Alexandra on the train back to Manhattan.

"You better believe it."

"Figured. You're gonna own the thing."

"Brüning and Burger are going to own it."

"The Reitschs are no fools."

"They don't have to be. The damned thing is worth something. We'll see to it that they get theirs. And we'll get ours."

IV

APRIL, 1992

Little Emily was curious, and her mother had allowed her to see the rings in her nipples—otherwise she would have had to explain why she didn't let the girl see her breasts anymore.

Little Emily was awed by the rings and wondered how old she would have to be before she could have any. She was maturing rapidly and already had the earliest beginnings of breasts. She raised again the subject of being painted nude—

"You said wait. I have waited, and I'd like to have a painting of me, like yours."

"What would you do with the painting?" Emily asked her.

"Hang it in my room."

"Would you then have to keep your room locked so Little Cole could not see it?" Emily wasn't sure she was doing the right thing for her daughter.

"Well . . . why not? And, Mother, I'd like to be called something besides 'Little Emily.' I mean, I'm a person. I'd like to have my own name."

Emily nodded. "Reasonable. So you are now Emily?"

"No, Mom. The kids at school call me Jenna. You know . . . Jennings. It's grown-up, Mom."

"Of course."

That evening Emily discussed Little Emily—now Jenna—with Cole. "She's growing up. Too damned fast."

"I suppose so. Too damned fast."

"They do nowadays, you know. She knows things you and I had no idea of twenty years ago. She asked me about condoms the other day—which she calls cockrubbers. She wants to know how old she has to be before she should start taking The Pill. Cole . . . the kid's got *tits*! They grow up younger now."

"Jesus Christ!"

"Her friends talk about these things. And we don't have any choice, Cole. We have to discuss these things honestly with her and try not to fill her head with bullshit."

"Meaning Judaeo-Christian morality?"

"Meaning that, exactly."

"Well . . . if she knows why she shouldn't do certain things and—"

"Valid reasons," said Emily. "Not horseshit. They won't buy it. This generation won't buy it."

Cole shrugged. "Did we, come to think of it?"

"She wants to be painted nude."

"Jesus, where does it stop?"

"I don't know." Emily shrugged.

V

Tony DeFelice sat in Cole's office. He was distraught.

"Margot's about to *die*," he said.

"What's the matter?"

"Her father has been arrested. He's out on bail, but he's charged with being part of a Mafia conspiracy."

"A conspiracy to—?"

"To control the sale—could you believe this?—of fuckin' *milk*!

Of milk in the New York market. Margot's dad could wind up in a federal slammer for the rest of his life!"

"What can I do for you, Tony?"

Tony glanced around. He stood up, stepped to the window, and looked down on the street. "The problem—one *part* of the problem—is that they've got a notorious Mafia lawyer. He . . . he'll let Daddy Donofrio go up as a sacrifice, to save bigger guys. I mean, he's talkin' right now to the New York DA, trying to cut a deal that lets Margot's dad and some others go in, so as to save bigger guys."

"So what can I do for you?"

"Let me have an honest lawyer on the case," said Tony.

"You don't mean me."

"You're damned right I mean you!"

"I don't try cases anymore, Tony."

"Don't have to. All you have to do is make that goddamned lying New York DA lay off Daddy Donofrio. Hell . . . *Pay him!* We can do that. It wouldn't be the first time he's been paid. There's nothing in this world more dangerous than a politically ambitious district attorney."

"I agree with that."

VI

A week later Cole sat in the office of Hugo Lyman, the attorney for the several men charged with conspiring to fix the price of milk in the New York metropolitan area.

"The bottom line," Lyman said, "is that we want you to stay out of this case. There are delicate negotiations going on, and we can't have them fucked up."

Lyman was an imposing man: bulky, with a bullet head and fierce eyebrows overhanging cold blue eyes. He was wearing a gray pin-striped double-breasted suit.

"Just who do you represent, Mr. Lyman?"

"I represent all the indicted men."

"Who retained you to represent Louis Donofrio?"

"The organization," said Lyman. "There's an organization involved."

"Fine. But *I* represent Louis Donofrio. So any arrangements negotiated will have to be cleared with me for my client."

"I don't think you understand. Donofrio can't have his separate personal lawyer. He's part of a group."

"Who made that rule?" Cole asked.

"Jennings . . . Lou Donofrio is affiliated with an *organization*."

"What organization?"

"The organization formed to control the sale of milk in this area."

"In other words, there *is* a conspiracy."

Lyman sighed loudly. "Call it what you want. Lou Donofrio is a part of it."

"Okay. But Louis Donofrio is represented by *me*, and I will have to consent to anything you negotiate."

Lyman nodded. "I guess you think you're a tough guy."

That was Wednesday. On Sunday the body of Louis Donofrio was found in the trunk of a car abandoned in the Vince Lombardi rest stop on the New Jersey Turnpike.

VII

"Goddamnit!" Dave barked. "When you've got a problem like that, you should check with me. I know ways to—"

"Cope with the Mafia?"

"It's not Mafia. Forget Mafia. I'm not sure there is any such thing. But there are groups of wiseguys who form conspiracies to—"

"Control, for Christ's sake, the sale of *milk?*" Emily asked.

"Any market. The sale of anything. Cole . . . They're moving in on the banking and securities businesses! There isn't any business they won't assault. And you know how they work it? *Violence*. Or the threat of violence. They're all standing up in line now, that bunch. And so are the guys who haul and sell milk. They take notice of what happened to Lou Donofrio, and they march to orders. That's the way it is."

"Well, what could I have done about it?"

"Cole . . . The key is *money*. We could have bought Donofrio out of the problem. We could have *bought* it! We could have bought off the wiseguys. We could have bought off the friggin' district attorney. He wouldn't be the first one bought off. And for small fry like Donofrio it wouldn't have cost all that much. You *confronted* those bastards. Their goddamned *honor* was at stake! No . . . forget honor. Their goddamned *credibility* was at stake. And *that* they can't risk."

Alexandra shook her head. "Cole. You can't play honest small-town lawyer in this league."

"Is there any league left where I can play it?" Cole asked bitterly.

"Yeah," she said. "*Minor* leagues. Very minor."

"You want to come in with me on a business deal?" Dave asked. "Alexandra and I have a deal in mind. It may be worth a hundred fortunes. You're too damned good a lawyer, Cole, to be screwin' around with a small-town practice in Wyckoff, New Jersey. How'd you like a share in a business that might come to . . . Well. It might become a significant new industry."

"I might as well," Cole said. "I sure didn't do Tony DeFelice any good."

"I'm damned sorry about that," said Dave. "You're a good lawyer, Cole. But, you stick with what you know. I'd like you to work on a corporate deal."

"I'm not a specialist—"

"My friend, you're a specialist as far as I'm concerned."

"But why me? There must be thousands of lawyers in Manhattan who—"

"I want somebody I can *trust*. I want a friend."

They were in the Sheas' Manhattan apartment, where they felt more comfortable, there being no children. Alexandra had not sent out for food. She had a pork roast in the oven. Their predinner drinks were half-frozen vodka. She had a Russian's taste for caviar, and a generous supply of it lay in a crystal bowl.

"You'll have to see a demonstration of the Reitsch software to see what business we have in mind," said Alexandra. "But . . . business. Enough for tonight. How do you like your rings by now, Emily?"

Emily took that for a clue, which it was, and lifted off her sweater and exposed her breasts. She smiled shyly.

"My engagement ring," she said.

She had in fact had the ring in her left nipple cut and her diamond engagement ring inserted in it. It hung from the nipple ring.

FIFTEEN

I

MAY, 1992

"The deal," Dave said to Hermann Reitsch, "is that we form a corporation. We issue shares of stock. I can find investors who will buy it. You will then have the cash to continue your development and build the system that will bring ships of any size into major ports in varying conditions of wind and weather."

"Who *controls* this corporation?" Reitsch asked.

"*We* do. You will be president and chief executive officer. I will have no office. My name will not be on the corporation."

"But it should be."

"No. I think I've explained that. My bank would take the position that I am investing in competition with it."

"But who will invest?"

"I have interested investors. Part of the money will come from overseas."

"I am happy to say that your friend Mr. Jennings was most impressed," said Reitsch.

"And his word will be accepted by some very wealthy people."

II

One of them was Julian Musgrave, the owner of Musgrave Enterprises, Incorporated, which now owned seven automobile agencies.

179

They sat over Italian food in a restaurant in Bayonne. Julian Musgrave was in his late sixties now. He had not lost his exuberance. Nor his taste for Chianti and Italian veal.

"You're looking for a hell of a lot of money," he said.

"I'm looking for ten percent of what's going into it," said Dave.

"Both of you guys are convinced that this damned thing is—"

"There's no such thing as certainty," Dave interrupted. "But if *I* believe in it and Cole believes in it, it's worth a commitment."

"Worth a risk," said Cole.

"What are you guys putting in it?" Musgrave asked.

Dave grinned. "You weren't born yesterday," he said. "You know I can't publicly invest in an idea my bank turned down on my recommendation. Hell, they wouldn't have underwritten the funding anyway. But they wouldn't take that into consideration."

Julian Musgrave invested a three million dollars in the Reitsch idea.

When he had left the restaurant, Dave shrugged and said to Cole, "Hell. He can afford it."

III

Alexandra sat across a table from Bob Leeman in a Czech restaurant on the Upper East Side.

Leeman looked at her. "It's okay. Y' know. I understand that Dave can't be seen talking to me."

"It's an idiot goddamned world," she said.

His bald head—she suspected he shaved what little hair he had left—gleamed even in the dim candlelight of the restaurant. As always he didn't drink and didn't eat meat, which was not the easiest thing to do in a restaurant known for its excellent food and wine. How he had managed over the years literally to rape the financial markets and never to be suspected or charged was beyond her. And his stable of little girls that he used and then educated.

One of them was an associate in a fine Manhattan law firm. One was an investment banker. Three were advertising executives. One was a confidence artist with no other definition. The world was a strange place.

"We have come up with an opportunity," said Alexandra. "I can explain it to you, or I can take you to see a demonstration of it. We are looking for ten million dollars. Dave and I think you could put in three. We ourselves are going to risk five."

Leeman grinned. "From Zurich?"

"From wherever. And I won't ask where your money will come from."

"I wouldn't consider an invitation to invest that much money if it came from somebody else."

She smiled. "We have a record, Bob."

"What are we going to do?"

"We are going to take control of a marvelous new technology that is potentially worth hundreds of millions."

"Not Sphere," he said sarcastically.

"No, and not the ladies' undergarments business."

"Don't scorn that. I wish I had been in that at the outset."

"They would have eaten you alive," she told him.

"You think so?"

"If they could have eaten us, they could have eaten you. Dave has gotten . . . reasonably powerful with assets since you and he did business. He's grateful to you, I might tell you. If not for the goddamned bank, you and he would be associates."

"But he needs Harcourt Barnham to—"

"You know why he needs Harcourt Barnham. Let's don't play around, Bob. You want to hear about this deal? Or not?"

IV

Leeman wanted to hear about the deal, but he also had something more in mind. He invited Dave to a lunch in a suite in the Waldorf, where he said other investors would be present.

No others were present. Dave was not quite sure how to take that. He accepted drinks and hors d'oeuvres and stared down at the street from the windows, wondering what Bob Leeman had in mind. The man did nothing without a purpose.

"Somebody is here to see you," said Leeman eventually.

He opened the door to a bedroom. A striking young woman came out, dressed in black: tiny minidress with deep décolletage and skirt halfway between her knees and crotch, black sheer panty hose, and shiny stiletto-heeled shoes. She was small, as he had not forgotten, but she had distinctly matured since the last time he saw her.

"Remember her, Dave?"

"Janelle . . ."

"All grown-up," she said.

She was in fact, grown-up. Twenty-four years old now and no longer the teenager Leeman had given Dave in 1983, Janelle had developed into an extraordinarily beautiful young woman.

She still worked for Leeman, though—apparently.

"Guess what she does now," said Leeman. "You said you wanted her to have an education and were willing to pay for it. I said I'd take care of that, and I did. Janelle graduated from MIT with a degree in mathematics. She's a systems designer. She's a hell of a lot smarter than I used to think she was."

"Systems designer . . . ?"

"You know the difference between an architect and a carpenter?" she asked, casually pouring herself a drink of Black Label scotch. "It's the same as the difference between a computer systems designer and a programmer."

"You've done damned well," said Dave.

"Well . . . he asked me to meet you again. I guess I owe him that much."

"She knows the name Hermann Reitsch," said Leeman.

The meeting began to be meaningful. "What do you know of him?" Dave asked.

"He's an eccentric computer guru," said Janelle. "He's developed the system you're asking Bob to invest in, and of course he's desperately short of money. From all I know of the thing, it just might work. It just might."

"In which case, it's worth the risk, she tells me," said Leeman.

Janelle crossed her legs. She was no more concerned about modesty than she had been when she was presented to him as a stark-naked teenaged girl. Her legs were slender and sleek, and she exposed them all the way to her hips. She took a pack of cigarettes and a lighter from her purse and lit a cigarette.

"She's developed a bad habit," said Leeman.

"I'll stop smoking when someone makes it worth my while," she said nonchalantly.

"Do you think Hermann Reitsch would let her see his idea?" Leeman asked.

Dave raised his chin high. "It could be arranged, I suppose."

"Okay. Why don't you do that? And . . . uh . . . I've got things to do. Why don't you two enjoy the bar and the buffet? I'll talk to you later."

Leeman left, abruptly.

"Well . . ." said Janelle. "I guess we should renew an old friendship."

She pulled her dress over her head. She was wearing a rigid black bra that forced her breasts up into unnatural points and formed her shadowy décolletage. She unhooked the bra and dropped it, loosing her big, firm breasts.

"God, girl . . ."

"We never got very far back then," she said.

"I couldn't take a chance on getting a fifteen-year-old girl pregnant."

"I was seventeen," she said.

"Fifteen, I checked it out."

"But didn't you want it? I mean, didn't you want to put your cock in me?"

"Of course I did. Sure I did."

"Okay. You're hung like a horse. And I'm a big girl now and on The Pill. Do you want to fuck me, Dave?"

He could hardly speak. He was mesmerized. He nodded.

She smiled lazily. "Well, then . . ."

She took his hand and led the way. She kicked off her shoes

and took off her panties. She left on her lace-topped hosiery. She lay on her back on the bed and spread herself.

He hurried to get out of his clothes. He was hugely, almost painfully, erect. He straddled the grinning young woman and lowered himself into her. Her black pubic hair was thick and coarse, and the rough feel of it almost got him off. Her slit was wet and smooth, though, and he was able to thrust deeply into her before he came.

Janelle sighed heavily. "You don't call that fuckin', do you?"

Dave chuckled. "It was for me. But now we get down to serious work. I'm good for four or five times."

"You better be," she muttered. "And how about doggy style next? I'm not much for the missionary position."

V

When Dave told Alexandra he was going back to New Rochelle to meet again with the Reitschs, she said she didn't care to go. He was glad. He wasn't sure how she was going to like Janelle. Also, he wanted an hour or so alone with Janelle.

Rain was windswept and pouring when they were to go to New Rochelle, so he rented a car, picked up Janelle at her apartment, and drove. Traffic was heavy on I-95, and tricky in the driving rain. It didn't help his concentration when Janelle opened his pants, put her face down in his lap, and began stroking and sucking his penis.

He had to wonder about something: Was she a nymphomaniac, or did she have a design to destroy his marriage and have him for herself? The latter idea was a good one, but he had to remember he was not just Alexandra's husband; they were partners, and she knew a lot about him. And he knew she would not let go of him.

When they arrived at the Reitsches' apartment Sara immediately offered Scotch to Janelle. The taste of what she had coaxed out of his cock still lingered in her mouth, and she hated to wash it away with Scotch whiskey and soda.

They were not invited to the apartment for dinner; it was too late for that; and Reitsch turned abruptly to the business at hand. "I am glad to see Miss Griffith," he said, "but please explain to me again just why you have brought her."

Dave nodded. "Miss Griffith is a graduate of MIT and a recognized systems designer. She works often as a consultant. In this instance, a man seriously considering investing three million dollars in your idea has retained her to look at it and make him a recommendation: Should he invest or not?"

Reitsch looked at Janelle. "You understand my caution," he said.

It was not easy to believe this very young woman, beautiful and stylish, was a heavyweight consultant in systems design. She had made no concessions and was wearing a shiny bright red minidress, black panty hose, and black shoes.

Janelle sipped Scotch and smiled casually. "You are afraid I will steal your idea," she said. "Not an unrealistic concern. But I doubt I could—particularly not after a single demonstration."

"I was not quite . . . thinking in those terms," said Reitsch.

"I'm pleased to hear it."

"I spoke of ten million dollars," Dave said. "I have six. The man she advises is ready to commit three million more, making nine. I don't know where we are going to get the other million, but—" He shrugged. "We will do it."

Reitsch switched on his equipment. The screens lighted up. The Verrazano Narrows entrance to New York Harbor appeared as it had before, and Dave noted with some concern that this was probably the only harbor entrance the man had programmed. That would mean also that the handling characteristics of what he fancifully called the Exxon Reitsch were the only ones entered in his computers.

Would ten million dollars bring the system up to market feasibility?

Well . . . Reitsch had spent what he thought was a lot of money to get this far; but it was probably not more than half a million dollars, if that. With ten million—

Janelle sat down at the keyboard. Reitsch put the ship in motion. She immediately grasped the concept, but she scraped a bridge pier just the same. On her third try she brought the huge tanker safely through to the pier—but crashed into the pier and presumably caused a spill and fire.

She lost interest in steering then and began to question Reitsch about how he designed the program and what equipment he was using and how.

"Will it offend you if I tell you I think you can probably make more effective use of resources?" she asked Reitsch. She accepted another Scotch from Sara. "There have been some very recent developments in data compression. You can shove data through the circuits faster."

Reitsch smiled tolerantly. "If you have the money," he said. "These things are dear."

"How much money?" Dave asked.

"Well . . . if we have access to millions as you are suggesting, we can do all of this and more."

"The big expense will be in collecting the data," said Dave. "You can't spend millions on jazzing up the machine and be left without enough to make the videotapes of the ports."

Reitsch looked at Janelle, as if to invite support. "A million and a half, maybe just a million and a quarter, for the machine," he said.

"Not unrealistic," said Janelle.

"Then you'll have to move into spiffy quarters," Dave went on. "You'll have to design and print sales materials. There are a lot of expenses."

"You think maybe it's not feasible?" Sara asked, crestfallen.

"I'm not saying that. I am saying you will have to accept cost control. You are a genius, Mr. Reitsch. You will be impatient with the bean counters. But you'll need them, and you'll have to do a lot of the things they say."

"It's a *dream*," said Sara mournfully.

"Dreams are made possible by money: the careful use of money."

"I see," said Reitsch, sadness and defiance mixing in his voice, "that I will *not* have complete control."

"But you will have a business. You will see your dream become a reality."

"Yes, Hermann," Sara whispered.

"Reality is also a matter of cooperation, teamwork," said Dave. "You've got a money man. That's me. You've got your first lawyer, who is Cole Jennings. You've got a design consultant, who is Janelle. You will have accountants and—the whole schmear."

"I know you are right, Mr. Shea," Reitsch said humbly. "I am grateful to you."

VI

"He who controls the schmear controls the business," Janelle said as they drove back toward Manhattan.

The spring storm continued, and the wipers strained to clear the windshield of the rented Oldsmobile. She had pulled off her red minidress, sat in her panty hose, and was smoking a cigarette.

"Bob made a big mistake when he talked so much in front of you, assuming you couldn't understand. Anyway . . . My question for you is: Is it worth controlling?"

"Yes, it is. He's got a real possibility there."

"You can make it work better," said Dave.

"There is nothing in this world that can't be made to work better," she answered.

"You know something? You're too damned smart for a girl of twenty-four."

"I've been taught by experts," said Janelle.

"I never knew how you got involved with Leeman and what went down from there."

"Simple enough," she said. "When I was fourteen, my mother realized I would never be able to realize my potential. I mean, I— Well, how to put it?"

"That you were and are a certifiable genius," said Dave.

"It's like Hermann Reitsch and his wonderful idea," she said. "You can't realize a potential from a basis of poverty."

"That's cynical."

"The truth is cynical."

"I guess I'd be hypocritical to disagree," he said. "I made some compromises to get away from what I was born into."

"My mother taught third grade in a public school. Still does. And we couldn't live on what she made, so she sold her tail, nights."

"Where was your father?"

"Who the hell knows. Anyway . . . Mom decided if she could sell *her* ass, she could sell mine. And maybe out of that I'd get the kind of chances in life that she never had. One of her Johns knew Leeman. I mean . . . I have to explain that Mom was never a bar hooker. She made dates with businessmen that she met like at PTA meetings. She confided in one or two of them that she had a nubile daughter who could go on the market to the right man for the right money. Okay. The guy sent her to see Leeman. She talked to him, and then she took me to meet him."

"Jesus!"

"I'm going to tell you something, Dave. Never once in my whole goddamned life have I felt any obligation to regard my body as a temple of God. It has always been something to make money with. And to have fun with."

"And you had brains."

She grinned. "And so do you. So business ethics mean no more to you than they do to Bob Leeman. Ethics and morals are for dummies. We can beat the world by ignoring their superstitions and climbing over their bodies. Bob has done it. And so have you, I figure. Hell, I sucked off a couple of MIT professors to assure my summa cum laude credential."

"Jesus, Janelle!"

"Tell me I made a wrong decision," she looked squarely at him.

"Anyway, I wasn't the first guy Bob gave you to."

"Or the last. But he was good to his girls. He didn't hand me over to drunks or bullies. He paid you a very big compliment when he gave you me."

"I offered to pay your tuition."

"I know. He told me at the time."

"I was very impressed with you."

"I didn't forget you, either. You were nice to me. And you had a world-class cock, which is something I already knew something about. You weren't the only one who thought that way. Technically I was a virgin when I went away to school. Hey! Remember what Marilyn Monroe said? Something like, 'I'm a big star now, and I'll never have to suck another cock.' And you know what Marlene Dietrich said? Something like, 'I'd much rather suck than fuck. Sucking, *I'm* in control, and I don't have the heavy, sweating bastard on top of me.' Marlene was smart. Marilyn wasn't."

"You're a compendium of arcane knowledge," Dave said dryly.

"We'll have—what?—an hour before you have to go home. Okay. I've sucked you off. We've fucked. Tonight I want to feel your tongue up in me. It's time I got some of that, don't you think?"

"You've earned it."

She laughed. "I'll pour some chocolate syrup in it. Or smear it with strawberry preserves. Which would you prefer?"

Dave nodded. "I'll think about it. In the meantime, we've got to make a deal. What do you want out of this Reitsch thing? A participation? Or a salary?"

"Both. We'll work something out."

"Okay, we'll—"

"DAVE! DAVE!"

He hit the brakes with all his might, to stop before he ran under the rear of a huge semi. The Oldsmobile spun, went off the pavement sideways, turned over, and broke through the guardrail rolling. It rolled side over side down a slope and into water, disintegrating as it went.

"Janelle . . . Is she all right?" he asked frantically as the emergency squad people were pulling him out of the totaled car. The water they had rolled into had put out the fire that burst from the ruptured gas tank. *"Don't let her die!"*

A squad woman wiped blood from his face as a man injected something into his arm.

"We'll get you to a hospital as fast as we can, sir."

"Columbia Presbyterian . . ." he sobbed. "Take us to Colum—"

The last words he heard were those of the squad woman. "Well . . . he knows where he wants to go. Best hospital in—"

VII

Janelle did not die. She suffered four broken ribs, a punctured lung, and a fractured pelvis. Dave suffered a broken arm, a broken leg, and skull fracture. She remained in the hospital for three months. Dave was released after five weeks.

With one arm in a sling, he could not hobble around on crutches. He worked the phones. That was all he could do. Alexandra was not speaking to him.

Harcourt Barnham was sympathetic. The bank continued his salary and even referred clients to him, whom he could advise and maybe earn commissions. With the computers in the apartment, he kept abreast of as much market information as was made public.

But—

"Cole . . . you're my lawyer. Right?"

"Right."

"You've got to deal with Reitsch for me. Get him on the right track and keep him there. Okay?"

"Okay."

"Now I'm going to confide in you about something you have to know, sooner or later. Client-lawyer communication, right?"

"Right . . ."

"Okay. I want you to fly over to Zurich for me."

VIII

AUGUST, 1992

Cole sat down in the impressive office of Axel Schnyder. He had already noticed how hierarchical status in Trust Management AG was manifested by clothing: suits, ties, shirts, length of skirts. Coffee was served by a comely blond in a microskirt. The woman who sat with Schnyder and took notes wore a skirt to her knees. She was stiff and brusque. Cole didn't ignore her, but paid her little attention.

"I was very sorry to learn of the automobile accident," said Schnyder. "I do understand that he is recovering slowly but nicely."

Cole nodded. "I believe that describes it accurately."

"It is apparent that he places complete trust in you. I knew that when you said Reinhard Brüning wanted to talk with me. I imagine he has acquainted you with all the facts of our relationship, including especially the confidential."

"He has."

Axel Schnyder smiled broadly and turned to nod toward the woman who was taking notes. "I believe, Frau Hess, we will not need notes. We can extend to Mr. Jennings the same kind of confidence our American friend obviously places in him."

She nodded, put down her notepad, and reached under the corner of his desk and . . . Cole did not guess, but she switched off a recorder.

"So. This Mr. Reitsch. I have gained more and more respect, over the years, for Dave Shea's business judgment. He has matured, become more careful. He really does believe he should commit a major investment to the Reitsch project?"

Cole nodded.

"And he thinks I should channel other clients' funds into this . . . computer system?"

"He recommends it."

"It is not entirely automatic," said Schnyder.

"I have powers of attorney," said Cole. "To act for Reinhard Brüning and for Friederich Burger."

"Ah . . . He *has* complete confidence in you. Then . . . let us review all of this. And then we will augment our acquaintanceship over dinner this evening."

•   •   •

Frau Hess turned out to be Frau Hanna Hess, and she joined them for dinner at a private club. Her skirt was not as long as the one that had declared her seniority in the office, nor did she wear the dark jacket and white blouse she had worn there, instead appearing in a white silk pantsuit that clung to her husky, mannish form. She wore her blond hair brush-cut, so short that it stood up in bristles and showed her scalp all over except for the very top of her head. She wore little makeup, though she did wear handsome pearl earrings and a strand of pearls around her neck. She smoked a black cigarillo and drank brandy.

Cole made a snap judgment that she was a dyke.

"I gather," said Axel Schnyder, "that Dave Shea is a long-time friend of yours."

"Since childhood," said Cole. "We grew up together in a small town in New Jersey."

"You are his personal attorney?"

"Not exactly. His *business* attorney. The only time I was ever involved in a personal matter, I represented his first wife in their divorce."

"What does he want, Mr. Jennings? Do you know?"

"He wants to be a big player."

"I detect that he is more interested in *power* than in money."

Cole shrugged. "Money brings power."

"He has done very well. I can tell you this because he has so much confidence in you that he has given you access to his accounts. But let him beware. He is nothing so big as Milken was, or Boesky. And let him remember what happened to them."

Hanna Hess asked to be excused and left their table to go to the ladies' room.

"She is giving me an opportunity," said Axel Schnyder, "to explain to you that she finds you attractive and may ask you to go home with her tonight."

Cole smiled. "I got the impression that she may not find *men* attractive."

"Everyone attracts her. Men, women . . . I have even heard it said—though I cannot confirm any such thing—that left alone she finds her big dog attractive."

"I am a married man."

Schnyder grinned. "Aren't we all? But I must tell you—if you don't want to go with her, assuming she asks you, you are going to offend her very deeply if you refuse. She has a sense that she is not a beautiful woman and assumes she is being rejected."

"Well . . ."

"I don't think you will regret it, Mr. Jennings."

After dinner, after much more talk about business, Hanna Hess spoke quietly to Cole, even realizing that Schnyder could hear. "I vould like to show you my flat. I have some . . . interesting things dere, including a razor so you can shave in the morning."

Cole glanced at Schnyder. "I would be honored, Frau Hess."

IX

She did have interesting things in her apartment, including a huge German shepherd dog—a *Schäferhund,* she called him. His name was Schatzi, meaning sweetheart. Schatzi might have been menacing, but he was exorbitantly friendly and happy to welcome home his mistress and whatever friend she brought with her.

Their night began with a walk in the nearby park, taking Schatzi out to do his business. In the park they met Trudi, a girl Hanna had called just before they went out. When they returned to the apartment they were three persons.

No sooner were they inside the door than Hanna and Trudi stripped. Neither wore panty hose. They wore thigh-high stockings supported by garter belts: Hanna's white, Trudi's black. They tossed aside bras and panties. Hanna showed that she was a true blond, though she had clipped her pubic hair, not shaved it off, and a narrow strip of it stood along the sides of her cleft. The diminutive Trudi was smoothly shaved.

"Vell, Mr. Jennings? May ve call you Cole? You, too, please. Down to your underpants anyway."

Unsure of himself, wondering what he had gotten himself into, Cole stripped to his slingshot underpants.

Hanna grinned. "Trudi has some special interests, vich ve hope you vill find interesting."

She beckoned him to walk into the bedroom with them, where he saw a big, heavy X-frame standing in the middle of the room and supported in its upright position by ropes to rings in the ceiling.

Trudi went immediately to the frame and stood against it with her arms extending along the upper parts of the X. Hanna smiled at Cole and quickly used leather straps with buckles to fasten Trudi's arms to the frame. Then she squatted and buckled the girl's ankles to the lower parts of the X. Finally, she ran a belt around Trudi's middle and the intersection of the X, and Trudi was firmly immobilized.

Hanna picked up a cruel-looking whip from the dresser. "Don't vorry," she said. "She *vants* it. Tell the gentleman, Trudi. You vant to be vipped, no?"

Trudi looked back over her shoulder and nodded at Cole. "*Ja,*" she said. She understood English but was uncomfortable with it. "*Schlagen Sie mir, bitte, Hanna . . . Schlagen Sie mir gut!*"

Hanna stepped back and slashed the girl across her bare buttocks. Trudi stiffened and moaned.

Hanna shook her head. From the dresser she picked up a red rubber ball with a narrow leather strap through it. She shoved the ball into Trudi's mouth and drew the strap around the back of her neck, where she fastened it with a buckle. Trudi was gagged.

Hanna lashed her, across her bottom, then across her shoulders. Trudi writhed and tugged on her bonds, and she wept.

"Uh . . . Are you sure she wants . . . ?" Cole asked.

Hanna spoke in the girl's ear. "*Genug, Trudi?*" she asked. Enough.

Trudi could mutter words past her gag. She shook her head and said, "*Mehr, bitte.*" More, please.

"Vould you like for Cole to vip you some?"

The girl looked over her shoulder at Cole and nodded.

He was reluctant. But he took the whip and gave the girl a stroke across her bottom.

"Trudi . . . ?" Hanna asked.

The girl looked back over her shoulder and spoke to Cole. "*Schwerer, bitte,*" she muttered around her gag. Harder.

"Mitout the oonderpants, please," said Hanna. "She's entitled to look back and see your paynis."

Cole felt caught up in a situation he never could have imagined. He took down his underpants.

Hanna had, apparently, an unending supply of straps. She seized his parts and ran a thin, soft-leather strap under his scrotum and up over the base of his penis. When she pulled it tight and buckled it, his confined penis grew yet more. His erection strained and throbbed. His balls were pulled up and forward.

Trudi turned and looked down. "*Gross,*" she mumbled.

Hanna now circled the shaft of his penis with still another strap and hung from it a little brass bell. When he moved, his penis swung the bell and rang it.

Hanna laughed.

"Now, our American friend. *Flog her!*"

He swung the whip. It cracked across Trudi's buttocks. Her scream was stifled by the rubber ball, but it was real. Hanna grinned and nodded. He slashed the girl across the shoulders. She tried again to scream. She jerked on the straps that held her to the X-frame. She lowered her head and moaned and sobbed.

Cole tossed the whip on the floor.

Hanna laughed again. She unfastened the gag. "So, Trudi . . . How did he do?"

"*Gut.*"

Cole ran his hand down the back of her head. "I hurt you," he said.

"*Es machts nichts aus,*" she sobbed. That is nothing. "*Danke, Cole. Danke!*"

The night had only begun. Eventually he slept between them in Hanna's wide bed.

SIXTEEN

I

SEPTEMBER, 1992

"You're out of the hospital," Alexandra said coldly to Dave as he hobbled into their apartment.

He was able now to get around, haltingly, with a cane.

"Is the little girl better?" Alexandra asked acerbically.

"Yes. She'll be out of the hospital in a few days. Complete recovery, actually."

"I suppose you'll be seeing her again."

"Not necessarily. She was working on the Reitsch matter, and now that we've decided to go ahead we really don't need any more consulting services of the kind she offers."

"Ah. Consulting services. What kind does she offer, really? Does she consult with her clothes on? Or off?"

"What does that mean?"

"Only that I've read the accident report." Alexandra grabbed a document off the coffee table. "Quote: 'When the emergency squad personnel removed Miss Griffith from the car, they observed that she was nude except for her hosiery. Her dress lay on the floor in the rear.' Close quote. Just what kind of consulting was she doing, naked?"

Dave shook his head. "Her dress must have come off as the car was rolling," he said weakly.

"You'll have to do better than that, buster."

"Alexandra—"

"I've done a little checking on her. She graduated summa cum laude from MIT. She's a genius in math and a recognized systems designer. So little Janelle was no hooker you'd picked up. You've had something going on the side. For some time. *YOU BASTARD!* After all I've done for you! After all we're supposed to mean to each other!"

"Alexandra—"

"She's younger than I am. She's a certifiable genius."

"Alexandra—"

Her eyes were hard and unforgiving. She walked into the bedroom and came back with a snub-nosed revolver.

"NO!"

"You bastard! I did every thing I could for you and this is how you thank me!"

He struggled up and hobbled toward the door. *"ALEXANDRA!"* He tripped over his cane and fell.

And that may have saved his life. She fired a shot that passed above him and punched through the door of the apartment. He crawled. She fired again and missed him. That slug shattered a picture window and sent shards of glass plummeting to the street. She fired still again, and the bullet grazed him, tearing through his clothes and ripping the skin from the ribs under his right arm.

When Alexandra saw his blood she was terrified. She supposed she had killed him. She dropped the pistol and ran to the bedroom to get her purse. She ran out of the apartment, leaving the door wide open.

II

NOVEMBER, 1992

Cole went to visit Alexandra at the Correction Center for Women on Rikers Island. He had contacted her lawyer and obtained his consent to have a conference with her.

She sat slumped behind the chain-link barrier that separated inmates from visitors. She wore a drab gray uniform dress, stenciled in black ink with the word PRISONER.

"He wouldn't come himself," she said dully.

"I'm not sure they'd let him," said Cole.

"You know what's going to happen to me?" she asked. "My lawyer tells me I'm going to Bedford Hills for ten to twenty years. That is, if I'm a nice girl and plead guilty."

"Using an unlicensed handgun was an aggravating factor."

She sighed heavily. "So I hear."

"Dave wants you to know he's sorry. Even though you tried to kill him, he's sorry."

"He's not as sorry as he's going to be," she said. "When I tell the feds what I know about him, he's going to wind up just like I'm winding up: in the slammer. Let him see how he likes living the way I'm living: in a fuckin' *cage*."

"Let's talk about that, Alexandra. You're forty years old, and you're going up for ten to twenty. You'll be out on parole in eight or nine years. Dave wants to make a deal. You keep the secrets, and he'll pay you ten percent of his income every year for the rest of your joint lives."

"Ten . . . Oh, how *nice!*"

"Think it through. Where you're going, you'll have no expenses. After taxes, you'll have whatever it amounts to, to invest and accumulate. When you get out, you'll be a wealthy woman, maybe fifty years old. If you destroy Dave, you'll get out poor."

Alexandra raised her chin high. "*Twenty* percent."

"Fifteen. That's all I'm authorized to do."

"How can I audit him?"

"Easy enough. You know where the money is. I've been Dave's friend since we were kids. I'm his lawyer. But I won't let him cheat you. Anyway, if you get a million a year for the rest of your life, what the hell?"

She pressed her hands against the chain link. "He's going to make that much?"

Cole shrugged. "You know Dave. Maybe more."

Alexandra dropped her chin to her chest. "Oh, yes. He'll be sitting in places like Sparks, where I met him, eating big thick steaks and drinking wine, with his little consultant chippy . . . while I sit in a prison cell."

"You shouldn't have tried to kill him, Alexandra. It could have been settled some other way."

Her face turned rigid and distorted. "I'm only sorry I didn't kill him," she snarled. "I'm going in for ten years . . . whatever. If I'd killed him, it would have been for life . . . It would have been worth it. I'm Ukrainian. We don't take these things easy."

Cole nodded grimly. "Will you buy the deal?" he asked.

"If I don't—?"

"You go to Bedford Hills for whatever and you come out with nothing to live on." He shook his head. "Not employable, either. You gonna be a waitress?"

She smirked. "Whatever happens, he's always got everybody by the short hairs. He makes enough money to buy God."

"And me," Cole conceded sorrowfully. "And you. What's it gonna be? You can have your revenge, but it will be at a terrible cost to you."

"How's this deal get formalized?" she asked.

Cole sighed. "Well, that's another thing. It will be a part of the court order incorporated in the divorce decree. I've discussed that with your lawyer."

"Divorce . . . ?"

"It's automatic. A person is entitled to a divorce from a person incarcerated as a felon. Without the circumstances we've talked about, he could take his divorce and walk away. As it is, he's willing to give you the fifteen percent."

"So he can marry his chippy."

"He has not confided to me his plans about that."

Alexandra grabbed the chain link with her fingers. A matron barked and shook her head.

"So . . . Janelle. They going to live in my apartment?"

"He's already moved out."

"I bet. Into a great place. While I sit in a little cell and do my time, he's going to live like a prince."

"If you hadn't tried to kill him, it would be a very different deal."

She blew a sigh. "Tell the bastard I buy his deal. I've got no choice. That's the way he arranges things, isn't it? So people have no choice."

Cole nodded. "He's a clever guy, Alexandra."

"Yeah . . . Say good-bye to Emily for me. Maybe they'll let us write."

"I hope so. And we'll pray for you to get out on your first parole hearing."

"Yeah . . ."

Because her case was notorious, the media covered it in some detail. Alexandra refused to say why she had tried to kill Dave. She acknowledged that she did. Her lawyer arranged the best plea bargain he could get and she was sentenced to a term of ten to fifteen years. The media noted that she could hope for parole in about eight years.

Early in December she was transferred from Rikers Island to the state prison for women at Bedford Hills. Television cameras caught her stumbling in shackles to a prison van, her hands chained to her waist by a belly chain and handcuffs. They also caught her tears, and their microphones picked up her sobs.

III

FEBRUARY, 1993

Janelle handed Dave a letter. They were not yet married but were living together in an apartment he had leased overlooking the East River.

"Cole Jennings stopped by and dropped off this letter. It's a letter to Emily. You can see who it's from. Cole and Emily want you to read it."

The envelope was imprinted "Bedford Hills Correctional Institution." Alexandra had been allowed to use a typewriter, and her letter said:

Greetings from the crowbar hotel. My accommodations here are luxurious. I live in a little cell. I eat in the prison cafeteria. The woman Dave trusted to supervise investments now supervises a mop and broom and is part of a crew charged with keeping our accommodations spotless. I am gradually settling into the role of convict. I had better. I am going to be just that for a long time.

I would be grateful if you would tell Dave the following. I am paying what I suppose is an appropriate price for what I did, no matter how grim this is, no matter how bleak the future I face. I am not sure I wouldn't rather be dead. In any case, I want to apologize to Dave, deeply and sincerely. He is not on my list of approved correspondents, so I can't write to him directly. Maybe you can understand and maybe he can that when I found out about Janelle, I just went wild.

Tell her I don't blame her for anything. In fact, I hope they are happy.

Incidentally, they cut off all my rings. They discovered them during my first strip search. They are not allowed here. Nothing much is allowed here. I am allowed to write to you and to receive letters from you. Please do write.

Alexandra

While Dave was reading the letter, Janelle had mixed him a martini, which he now accepted and sipped. She had stopped smoking—on which he had insisted.

She already had a Scotch for herself, and she sat with the glass in both hands, wearing just bikini panties and a sheer little bra—an outfit she knew he liked. She nodded at the letter, which he had put down on the coffee table, and said, "Pitiful."

"If she'd been a better shot, it would be worse than pitiful."

"You have to forgive her, Dave. I hope you'll tell Emily to write that you do. It can't hurt you to say you forgive her."

"We'll be seeing Emily and Cole Saturday evening. You can tell Emily to say that when she writes to Alexandra. As for me, I don't want to think about her. I hope I never see her again."

"You sure as hell won't for the next eight or ten years."

"Good," he said coldly.

"Incidentally, what is she talking about when she says they cut off her rings?"

Dave lifted his chin and his eyebrows. "She had her nipples pierced and wore rings in them. She—"

"Ugh!"

"More than that. She had her inner labia pierced and wore weights attached to the rings to stretch them."

"Did they stretch?"

"They looked like a rooster's wattles hanging out of her crack."

"Oh, Jesus Christ! She must have been some sexy babe."

"She was. Smart as hell. Beautiful . . . And aggressive."

"You took a chance, with me. She'd have found out one way or another, sooner or later."

"You underestimate us."

Janelle nodded. "So does Reitsch. I don't think he realizes he has lost all control."

Dave grinned. "Navigation Simulation, Incorporated. Next week a supertanker is going to come through the Verrazano Narrows under control of a harbor pilot who learned how to do it on a simulator. He'd brought in hundreds of other ships, but he'd never brought in a supertanker."

"We ought to program the thing to dock the QE II," she said.

"No. There's only one QE II. No market there."

"Think of the public-relations triumph," said Janelle.

"Uh . . . I guess you've got a point. Right now Hermann is working on other approaches to New York docks. And . . . you know
the next port he's going to work on? Hong Kong. One of the busiest
ports in the world. Then Rotterdam."

"Then airports?"

"Kennedy first."

"Okay. We going out?"

"Sparks," he said. "I could use a nice thick, rare steak."

Janelle nodded. "That's where you met Alexandra. Gimme some,
kid, before we go."

He loved the taste of her cunt. He got on his knees and knelt
before her as she pulled down her panties. Anyway, he had learned
more about female anatomy than he had ever guessed: all the folds
and flavors and the way the colors changed as he stimulated her.
He had learned definitively, for once and all, just what a clit was
and how sensitive it was to the touch of his tongue. Hers was
prominent and stuck out like a tiny penis. She had taught him
that the outer parts of her were where the sensitive nerves were,
just as the most sensitive nerves of his penis were in the foreskin;
and he learned that shoving his tongue in deep was not as good
as licking the outer, visible parts. But he knew it did not mean
that taking his oversized organ all the way in her wasn't as satis-
fying, her real satisfaction came from the touch of his stiff shaft
running in and out of her vestibule and hitting the exotic nerves
that ran inside her.

Janelle was an education.

IV

MARCH, 1993

Alexandra sat on the narrow cot in her cell, reading for the fifth
or sixth time a letter she had received from Emily Jennings. She
read aloud—"Dave told me to say that he forgives you entirely. He
understands why, and he is sorry you are where you are. He really
wishes it could be some other way." Alexandra sobbed quietly.

Her confinement was hell. The walls of the cell were concrete block, smeared repeatedly over the years with institutional greenish paint. The door was steel, solid except for a tiny window at face level. She had been in lockup since six o'clock, which was the time when the women were sent into their cells for the night. They would open the doors, and the women would march to the cafeteria for breakfast at seven in the morning.

She had taken off her uniform and hung it in the little cubby where her several uniforms hung. Coveralls with short sleeves. Today had been green. Tomorrow would be blue. Another day would be yellow. Alexandra sat on her cot in her cheap cotton underwear. All the women did. They did not wear the demeaning uniforms more hours than they had to. It was chilly, though, and she had her wool blanket wrapped over her shoulders.

She was tired. She had spent her five work hours mopping floors. It was not the kind of thing she had been accustomed to. Nothing was anything like what she had been accustomed to.

The routine was GO THERE, DO THIS, DO THAT, DON'T DO SOMETHING ELSE, SNAP TO AND OBEY, LADIES. Many of the rules were petty and irrational. That made no difference. Violations were punished. She had been punished once already, for speaking up sharply to an officer. That had cost her two days in a disciplinary cell. Disciplinary cells were like other cells, except they had barred doors, and no books, magazines, newspapers, or writing materials were allowed. The disciplined prisoner simply sat there, twenty-four hours a day, with nothing to do but stare at the walls.

In her regular cell she had a few paperback books, weekly and monthly magazines, some watercolors and a pad of paper, and a battery-powered shortwave radio with earplug. These things were life.

She had made a few friends. Some of them were serving life sentences, some only a year or two for some petty offense against the peace and dignity of the State of New York. She had met one upscale society lady who was serving a long sentence for the murder of her husband. She had been there long enough that she was allowed to wear civilian clothes, even with a string of pearls. Even so, she was locked in a cell just like this one at six.

A bell sounded. It was the signal for a count. Alexandra sighed and rose. She stood at the door and pressed her palm against the glass of the little window. A matron passed by and tapped on the door with her baton. Alexandra had been counted and could sit down.

She sat down, glanced over Emily's letter once more, and wiped away tears. The goddamned door was locked. Even if it were not, the barred gate down the corridor was locked and guarded. This was no reformatory. This was a *prison*. She could not believe she had wound up this way. Eight years, or nine, or ten—conceivably even fifteen—living like this. She had written she might better be dead. Maybe she should be.

The newspaper said that tomorrow a supertanker would berth at the Jersey docks, having been steered by a harbor pilot who had learned the technique from a Reitsch simulator. She supposed the Reitsches knew where she was, and why. Everyone did.

V

Dave and Janelle, with Hermann and Sara Reitsch, stood on the bridge of the immense tanker as it passed under the Verrazano Bridge, under the control of a harbor pilot who had learned how to maneuver the huge ship by working with the Reitsch simulator. The pilot had steered hundreds of ships into New York Harbor, but this was his first experience with a supertanker. Like Dave, he had maneuvered badly at first, but he had learned. He had learned by steering a highly realistic simulated ship on a screen, not by risking a real ship.

The trial was a triumph. There were television cameras on the bridge, television cameras in helicopters, and television cameras in small boats running alongside the ship. The news coverage was everything they could have asked for.

Cameras were not present for the meeting of the stockholders of Navigation Simulation, Incorporated.

Hermann Reitsch presided over the meeting. He learned in minutes that he had no control over the company and none over his invention. Cole Jennings held proxies for a substantial majority of the shares of stock. He voted them as Dave had specified. The board of directors, which would control the business, included Reitsch himself, Janelle Griffith, and three others whom Reitsch had never met.

In the subsequent directors meeting, the board elected Hermann Reitsch president, Cole Jennings vice president and general counsel, and Dave's nominees as secretary and treasurer.

Dave was not present.

SEVENTEEN

I

On Janelle's twenty-fifth birthday, a Saturday, Dave drove her to Wyckoff to meet his parents and his brother. He had arranged a gala party at the Four Seasons for that evening, but for lunch they would sit down with his family, whom she had not met.

They weren't married, but they planned to be, before the month was over. It was as if he were bringing his intended to gain his family's approval.

"We will have to be married in a church here," he said to Janelle as they drove into the little town. "They never quite accepted Alexandra because we were not church-married. I suppose they think she is where she belongs and should stay there."

"It would be hard to forgive a woman who tried to kill their son."

Janelle had dressed modestly for the occasion, in an off-white pantsuit. Having given up smoking at his insistence, she chewed gum, which she now took out and tossed through the window as they drove up the street toward his childhood home.

"Don't worry," he said. "They are not teetotalers. There'll be drinks."

"I could use something."

The Shea family liked her. She was little and cute and ingratiating. They did not guess, as she whispered to Dave, that when he met her she was fifteen years old and stark naked.

In the kitchen his mother talked to Dave alone. "She is a very nice little girl. I hope she is the end of your womanizing. That other one, the Rooshyan, should spend the rest of her life in prison."

"Well . . ."

His mother was peeling potatoes. "I do wish you would drive over here now and then and visit your children. You do owe them that much."

"I don't want to confuse them," he said. "Amy has probably taught them I'm a villain, and I shouldn't deny her that. They have the money to live comfortably and be well educated."

"And that is all your obligation?"

"We live different kinds of lives," he said.

He looked around the modest kitchen of his childhood home, which had once been his motivation to do better: the linoleum floor, the sink with two taps, the simple cabinets, the table on which most family meals were eaten, the gas range, the fridge; and he compared it to the kitchen in the apartment he shared with Janelle now. His mother had not seen it and would not like it.

"You have moved away, David," she said, "in more ways than one."

"Janelle and I would like to be married here, in the church."

"If you wish. But I don't think that is a good idea. It would be the first time you have set foot in the church in . . . in how many years? You are not a Christian, my son. I think it would be better if you were married by a magistrate, somewhere in New York."

II

The guests who would go to the Four Seasons gathered in the apartment Dave and Janelle shared.

Cole and Emily were there. Tony and Margot DeFelice came. Julian Musgrave had been invited and appeared, somewhat to Dave's surprise. He had also invited Bob Leeman, and Bob had come, bringing with him a fifteen- or sixteen-year-old girl wearing a microskirt that exposed the crotch of her panty hose when she uncrossed her legs.

Most interesting to Dave was Alicia Griffith, Janelle's mother: the woman who had sold her teenaged daughter into social slavery.

They had not met until now. The woman was only a little older than Dave, say forty-one or-two. She wore her blond hair short. She had contact lenses in her eyes, as Janelle had told Dave. She was a solid, compact person, with a figure that would appeal to the men she allowed to toy with her—and still did, as Janelle had confided. Her breasts were much larger than her daughter's, her belly prominent, her legs stocky. She wore a colorful brocade dress. Her skirt was mini, not micro. Dave's impression was that she was not showing herself this evening as she showed herself at PTA meetings. She was liberated here as she could not be as a third-grade teacher in a public school.

"Janelle has done well for herself," she said to Dave. "I guess I haven't been too bad a mother."

"I guess not," he agreed.

"Will you invite me to the wedding?"

"Of course. Of course we will."

Alicia Griffith took a big gulp of Scotch. "You're an operator, Dave. Take care of her."

"I will, but I don't think she needs anyone to take care of her. Janelle is too smart to depend on anybody."

"We're vulnerable, Dave, all of us. Maybe you, too."

"I love her, Alicia. There is no question about that."

"I know how you met her. That guy over there—"

Bob Leeman saw her nodding toward him and came over. "I am very grateful to you, Alicia," he said.

The three of them looked toward Janelle. She was delicious in a little dress Dave had helped her pick out. It was black velvet, miniskirted, and clinging. When she showed her legs she did not show panty hose but the tops of black laced stockings held up by black straps from a garter belt. She did not allow the skin of her legs above the stockings to be seen casually, but occasionally it was visible. Dave had prescribed the costume.

Alicia moved over to talk to her daughter.

"I introduced you to Alexandra also," Leeman said to Dave. "I am sorry how that one worked out. But this one—"

"I owe you, Bob,"

Leeman grinned. "We are going to make a bundle on the Reitsch thing. Just keep the stupid son of a bitch at work."

Emily replaced Leeman. "I went up to see her, Dave."

"I'd as soon you didn't."

"You can't imagine what's happened to her. She has been *destroyed.*"

"She did it to herself."

"She doesn't deny it. She knows why she's in prison. But . . . They've cut off her hair. I don't mean they've shaved her head, but they've cut it so it's above her ears: her beautiful hair. That wonderfully intelligent woman *mops floors!*"

"Emily . . . what do you expect me to do? I crawled around on the floor while she fired shots at me."

"She was grateful to know you forgive her. She'll pay the price."

"Do you expect to see her again?"

"Yes. She has no other visitors."

"Tell her to count on the money. I'll see that she gets it. When she is released, she'll be comfortable for the rest of her life."

"And that's all there is to it?"

"What else, Emily? What more can I do?"

"Dave, sometimes I think you have no feelings."

He stared back at her blankly.

III

Ben Haye sat at a table with Dave Shea in the Pen and Pencil, on Forty-fourth Street. He was a man roughly Dave's age. They had known each other, distantly, for many years, since Haye had played football for West Virginia and had opposed Dave on the field and then met with him for a beer afterward. He had come to New York directly from the university and had taken a job with Kidder, Peabody, where he was an investment banker. The two men had shared lunch twice or three times a year in recent years, talking mostly about football.

"We are now a subsidiary of GE, you know," Haye said. "The place used to be . . . how would you say? Collegial? Well, it's not anymore. I was called in to hear my bonus number. Two million. Can you believe it? *Two fuckin' million!* I generated ninety-four million in business, and they hand me *two million?*"

Ben still spoke with the West Virginia accent he had brought from home. He had never taken any pains to change it.

Dave nodded sympathetically. He knew that Ben and his family lived in Greenwich, Connecticut, where two million dollars was not going to make any great splash. Though he had never met her, Dave knew also that Ben was married to a fecund Ohio Valley princess, the daughter of a man whose company manufactured glassware that was respected and bought all over the western world. Ben was the father of six children.

"I felt like telling them to shove it and walk out the door. Then I decided—"

"Don't get mad. Get even," Dave suggested.

"I'm looking for someone who can take a position in a company. I mean, buying or selling on some insider information won't be enough. The way this has got to work is, I give you detailed information, you trade through your contacts, you make one hell of a profit, and you pay me the bonus I didn't get from Kidder, Peabody."

"What are we talking about, in money?"

"A hundred million."

"I can't swing that, Ben."

"I didn't expect you to. But you know people who can."

"I'll look into it. You and I can't be seen together. You can call me and say you're Mr. Blivins. If I call you, I'll say *I'm* Mr. Blivins."

"Deal."

IV

Bob Leeman sat down over hors d'oeuvres in Dave and Janelle's apartment. Because he didn't drink, Janelle had put before him a bottle of Perrier water, with a bucket of ice. Because he didn't eat much, there would have been no point in inviting him for dinner, or inviting him out for dinner. He came alone, without one of his little girls.

Harcourt Barnham would go into orbit if they knew Dave was playing host to Leeman, so it was the first time he had seen their apartment.

"Lovely," he said, looking around. "It takes a bit of chutzpah to display that."

He referred to the nude painting of Alexandra, which was about the only item from that marriage that appeared in the apartment. Janelle had demanded it. It hung prominently in their living room. Alexandra faced the viewer defiantly, with an open, amused smile, her hands clasped behind her head, her hips tilted forward. Janelle called her the bitch and never failed to identify her to visitors—

"She's the woman who tried to kill Dave. She's doing big time in Bedford Hills."

Here, that evening, Janelle was modestly dressed in a black knit pantsuit.

"Jesus, man, you're talking about a hundred million!" Leeman said. "I don't have to tell you the difference between that and ten."

"Ninety," said Janelle dryly.

"We're not small-timers, Dave," Leeman went on. "But I can't raise a hundred million. And you can't. I guess I know a guy who can. But—He might decide to eat us alive."

"Nobody ever won anything without taking a chance."

Leeman nodded. "I'll try to set it up. A meet. I'll try."

After Bob Leeman left, Janelle pulled off her pantsuit. "I want to go out somewhere good," she said. "Like Sparks. Like . . . well, somewhere. I'll give you head first. And you give it to me. I'm horny. You maybe and then me. Okay?"

She leaned back on the couch and spread her legs. He knelt before her and began to dart his tongue around her already engorged clitoris. She tasted different tonight, for some reason. It was all right. He ran his tongue over all her parts. She stiffened and moaned. She shook with her orgasm.

Then she returned the favor.

V

Dave met Lawrence—never called Larry—Doubler at his estate in Back Country Greenwich, where he had a house that stood on a high hill and had a view of Long Island Sound five or six miles away. They sat down on white-painted wrought-iron chairs on a stone-paved terrace.

The man was a legend. It was a privilege to meet him. He had replaced Ivan Boesky and Michael Milken as the king of junk bonds and mergers. It was said of him that he probably had access to a hundred billion dollars.

Doubler might have been an unprepossessing man except that his light blue eyes could fix and stare so hard that it was a rare person who was not disconcerted. Summer afternoon it might be, but he wore a black three-piece suit, white shirt, rep tie, and polished black shoes. He was slender and tall. His clothes were tailored and fit him perfectly. He was completely self-contained, totally self-confident. He liked his estate, obviously. He said nothing, but his pride was obvious.

He smoked a cigarette and sipped from a martini mixed with Bombay gin. He had offered the same for Dave, who accepted it though he would rather have had Beefeater.

Dave had not come to this meeting with no idea who this man was. He was a Mormon from Las Vegas, though obviously no longer faithful as his martini and cigarette testified.

"I know who you are," Doubler said suddenly, after a few minutes of polite chat. "You've done well. I met Alexandra Fairchild a few times. I guess I won't see her again. Tragedy. I understand you're married now to one of Leeman's little girls. Strange, that man. He abuses children, then makes them stars. The one you've married is a triumph for him. A triumph for you, I imagine."

"She's a genius," said Dave.

"I'd like to meet her. Let's set up a dinner."

"We'd be honored."

"Well . . . what is it you have? Information that can lead to— what?" Doubler looked at him inquisitively.

"I have a very unhappy friend at Kidder, Peabody. He wants to use what he knows to make himself the big bonus they didn't pay him for last year. He's not talking about playing a stock. He's talking about taking over a company. I don't have that kind of money. I don't have access to it."

"So we are talking about a major move."

Dave nodded.

"Out of which, you expect to get . . . ?"

"Can we call it a commission? I will get the information. You will move as you see fit. You will pay me—I will trust in your discretion. Out of what you pay me, I will take care of my friend, I may tell you that he is ready to betray Kidder, Peabody because his bonus was only two million dollars."

Doubler grinned and shook his head. "When I broke into this business, a two-million-dollar bonus was a *dream*. Now your friend is angry because that's all he got."

"He generated a hundred million."

"So. Let's see what he has. Do you know?"

"He hasn't told me yet."

"Obviously neither of us can make a decision until we know what he is talking about."

"When he hears that *you* are interested, he will tell us everything."

"Good. We will have to be entirely circumspect, of course. I want you to bring your young wife here to dinner. I want to meet her. But it will have to be . . . confidentially. Officially, publicly, you and I have never met."

"And never will, I suspect."

"Well . . . 'never' is a big word. We'll see."

VI

Ben Haye came to the Sheas' apartment for dinner—Chinese food to be delivered, because Janelle didn't cook much. He didn't trust his fecund princess wife in business discussions and hadn't brought her with him, though she was included in the invitation.

Janelle was wearing her little black minidress and occasionally showing the bare skin above her stockings. She had decided she enjoyed that.

He glanced around, taking in the painting of Alexandra. "You're a lucky man, Dave. I wonder if you know how lucky you are."

Janelle smiled. "Remember the line in *Twelve O'Clock High* when the general says something to the effect, 'I don't believe in luck. I think a man makes his own luck.' Something like that. Well . . . Dave is not especially lucky, Ben. Dave makes his own luck."

"Which has taken courage, a willingness to take risks, that I've never had," Haye said sorrowfully.

"Okay. Maybe you will now. Lawrence Doubler is interested in whatever proposition you may have. You talked about taking a major position. I can't. He can. But he's not going to do it without full disclosure."

"Okay. Here's the deal. I don't have to tell you what Otis Mining and Manufacturing is. OMM. They have a money-making, successful operation, but they've invested heavily in opening new mines in South America, and they're short on cash. Raiders have taken notice. OMM wants to float a stock issue and has come to Kidder, Peabody. KP is not averse. Montgomery has suggested he might just buy the whole issue. If he did that, his position in OMM would not be control but close to it. You know what he did to TWA."

"Does OMM know he might do this?"

"No. KP doesn't know it. There are others, who have been a little more public. Anyway, OMM is ripe for a takeover raid. If Doubler outbid Montgomery . . ."

"Okay. What's in this for us?"

"I assume, Dave, that Doubler will pay you a—What shall

we call it? A commission? Out of which you pay me what KP didn't."

"It's a felony, you know," said Janelle.

Haye's face hardened. "Maybe it's been my mistake that I've never committed one before."

"Implying that I have," said Dave.

"I don't imply anything, Dave. I offer an opportunity."

VII

Dave rented a Mercedes for the drive to the Doubler estate in Greenwich. He didn't believe in owning cars. Living in Manhattan, he didn't need one. Anyway, they tied up capital that could be put to better use. Besides that, they identified a person. Someone could note the license number and find out that you were at such a place at such a time.

They arrived at seven. Dave had warned Janelle that Doubler was never casual. He appeared for dinner in a dark suit. She wore a rose-colored cashmere dress that fit her like a coat of paint but had a skirt long enough that she would not show the skin between the tops of her stockings and her panties.

Lawrence Doubler waited for them on the terrace where Dave had met him. His wife, Helen, was with him. She was a construct. Everything about her had been done by professionals: her hair, her makeup, her clothes . . . maybe even her postures and tone of voice. Her blond hair was too perfect and could not have been long away from the hands of a coiffeur. It was sculpted: medium length, just covering her ears. Her brows had been plucked into two fine lines, as though drawn with pencil. She wore a faint coloring of purple eye shadow. Her lashes were stiff and black. Her pink lipstick gleamed. Her white lace dress might have been a bridal gown except that few brides her age, which had to be in her forties, would have been wed in miniskirts. Nor in stockings dramatized by a dark floral pattern.

She offered Janelle a cigarette, which Janelle accepted, even knowing Dave wouldn't like it. The cigarette was custom-made, in lime-green paper. It was even imprinted with the name, and Janelle smoked a Helen cigarette.

The drinks and hors d'oeuvres, then later the dinner, were served by two young women anachronistically dressed as French maids: that is, in white caps, white serving aprons over black dresses with microskirts flared out by white crinoline petticoats, dark sheer stockings, and black pumps.

It came to Dave's mind that everything about Lawrence Doubler was an anachronism. Even his control of a vast amount of money, which he had acquired by anachronistic means. He had heard he still had connections in Vegas. He was not anonymous, but his name occurred infrequently in the business press. He tried to avoid notice.

That he was a power could not be doubted. His business judgment would be conservative. He did not give money to politicians. He didn't own any. He did no lobbying. He acted as if government were extraneous, useless; he didn't need it.

"We are very glad to meet you, Mrs. Shea," he said. "May I call you Janelle? Of course, you call us Lawrence and Helen."

"Lawrence . . ." said Janelle. "And Helen."

"Unfortunately, the nature of our business relationship will make it obligatory that we not be identified too closely with each other. I am afraid we will not be seeing you often. But I think we are going to make a nice profit on the deal Dave has brought to me."

It was also true, as Janelle quickly concluded, that the Doublers were boring. "Oh, I hope it will work out so we can see each other often," she said, but she didn't mean it.

"We will work something out," said Helen.

On the way back to Manhattan, Janelle did what she had done the night of the accident. She put her face down in Dave's lap, pulled his cock out of his pants, and gave him head.

"Drive carefully, goddamnit," she said.

Dave drifted as she worked vigorously on his penis. "Did you know Doubler when you were with Leeman."

Janelle was busy; she didn't answer.

VIII

OCTOBER, 1993

Janelle walked into the lobby of the Waldorf, wearing what she had been told to wear: the rose cashmere dress she had worn at the Doubler estate in Greenwich. She glanced around the lobby, and immediately she identified the courier: a woman in her fifties, elegantly dressed and looking as if she lived in the Waldorf.

Their eyes met, and the woman walked over to Janelle.

"Odd weather for this time of year," she said.

"It happens," said Janelle.

"I'm from Ohio, where weather is more seasonal."

"I'm from Connecticut, where you can expect anything."

The woman was carrying a suitcase, which she handed to Janelle.

At home in their apartment, before Dave came in from the bank, she opened the case and counted the money. She had never seen so many bills before. There were bundles of them.

"Dave . . . Here is six million dollars."

"Three for us and three for Ben."

IX

NOVEMBER, 1993

Axel Schnyder sat opposite Dave Shea in the dining room of a Zurich club. "I asked you to come here," he said, "because your Internal Revenue Service has been nosing around."

"Nosing around?"

"They aren't asking for you by name. We've not been obliged to tell them anything. But they are interested in the Otis Mining business. I don't have to tell you, Dave, that your friend in Greenwich, Connecticut, has lots of money in various funds here. Those funds bought heavily in OMM. I'm talking about very large money, Dave. That man controls *very* large money, in a hundred ways. It isn't his, of course, any more than what you have is mine. But he *controls* it. His friends now control OMM. It's not just your tax people who want to know how that happened. Your Securities and Exchange Commission wants to know. I have to take note of the fact that very shortly after the OMM deal was accomplished, you deposited three million dollars. Were you involved in that, Dave? If you were, you had better be careful."

"I'm always careful."

"Do be. This can get very sticky."

"I am always careful."

"I don't want to know more. I know, though, unhappily, that the beautiful and intelligent second Mrs. Shea is imprisoned."

"She tried to kill me. I didn't want her to go up for a long term. I'd have lied and said it was an accident or something. But she . . . blew a hole in the door of our apartment and one in the window. And she meant to blow a hole in me. Then she tried to run away. The neighbors went into hysterics. She is in prison for ten to fifteen years."

"American sentences are harsh."

"Well . . . she'll have a parole hearing after about eight years. I'll go to that hearing and testify that I forgive her entirely and would like to see her out."

"And I understand you are remarried, to an exceptionally beautiful and talented woman."

"Yes. Exceptionally beautiful and talented."

Schnyder nodded. "You are a lucky man. If you were not so lucky, you might like to spend some time with an associate of mine, Hanna Hess. She has noticed you and . . . Well, I can promise you an interesting night."

Dave smiled. "I can hardly refuse an interesting night."

EIGHTEEN

I

CHRISTMAS EVE, 1993

Amy had a sense that maybe Dave would visit her and their children this Christmas. She really had no reason to think this would happen but she always fantasized that he would come back to her. When the presents arrived, she knew he wouldn't. Delivered by UPS, they were generous, in the money sense, but impersonal.

Cole came by the house in the afternoon of the day before Christmas. The kids were out, at parties. Amy was alone.

"Well, his second wife is in prison, as I understand. She tried to kill him. Maybe that's what I should have done. But . . . no. The kids—"

"Alexandra has been destroyed as a personality. She's been in a year and has six or seven more years to go, at a minimum. She's pitiful. Emily drives up to see her once a month." He paused. "I'm sorry, Amy, but she was a brilliant woman . . . beautiful . . . smart."

"Now he's married a third time. He'll never stop hurting people—using people."

"You wouldn't want to meet Janelle. She's beautiful, too, in a very different way. And a *genius*."

"I was never woman enough for him, was I, Cole?"

"No one is enough for Dave. Man or woman."

Amy shrugged. She looked down at herself. She was heavy, the word used about her in Wyckoff. She was unstylish. There was nothing wrong with her clothes, but they were not daring; they were what a matronly woman, the mother of teenaged children, would wear.

"Cole . . ."

She unbuttoned her sweater and pulled it off, revealing her standardish white bra.

"Amy . . ."

"I want a Christmas present from you, Cole. I didn't get much of one from Dave. I want one from you."

She unhooked the bra and dropped it. Her breasts were big and white, with dramatically pink areolae and prominent nipples.

"Amy!"

"I want a Christmas present, Cole. I want you to fuck me. I want to be fucked, more than anything else in this world."

"Me?"

"Who else can I trust?"

She took off the rest of her clothes. She walked around the room, showing herself to him. Cole could understand why Dave had moved from her to women like Alexandra and Janelle. Amy was a woman, true, a little loose and heavy, but she did not have the elegance of Dave's two subsequent wives.

"Amy . . . ?"

"I'm not so bad, am I? Am I so ugly you couldn't think of fucking me?"

"What if I got you pregnant, Amy?" He was trying to think of anything.

"I'm not dumb. I know how to take care of that. If it happens, I'll take care of it. I won't embarrass you. Emily will never know. I mean . . . from time to time, Cole. From time to time. I don't know another man I can trust the way I trust you."

"Are you saying you have never . . . ?"

"No. But they've been bastards. All they wanted was a hole to stick themselves in. I want to be fucked by a man who respects me. I want *you*, Cole. I want you in—me. I want a man who thinks of me as a human being and not as a cunt hole. And I don't know anybody else."

"Amy, it's not going to make you feel any better."

She looked at him desperately. "Please . . ." she said in a small voice.

Reluctantly he followed her into the bedroom.

"Oh, God, Cole! Oh, GOD!"

He had to go home eventually. But not before he'd had her twice more. Sometimes he really hated Dave. Sometimes he hated himself.

II

The Jennings family gathered around their Christmas tree. Cole was uneasy, trusting that Emily would not guess what he had done with Amy two hours before. He trusted that his batteries would be recharged before she would expect anything from him.

Emily, in any event, was less demanding than she had been. She seemed to be weakening. She had seen a doctor, who had found no reason why she should feel her energy diminishing. And that night they dismissed that concern and celebrated the evening.

Little Jenna was thirteen, almost fourteen. She was not a child anymore, really. When Cole poured champagne, she drank hers and was ready for more. Her brother took a sip, swallowed it, and pronounced it "strong." Jenna laughed.

They had their Christmas dinner on Christmas Eve. Tomorrow they would open their presents. The dinner was a turkey with all the trimmings, the same as they'd had on Thanksgiving.

"God must love us," Emily said as they began to eat. They had not said grace and never did, but she said this just the same.

Both parents were a little concerned about Jenna. She wore a bra now. She was proud of her maturing body. She had grown up fast, too fast maybe.

She asked her mother sometimes to let her look at the rings in her nipples, and she insisted that she wanted her own to be installed as soon as possible. Emily was becoming sorry she had ever let Jenna see them.

After dinner, sitting around the tree, they sang Christmas carols. It was a tradition with them.

They went to bed early. They knew they would rise early to open the presents. Emily, who had not worn a nightgown to bed in years, as Cole had not worn pajamas, snuggled close to him in bed but did not ask for sex. She fell asleep quietly.

III

On Christmas Eve, Janelle dressed as she knew Dave liked: in a black garter belt holding up beige stockings. She had arranged delivery of an extraordinary dinner—the Chinese food that both of them enjoyed. They had champagne.

They looked at their Christmas presents. Janelle's mother had sent a large poinsettia. Dave's parents and brother had sent a different floral setting, of flowers out of season. Cole and Emily had sent a huge assortment of cheeses and wines. Bob Leeman had sent a nightgown: sheer and lacy. Ben Haye had sent a selection of Belgian Chocolates. The surprise was that Lawrence and Helen Doubler had sent a mink coat.

Touching to both of them was a Christmas card from Bedford Hills. Alexandra had been allowed to go beyond her usual mailing list and send cards to other people.

Greetings. I ope you are having a happy Xmas.

IV

Alexandra spent Christmas Eve locked down at Bedford Hills. Worse than that. She was locked down in disciplinary confinement. Try as she might, she could not make herself a good, quiet, obedient prisoner. It was simply not in her nature to be a prisoner. She had, as they put it, "smarted off" at a matron, for which they had sentenced her to spend three days in disciplinary lockup, which would include Christmas Eve, Christmas Day, and one day more. They had ordered her to strip, given her a white cotton smock stenciled in black ink with the letters NYDC, meaning New

York Department of Corrections, handcuffed her, and led her to the disciplinary wing.

The discipline was being confined in a barred cell with nothing to read, nothing to do. As the officers put it, "ladies" in disciplinary confinement were given time to reflect and repent.

Worse, it would go on her record and might make her be "flopped" at her first parole hearing. She gripped the bars and stared out into the corridor, as if there were something more to be seen there than inside. She sobbed.

"Take it easy, Shea," said the woman in the cell to her right. "You got three days in here. Well, I got seven, by God. You've got to do ten years or so. I'm in for life. You don't get used to it. You never will. But *you're* gonna get out. Think about some of us who aren't."

"I'm sorry, Emma."

"Don't think you can beat the system. Just keep your mouth shut and do what they tell you. That way you'll get out. Someday."

"Hell of a way to spend Christmas," Alexandra whispered tearfully.

"You were in last year, too."

"Not in *here*."

Alexandra sighed hard. She guessed that Emma had left the bars and had sat down on her cot.

They brought Christmas dinner: turkey and dressing, all cold. She had to get down on her hands and knees to pull the tray through the slot at the bottom of the door. She wept silently as she ate. She had to eat. There would be nothing more until tomorrow.

A hell of a way to spend Christmas.

She'd had a letter from Emily. Dave had made a big deal of some kind. He'd get a percentage, and then she'd get a percentage. Emily wrote in code, knowing Alexandra's mail was read, but she knew Alexandra would understand.

Alexandra would have gladly given up her percentage, or anything else, not to be in prison.

V

Alicia Griffith, Janelle's mother, earned two hundred fifty dollars on Christmas Eve. She spent it in a hotel room with the newly divorced father of one of her third-grade pupils. She had met him at the school when he came for parents' night, and how he had learned she would be amenable to sex for money she did not know.

Like most men, he wanted her to take him in her mouth. That was all right. She was used to it. In fact, she took a certain pride in being good at it. She ran her tongue over his parts and slipped him back and forth between her lips. She had spent a lot of Christmas Eves like this.

VI

CHRISTMAS DAY, 1993

Alicia had to leave the hotel early in the morning, in time to bathe and dress herself for the drive to New Jersey, where she was to meet her son-in-law's family. She dressed modestly, in a white pantsuit, as befitted a mother-in-law.

"I bet I know what you did last night," Janelle whispered to her as they entered the rented Mercedes Dave would drive to Wyckoff.

"I made two hundred fifty bucks," Alicia murmured.

Dave had in the trunk of the car the Christmas presents he had bought for his family. The chief one was a microwave oven. He had bought a black cashmere dress for his mother and a Rolex wristwatch for his father.

Alicia went to the kitchen with Dave's mother, to offer help. She could cook. She had done it all her life.

Dave's mother shook her head at the microwave oven, which now sat on the counter. "I'll have to learn to use it. I guess most people have them. But I can't for the life of me figure out what it's good for."

"Read the instructions," said Alicia. "Pick up a microwave cookbook. Pretty soon you'll wonder how you ever lived without it."

Mrs. Shea smiled and nodded. "I am very pleased . . . We are all very pleased, at Dave's marrying your daughter. She's the kind of woman he always should have had. The one who's . . . locked up . . . I never could understand that. His first wife was just a small-town girl, and Dave's not a small-town guy. Amy is nice, but he needs a woman who's more than nice."

"I'm happy with the marriage, too," said Alicia.

In the living room, Dave sat apart with his father, who engaged him in earnest conversation, quietly so that others in the room would not hear.

"I know nothing about your business, which is obvious. I can't understand it. I wouldn't begin to know how to do it. But . . . Dave, you do file complete returns and pay your taxes, don't you?"

"Of course."

"So many people have gotten in trouble. I read the newspapers. People in your line of business are in penitentiaries."

"Don't worry about it. Don't even think about it. I've got accountants who make sure that everything is done right."

His father nodded, apparently satisfied. "I like your new wife," he said. "How old is she?"

"She's twenty-five."

"And you're thirty . . . seven. You devil! And she's not pregnant?"

"No."

"Let's hope she will be, soon. You're a little old to be starting another family."

VII

On Christmas afternoon, after the presents had been opened, another heavy meal eaten, some wine drunk, the Jennings family settled into a torpor. Except for Jenna. She walked to the home of a junior high classmate named Bill Morris, the son of the Bill Morris who had been with Dave Shea the night when Jim Amos was killed. They went to the recreation room in the basement to play pool. The Morrises were away, visiting grandparents.

Also there was Bob Hupp, a sixteen-year-old who had a reputation for playing pool very well. He liked coming to the Morris
rec room and playing on the table.

Jenna played pool well, too. Hupp had taught her. They did not
play eight-ball, which they regarded as a children's game, or nine-
ball, which they thought was a gambler's game and beneath their
skills. They played fifty-ball straight pool. Players had to call their
shots, and the first one to pocket fifty balls won. Hupp would win
usually, but Jenna did occasionally, and Bill Morris did rarely.

This game was the first they had ever played that was marked
by a new and different condition.

Jenna was naked.

"Hey, Jennings," Hupp had challenged her. "Why don't you take
it off and let us see? I mean, we've seen your painting."

She was not supposed to let anyone see her nude painting, but
she had let these two boys see, because they were very good friends.

"Oh, you guys, c'mon!" she teased. "You don' really want me to
take off my c'othes. C'mon!"

"C'mon is right. Couldn't hurt you, and it'd be a great Christmas
present."

Jenna stiffened her shoulders and blew a loud sigh. "Well . . .
Maybe . . . Look but do not touch."

"Absolutely," Hupp assured her, eyes wide.

"You guys are gonna get hard-ons." She smiled seductively.

Morris grinned. "We've got 'em now, just thinking about it. But
we haven't attacked you."

"Well . . . And it's our secret."

"Absolutely."

She thought about it for a moment, then pulled off her sweater.
She pulled down her jeans. At this point, in her bra and panties,
she paused. "Maybe . . . just this much? Okay?"

Hupp shrugged. "You show more than that in your bikini."

"Well . . ." She unhooked her bra and dropped it. Then her panties. Stark naked, she picked up a cue and asked, "Are we gonna
play pool?"

They played pool. Jenna—thirteen years old, about to be fourteen—was only a little embarrassed, and that only at first. She was proud of her youthful, developing body and quickly discovered that she enjoyed showing it.

Her breasts were small and round. They were white against her tan lines from the summer. "God, they've gotta grow," she said. She lifted them in her hands. "I wouldn't want to live my whole life with little tits like this."

She noticed after a while that the two boys moved around the table to watch her shoot. When she leaned over the table, her breasts, small though they were, hung down a little. When she had to stretch over the table, the boys would move behind her. That posture showed off her upturned butt and some of the pink fleshy parts of her pussy. She made a point of playfully spreading her legs when she stretched over the table.

She laughed. "Hey, you really wanta see?" She hopped up on the table, sat on the rail, and spread wide. She used her fingers to push aside her outer lips. Now they saw all they had dreamed of seeing, and more: her shiny pink inner lips, a tiny clit, and the shadowed furrow that opened into her deeper parts. She sat and grinned at them for a long moment, then hopped down. "Show's over."

They both had seen more than they knew what to do with, all they could do was stare.

NINETEEN

I

Alexandra was led out of the prison, wearing civilian clothes: that is, a stylish black pantsuit. She was wearing a little makeup, too. But she was also wearing handcuffs attached to a belly chain, and shackles on her ankles. She was apathetic about the restraints. They were nothing more than she had expected when she was told she would be going down to New York to testify before a grand jury.

Seated in a prison van, she was driven the hour or so it took to reach Manhattan and the federal courthouse. Conducted through the courthouse, she was unchained and locked in a detention cell until they were ready to hear her testimony. The detention cell was a tiny chain-link cage with nothing in it but a shelf on which the prisoner could sit. About this, too, she was apathetic. What difference did it make?

An elderly man with a bald, liver-spotted head came to the cell and asked if she would like a cup of coffee. She said she would, and he returned in a few minutes with a paper cup of hot coffee. He unlocked the padlock that secured the cell, opened the door and handed her the coffee, then locked the padlock again.

"You don't remember me, do you?" he asked. "I remember you as Miss Fairchild—actually as Miss Krylov."

"I'm sorry."

233

"Well . . . I've never been a famous person. But you were very kind to me once, when they tried to deport me. You went to bat for me and others and made the point with the newspapers that not all Russians were Communists and almost none were spies."

She nodded. "I remember."

"I'm very sorry to see you in the circumstances you're in."

"I'm sorry, too," she said.

They wanted her testimony on the question of whether or not her former husband, David Shea, maintained overseas accounts.

"If he did, I didn't know it," she said under oath.

"I remind you, Mrs. Shea, that there is a very severe penalty for perjury."

Alexandra shrugged. "To get out of prison I would swear to any script you wrote for me."

"You are not in prison for tax evasion or securities manipulation. You are in for trying to kill your husband."

"I lost my head."

"Is it going to be your testimony that you knew nothing of overseas accounts your husband maintained?"

"That is my testimony. He and I had a close marital relationship, with mutual respect; but he did not confide in me anything much about his business. He is a banker with Harcourt Barnham."

"Why did you try to kill him?"

"Because I found out he was seeing another woman."

"Mrs. Shea . . . do *you* have an overseas account?"

"Sir. I am an inmate in a state prison, serving a long term. How could I have an overseas account?"

"Your ex-husband is not paying you for your silence?"

"I would testify to anything anyone asked if it would get me out of prison. No one could pay me enough for the years I am spending in confinement."

Dave was not there, or anywhere near. Neither was Cole. But when she was taken out of the courtroom and the handcuffs were being locked on her again, Alexandra saw Emily standing unrecognized in the small assemblage that watched. Both of them were careful to show no sign of recognition. As a matron squatted before her and locked the shackles on her ankles, Alexandra risked a small, subtle smile.

II

"Goddamnit," Cole said. "They're closing in."

Dave shook his head. "They can't find anything because they don't know what they're looking for."

"From all I can find out, Alexandra told them nothing. She perjured herself. If they can prove she lied under oath, she'll get a sentence on top of the one she's serving and will probably spend the rest of her life in one prison or another."

"Won't happen," said Dave. "How could they prove she knew anything? Her name's on nothing. Nor is mine, for that matter."

"Do you feel sorry for her?"

"Yes, and I want to ask you something. Do you want to work on it, or should I get another lawyer to work on a plea for commutation of sentence?"

"Dave . . ."

"Okay, I'll get somebody. Somebody with political influence. But when Emily goes to see her, I want her to tell Alexandra I'm working on it."

III

The raid on OMM became notorious. The *Wall Street Journal* covered the subject:

> Control of Otis Mining and Manufacturing has passed to anonymous purchasers of its stock, several European conglomerates with ownership no one seems able to discover. Rumors abound. Among the possible owners is Lawrence Doubler, who denies knowing anything about it.

Whoever now owns the controlling interest in OMM has not made any radical changes in its business policies.

William Foster, CEO, insists he has had no instructions from his new shareholders to change anything. He will only say that the company is now much more soundly funded and that he is grateful to his new investors.

The SEC and the Justice Department remain determined to discover who did what to whom. Old owners of the stock are deeply concerned about loss of control.

Ben Haye proved to be a source of more insider information. He liked the three million Dave had paid him, and he wanted more.

He invited Dave and Janelle to dinner at his Greenwich home—where they had to come in confidence because knowledge of a relationship between them could prove disastrous to both. Dave rented a BMW, which would be inconspicuous in that town and drove to the Haye home on North Street.

It was apparent why Ben had to make money and had scorned the two million he had been given as a bonus by Kidder, Peabody. The home was by no means the most luxurious in Greenwich, but it was something beyond the dreams of a boy from West Virginia, or a boy from Wyckoff. The glassmaker's heiress was in love with antiques and had furnished the place with a collection of expensive antiques, all but a few items purchased right there in Greenwich.

"This house was built in 1912," she explained. "It didn't seem right to fill it with modern stuff."

"Oh, no. No. That wouldn't have been appropriate at all," said Janelle, the daughter of an elementary school teacher who still practiced prostitution.

Dave was amused and said, "Janelle does know a little about antiques."

Janelle smiled at him. She knew nothing about antiques.

Deborah Haye was a heavyset woman. She tried to be stylish. She was dressed that evening in a low-cut red dress that showed her oversized breasts down almost to the nipples, and it was obvious that she and her husband were proud of them.

Ben made a point of separating himself and Dave from the two women. "I can't talk about things in front of Debbie," he said quietly. "You'll understand. She doesn't know I got three million from you, and she has no idea what I did with it."

"Let me guess," said Dave. "Bahamas."

"Well . . ."

"Fine. But get it to Europe. Think of Zurich or Vienna or Luxembourg."

"Okay. But I know of another deal that can be worked. This won't be for control of a corporation, just for one hell of a nice profit. We don't need to bring in your multibillion friend. We can just invest our own money."

"The deal is? Quickly, before the women come back."

Ben glanced at the two women. Debbie was explaining to Janelle where she had bought, and why, an antique table that sat across the room.

"Michigan & Minnesota Corporation has come to Kidder for help in financing the development of a find of high-quality ilmenite. Do you know what that is?"

"No."

"Titanium ore. Ilmenite is a common mineral, but this is exceptionally high in titanium quantity and exceptionally free of contaminants. They want to mine it and build a plant to refine titanium. They're going to get the money. You can buy a share of Mich and Minn for 18⅜, today's quote. When they get the backing and announce what they've got and what they're going to do, that's going to double, at least. I'm going to put part of my three million into it, out of my offshore account. You can do the same. But we can't be greedy, and we've got to be careful. Big trades in the stock will be suspicious. And it will be too plain that the information could have come from Kidder, Peabody."

"It could have come from anybody at Mich and Minn," said Dave. "And no doubt from others."

Ben nodded. "But big moves on the stock in the next couple of weeks are going to look suspicious. The SEC will be on it for sure. This has got to be *our* deal, handled very discreetly."

"Don't make a big buy all at once," said Dave. "Buy five hundred shares tomorrow and five hundred a couple of days afterward; then a hundred or two next week, and so on until the announcement is issued. Then we sell, a little at a time. We're not going to make millions, but you can't always do that. Suppose you get two thousand shares and the price doubles. Well, you make thirty-six thousand dollars."

"I've got another idea," said Ben. "You've got—what?—multiple accounts in Europe. Suppose I transfer part of my three million to *your* accounts. You can trade better than I can. You're much more remote from K-P and the information. And you've got other contacts, who can invest discreetly for themselves and us."

"Deal," said Dave. "We'll work it out."

IV

A few days later Dave came home to find Janelle wearing the shortest mini he had ever seen on her. She was wearing stockings and a garter belt. When she sat without keeping her legs crossed she showed her crotch. But not a bare crotch. She was wearing panties. As he stared he saw something that surprised him—her bikini panties were slit, and when she spread her legs even a little, the panties separated, and everything was exposed.

"I went shopping this afternoon," she said as she handed him his martini. "Out of curiosity mostly, I went to see one of the Coopers' Cheeks stores. They have some interesting stuff. This dress. Crotchless panties. I bought three pairs. Bras with holes for the nipples to show through. I have one on. I'll show you in a little while. And, you wouldn't believe—" She reached down and opened a shopping bag. "Look."

She showed him a pair of black leather wrist cuffs lined with fleece and linked together by about a foot of shiny steel chain. They fastened with buckles, and the hasps of the buckles were looped at the ends, so that very small padlocks could prevent the person wearing the cuffs from taking them off.

"And finally—"

She showed him a wide leather collar, also lined with fleece and equipped with a buckle and a little padlock.

Dave frowned and smiled at the same time. "What are we going to do with those?" he asked.

"Well . . . you can put them on me. I may hate the cuffs and ask you to take them right off. But I think the collar is sort of nice. Sexy. Why don't you put it on me right now? The cuffs later."

Gingerly he put the collar around her throat. The leather was soft, and he could see it wouldn't hurt her. He buckled it, not too tightly, and locked the padlock.

"Ha . . . your love slave, baby."

"I can't think of you as a slave, love or otherwise."

She went to a mirror and looked at herself. She tugged on the collar, moving it around so the buckle and lock were at her throat.

"Tell me it doesn't turn you on. Not that you need to be turned on."

He had known it would turn him on, and it did. It forced him to remember how he used to tie Amy with clothesline rope. That had turned him on. He had never hurt her, but he had made her sit evenings after the kids had gone to bed, with her wrists and ankles bound. She had tearfully called it demeaning and humiliating. Janelle lifted her chin and posed with the collar around her neck. She was pleased with it, even proud of it.

She took off the dress while they microwaved the frozen pizzas from the fridge and opened the wine. She was wearing the bra she had described, with her nipples sticking out through holes. He fingered her nipples until they became erect.

When they had eaten she told him he could put the cuffs on her. He did.

"Well . . . ?"

She stared at them for a moment, raised her hands and stretched the chain, then grinned. "They're okay. I don't think I'd want to wear them very long or very often, but . . . they turn you on, don't they?"

"I won't deny it."

She twisted her shoulders. "Kind of imaginative lovemaking, huh? I'm a sight."

The bra with her nipples sticking out was black. The crotchless panties were black, as were her garter belt, her sheer stockings, and her black stiletto-heeled shoes. She walked around the room, turning and showing herself off to him.

"It's better than just naked, isn't it?"

Dave grinned and nodded.

Suddenly she smiled wickedly and asked, "What would turn you on even more?"

"Well . . . I wonder if a naughty girl like you shouldn't have a little spanking."

"You've . . . got . . . to . . . be . . . kidding."

"Don't knock it if you haven't tried it."

She arched her shoulders. "Maybe just one or two experimental whacks," she murmured.

"Over my knees," he said.

He was sitting at the center of the couch, and Janelle stretched out, with her hips on his lap. Her tiny panties did not cover her butt. He lifted his hand and gave her a sharp smack on her right cheek.

"OW!"

He did it again, on her other cheek.

"OW! Hey! Not so fuckin' *hard*!"

"Okay. Six more, three on each half of your beautiful ass. Not so hard. Okay?"

She drew a deep breath and nodded.

He spanked her. She grunted with each slap, but she did not yell or try to roll off him.

Dave pressed a finger through the gap in her panties and ran it over her parts. "You're wet," he muttered. "You bitch. You like it. I'm going to spank you till you beg me to stop. A little harder again. I bet you come."

"OW! OW!" But she did not ask him to stop. Her cheeks turned a glowing pink.

Finally—"Okay! OW! Oh, Jesus, stop! I'm coming! I'm coming! I'm coming!" She moaned and she pressed her face into the seat of the couch.

When she relaxed, he turned her over and lifted her. Then he kissed her. Tears wet her eyes and cheeks, and her face was flushed. She tried to reach behind and feel her hot backside, but the cuffs and the foot of chain wouldn't let her.

"Get your pants down," she whispered. "The girl you've just abused is going to give you the greatest head you've ever had. Get ready for it. It's going to take a while."

She teased him with her tongue. When she knew he was on the verge of coming, she would draw back and reach for a glass of Scotch and take a swallow. After a minute or so, she would go back to work on him, licking gently, raising him little by little. Then: another break. Then more licking. And so on, until he all but exploded in a powerful orgasm, shooting into her mouth. She did not swallow but allowed his ejaculate to seep out of her mouth, run down over her chin, and drip on her breasts.

Janelle grinned as Dave tried to regain his senses.

TWENTY

I

In the ensuing two weeks, Reinhard Brüning and Friederich Burger invested in shares of Michigan and Minnesota Corporation. So did Bob Leeman.

Bob sat over dinner with Dave and Janelle in an obscure little Italian restaurant on the Upper East Side. They still did not want to be seen together.

Janelle was wearing a microdress she had bought at Cheeks. Dave was wearing a cashmere tweed jacket—subdued gray and maroon check. It was a jacket he never let the officers of Harcourt Barnham see. Leeman noticed Janelle's dress and Dave's jacket and complimented them, but he himself was wearing a nondescript suit as usual, because he cared nothing about clothes.

Or about food and wine. He ordered a salad and Perrier water, while Dave and Janelle lingered over the menu and finally chose veal with pasta primavera on the side, with a bottle of fine Chianti.

Bob turned mournful. "It's the first time you've steered me wrong, Dave. Ilmenite! The world is full of the goddamned stuff, and theirs isn't any better than anybody else's. I paid eighteen and change for the stock, and it's down to twelve."

"They had a lot of smart people fooled," said Janelle.

"Honey, there aren't any smart people in this world. Not professors, not politicians, not industrialists, and sure as hell not New York investment bankers and securities dealers."

"The geologist and chemist they relied on were paid off," said Dave.

"So we got suckered. Was it too much to ask that somebody hire an independent examiner to look into these claims about the ilmenite? But they didn't. And you know why they didn't? Because these guys in the New York financial district think they are big brains, all but infallible."

Dave smiled. "That's what makes life possible for us, Bob. Isn't it?"

"Well, we might not be the smart people either," Bob said as he poured Perrier over ice. "The movements in Mich and Minn during the week or so when it looked like something big was going to happen didn't go overlooked by the SEC. We put in money because we thought the value of the stock was going to double. They're asking why we thought so."

"They asked you?"

"I have a reputation. I didn't buy much, only a hundred thousand worth; but they thought that was significant. They wanted to know why I bought."

"And you said?"

Bob nibbled on a bit of lettuce. "I said I thought it was a good stock, with potential. Then they asked why I'd never invested in it before. I didn't have a very good answer. I just said I dabbled in a lot of stocks."

"To which . . . Who was asking?"

"A guy from the SEC, plus a guy from the New York DA's office."

"How much did they know?"

"Who could tell? They asked me if I knew a couple of guys named Reinhard Brüning and Friederich Burger. I said I never heard of them. I never did, either." He stopped and smiled. "I figure one of them is *you.* Maybe both of them."

"I have no idea who they might be," Dave said.

"Well . . . one thing for sure: I didn't mention *you.*"

"How much did these guys, Brüning and Burger put in?"

"They didn't say. They weren't giving out information. They asked the questions."

Dave drew and released a deep breath. "I didn't tell you where the information came from."

"I didn't want to know. Then they can't force it out of me."

"They've got nothing on you, Bob. You bought some stock. They suspect you had insider information, but you don't know where it came from; and so long as you don't mention me—which I know you won't—they'll never figure it out."

"If Dave gets in trouble, you're in trouble, too, Bob," said Janelle.

"I know that. But I don't like how close they're getting. I'm going to be under a magnifying glass."

"You need an overseas account," said Dave. "Maybe more than one."

"I've never worked that way."

"Well, think about it. And if it makes you feel any better, the guy who supplied the information that turned out wrong lost a big piece of money himself."

"And you?"

Dave grinned. "Me? Would I trade on insider information?"

II

As they lay in bed together that night, Janelle asked Dave, "Don't you ever worry?"

"I worry. I try not to show it."

"You've got it all well covered, haven't you?"

"I look like an ordinary banker with Harcourt Barnham, a little flamboyant maybe but not a big risk-taker. I pay the taxes on my salary and bonus. We don't live better than that income would allow—taken with yours as a computer consultant. Unless somebody some way figures out who Brüning and Burger are, we're safe."

"You're not afraid Alexandra will crack? Emily says she's completely detached from reality."

"The lawyer I'm paying to make her appeal for commutation says she's settled into being a docile convict. Her reality is a cell, blue or yellow jumpsuits, a job mopping floors—"

"Does that lawyer stand any chance of getting her out early?"

"No. But so long as she thinks he has and knows I'm funding the effort, she stays on our side. She would anyway. What would be the percentage for her in jumping the reservation? The only chance she has for a good life when she's out is the money I'm putting aside for her. I know Alexandra pretty well, you understand. She's an intelligent, rational woman. I'm her future, and she knows it."

"She wasn't rational when she tried to kill you."

"One bad moment, which turned out fortunate for you and me. She's basically rational—cold, calculating rational—and capable of enduring what she has to endure, particularly since she has no choice."

"When she's out? What happens when she's out?"

"It's a good eight years before we have to think about that. Maybe more. Meanwhile, she's locked up. She's out of the way."

Janelle shook her head. "Talk about cold, calculating rational."

III

Fourteen-year-old Jenna Jennings sat in the back of a car on its way from Wyckoff to Rockaway, where the high school basketball team was playing that evening. In the backseat with her were Bill Morris and Bob Hupp. None of them was old enough to drive, so they were in a car belonging to the family of Susannah Wilkins, who was sixteen and had her driver's license. Susannah's date, Dick Muggrage, sixteen too, sat in the front seat, beside her. Muggrage sat with his arm over the back of his seat, watching what was going on with Jenna and her two boyfriends.

Jenna had pulled off her sweatshirt and bra and sat with her breasts exposed.

"You're something, Jennings," said Susannah, keeping her eyes on the road and taking an occasional quick glance at the backseat.

Jenna lifted her butt from the seat and pulled down her jeans and panties. "The guys like it," she said. "Muggrage likes it, too."

"Tell you something more," said Bob Hupp. "Jennings likes it. She really likes letting us see her."

"Right?" Susannah asked.

"Well . . . sure. Try it, Wilkins. Don't knock it if you haven't tried it."

"I'll do it in private, thank you," said Susannah.

"*I'm* doing it in private, with guys I trust. Which includes you."

Susannah glanced again. "You got hair on your pussy," she said. "I don't think I had any when I was fourteen."

"You don't remember?"

"Yeah, I remember. But not a bush like that."

"Whatta ya do for Muggrage? You show it to him?"

"I do better than that," said Susannah.

"Like . . . ?"

"I jack him off. Don't I, hon?"

Dick Muggrage grinned. "You sure do."

"Jesus!"

"Why don't you jack those guys off?" he asked. "Both of them."

Jenna glanced back and forth between Bill Morris and Bob Hupp. They had talked about things. She showed herself to them, but it was still understood among them that they were not to grope her. She had shown them her breasts many times, but they had never touched them. She had shown her pussy, and they had never tried to feel that.

"Hey," said Susannah. "Both of them at the same time. Let's see if you're ambidextrous."

"We never touch each other . . ." Jenny murmured uncertainly.

"What are you a prude?" Susannah asked.

IV

JUNE, 1994

Hermann Reitsch began to complain that he had lost control of his corporation and his idea. Dave had turned it into a billion-dollar business, but Reitsch was a man to whom his ideas were more important than the money.

"Look, damnit. Ships are coming into Hong Kong, Rotterdam, Tokyo, and San Francisco, not even to mention New York, on the basis of your computer program. Planes land at Kennedy with pilots practiced on the approaches by your program. Your idea was brilliant. But it would never have gone beyond the experimental stage without money. I raised the goddamned money, Hermann."

"It's a question of—"

"Don't tell *me* what it's a question of. You're a wealthy man. You can move out of that apartment and into a fine home."

"I don't know . . ."

At the same time, a query came. Liz McAllister, who had worked for the Coopers for a long time, inquired of Cole Jennings if she might not have a place in some enterprise run by Cole and Dave.

Remembering the enthusiasm with which she had gobbled his cock and balls—though not anxious she should do it again—Cole knew she was a capable woman, knowledgeable about computers; and he suggested to Dave that she be placed with Hermann Reitsch, who might find her less than threatening and a fellow enthusiast about computer science.

Janelle was as competent, or more, but she was young, beautiful, erotic, and challenging. Maybe Liz would not be. Maybe she was the person who would soothe Reitsch's apprehensions and keep him on the road to further development.

Dave accepted the recommendation, and Liz became a vice president of the corporation.

She remained the exuberantly friendly woman that Cole had met in Houston. She stood behind Reitsch in his chair at his keyboard, leaning against him, her big breasts pressing against his neck and distracting him.

"You see, honey," she said, "I'm a practical type. You are a genius, but you aren't always practical. I think you could make that little thing there work with less memory space. Can I make a suggestion?"

They worked closely together and it was not long before Liz offered her sexual services.

"Liz . . . Sara must never, *never* find out."

"It's just friendship, Hermann. Friendship between two coworkers. I'll make no demands."

V

Ben Haye, distressed at the outcome of the Mich and Minn deal, offered new information. He came one evening to Dave and Janelle's apartment.

Janelle had ordered in Chinese food, and they sat over it, with chilled Chablis, and ate with chopsticks. Janelle wore a pink cashmere sweater with a tiny black skirt that crept up and showed her bare legs above the tops of her stockings. If it had crept up a little more he would have seen that she was wearing no panties. She rarely did.

"You can't let Leeman in on this," said Ben. "The SEC watches his every move."

"Agreed," said Dave.

"Okay. This is not a takeover. We can't hope to take control of this company. We can only trade in its stock and make a profit."

Dave nodded.

"You know how I know. You know how I found out. This time again, I've got to ask you to trade through your European accounts, so it can't be traced to me."

Janelle smiled. "It can't be traced to *us* either. Dave's got that under control."

"Great. Now. I lost almost half my three million in the Mich and Minn deal. I'm so sure of this one that I'm willing to risk the rest of it."

"I hope you're right, for Christ's sake."

"All right. Silicon Valley."

"Damned risky, that," said Dave.

"Not this one. What do you know of the Internet?"

"Nothing much."

"Find out about it, Dave. Within as little as two or three years it's going to be one of the biggest businesses in the world. Within five years nearly every American will have access to the Internet or will think he *has* to have access. Internet service providers are going to be a big, big business."

"Well, I have read a little about it, now that you bring it up."

"Okay. There are two companies: US Online Services and Eagle Internet. They are going to merge. It will be a friendly merger. US Online is going to buy Eagle Internet stock and take control. The resulting company will be the biggest single producer of Internet services in the world. The two managements are going to merge. The Eagle guys will get stock and options and golden parachutes. US has agreed to pay 35⅝ for the Eagle stock. It sells right now at 20½. So . . . we buy Eagle Internet. That is, your overseas accounts buy it."

"That's goddamned obvious insider information, Ben."

"You're well hidden. You know how to keep it hidden."

"They're going to be looking."

"Have you got it covered, or not?"

Dave nodded skeptically. "Fifteen points. No goddamned coup."

"I'll bring you more."

"All right. I'll take a chance on it."

VI

OCTOBER, 1994

After two years spent mopping floors, Alexandra had been transferred to a typing and filing job in the administrative offices at Bedford Hills. They recognized that she was a literate, educated woman whose skills could be better utilized. She was relieved even of wearing the prison dungarees and sat at a desk in the office wearing a drab gray dress that was conspicuously a uniform but was not the demeaning bright-colored dungarees she had worn for two years. At the end of each workday she had to undergo a strip and body-cavity search, but she had become used to that.

She had become used to most of it. At first, uncertainty and even fear had plagued her. She had been uncertain about what was going to happen to her next. Now she knew the routine. She knew how she would spend each day. She hated everything about it of course, but she did not fear any longer. She was assimilated to prison life. Each day was one day more.

Dave had a lawyer working to get her a commutation. She had no confidence in that. It was a remote hope. But that ruthless, manipulative son of a bitch could do anything, just about. Anyway, if the effort was being made, it was being made. It was more than *she* could do.

That was the worst of it. She was helpless here. She had no control over anything. She had been a woman who made things happen. Now things happened *to* her, and she had no influence over them.

In her cell at night, Alexandra ran her fingers into herself and managed to come. It was all she had. While she was doing it, she filled her mind with images of Dave fucking her. Now he was fucking another woman. She should have understood that he would and learned to live with it.

An assistant to the superintendent came to her desk.

"Mrs. Shea, here's a newspaper article you might be interested in."

She handed Alexandra a copy of the day's *New York Times*, open to a page where the article appeared.

Mr. and Mrs. David Shea are shown in the above photo at Kennedy Airport as they boarded the Concorde for a flight to Paris. They described the trip as the honeymoon they never had.

Mr. Shea is an investment banker with Harcourt Barnham. Mrs. Shea is a computer systems designer and consultant.

Before leaving for Paris they were hosts at a dinner for some forty friends, held at Four Seasons.

Mrs. Shea, Janelle, is widely regarded as something of a fashion archetype. She rarely wears any sort of slacks, saying that skirts are more flattering to a woman. She wears stockings and not panty hose, a custom that is coming back into style.

The couple plan to spend a week in Paris before proceeding on to Rome, then to Venice, Vienna, and finally London.

VII

What the newspaper article did not say, because the society writer had no idea of it, was that Dave and Janelle would also visit Zurich.

"This is small, Dave," said Axel Schnyder. "And it risks trading in insider information again. Any big move in this stock is going to bring down your SEC. If you will take my advice, you will not do it."

Dave nodded. "Very well. But I have an associate who is going to be very upset."

"You will risk a great deal for returns that cannot be much."

In their hotel room that night, Janelle said to Dave, "That man is your mentor. Take his advice."

"What am I going to say to Ben?"

"Tell him to quit coming up with peanuts. Tell him we need something big."

She was licking his penis. He arched his back and tried to focus on what she was telling him. Janelle . . .

TWENTY-ONE

I

"Dammit!" said Janelle. "I could wind up where Alexandra is."

"If Alexandra hadn't gone nuts, she wouldn't be where she is," said Dave. "Everything is covered. You know that. You think I'd risk *you*? C'mon!"

"The timing will be critical," said Ben Haye.

Mrs. Haye was in the kitchen, happily working on their dinner. This allowed a few minutes business conversation she was not to overhear.

"Very critical," Dave agreed.

It was difficult for Ben to focus on business when Janelle was dressed as she was: in a yellow microskirt, with stockings not panty hose. He had quit pretending he did not stare at her legs.

"You could buy a call," said Ben.

"No. If I exercised an option, that would tell too much. We'll *trade*. Fast. I'll get it all set up. My European—"

"Are you ever going to tell me who your European contacts are?"

"No. What you don't know, you can't tell . . . if something went wrong. Which it's not."

"Not like insider information," said Janelle. "We're going to make our own information."

"And all I have to do is identify the company," said Ben skeptically.

"That's the idea, Ben. That's the idea. I have companies in mind. But you have others. We'll work together. I'll trade for you. You can never be identified." Dave shrugged. "And neither can I."

II

"Dave wants me to go to Zurich," Cole said to Emily. "*Toute de suite*. All I have to do is receive certain signals from him and convey them on. He's gonna make a *coup*, honey. He's gonna make a goddamned coup. And we'll get a piece of it."

Emily shook her head. "We're playing with fire."

"The way he's got it set up: the levels of protection. Dave has always been a manipulator. And he's damned good at it."

"God, I have to hope so."

They were in their bedroom. Emily was naked. The rings Alexandra had encouraged her to put in her nipples still hung there. She was proud of them. She was really very proud of them. Jenna asked to see them occasionally and kept asking when she could have *her* nipples pierced. It was difficult to deny her, since her mother had pierced nipples and wore rings.

Emily had made a concession to Jenna. The girl was almost fifteen now, and Emily had agreed she could have a ring installed in her navel. It was a public thing. When Jenna went swimming in her bikini, the ring in her navel was conspicuous. And . . . and the girl loved the attention it got. She was known for it.

Emily and Cole could have wished she was known for something else, but that was what she was known for. The fact that she might be valedictorian of her high school class was all but overlooked. She was the girl with the ring in her navel.

"Exactly what is going to happen, Cole?" Emily asked.

"I don't know. All I know is that I am to be in Zurich and waiting by the phone. I'll get a call. I'll call Schnyder, and then something will happen."

He did not tell her that the call from Dave was to come to the apartment of Hanna Hess. It would be evening in Zurich, and that is where he would be. Axel Schnyder had so arranged it. The telephone number was in another name.

Hanna had arranged to make the evening recreational, also.

III

The corporation involved was CallNet, California Internet Services. It was a NASDAQ stock, trading at 103.

At one o'clock on the afternoon of February 1, Janelle, who knew exactly how to do it, used a computer at a friend's apartment in Cambridge, Massachusetts. She had a key Ed Atkins had given her years before. She entered wearing blue jeans and a gray sweatshirt, to be taken for a student. He never knew she had entered the apartment and used his computer. She used his AOL account, went on the Internet, and posted a news release on the website of NetWire, a business news service. It read:

> California Internet Services has issued a report of earnings for the last quarter of 1994 that are substantially below expectations. At the same time CallNet issued a statement that first quarter earnings for this year will fall below previously expected numbers.
>
> The problem, according to officers of CallNet, is that the company has been bleeding talent. Key personnel have left, accepting positions with other companies.
>
> Apparently these key employees have lost confidence in CallNet and have been seeking other opportunities.

NetWire distributed the report to its hundreds of subscribers. Within an hour, CallNet had fallen from 103 to 91 and continued tumbling fast to 31.

At that point, Janelle called the Zurich number.

Hanna Hess answered but immediately put Cole on the line.

"Climb Mount McKinley," she said.

"Climb Mount McKinley," he repeated.

She hung up.

He dialed Axel Schnyder. "Climb Mount McKinley."

"Climb Mount McKinley."

Through Dave's accounts, and through his own, Schnyder bought CallNet at 31. It was two P.M. in New York.

By two-thirty CallNet had posted on PR Newswire a release denying entirely the story that had come through from NetWire. The company called it a fraud and threatened a major lawsuit against NetWire. By four, when the market closed, CallNet had recovered to the 103 where it had begun the day and had in fact risen to 105⅜.

Before then Janelle had called Zurich a second time. "Come down from Mount McKinley," she said.

"Come down from Mount McKinley."

Schnyder dumped all the CallNet stock. Some of it went for 103, some for 104, and some for 105⅜.

It was the coup Dave had wanted. He risked four million dollars on it and made more than a million. Ben Haye made a quarter of a million. No one asked how much Axel Schnyder had made.

But it had been very risky. The SEC and the Justice Department immediately identified it as a bold fraud and initiated an investigation. All would depend on how well Dave and Janelle had covered themselves.

IV

Dave went to Zurich to meet with Axel Schnyder. He spent the night with Hanna Hess and Trudi. When he arrived at her apartment, he found Hanna naked. She demanded he make himself the same. When Trudi arrived they stripped her and fastened her to the X-frame. They strapped a rubber-ball gag in the girl's mouth. Hanna gave Dave the whip, and he whipped Trudi.

By now he understood that the girl loved it. He put a finger in her crotch and felt how wet she was. So he whipped her hard—hard enough to raise welts, not hard enough to cut her skin and make her bleed.

When he finished, her head was hanging and she was crying. They left her there, strapped to the frame, while they poured drinks and Hanna began to make dinner. Dave took the ball from the girl's mouth, brushed back her hair with his hand, and gave her a sip of brandy.

"*Gut. Gut*, Dave. *Danke. Sie schlagen mir gut.*"

They unstrapped Trudi. She sat with them and ate and drank wine. Then he said, "I think it's time Hanna was whipped."

Hanna shook her head doubtfully. "Trudi likes it," she said.

"Have you never been whipped?"

"No, never."

"You have the equipment for it," he said, nodding at the X-frame.

"A man had dot built. He likes to be vipped."

"And you accommodate him."

"Yes."

"And Trudi."

"She likes it."

"How do you know *you* won't? Let's strap you on the frame and see how you like that, anyway."

Trudi led the dog into the bedroom and shut him in there. He might get excited seeing his mistress bound and maybe whipped.

Hanna submitted to being strapped on the X. Trudi helped, and Dave fastened her tightly by the wrists and ankles and with the belt around her middle.

"Dave," she muttered. "You are an eefil man. I don't vant to be vipped. Make me stand here like dis, but don't vip me."

"Well . . . let's put the gag in anyway. You need to know what that's like."

She tried to resist, but he shoved the rubber ball between her teeth and strapped it in tight.

"No vip," she struggled to say past the ball.

"Just a test," he said.

He stepped back and swung the whip. It whooshed through the air and smacked her hard on the butt. Her flesh shuddered, and she strained against the straps.

"AAH! AAHH! NO!" She could not scream past the ball, but she shook her head wildly, moaning. "NOO! STOP!"

"You thought it was fun when Trudi took it. Maybe you'll like it better after you get a little more used to it."

"No . . . No . . ."

He swung again. Her fleshy nether cheeks jumped under the impact. "NO! *GOTT!* NO . . . NO . . ."

Dave handed the whip to Trudi. "She enjoys whipping you. Maybe you'll like whipping her."

Trudi smiled an evil little smile and swung the whip. The flesh of Hanna's butt bounced. Trudi swung again. The whip cracked against Hanna's tush. Welts began to show.

Hanna began to weep hysterically. Trudi swung again. Then Hanna choked and vomited.

"Maybe that's enough," said Dave quietly. "Apparently she really can't take it. Give her some brandy to clean her mouth. We'll leave her where she is until she settles down."

"You are an eefil man, Dave," Hanna sobbed. "I don't vant to be vipped. It *hurts!* I gif you anysing. I suck you. But not vip. Pleasse! No more!"

They left her on the frame for an hour, giving her sips of brandy from time to time. She hung limply on the straps and sobbed quietly.

V

MARCH, 1995

The doorbell rang in Edward Atkins's apartment. He went to the door. A grim man showed him identification.

"FBI."

"Come in. What can I do for you?"

"We've traced a news release placed on the Internet. It came from your computer, your AOL account."

Atkins shook his head. "I have no idea what you're talking about."

The FBI man sat down on Atkins's couch. "It's a multimillion-dollar stock fraud, based on a news release posted by you on NetWire."

"I have no idea what you're talking about."

"You could wind up in the slammer very shortly," said the agent.

"*For what?* I don't know what you're talking about."

"Okay. Play it tough. Where were you on the afternoon of February first? Say, one o'clock?"

Atkins shook his head. "I don't know. I . . . Well. All right. What day of the week was that?"

"Wednesday."

"At one o'clock on Wednesdays I meet a class. I teach at MIT. Before that I would have had lunch with one or two friends in the cafeteria. Then—"

"Can these friends vouch for that?"

"I don't know. Who remembers what he was doing on February first? But if I missed the class, the university would have a record of that."

"Does anyone else have access to your computer?"

"No. No one."

"Even without your knowledge?"

"No. No one."

"Does anyone have access to your apartment?"

"Well . . . c'mon. Yes, I have a girlfriend, and she has a key. But—"

Atkins honestly did not remember that he had given a key to Janelle Griffith years before.

VI

Lou Beth Simpson answered her doorbell. She was wearing blue jeans and a gray sweatshirt, what a witness had described the young woman who entered the Atkins apartment on or about the first of February had been wearing. Shortly she found herself handcuffed and in a car on the way to the office of the United States District Attorney, Boston.

She cried. She had no idea why she was under arrest, and she was terrified.

"What have I done?" she sobbed in the office of the DA. "What am I supposed to have done?" She covered her face with her locked-together hands and wept.

"A multimillion-dollar stock fraud," said an assistant district attorney grimly.

"I don't own any stocks. I don't know anything about stocks."

The girl, an attractive blond, was a graduate student of mathematics at MIT.

When she persisted in protesting her innocence, she was taken to lockup. Her parents arrived and retained a lawyer. Lou Beth was arraigned, but paper work was fouled up, even though her attorney was yelling and screaming. It was three days before the DA decided he could not make a case against her and the paperwork appeared. She left the jail shaking, frightened.

The DA and the FBI had made no connection to Janelle and Dave.

VII

MAY, 1995

Alexandra sat in her cell in the evening, locked down. She had a block of watercolor paper and a set of paints and brushes and was trying to paint a picture of a church in Kiev as she remembered it. She had to work from memory. The prison library had no books with pictures of her home city.

The lawyer Dave had hired had made an appeal for a commutation of her sentence, but he had not succeeded. She was resigned to the fact that she would be in prison until 2002, if not even longer.

The lawyer had given her, quietly, a statement of how much Dave had placed in her Swiss account. She was a wealthy woman. But . . . that didn't unlock her cell door.

Her cell had become her home and her refuge. She was actually glad when they locked her in. Locked, she was alone and did not have to react with the loathsome women who lived in Bedford Hills.

She read in the paper the account of the major fraud perpetrated on the CallNet stock. It had the mark of Dave on it, and she wondered if he had managed it. If he had, she would get her share of the profit. She smiled grimly and congratulated the manipulative man who was out there functioning while she sat here.

She believed he was sincerely trying to get her out. That was Dave. He forgave her for trying to kill him. The State of New York wouldn't.

But . . . They called for a count. She stood and pressed her hand to the little glass window in her cell door. The officer looked in. He was a man. She was wearing nothing but her panties. That made no difference, either. No one had ever touched her, or suggested he might. Maybe the officer liked seeing her. Maybe he only looked in to see . . . whatever. She was not going to try to kill herself, if that was what he had in mind. She was going to serve her time and get out.

VIII

Janelle walked around the apartment in a pair of dark stockings held up by a black garter belt. She wore stiletto-heeled shoes.

"Don't forget we're going out for dinner," Dave said.

"Lutece," she said. "With the Jenningses. You know, they're not the world's most interesting people."

"Cole did what we asked him to."

"If he hadn't, who would you have used?"

"I don't know."

"I guess he has his purposes. He's entirely loyal to you."

"In more ways than you know. And Emily . . . She's not so dull. Ask her to show you the platinum rings in her nipples."

"Alexandra had them. And in her pussy, too. Didn't she?"

"Yes."

"You want me to have that done?"

"You're perfect, and I love you the way you are."

"I'm glad you think so, because I don't think I'd want—"

"They're downstairs," he said, nodding toward the call box that brought word from the lobby. "You want to get dressed?"

Dave carried an attaché case to Lutece. At the door he handed it to Cole and told him to check it. Cole did. When they left, Cole retrieved it. He did not open it until he and Emily were at home in Wyckoff. It was crammed with what Cole had known would be in it: bundles of hundred-dollar bills.

"You can't report that," Emily said.

"Hell no."

"What are we gonna do with it?"

"I've got my own overseas account," said Cole. "You have to fly to Zurich with it. I'll tell you who to see. He'll be expecting you."

"We're in up to our asses, Cole," she whispered.

TWENTY-TWO

I

Ben Haye had another idea and invited Dave and Janelle to Greenwich to hear it. As always Ben would not talk business within Deborah's hearing.

Debbie Haye was a determinedly happy woman. She invited Janelle to join her in the kitchen, where she was cooking their meal. She was not fat but plump, and this night she was wearing a red minidress that really did not suit her. It showed her thick legs. Scooped down at the top, she showed as much as she thought she dared of her ample breasts.

"My father makes beautiful things," she said. She held up a tumbler of studded milk glass. "He taught me to appreciate beautiful things."

Janelle grinned. "Did he ever consider making a bowl based on a molding of one of your boobs?" she asked.

Debbie blushed. Not many people could blush anymore, but she did. "My father has never seen them," she said.

"I wonder . . . You're proud of them, aren't you?"

"Well . . . I'm not the world's most beautiful woman, but—"

"I bet we could find an artist," said Janelle. "I mean, maybe he could put one of them in clay or latex or something and make a model. From that model, he could do—How would you like to have a bronze reproduction of one of your tits? Or both?"

Debbie Haye laughed nervously. "You're making fun of me, Ja-nelle."

"*Not at all.* Someday they'll be . . . droopy. But not now. We've got a painting hanging in our apartment. It's of Dave's second wife. A nude. You know where she is. She'll never again be what she was when that picture was painted. But it's a permanent remembrance of what she was."

"You're serious?"

Janelle nodded.

"Jesus!"

In the living room, Dave and Ben talked.

"Hey, look," Dave said. "They're on it. They came damned close at one point. Don't ask me any questions about this. The feds held a poor little girl in jail for three days, to sweat her. They kept her in handcuffs when they were interrogating her. She couldn't have told them anything. She didn't know anything. Which didn't discourage them. God save us all from runaway prosecutors."

"You've got levels and levels of protection," said Ben.

"Yeah, but it would not be impossibly difficult to reach the conclusion that the leaks are coming from Kidder, Peabody, which is just a step from you. We don't dare be greedy, Ben. I'll let you in on things. But right now we've got to lay low. For a while."

II

Fifteen-year-old Jenna remained a virgin, with an inflexible determination that she was going to remain that way. She had, though, a reputation for being willing to show herself. It had become common knowledge in Wyckoff that Jenna Jennings could be persuaded to show her breasts, and more, to boys. She wouldn't do it for anybody. She did it for friends she trusted, and that circle of friends expanded.

Her mother and father suspected something of this but didn't know how far it went. Jenna continued to be an all-A student. There seemed to be no reason to get therapy for her.

They might have if they had known—

One summer afternoon Jenna was in a car with three boys and said she had to go to a bathroom. Bill Morris said, "Why do that? Let's just walk down in the woods here, where you can pee."

She laughed. "Hey, c'mon, guys!"

"Why not, Jennings? It'll be fun to watch. We've seen your snatch. Why not let us watch you pee?"

"Well . . ."

They walked down among the trees and brush a short distance, and she took off her jeans and panties, tipped her hips so her urine would not fall on her feet, and shot her warm stream on the ground, while the boys watched.

After that, it became a now-and-then thing with her. Boys watched her sit on toilets, though they liked it better outdoors. She decided it was fun to let them see her. She would laugh and pee. She let them take Polaroid pictures of her—from the navel down only—as her urine spurted.

One day a boy brought her a pair of his sister's panties and asked her to put them on, then wet them. She did. That was fun, too. Then one of them brought her a pair of his own blue jeans and asked her to wet them. Two clapped their hands and two took pictures as the stain spread over the crotch of the jeans.

Jenna enjoyed it. She knew it was an odd habit, but she enjoyed it. It was harmless anyway. Some of the boys propositioned her, but they knew the answer would be no. It was always no. Looky, no touchy.

III

OCTOBER, 1995

Alexandra had gained weight in prison, and the black dress she wore when she was taken into New York was a little tight on her. For this trip, she wore handcuffs only, no other restraints, and sat behind a screen in the backseat of a Ford Crown Victoria.

They took her to the office of the United States District Attorney, where a woman assistant district attorney interviewed her in her office. The woman was named Tabatha Morgan. She was probably forty-five years old, and she had oversized, prominent breasts and thick legs.

"Mrs. Shea, what I want to ask you is really very simple. What do you know about CallNet?"

Alexandra shook her head. "What I read in the *Times*. That's all."

"You never heard it mentioned? By your ex-husband?"

Alexandra lifted her hands and wiped her eyes. They had not taken off the cuffs, and she had to raise both hands. "I've read there was a fraud on that stock. But that happened this year. I've been in prison since 1992. If my former husband had anything to do with it, I wouldn't know about it. Do you think he comes up to Bedford Hills and talks to me about his business? He's never even visited me. Not once. And he writes no letters."

"Mrs. Emily Jennings visits you. She tells you nothing about what Mr. Shea is doing?"

"Nothing much. I very much doubt she knows anything. She's a wonderful woman. Kind. She's the only visitor I get." Alexandra sobbed once, then subdued it. "The only one . . ."

"Her husband has been in Zurich several times. What does he do over there?"

"I have no idea."

"And you don't have an overseas account of your own?"

Alexandra sighed and again wiped her eyes. "How could I have an overseas account? I'm *locked up* in prison!"

The woman nodded. "We had better not find one. You'll stay locked up the rest of your life if we do."

IV

"I don't like this at all," Dave said to Janelle.

"Why would they ask *her* about CallNet? This is getting too close."

"What the hell made them think *she* could know anything?"

"I have a suggestion."

"Which is?"

"Let's lay low for a while. I don't know exactly how much you've got in those accounts. But plenty. And I have to wonder what we're going to do with it. I mean, it's like that money is lost to us. You don't pay taxes on it—"

"No way."

"We live on what you and I make from Harcourt-Barnham and my consulting business. I'm sure the IRS watches to see that we don't live higher on the hog. What good is the money in the European accounts?"

"I'll tell you," he said firmly. "I'm a big player now. I can make things happen. That's what I always wanted. I can move money around . . . and make things happen."

"I'll tell you what I'd like to do. Why don't you transfer some money to, say, Hong Kong? Then we can go out there for a nice vacation. Never go near Zurich."

"The Coopers are out there," he said.

"So?"

V

Dave Shea was incapable of taking a vacation. No sooner had they arrived in Hong Kong than he contacted Len Cooper. He invited him to lunch.

Dave and Janelle were staying at the Mandarin Oriental Hotel, the finest and most expensive hotel in Hong Kong. Dave would stay nowhere else. His pride would not let him.

To his surprise, Len did not appear alone. His father Jerry was with him—Jerry who five years ago had threatened him with all kinds of trouble if he did not keep hands off the Sphere computer deal.

This time Jerry was cordial. He shook hands and told Dave he was glad to see him again. Dave knew why. He was a bigger player than he had been four years ago.

"And this is my wife Janelle."

Both Coopers smiled appreciatively at her, taking note of the brocaded emerald-green silk cheongsam she had already bought in a hotel shop. The skirt was split almost to her hip. "You're a damned lucky man, Dave," Jerry said.

Dave squeezed Janelle's hand. "Don't I know it."

"Forgive my mentioning it," said Jerry, "but I believe your first wife is—"

"Second wife. She's in Bedford Hills. She shot me, tried to kill me. And did it with an unlicensed handgun. She'll be in for several more years, minimum."

"I met her, of course," said Len. "You were a lucky man then, too."

"Until she found out about *me*," said Janelle dryly.

"Well . . . congratulations to you both," said Len. "What brings you to Hong Kong?"

"It's supposed to be a vacation," said Janelle.

"Let us lend you a car and driver," said Len. "There are lots of things to see in Hong Kong."

"That's very kind of you," said Dave.

"What do you know about us that you didn't know before?" Jerry asked bluntly.

Dave shrugged. "Nothing much. You married your late wife's sister."

Jerry nodded. "Biblically forbidden, I suppose. I don't give a damn. She's a good woman. I'm seventy-two years old. We have a home in Florida, on a canal where alligators would come into our swimming pool if it wasn't fenced, and Therese's a wonderful, caring wife."

"Then *you're* a lucky man," said Dave.

"I know it. Anyway . . . It was you that shot down Charlie Han, didn't you? I guess you play rough, Dave."

"Don't you?"

"Goddamnit, I had to. I was fucked bad when I was young. I make my luck, just like you do, Dave. But . . . we've got a business now."

"Several businesses," said Len. "Did you come to Hong Kong looking for business opportunities, Dave?"

"He came here for a *vacation*; it's supposed to be," said Janelle.

"Okay. Let me make you a suggestion, just the same. Put a little money in the Shanghai and Hong Kong Bank. You think the Swiss can keep secrets? You don't know Hong Kong banking."

Dave grinned. "I know a little. I transferred some money here before we left the States."

"This is where it's at, Dave. The Far East. This is the future. I can introduce you to some guys—But be careful. Wasn't it Bret Harte who wrote, 'For ways that are mean and tricks that are vain, the Heathen Chinee is peculiar'? You've got to watch them every minute."

"What about the return of Hong Kong to China?"

"The Beijing Communists may be a lot of things, but they are not stupid. There's a saying: 'The horses will run, and the clubs will dance.' They don't want to close things down. We are going to stay."

VI

Two days later Dave and Janelle boarded a yacht owned by a Chinese businessman named Chen Peng. They were to have dinner aboard the boat as it crossed to Macau, where they could visit the casinos.

Chen Peng was a Hong Kong billionaire who lived in an estate on The Peak, the highest spot on the island, where many very wealthy families lived. There, as Len had explained, he maintained a group of armed security guards.

Chen was on the bridge, talking to his captain.

"Triad gangs try to kidnap men like him and hold them for ransom," said Len. "That's the big crime in Hong Kong."

"Triad?" Janelle asked.

"Chinese criminal syndicates. The police try to crack down on them from time to time, but they continue to exist. They have elaborate rituals and even costumes. If the Mafia tried to move in on Hong Kong, the triads would simply wipe them out. They are absolutely ruthless."

Janelle had noticed, somewhat nervously, four ominous little men on board.

"Gurkhas," Len explained. "From Tibet. Fierce fighters. They served in the British forces here, but they're being phased out now as the Handover approaches. Some of them have stayed on."

"How can you do business in a place where—?"

"The triads have not moved in on business the way the Mafia has. They kidnap, sometimes kill, smuggle, handle the drug trade; but *we've* never had to resist them or pay them off. And when Beijing takes over, it's going to be much tougher for them."

Chen came down from the bridge. He was a short, chubby man with shiny skin, wearing a yachting cap.

He clapped his hands, and two Chinese girls came out to take orders for drinks. They did not understand English, and he translated for them. Neither was more than seventeen years old, as Janelle judged. They wore tiny bikini bottoms, nothing over their breasts, and their heads were shaved.

Chen smiled and explained, "So they won't jump ship. Nobody wants a bald girl, except for a whore; and these girls don't want to be whores. So we shave them every week or so. They'll be leaving me one day, and we'll let their hair grow the last few months."

Janelle glanced at Dave and knew what he was thinking: that when he first saw her she was younger than these girls and was stark naked.

"Where do they come from?" Dave asked.

"Back-country China," said Chen. "There's a regular market for them in the western part of the country. They are displayed and auctioned, actually. Most of them wind up as wives of industrial workers in Shanghai and cities like that. They can't run off and go home, because they don't know where they come from. An agent of mine bought these two from their parents. They're sisters. Another two or three years, I'll arrange marriages for them. They're very happy, believe it or not. They eat as they never dreamed of eating and live in what for them is unimaginable luxury."

"They do sex?" Janelle asked bluntly.

"No. They're virgins. And will be when they marry—which is important to some men."

Dave muttered to Janelle, " 'The heathen Chinee are peculiar.' "

Chen grinned. "I know the quote, Mr. Shea. We find some of *your* practices peculiar. Which should not prevent our being friends."

Dave smiled. "It does not, Mr. Chen."

"I understand you are looking for investment opportunities," said Chen.

"Yes."

"What would you think of putting some funds in a new bank?"

"Here?"

"No. In San Francisco."

"Mr. Chen, I am given to understand you could buy me out of pocket change. Why would you want me to invest in your bank?"

"I have a colorable reputation," said Chen. "I would have difficulty getting the necessary government approvals. You could put in money from your European accounts, which I would have enriched hugely. You could put in a modest amount of your own money and become the CEO of the new bank."

"And then?"

"We would become major lenders. We would take control of corporations. We would become big players in America. I understand from our friends the Coopers that you want to be a big player."

Dave nodded.

VII

That night in their cabin on the yacht, Janelle whispered in Dave's ear. "I have a suspicion that everything we do is being taped by a hidden camera. And everything we say is being recorded. So let's let them think we are just a loving couple. Let's give them a show, baby. A show they'll remember but which won't do them a bit of good."

He nodded. They lay on the bed, and she put her tongue against his penis. And began bobbing her head up and down, licking and nibbling and sucking.

They had visited Macau, visited two casinos, and Dave had won two thousand Hong Kong dollars—less than three hundred American. They retired to their cabin about two in the morning, to sleep while the yacht returned to its dock in Hong Kong.

Janelle nibbled on his foreskin and murmured again, "I can't tell you how glad I am you're not circumcised."

"I've always been grateful to my father, who wouldn't allow it."

She ran her tongue around his tip, slipping the skin back just a little to let her lick his glans, which already glistened with pre-orgasmic seepage.

She whispered in his ear again. "Tomorrow night *you're* going to do *me*, lover. Right now, let's let them think I'm just a horny slut you married to get what you're getting now."

VIII

She was right about the hidden camera. In another cabin, Chen Peng and Len Cooper sat sipping brandy and watching a big color television screen.

"I'm happily married," said Len, "but, God, look at that!"

"He is a fortunate man," said Chen. "I am sorry I didn't bring with us any woman I could offer you. My two little girls are virgins, as I said. Maybe . . . maybe they could do you by hand. I can't ask of them anything more than that."

"Christ, look at her! She loves it!"

"She is beautiful and skilled. She uses her tongue like an artist."

"My wife likes it, too, and is good at it. But—"

"Will he accept my proposition?" Chen asked.

"He'll take care of himself," said Len. "That man is no fool."

Chen pointed at the screen. "*She* can make a fool of him."

TWENTY-THREE

I

JANUARY, 1996

Established in San Francisco, the bank was named Enterprise Bank. Chen, as he had promised, put a billion dollars in Dave's European accounts and others. The money was funneled into Enterprise Bank. The state of California and the federal government examined thoroughly. The money was there, in federal bonds and blue-chip investments. Enterprise Bank was sound. Examiners found no fault in it.

It was an investment bank, not just a depository. Shortly it owned controlling interests in corporations that borrowed money from it.

Dave found himself a minor player in Enterprise Bank. His investment was not great. He was a front man. Not even that. He knew how to identify people who could act as fronts. He didn't use Cole Jennings. He did use Ben Haye, who left his firm to become CEO of Enterprise Bank.

"One serious problem," said Axel Schnyder. "Your country, my country, and others are asking where all this money came from."

"From the Far East," Dave told him.

"Yes. The transfers came from banks in Hong Kong, China, Japan, and Singapore. It is an international scandal."

"If the bank operates legally and ethically—"

"Still, people wonder who is really behind it."

"Do you want to know?"

"I believe I don't."

"Well . . . I have to tell you. There is money in Hong Kong that you and I never dreamed of. God knows how much of it is legal. You should go out there. There is shipping that makes the port of Rotterdam look small. I sat on a terrace one day and had lunch overlooking a ship channel. The ships coming in and going out were a *stream*. Container ships. Tankers . . ."

"You have put a lot of your own assets in this bank."

"My accounts—?"

"Are sound. But much depleted. You have taken a huge risk."

"Nothing risked, nothing gained."

Schnyder nodded. "Frau Hess is at home tonight, if you want her. She tells me you whipped her. I did promise you an interesting woman. She said to tell you that you can whip her again, if you want."

II

To her very great surprise, Janelle received a call from Chen Peng while Dave was in Switzerland. He was in a suite at the Waldorf, and he invited her to join him for lunch.

She expected to be one of a party, but she found when she arrived that she was the only guest. Chen Peng was cordial. He was dressed in a tailored dark blue suit, white shirt, rep tie, and Gucci loafers. She was wearing one of her favorite minidresses, this one white.

"You are an exquisitely beautiful woman, Mrs. Shea. I should like for us to become better acquainted."

"In what sense," she asked bluntly.

"After we drink some champagne I would like to show you a videotape."

"I think I know what that videotape is."

He frowned. "You mean you know? You guessed?"

"I am not a bashful woman, Mr. Chen."

"Yes. I know your history with Mr. Leeman."

"I imagine you know everything, about everybody."

"Who said knowledge is power? I forget the origin of the quote, but it is quite famous, isn't it? Yes. Knowledge is more important than money."

"I agree."

After they had emptied their champagne flutes, he switched on a big television set and its VCR. The tape was what she expected.

"That is a remarkable performance," he said. "Would you like to repeat it?"

"With you?"

"Yes. With me."

Janelle sighed. "I don't think so, Mr. Peng. I am faithful to my husband."

"I trust you will not dislike me for asking."

"I trust you will not dislike me for saying no."

Chen nodded and smiled. "Then let's talk business. Your husband's European accounts enabled me to transfer funds to The Bank. I will want to transfer more, through him, to various businesses in the States. I can't have a presence here. I would be resisted. Your government would move to block me. But Mr. Shea, through his European accounts—and maybe he should establish more—can facilitate my moving as I wish to move. I will see to it that he receives generous shares. But . . . I detect some hesitancy on his part. Why is that?"

"I can think of two reasons," she said. "In the first place, it's dangerous. The risk is great. Besides that, Dave wants to be independent. What you're talking about is his becoming a satrap of yours. He can't think of himself that way."

"You must have great influence over him. I mean . . . seeing how you . . . on the tape. You can persuade him."

Janelle smiled and shook her head. "Mr. Chen, how much influence would you give a woman who did that for you? You would appreciate it. You might even love her for it. But would you take her advice? Because of that?"

"You are not just any woman. You are exceptionally intelligent as well as exceptionally beautiful and erotic. I do think you can influence him."

"I don't know," she said skeptically.

"I will establish a special account for you in the Hong Kong and Shanghai Bank. Your husband should not know about it. But the money will make you independent, of him and everyone else."

"If—"

"If he does what you influence him to do."

III

FEBRUARY, 1996

Janelle sat with Dave over dinner at the Four Seasons. She was wearing one of the little microdresses that she favored, with stockings, not panty hose, and attracting attention. Dave was proud of her.

"Your Chinese friend had an idea," she said.

"Yes?"

"They've been in touch with me. Chen Peng was in New York and talked to me when you were in Zurich. You remember the night on the boat when I told you I suspected they were taping us? Well, they were. He showed me a copy of the tape. It was one hell of a performance, if I do say so myself. But . . . He is suggesting that they can make me a multimillionaire woman. They are not entirely clear about how, but the idea is that I would betray you."

"Betray me how?"

"He wasn't entirely specific."

" 'The Heathen Chinee is peculiar.' "

"All right. But let me tell you something. You can't fight him. He's got too much money. He's too powerful. We've got to make peace with him."

"I thought we *were* at peace with him."

"I never thought so. I never trusted Chen. I know what he wants, and whatever it is, we've got to negotiate. We can't fight him."

Dave nodded. "Axel Schnyder said something of the same thing. He doesn't trust the Hong Kong billionaires."

"Our relationship with them has opened up a whole new world. The opportunities are endless. The risks are, too."

IV

Emily let Jenna examine her nipple rings again. Again the girl asked permission to have her own nipples pierced and rings installed.

"She's big enough," Emily told Cole.

"Christ, she's not yet sixteen. She couldn't have tits big enough."

"Even so, she's got 'em. She has matured very early."

He shook his head. "I can't believe—"

"Jenna! Come in here, please."

The girl came in from the kitchen, where she was loading the dishwasher.

"Show your daddy your titties," Emily said quietly, suggesting, not demanding.

"You don't have to do that, honey," Cole said quickly.

"I don't mind," Jenna said.

She lifted her sweatshirt. It was true. She had fully developed breasts.

"She wants rings," said Emily. "It's a little hard to say no, since I've got them."

"At your age?" he asked.

Jenna, all but unconsciously, lifted her breasts and squeezed her nipples, which immediately became erect. Cole could see that they were big enough for rings.

"I think they'll be pretty," said Jenna.

"You'll be the only girl in your school with rings."

Jenna grinned. "Probably," she said.

V

MARCH, 1996

It was bonus time at Harcourt Barnham. Dave went into the office of the CEO to receive his check. It was four million dollars. He hadn't done badly, for the bank or for himself.

The CEO, Charles Emmit, was a suit, about sixty years old, a bulky man with a flushed complexion, whose hair had not begun to turn gray. His reputation was for being smart, competent, and maybe a little too solemn.

"I am sorry to have to talk to you, Dave, in the terms I am about to; but we have a problem."

"Mr. Emmit . . ." Dave said. He disliked hierarchy, but he still called Emmit "mister."

"Dave—" Emmit paused to light a cigarette, something he did when he was nervous. "You have done well here, and I think we have done well by you. But to be brutally frank, the board of directors has decided to terminate you. That bonus check is also severance pay."

"Am I allowed to ask why?"

"We don't have firm evidence of all of this, but we are satisfied that you are trading on your own. We think you have at least one overseas account. We think you went to Hong Kong, not for a vacation, but to establish a relationship with Hong Kong money interests. You go to Zurich often. All of that might not be . . . fatal to our relationship. But we detect that you are involved in conflicts of interest. Worse than that, we very much doubt that you report your outside income to the Internal Revenue Service. Harcourt Barnham thrives on its reputation for being squeaky clean. If you got in trouble with the IRS or the SEC, it would damage our reputation. That is a risk we cannot take."

"I've been here nine years."

"Which means that your name and ours are linked. That is why we will keep absolutely silent about what we think you have been doing. We haven't been asked any questions about you, and if we are we will say nothing about what we suspect."

"I suppose I should thank you."

"I'm sorry about this, Dave. Personally, I like you."

VI

APRIL, 1996

Alexandra sat across a table from Emily for their monthly visit. It was a contact visit. She had been strip-searched before she came into the visitors room, and she would be strip-searched when she went back inside. She was wearing the drab gray cotton dress that was her uniform now. Emily wore a black pantsuit. She tried not to be over-dressed when she visited Alexandra, thinking it would be painful for the prisoner.

"I would have been here last week, but—"

"I know. I couldn't have a visitor then. I was in disciplinary lock up for three days."

"Why? If I may ask."

"I took some pencils from the office, back to my cell, for drawing. That's theft. Small-time office pilferage. You know. I guess we've all done it, outside. But not here. I got three days in the barred slammer for it. The worst part is, it goes on my record, and when I come up for my first parole hearing they're going to turn me down." She shook her head. "I just don't make a good prisoner. It's a world I can't handle. I try, but—"

"Did you lose your job?"

"No. All is forgiven, I guess. It's like being a child. You take your punishment, and then everything's okay. Anyhow, how are things outside?"

"Well, I do have some news for you. Dave lost his job at Harcourt Barnham. He's really upset."

Alexandra shrugged. "He has other things going."

"He got four million dollars as severance pay. You'll get your share of that. But he needs a settled job, to justify his style of living for the IRS."

"Is he looking?"

"He's going to Zurich again. Cole wishes he wouldn't do that so much. It was those too-frequent trips to Zurich that raised suspi-cions with Harcourt Barnham."

"He'd better be careful," said Alexandra. "I don't think he could live with what I've got to live with. I'm not doing it too well, myself." She shook her head. "It's been so long . . . seems forever . . . Sometimes I wish I were dead."

"No you don't."

Alexandra nodded bitterly. "Easy for you to say . . . try it. See if you don't."

VII

Dave met with Axel Schnyder in Zurich.

"I understand. You need an affiliation. I imagine we can probably arrange it with Banque Suisse. You understand, they will expect you to make money for them."

"I made money for Harcourt Barnham."

"Banque Suisse is a little more liberal-minded. So long as you make money for the bank—"

"I will make money for the bank. I've made it for you, too, haven't I?"

Schnyder nodded. "But you take risks."

Dave shrugged. "How can you make money without taking risks?"

He sat later at dinner with Hanna Hess. She smoked a cigarillo and drank Courvoisier.

"You vill vip me?" she asked.

"He says you want it."

"Yes . . . I vas terrified dat first time. I sink fear was worse than pain. Trudi will not be viz us tonight. You vip me. Maybe not quite so hard."

Dave grinned. "Not quite so hard," he agreed. "Hanna, you're an interesting woman."

"*German* voman," she said.

"I doubt they all want to be whipped."

"Maybe. Not many know . . ."

They took Schatzi for a walk in the park, then shut him up in the second bedroom. Hanna took off her clothes and put herself up to the X-frame. He strapped her tightly.

She was a more interesting woman than he remembered. She was mannish with her close-cropped blond hair and her body was muscled and toned. But she did have breasts. He fondled them. He ran his hand over her crotch, where the hair had been trimmed until it was all but gone.

She grunted. "Oh, do dat, Dave. I like."

"You want the gag?"

"I sink maybe better. I scream, somebody hear."

He pushed the rubber ball between her teeth and strapped it behind her neck.

"Ja," she murmured. " 'Ip. 'Ip *gut.* 'Ot 'oo 'ard, 'ease."

He stepped back from her and slammed the whip against her bottom.

"Uhh . . . ohh!"

Then he lashed her back, between her shoulders, three quick strokes.

"Ohh! Uh! Oohh!"

It was more fun to whip her bottom. He liked to see her flesh jump. He gave her five strokes there.

Hanna hung her head and began to sob.

"You want me to stop?"

She nodded. "One or 'oo more on'y. 'En s'op."

He flogged her bottom two more strokes. She wept, and he unstrapped the gag and let her spit it out.

Dave could see the juices begin to flow from her.

"Oh, God, Dave. Some other time maybe again. But not more now. Ohh! Sore!"

"Well . . . We'll leave you on the frame awhile. Like some brandy?"

"Yes, please."

He poured brandy and held the snifter to her lips. She took it in gratefully.

He ran his hand over her cropped hair. "There aren't many like you in this world," he said.

"More zan you sink, maybe."

He put his hand in her crotch and shoved a finger in. She writhed and moaned. He began to knead her breasts. Suddenly, to his surprise, he found his hand wet. She was lactating!

"My God, Hanna!"

"Suck some of it and swallow it. Is good for you."

He sucked her left nipple. The warm milk flowed into his mouth, and he swallowed it. He didn't like warm milk, but he swallowed this. Then he cleaned his mouth with the brandy.

"I didn't know you were pregnant," he said.

She shook her head. "Never vas. Voman can make milk if she is sucked on and shtimulated. Ask doctor. Pregnant not necessary."

TWENTY-FOUR

I

SUMMER, 1996

Dave and Janelle moved into a new apartment, a luxury suite overlooking the East River. From there they had a view of the United Nations Plaza and all that fronted the river. It was the apartment that had once been leased by Truman Capote. Janelle was very conscious of that. Dave had never read Capote. He never read anything that did not relate to business.

"Goddamnit, you should at least read *In Cold Blood.*"

"Okay, I'll read it. Okay?"

He had trained himself to be a speed reader and finished the book in one evening.

"So?" he asked.

"The man who once lived here wrote that."

"Okay. He was a flaming fag. An alcoholic. Big deal. But the book is *great!*"

"Okay."

"Doesn't anything move you? Anything but money and sex?"

"Well . . . You could do worse."

She grinned. "I could, couldn't I?"

"Name the man who ever ate pussy like I do."

Janelle sighed. "Dave . . . there is more to life than that."

II

OCTOBER, 1996

Sixteen-year-old Jenna had her nipple rings installed. She was ex-orbitantly proud of them. Her father had paid for platinum, and they gleamed. They were a little smaller than quarters, and they dangled from her nipples. She let her close friends see them.

The word got around the high school that she had them. One day she was summoned to the principal's office.

"Miss Jennings, we have heard that you are wearing rings in your . . . breasts. Tell me it's not true."

"It *is* true."

"Do you think that's appropriate conduct?"

"My mother wears rings."

"Your mother is a mature woman. You are sixteen years old."

"So?"

"Well . . . we can't allow you to go to gym classes with rings where you have them. The other girls would see them in the shower. So . . . you can be excused from gym classes or you can take the rings out."

"I am not taking them out, sir."

"All right. Regard yourself as being on a sort of probation. Your father is a prominent lawyer and I suppose knows about this. He could make an issue of it."

"There is no issue," Jenny said. "My father paid a lot of money for them. They are platinum. I bet there are other girls in the school who have them. You just happened to find out about me."

"Very well, Miss Jennings. I guess I can't order you to have them taken out. But I can order you not to attend gym classes anymore."

She shrugged. "I like going to gym. But I don't have to. Ask the gym teacher. Am I the only girl in this school who has rings in her nipples?"

The principal sighed. "I don't want to know," he said weakly.

That afternoon, after school, she went down in the woods with three boys, showed her rings, and peed on the autumn leaves on the ground. She remained a virgin.

III

Dave's role with Enterprise Bank grew less mysterious. Chen Peng's motive was to gain control of American corporations. He expected Dave to identify possible takeovers and then facilitate the use of Hong Kong money to make loans and gain control. It was not complicated, though it had to continue to be entirely secret.

Chen Peng identified Arizona Oil as a company ripe for takeover.

"This corporation," he said, "has huge assets in potential lands. Maybe there is no oil there. But my sources say there is."

"It is widely held," Dave told him. "It will not be a matter of a few stockholders."

Chen Peng grinned. "Greedy stockholders. When they see an offer for their stock—"

"Who is going to make this offer? It can't be Enterprise Bank."

"That is correct. We must first acquire a company that can do it. Name me that company."

"Well . . . Petroleum of New Jersey has problems. They are short of capital. They are into too many loans."

"That is good. We buy their paper."

"Who does?"

"Messieurs Brüning and Burger."

"Which lands the whole damned thing on me."

"You will be well taken care of. Need I say that?"

Janelle was skeptical. "We can get burned. I don't need to tell you that Chen could care less. Hey, man. He's *using* us."

"The Heathen Chinee are not the only smart guys in the world."

"Well . . ."

IV

CHRISTMAS, 1996

In Bedford Hills, Alexandra had found a new solace. It was pro-hibited but was tolerated to keep peace.

The girl was nineteen and entered the prison under a life sen-tence. She was beautiful. She was assigned initially to mopping floors as Alexandra had been; but in time she was assigned to secretarial duties and came in contact with Alexandra. Before long, the forty-four-year-old Alexandra and the nineteen-year-old Lucy were in love with each other.

It was not easy to find opportunities to *make* love, but they took chances and made opportunities. Lucy wound up in the same cell range with Alexandra, and they did find chances.

It was solace at first, but in time Alexandra had to realize that eventually she was going to be released and Lucy was not. That made her solace a new agony.

V

JANUARY, 1997

Brüning and Burger gradually bought up the debt of Petroleum of New Jersey. Then a newly formed corporation, called United Gas & Oil, offered a premium price for Arizona Oil stock. The stock-holders leaped at the chance. United Gas & Oil took control of Arizona Oil.

"I ain't as dumb as Chen thinks I am," Dave said to Janelle. "*I* own United Gas & Oil. He doesn't."

"Be careful. Maybe he owns *you*. It's his money, after all."

Hermann Reitsch continued to complain that he had lost all con-trol of his inventions.

"How much are you worth, Hermann?"

"More than I ever dreamed, I must admit."

"And who made it that way?"

"You did."

"That is because you are a genius at what you do, and I am a genius at what I do."

"But I—"

"We sent you a woman," said Dave. "Liz likes to take a man's cock and balls all the way into her mouth. Has she done that for you?"

"Please!"

"We've got a good business going, Hermann. Let's not mess it up."

Chen seemed to accept the idea that Dave Shea was a partner, not a satrap. He asked him for advice. He had a New York travel agent deliver first-class tickets for Hong Kong on Cathay Pacific Airline, and when Dave and Janelle arrived at Kai Tak Airport, they were picked up by a limousine and driven to his home on The Peak, where they were guests during their stay.

Chen Peng lived in a magnificent mansion, Edwardian in style that had once been the home of a British millionaire. It was part of a heavily guarded compound with several homes inside.

The compound included a set of cabanas facing a big swimming pool. Hong Kong was subtropical, and the family spent much time in the pool. Janelle discovered immediately that Chen's wife, daughters, and daughters-in-law—as well as the wives of some of his executives—swam nude and lounged nude around the pool. Chen was quick to tell her that she didn't have to do that, too; but she would have been conspicuous if she hadn't.

Clearly, Chen Peng liked it; and clearly he liked seeing her naked. He stared, more at her pubic hair than at her breasts.

They talked business. Janelle participated. It was more than a little incongruous, especially in Hong Kong, that a woman, much less a naked woman, should take part in business discussions, but Dave wanted her. She was not just an ornament, he said to Chen.

"I have learned to understand this," said Chen. "American

women . . . Very different. Very different. Look at my women.
Pretty, are they not? But the whole collection of them doesn't have
the brains this woman has."

"They might if you gave them a chance," Janelle said to him.

Chen smiled quizzically, as if he did not quite understand her
comment. "Your friend Haye, at Enterprise Bank, has identified
a corporation he thinks might be promising. Texas Silicon makes
computer chips. They are good ones, as Haye promises and my
sources assure me. The company can be acquired. It will require
an investment. Not just a few dollars. I would appreciate it if you
would look into this and tell me what you think."

"High tech is risky," said Dave. "And the competition is fierce."

"*I* know the company," said Janelle.

"And *your* recommendation would be . . . ?"

She shook her head. "Don't do it. High-tech companies have
only one asset: brains; and Texas Silicon has a brain drain problem."

"Its people—?"

"Have lost confidence in it and are moving on. There is great
demand for systems designers. They move around a lot. And a lot
of them are moving away from Texas Silicon."

Chen smiled at Dave. "Do I need another opinion?"

"*I* don't," said Dave.

Chen nodded. "Good. Have you other suggestions, Mrs. Shea?"

"Not at the moment."

"Would you be so good as to look around and see if you can
find anything for us?"

"I'll be glad to."

VI

Chen's Edwardian mansion was equipped with Edwardian bathroom fixtures. Enough room for both of them.

Better than that was the shower stall. It was as big as a small
room, and the main shower head was out of reach above. Three
walls were marble. There was no front wall, and what water

splashed out ran to a drain in the tile floor. Tubes ran around the three walls. They were perforated with tiny holes, and when water was sent through them they sent tiny, high-pressure streams against the bodies. A needle spray. It was cleansing and stimulating.

Also, the shower was equipped with a bidet head. It shot a stream of warm water into Janelle's private parts. It was also steam-equipped.

"We've got to get one of these, baby," she said to him as she spread over it. "American plumbers can—"

"Sure. You used the one in the Zurich hotel."

"But over a potty. I want one like this, in the shower."

He remembered the Zurich bidet. As sophisticated as she was, she had never seen one before and was not sure if she should sit facing the wall or facing out.

As she turned and turned in the needle spray, she put her mouth to his ear and said, "I hope you realize that everything we do in this suite is being taped."

"I suppose. Let's give Chen another show."

VII

On their flight home, where their talk could not be recorded, Janelle had a question for Dave—

"Do I really try to find something for Chen?"

"Do you have anything in mind?"

"There is a company in California that has developed a voice-recognition system. Its technicians are still enthusiastic and aren't jumping ship yet. They will, though, if there's not an injection of capital. But of course it's a very high risk." She smiled. "We can risk *Chen's* capital."

"While retaining an interest."

"Exactly."

"*You* identify it to him. I know what he'll do, if he hasn't already. He'll set up an account for you somewhere. He'll make you independent. Independent of me. Maybe not independent of him. And maybe you ought to think about giving him what he wants."

"Are you serious?"

Dave shook his head. "He's got economic power that can make or break anybody. I don't say do it. I just say think about it."

VIII

Three days after their return from Hong Kong, Janelle was arrested, and threatened with charges. Two federal marshals, a man and a woman, served a warrant on her and she refused. They handcuffed her and took her to an office of the United States District Attorney. She sobbed most of the way in the car.

She was led into the office of Tabatha Morgan, the same woman who had interrogated Alexandra.

"Mrs. Shea . . . You are, I believe, the third Mrs. Shea. Anyway, tell us about CalNet."

Janelle sobbed. "What do you want to know about it?"

"What do *you* know about it?"

Morgan handed Janelle a box of tissues and waited while Janelle wiped her eyes. She did not offer, though, to take off the handcuffs. That was psychological.

Janelle sighed. "I'm a computer systems designer and a consultant. That's what I was educated to be—"

"Excuse me, Mrs. Shea. You were a teenage prostitute, weren't you."

Janelle shook her head. "No! I have never been a prostitute."

"Okay. Your mother is."

"I don't know about that. She was a good mother and took care of me. Maybe she made some money on the side. I don't know about that. What's it got to do with anything, anyway?" Janelle sobbed.

"Well . . . we're trying to figure out what your husband is doing. There is evidence to make us think he has huge overseas accounts, most recently in Hong Kong, on which he does not pay taxes and which he uses to play illegal games in the stock market. His second wife is in Bedford Hills, as I'm sure you know. She insists *she* has no foreign accounts. Now comes you. You want to tell us you're completely innocent of how your husband makes his money?"

"Harcourt Barnham paid him a bonus for his last year with them. He'd made so much money for the bank that they paid him four million dollars. That's on his tax return. You have to know that."

"We figure he made ten times that."

"Forty! I'd know. I would know. And I don't know. How can I prove a negative?"

"So you're not going to tell us anything?"

"What do you *want* me to tell you?"

"Why don't you volunteer something?"

Janelle thrust her hands forward. "Take these things off me! Please! Take them off . . ."

The woman nodded at the marshal who sat behind Janelle, and the marshal used a key and unlocked the handcuffs.

"Now do you want to tell us something?"

"What do you want me to tell you?"

The assistant district attorney grinned. "You're a tough bitch, aren't you?"

Janelle shook her head.

"Just keep it in mind, kiddo. We're looking at David Shea. And at you. Anytime you want to square with us, you can do it."

IX

"You owe me big time, mister. I sat there in goddamned *handcuffs*, and I didn't tell a thing."

Dave sighed loudly. "If I'd wound up in trouble, you'd have been in the same kind of trouble."

"I thought they were going to lock me up. I was scared out of my wits. But I didn't *lose* my wits. That woman . . . that district attorney woman. She's got it in for you. She called me a tough bitch. She talked about Alexandra, too."

"I think we've got to use the Hong Kong connection."

"Without going out there. Your trips to Zurich have raised suspicions. Trips to Hong Kong, same thing."

"You're probably right. Of course, you can go."

"And fall into bed with Chen? Is that what you want me to do?"

"I want you to use your own best judgment."

"Christ, man, you are a bastard!"

X

MARCH, 1997

At age thirty-nine, Emily had begun to worry about whether or not Cole was becoming bored with her. He was attentive. He was loving. But she could not help wondering if their love affair had not gone stale. He didn't want sex as often. It wasn't because of his vasectomy. He insisted he got as much pleasure as ever.

She became more adventuresome. She wore high heels and stockings with garter belts. Also crotchless panties and bras with holes to display her nipples. With children at home, she had to confine all this to their bedroom. She wished she could wear those things around the house. When they traveled, she took them with her and wore them in their hotel room.

Finally, without saying anything to him, she returned to the doctor who had pierced her nipples, and Jenna's, and had him pierce her inner labia and install rings. As a young woman she had been embarrassed by her shiny pink petals, which showed outside her. Now she decided they were erotic.

She would not hang weights on them as Alexandra had done. But she bought big rings; an inch in diameter. Cole was in San Francisco, and when he came home she was healed and ready to show them. No weights. But she had done something else. She had bought a delicate silver chain that went through the rings and back around her butt and held her spread open. If that didn't arouse him, she couldn't imagine what would.

XI

APRIL, 1997

Jenna, now seventeen, was a confirmed exhibitionist. Her greatest thrill was to let the boys who were her good friends see her. She had said nothing about it to her mother or father, but she wanted to try nude dancing, or maybe just figure modeling. She figured she could do it if she went away to college, somewhere distant from Wyckoff. As the time came to begin looking at colleges, she took an interest only in ones hundreds of miles away, in places like Ohio and Michigan.

She had no notion that nude dancing or modeling would be her career. She thought she wanted to be an architect and intended to study for it.

She remained a virgin. She was also going to graduate valedictorian of her high school class. The high school didn't like it—the girl with rings in her nipples, who reputedly let boys see those rings—but they couldn't deny her academic record.

TWENTY-FIVE

I

JULY, 1997

When Janelle arrived in Hong Kong, it was now a Chinese city, the Handover having taken place on July 1. The flags were different. The royal symbols had been removed from public buildings. The money and the postage stamps no longer bore the image of the queen. But there was no conspicuous troop presence in the city. The same police were on the streets, polite and helpful, only with red badges on their caps. She had come through immigration as easily as before. The officer who stamped a visa in her passport spoke English.

"May I inquire, Mrs. Shea, if there is any significance in your traveling to Hong Kong alone, without Mr. Shea?"

She sat over dinner with Chen Peng, in the dining room of the Mandarin Oriental Hotel. She was wearing the emerald-green silk cheongsam she had bought on her first visit to Hong Kong. It was the only one she had, but she judged it appropriate for this meeting.

"We have a runaway prosecutor on our tails," she said. "Do you know what that is, Mr. Chen?"

"I do. I also know who your runaway prosecutor is. Miss Tabatha Morgan. Guilt or innocence mean nothing to those people." He smiled. "Maybe she wants to be mayor of New York."

"You seem to know everything," said Janelle.

"It is my business. And, Mrs. Shea, can we drop the 'mister' and 'missus'? Why don't you call me Peng? And may I call you Janelle?"

"Of course . . . Peng."

"I have taken a liberty," he said. He handed her a passbook and a bank card. "I have established an account for you in the Hong Kong and Shanghai Bank. As you can see, it is in the name Lily Hu. I have made an initial deposit to it in the amount of one hundred thousand American dollars. Your Internal Revenue Service will be entirely unable to trace that. Whether or not you choose to tell your husband about this is entirely your affair. May I suggest you don't? If the runaway prosecutor somehow nails him—isn't that the American term?—you will have . . . Well, we shall see how much you have. I am doing something else. I am having a Chinese passport forged for you. I can do the same for your husband if he should need to take refuge here."

"You are a very practical man, Peng. I sense that all Chinese are. Why are you doing this?"

"I want you to help me identify American high-tech companies that I might want to invest in. I venture to hope as well that we can be yin and yang."

"Yin and yang," she said. "I know what that means."

"It is not a condition. We have a business relationship."

"I've heard that the Chinese have made an art of fucking . . . better than anyone else in the world."

"Well . . . we learn what are called the Emperor's Glorious Postures. What you call the missionary position is not one of them. Anyway, some of the nine require the agility of acrobats. I'm afraid I can't do those. Some require special furniture. I have that in my hotel suite. While . . . there is no reason why you should accept anything of the kind. I would be honored if you would."

"Let me think about it," she said. "In the meantime, I have been thinking about companies you might want to acquire."

II

In spite of the reservations and apprehensions of the staff of her high school, Jenn had graduated at the head of her class and made a brief valedictory speech, as was expected.

"We are *people*," she said. "We have become what our parents made of us and gave to us—and what our teachers have given us. But now we move along. Now we take responsibility for ourselves. We hold our future in our hands."

Hardly anyone in her audience hadn't known that the valedictorian had platinum rings in her nipples. Some of the other girls in the audience had rings, too, most of them silver. Others determined that they would get theirs.

She had been accepted by the University of Michigan, one of several universities that had accepted her; and she had been awarded a tuition scholarship.

In July, she was in the woods with four girlfriends, including Amelia and Linda and four boys. They sat on the grass at the edge of a tumbling stream. The three girls were naked, though the other two were diffident but willing. They compared breasts. Amelia, had very big ones. She complained from time to time that they defined her, that nobody knew her except as the girl with the big hooters.

"It pisses me," said Amelia, "that you guys get to see us naked but we don't get to see you. How about pulling out your pricks, anyway, and letting us see them? Maybe one of you guys will get to be known as the one with the big dong."

The four boys who were there opened their flies, none of them with enthusiasm, and pulled out their penises. Bill Morris, Jenna's favorite, with whom she had smooched and had allowed to grope her, had an ordinary one, neither very big nor very small.

"Okay, girls. Now you see them. Now let's see you kiss them."

Amelia knelt and kissed each one in turn. So did Jenna. She kissed each boy's penis. All she did was put her lips to each one and kiss it, the same as if she were kissing his mouth. Linda wanted no part of what was going on.

Bill Morris felt the blood rushing to his groin. He asked her to lick his. She did that. She ran her tongue over the skin of his shaft and over his glans.

"Take it inside your mouth, honey," he begged.

"Dream on, lover," she said as she stood up and reached for her clothes.

III

Everyone in Hong Kong carried a cell phone, even schoolchildren. Chen provided one to Janelle, and she took it wherever she went. She used it to talk to Dave at home.

Sitting on a bench on the Hong Kong waterfront, she dialed their apartment. It was noon in Hong Kong and would be midnight in New York.

"He is especially interested in high-tech companies. I'm thinking about Drake. What do you know about Drake?"

"Not a hell of a lot, but I can find out."

"I can tell you this much," she said. "Drake is another genius. But he is more realistic than Reitsch. He won't be a pushover like Reitsch was. He's the guy I mentioned to you before, in Silicon Valley. Voice recognition. He can make your computer work without touching keys. You just talk to it. Two things are coming in the high-tech world. Miniaturization, so you can carry a computer in your pocket or purse. That and voice commands. The whole damned world is going to be run this way."

"Where are you, honey?"

"I'm sitting on the waterfront. The Star Ferry just pulled out, going over to Kowloon. There's a big cruise ship in the harbor. It's beautiful, Dave."

"I remember some of it. Have you seen the Coopers?"

"Not yet. They know I'm here. I'm invited to dinner with them."

"Has Chen come onto you yet?"

"Sort of."

"What are you going to do?"

"What do you want me to do?"

"I want you to use your own good judgment, as I said before."

"Get me a full report on Drake, Dave. Send it to me e-mail. The address will be at the hotel. We can trust the Mandarin Oriental to be confidential. Be a little careful, but I think we can count on confidentiality."

IV

His report came through the next day and was handed to her by the hotel. It read:

Willard Drake has formed a corporation, as you supposed— Drake Research Services, Incorporated. He is in search of money. He intends to keep control, but he has put out shares of stock to people who are willing to invest in him.

If Malloy was an egomaniac about Sphere, he was nothing compared to this guy. It's going to be his way or no way. He'd rather lose the thing than give away any control. We will have a problem with him. You may want to suggest something else to Chen.

Janelle returned to the waterfront, which she had come to love—in fact, she had learned to love Hong Kong—and pondered on what she would do. Drake was the only investment she really had in mind.

That night she had dinner with Jerry and Len Cooper at Mozart Stub'n, a distinguished small Austrian restaurant not far from their apartment.

"That is a beautiful dress," Jerry said to her.

"Thank you. A gift from Mr. Chen."

It was a blue cheongsam, this one only knee length, with of course the skirt split to her hip. It was embroidered with gold and silver thread. She wore no panty hose or stockings under it, only a pair of white bikini panties.

"You are forming an alliance with Chen, aren't you?"

"It's possible."

"If we risked that, he'd eat us alive. He's a predator, Janelle."

"You are lucky he doesn't want your company. I think he'd take it if he did. The money on The Peak is awesome."

"Well . . . he's not the only billionaire up there."

"I think," said Len, "that we Americans had better be giving close attention to our own interests, before the Chinese come to dominate the world's economy."

"They've got a long way to go before they do that," she said.

V

With Janelle in Hong Kong, Dave decided to see if he could do anything about Tabatha Morgan. He had a little investigating done and found out where she lived and where she usually ate. She favored an Italian restaurant on the Upper East Side and ate there two or three nights a week—always alone. He visited the place on a Monday night, and she was not there. He laid a fifty-dollar bill on the maître d', and on Wednesday evening the man called to say that Miss Morgan was in the restaurant. He went there, and the maître d' identified her for him.

"Oh," he said as he walked past her table, ostensibly on his way to a table of his own. "I believe you are Miss Tabatha Morgan."

She looked up. She was a thickset woman, not very attractive but not repulsive, dressed in a green knee-length dress that showed too much of her heavy legs. She laid a frowning, skeptical eye on him.

"And you are?" she asked.

"I believe you know my name. I'm Dave Shea."

"Aahh . . . Mr. Shea. I have looked forward to meeting you, though in very different circumstances."

"So I am told. Would you mind if I joined you, so we can talk a bit?"

She shrugged. "I suppose not. Why not?"

She was having a drink, apparently Scotch. He sat down and gave the waiter an order for a Beefeater martini on the rocks.

"You have met two of my wives—in those very different circumstances you mentioned. I do wish you hadn't had Janelle handcuffed. It upset her terribly."

"The marshals did that when they served the arrest warrant. I had nothing to do with it."

Dave smiled. "I hope you won't mind my saying that's a little disingenuous. You could have had them removed when she first entered your office."

Miss Morgan returned the smile, weakly. "Well . . . sometimes it helps."

"Of course. It frightens them. Of course, it didn't frighten Alexandra. She's been locked up and chained up so much that she's almost used to it.

"Anyway, I believe you called both my wives tough bitches. And maybe they are. What other impressions did you form?"

"They're both smart as hell."

"Well, Alexandra—"

"I know. Fit of jealousy."

"She's a fine woman. Ukrainian. We went there and visited Kiev, where she grew up. It's a damned tragedy, if you don't mind my telling you, that she did what she did and got herself where she is."

"I guess, uh, that *you're* the smart one."

"Oh, I don't know. I do what I have to do to avoid being what I was born as."

"You've covered your tracks admirably. So far I've been frustrated in trying to track down just what you are up to."

"Did it ever occur to you that maybe there are no tracks to cover?"

Miss Morgan sighed. "Why so many trips to Zurich? Why do you go to Hong Kong?"

"Miss Morgan, I am an investment banker. I advise other people on how to invest their money. I am always looking for something promising. Not everything is to be found in the States. You can check with Harcourt Barnham. I recommended many European companies as likely subjects for investment. I am doing the same at Banque Suisse. And Hong Kong is a very promising place for careful investment."

He studied the menu.

"I recommend the veal," she said. "I eat here often."

"I'll do what you suggest."

"Hong Kong must be an interesting place," she said. She had finished her drink and signaled the waiter to bring her another one.

"It's fascinating," he said. "You should make a point of going there sometime."

She lifted her eyebrows. "A little difficult to do on the salary of an assistant district attorney."

He grinned. "Maybe you should become an investment banker. It's not too late for a career change. And I imagine you've learned a lot about the business during the course of your investigations."

"It would be a scandal," she said. "I could be disbarred, maybe even prosecuted for going to work in the business I've been investigating."

"I would judge you've got the guts for it," he said.

He continued to tell her stories, impress her, flatter her in a very subtle way. As only Dave could.

Two hours later they arrived at the door of her apartment. She had invited him to come in for a drink.

Things went on from there. Half an hour later she was nude, and shortly they were in bed. They got up eventually and returned to the living room. He relaxed in a corner of the couch, and she put her head down on his chest.

"No man has ever done that for me," she whispered. "I've been abused but never made love to."

"Shame," he said. "You deserve it."

"For my oversized titties?" she asked.

"No. You're not the conventional beauty, but you're an intelligent and loving woman. In my book that counts."

"You came to the restaurant looking for me, didn't you?"

"How could I have done that?"

"You'll have to forgive me for being suspicious."

"Tabby . . . your career is being suspicious."

"Will we see each other again?"

"I hope we will."

"Until Janelle comes home."

"Well . . . it will be more difficult after that."

VI

The night after she had dinner with the Coopers, Janelle had dinner with Chen Peng. To her surprise, he had a luxurious suite in the Mandarin Oriental Hotel, and he welcomed her there. That she was the only guest was significant, she imagined. He had no bar in the suite, just ice buckets chilling champagne—Dom Pérignon.

He poured champagne and toasted her. She returned the toast.

She was wearing the blue cheongsam he had given her.

"Dinner will be brought in," he said. "I was wondering, though, if you might first allow me to share with you one of the Glorious Postures."

"I have to confess I am intrigued."

"Notice the chair," he said, pointing to an oddly shaped piece of furniture. "It is for one of the postures."

She frowned at the thing. It was elegantly upholstered with shiny red silk. Two wooden rods or posts stood up from one end of it.

"How does it work?"

"You put your hips over the end and make yourself comfortable with your upper body relaxing on the shallow slope that leads down to the nest of pillows. Then I will move your legs outside the posts. This leaves you with your bottom up in the air and your parts spread wide. With you in that position I can achieve very deep penetration. I can assure you delicious sensations and total satisfaction."

"I'm not tied to it or anything?"

"Of course not. Nothing like that."

"I suppose I must take off my clothes."

"Only your panties. I will take them before I spread your legs."

"Peng . . . All right. I am fascinated by the idea."

She pushed her hips against the chair and let her body slide down toward the pillows. The device was softly upholstered and not at all uncomfortable.

In fact he asked her, "Are you quite comfortable? Not strained?"

"I'm all right."

"Then have I your consent to take down your panties and spread your legs."

"Yes . . ." she murmured.

He gently pulled down her bikini panties and knelt and slipped off her shoes so he could get the panties past them. Then he carefully lifted each leg and put her knees outside the posts.

"Are you quite all right? Are you quite comfortable?"

She turned, looked at him, and nodded. He was taking down his pants. She smiled feebly. "I must be a hell of a sight," she muttered.

"You are an exquisitely beautiful sight," he said.

He entered her slowly, and he was entirely right that the chair put her on an angle to receive him deeply. He did not thrust into her. He just slid back and forth, and she had the impression that he was rotating his hips. She began to understand that this was not going to be over in a few minutes. The Glorious Posture was designed to make the act last a long time.

Her tension grew. The sensations became more and more intense. From the sound of his breathing, she understood that his were, too. She reached an orgasm, as complete as any she had ever known. But it was not over. He hadn't had his and was apparently holding back to keep the thing going. She came again. Her muscles contracted on him and tightly made him reach his climax. He pulsed, and she felt his warm, slippery ejaculate spurt into her. He moaned. So did she.

Very considerately, he took a wad of tissues and wiped her clean. Then he offered his hand and helped her up from the chair.

TWENTY-SIX

I

JUNE, 1997

Waiters delivered a magnificent Chinese dinner. She had never heard of most of the dishes served that night. They began with fresh prawns mixed into a fruit salad. That was not so unusual, but the next course was shark's fin soup, which was delicious. After that, egg white served with bird's nest and crabmeat. Bird's nest was not, of course, straw and twigs but was the lining of the nest: a soft, moist secretion produced by a bird native to Asia, which the bird used to line its nest. After that they had sautéed slices of sea whelk, which was a marine snail, served with scallops and broccoli. Next they had a fish meat that she could not identify and Peng did not offer to identify, with bits of goose webs mixed in. Peng explained that after a goose was slaughtered they very carefully cut the webs from its feet. The webs were a delicacy.

All this they ate with champagne.

The meal was an adventure.

"I have been looking into your suggestion that we try to acquire control of Drake's voice-recognition system," Peng said. "I think you have done me a very great service. I know I don't have to tell you why it's so important."

"Potential," she said. "It's something everybody wants to do, and Drake has come closest of anybody."

"Microsoft," said Peng. "If we don't get Drake, he'll be eaten alive by Microsoft. If we do get him, potentially we could be as big a player in the world computer markets as Microsoft."

"My husband reports that Drake is a genius and a complete egomaniac. Also, his system is becoming widely recognized, and he is going to be able to get money from various sources. Malloy, in Texas, was cash-hungry. Drake will not be."

"The Coopers acquired Malloy, didn't they?"

"They and some Chinese associates."

"Their success has been modest," said Peng. "Their profits have been modest. They expected to be bigger than Apple, bigger than Hewlett-Packard, bigger than Dell. Well, they're not. They've found a niche, but they are not a major player in the information industry."

"I know," she said. "The Coopers threatened Dave to keep him away from Malloy."

Peng shrugged. "The Coopers are crude. With you and your husband's cooperation, we will take over Drake Research Services, Incorporated, before Willard Drake realizes what's happening."

II

AUGUST, 1997

Willard Drake was a forty-four-year-old man: scholarly, intense, wiry and always wore jeans. He had solved the problem of taking the time to worry about hair by shaving his head and now had no hair at all. He had been a professor of mathematics and computer science at three universities, until his parents died and left him a little money, which he used to equip a laboratory and devote almost all his time to the research he had begun in university labs. He was an adjunct professor at Stanford University, but he went there only two afternoons a week, to preside over graduate seminars.

His wife was an extraordinarily beautiful woman, eleven years younger than he was. He had met Julie Drake in Jamaica, and after only a few weeks acquaintance they were married. She was black, with a velvety chocolate-brown complexion. Taller than her husband, she carried herself with erect dignity. She wore no makeup. Her hair was cut to a bristly half inch of her scalp.

When she was twenty years old, her parents had sent her to live with relatives in London, where she was educated at the London School of Economics. She spoke with a distinct accent that was a combination of Jamaican and Oxonian.

Drake was a bristly personality, quick to take offense at anyone who disagreed with him—so much so that some of his colleagues would have liked to see the university terminate him. Others, though, believed it would hugely enhance the reputation of the university's math and science departments if one of their professors, even if now just an adjunct professor, developed the world's first true voice-recognition software.

His computer, in the lab he maintained off campus, could recognize some thousand words. What was more impressive, it recognized them when Mrs. Drake spoke them in that idiosyncratic accent of hers. Witnesses to the system had tried speaking to it themselves, using their own natural voices and accents.

"Marry," someone would say to the computer.

A question would appear on the screen:

Mary? Merry? Marry?

Using a mouse, the witness would move the cursor to "marry" and click. Then he would speak the word again, and it would appear on the screen: **marry.**

The point of the program was not just to give the computer commands, but to enable the user to dictate documents.

He was showing his system to several visitors who had traveled from other cities to see it.

A visiting UCLA professor with an accent said, "Villiam iss a good fellow."

William? Is?

The professor ran the cursor to those words and clicked. His sentence then appeared on the screen: William is a good fellow.

"If you had this program in your office and spoke to the computer a few times," Drake explained, "it would learn to recognize you and your speech idiosyncrasies, and you would receive fewer and fewer inquiries. That's a feature I haven't entirely worked out. But it has learned to recognize two speakers, myself and my wife. She has an idiosyncratic accent, as you have heard, but the system has learned to recognize her. It asks her almost as few questions as it asks me, even though we pronounce words very differently."

"It iss marvelous," said the professor from UCLA.

"Well . . . there is work to be done. But I know I'm on the right track."

III

Drake sat over dinner that night with Julie and their two children: a boy eight and a girl seven.

"Impressed, then?"

"Impressed. And they understood. They'll spread the word. Our stock will rise tomorrow or the next day, I am confident."

"And fall again in a week or so, maybe. Tech stocks are notoriously volatile."

"You are my financial genius."

"And you are just a genius, period."

"I am concerned about Greenleaf. He would love to see the whole thing go to hell."

"Jealousy," she scoffed.

"He has his own idea. He resents the idea that I was able to accumulate the money to get ahead of him. He resents having to use the university computers, instead of his own."

"He can go to ding dong bell," she said. It was a bit of rhyming cockney slang she had picked up in London. It meant that he could go to hell. The children would not understand what she meant.

IV

Janelle was at home, having spent three weeks in Hong Kong. She sat in their living room, wearing the black garter belt, dark stockings, and shiny black shoes she knew Dave liked.

"Chen."

She called Chen Peng by his patronymic, knowing the use of his given name would suggest a friendship having developed further than she wanted Dave to know right now. They had tried two more of the Glorious Postures. Their relationship had two components: business and erotic.

"Chen took me over into China. We went to Guangzhou. I ate something I never expected to eat in my life. A snake. They were in cages on the sidewalk, and Chen invited me to choose one. They were in three cages, according to size. He suggested I take a medium-size one."

"Alive?" Dave asked.

"Oh, yes."

"Venomous?"

"I don't know. I doubt it. Anyway, it was carried to the kitchen, squirming on a waiter's arm, and after a little while it was served as an appetizer. We shared it."

"Ughh!"

"Actually, it was tasty. What they do is cut off both ends, slit it down the middle, rinse it out with rice wine, deep-fry it, and cut it in bite-sized pieces. It's served with dipping sauce. The only difficulty I had was with picking up pieces with chopsticks."

"It sounds like you had quite an adventure."

"I did. What have you been doing?"

"I may have gotten your friend Tabatha Morgan off our backs."

"I don't think I want to know how. It must have taken courage."

"She's so damned *grateful*."

"I suppose. Was it Samuel Johnson or Winston Churchill who said that about fat old women? Anyway, I meant not to ask if Chen came onto me. But—You said to use my own judgment. Can we leave it at that?"

He frowned, but he nodded. "Maybe you needed courage, too. Anyway, otherwise I've had an exciting time checking out Drake. It's going to be a little complicated, but I think I know a way. In the first place, Drake Research Services stock is traded on NAS-DAQ. Have you ever heard of a professor of computer sciences at Stanford named Greenleaf?"

"No."

"Well, Ben Haye is of course in San Francisco now, and I asked him to be confidential about it but to get me all the skinny he could on Drake. He came up with a lot of stuff we already knew. But he came up with something interesting. It seems that Professor Greenleaf hates Drake's guts. He is also a respected systems designer on his own. He might—just might—be motivated to issue a report to the effect that Drake's program is fatally flawed. The DRS stock took a little jump on Monday. It went from 23½ to 28⅛ in one day. That seems to be because a professor at UCLA made a state-ment that his system is 'marvelous.' Now . . . if this fellow Green-leaf would issue a report, supported maybe by some others who despise Drake—and there seems to be quite a few of those—it might drive the stock down very substantially. At which point Hong Kong and Zurich jump in and buy a substantial minority interest. That will put somebody—Chen—in a position to apply pressure to Drake."

"How do you know Greenleaf will cooperate?"

"I don't. But the story is that he has an ego only a little smaller than Drake's. Suppose somebody should endow a chair in computer science, maybe at Stanford, maybe somewhere else, and make it a condition that Professor Greenleaf will be the first occupant of that prestigious chair. I don't know that it will work, but I think it's one way of going after DRS."

"Chen thinks Microsoft will also be after DRS."

"I doubt that. Microsoft is under an intense investigation by the Anti-Trust Division of the Justice Department. If they are seen as trying to take control of still another technology, it could strengthen the case against them. We might be able to counter that, too. If Microsoft makes a move, maybe somebody could prompt Drake to complain. We'll have to think about that one."

V

SEPTEMBER, 1997

Cole and Emily rented a station wagon and drove Jenna to Ann Arbor and the University of Michigan—a station wagon for her foot locker and other baggage. They moved her into her dorm room, and that evening they had dinner. In the morning they left for New Jersey. It was a wrenching experience for them to leave her.

It was more wrenching for Jenna than she had expected. But she was so busy with the processes of orientation and registration that she had little time to think about it. She was on campus a week before classes began. She found she had to take courses she had not expected: required courses. She learned that she could not declare a major in her freshman year but had to go through something the university called a core curriculum.

She found herself in a one-semester course devoted entirely to studying Plato: a Greek philosopher she had never heard of before. They studied *The Republic*. She learned that the question, What is justice? was not as simple as she might have imagined—if she had ever thought of it before. It was not so simple as, "Speak the truth and pay your debts."

When her roommate saw that she had pierced nipples and wore rings in them, she was fascinated. Girls came to their room to see them. Not all her fellow students were midwesterners, but most of them were; and she discovered that they came from a very different cultural background from what she came from.

Mary Straughn, her roommate, was from a town on the Ohio River, called Marietta. She was not only fascinated but a little repulsed by the nipple rings. But she was not a virgin, as Jenna was.

Jenna was probably the only girl in the dorm wearing rings in her nipples, and the least sexually experienced on her dorm floor.

"Hey, Jenna, do you like to give head?" Mary asked one night when they were lying in the dark, Jenna on one of the two beds in the room, Mary in the other.

"I've never done it."

"Never—You take 'em all in the twat?"

"I've never done that either."

Mary rolled out of bed and switched on a desk lamp. "Hey! Are you serious? You want me to believe you're a virgin?"

"Well . . . I guess I just never met the guy I wanted to do it with."

Mary grinned. She was a pudgy, dark-haired, dark-eyed girl, eighteen years old. "You're gonna have to, sooner or later." She sat on the edge of her bed, naked, shaking her head.

"I suppose so."

"Take it from me, Jennings, head is best, until you're married and want to have kids. When you don't want to get pregnant, suck him off. He'll love it and get off your case. I've had four guys. The first one, I didn't know about giving head and almost got knocked up. He used rubbers. You can't rely on 'em. Of course, now I'm on The Pill, so I can go either way. The university health service will provide. I think you have to have a letter from a parent, authorizing. I don't know. I have my prescription, and my mother will mail 'em to me each month."

VI

OCTOBER, 1997

Professor John Greenleaf was as big an egomaniac as Willard Drake. It was probably inevitable that a rivalry between two such personalities would turn petty and bitter.

Greenleaf sat at breakfast with his companion Douglas Livermore. Greenleaf was fifty-five years old, a muscular, athletic man who played tennis and swam daily. Three evenings a week he worked out in a gym. He was a graduate of Harvard and a recognized authority on computer science. Livermore was twenty-four years old, a graduate student, who in his own right was becoming known for his ingenious systems designs. He was tall and slender, a blond with striking light blue eyes, which some people found disquieting, discerning a suggestion of determination, even of cruelty, in them. He was the latest in a series of graduate students who had lived in Greenleaf's apartment and shared his bed.

This morning he was naked, as he usually was in the apartment. Greenleaf liked that. So far as the younger man was concerned, this and the rest of the relationship he had with the famous man was a fair price to pay for his sponsorship.

Greenleaf stabbed a finger at the morning newspaper. "His goddamned stock has gone up! Those out-of-town idiots who came to look at his system went around and shot off their mouths about what a marvelous thing he's got, and the silly market bought DRS without knowing a damned thing about it."

Livermore went to the counter beside the sink to pour more orange juice into his glass. "Want some, Professor?" he asked.

"Thanks."

The young man returned to the table with his glass and picked up Greenleaf's. The professor looked up from the newspaper and watched him. The view of the young man's taut, twitchy butt aroused him. When Douglas turned and came back toward the table, the professor stared at his body.

"All he's got that we don't have is goddamned *money!*" Greenleaf groused. "His inheritance seeded this thing of his, and he floated a fraudulent stock issue. Doug . . . if we can just somehow get it going, *our* idea is superior. It is more economical of resources and will be cheaper to operate. Drake's system is going to look clunky beside ours, if we can just get it out."

VII

Sitting on her cot, in lockup, Alexandra took notice that five years had passed since she arrived at Bedford Hills. She watched the evening news on her little television set. All she could get were the networks, and everything they broadcast was boring. She watched the local and national news, just the same, on the chance she would hear some reference to Dave. Once in a very long time, she did.

She had begun to take an interest in baseball, also in football, and watched every game that was broadcast. At eleven o'clock they switched off the electricity in the cells. The light went out, and the television set went dark, and she had no choice but to stretch out and try to sleep.

Which was not easy. Her thoughts were not pleasant.

Apart from the simple oppression of confinement, imprisonment was burdensomely boring. Hours and days crept.

Emily came once a month, faithfully. Emily said nothing about it, but Alexandra was aware that she had become fat and slovenly. What difference?

"I suppose Janelle is beautiful as ever."

"I don't see her. She spent some time in Hong Kong and China recently. They are establishing a Far East connection of some sort."

"Let's hope they make ten fortunes."

Not confident that their conversation wasn't recorded, they never mentioned Alexandra's percentage.

"If we know Dave, we can be sure he will."

TWENTY-SEVEN

I

NOVEMBER, 1997

Ben Haye was still serving as CEO of Enterprise Bank. Dave told him to look at Professor Greenleaf and learn everything he could about him. It took Ben very little time to discover the relationship between the professor and his graduate student Douglas Livermore. It was well known around the campus, which was tolerant of it.

Graduate students were exploited in many ways, and this was only one of them. If Livermore had been a woman, the case would have been different. But this graduate student was a man—one building a record for brilliance and success—and it was obvious that the relationship was entirely consensual. In fact, some would have said that Doug Livermore was exploiting Professor Greenleaf as much as the professor was exploiting him.

On the basis of information obtained, Ben had a young lawyer for Enterprise Bank—Joseph Giannini, who was distantly related to A. P. Giannini, founder of Bank of America—contact a young woman named Sydney Toller, herself a graduate student working toward her doctorate in mathematics. He invited her to dinner at the Top of the Mark, which he hoped would impress her. Maybe it did, but she was no unsophisticated young woman; she ordered a double Glenfiddich straight.

"I suppose you have some reason for inviting me to dinner, Mr. Giannini."

"I have. It's a privilege, in any event."

Sydney Toller was a pretty young woman, not delicately pretty but very attractive. She had glossy, dark brown hair, thick eyebrows, brown eyes, and a wide mouth with rather thin lips. Hers was a strong face. She had a well-toned body. She was wearing a black cardigan sweater over a white blouse, also a short black skirt.

"May I call you Joseph?"

"You may call me Joe."

"I am Sydney. I prefer not to be called Sid."

Joe was drinking a martini. It was said that the martinis made in the Top of the Mark were the best in the world. He was a tall, slender man, thirty years old, with black hair and an long, strong face, emphasized with penetrating blue eyes.

"I understand you are working on your Ph.D. in math," he said.

"You seem to know a great deal about me. Why?"

"Nothing sinister. Enterprise Bank thinks you may have some information we could use."

"Specifically?"

"Can we talk in confidence?"

"That depends on what we are going to talk about."

"Well . . . as I said, it's nothing sinister. I am sure you know that Professor John Greenleaf is working on a voice-recognition system to rival Willard Drake's. His chief problem is lack of money. Enterprise Bank might be willing to lend him money. But we need to know a great deal more about him and about what he's doing."

"So what would I know about that?"

"Maybe very little about his system. But maybe a great deal about his character."

She drew a deep breath. "I follow you. You really have been sneaking around."

"Not I. I was handed the information. I don't like the people who got it, and I don't like the *way* they got it. None of them could possibly have been allowed to contact you."

"Sleazeballs?" she asked, sipping from her Scotch.

He nodded. "The officers of Enterprise Bank thought maybe I

could talk with you on terms of some mutual respect. At least, I wouldn't offend you on sight."

She chuckled.

"So you know what I'm interested in—that is, what Enterprise Bank is interested in."

"Doug Livermore," she said. "Your sleazeballs really did check around. Private detectives, I suppose."

"Professional sleazeballs," he said.

"So why do you ask me? You already know."

"Only the superficial facts."

She sighed. "Let's order dinner. Then I'll tell you the whole story."

Joe summoned a waiter, and they ordered.

"Okay," she said. "Doug places ambition ahead of all else. Greenleaf is in a position to advance his career. Doug and I were living together. He moved out and moved in with the professor. Were we in love with each other? I don't know. Were we thinking of marrying? We hadn't talked about it. But he left me and went to live with Greenleaf. He's bi. He'd had other relationships, both kinds. The professor isn't. He's strictly a fag."

"What relationship do you have with Livermore now? I mean, is he still a friend?"

She smiled. "When the professor's out of town . . . You follow me? I'm surprised you didn't know. You know everything else. Of course, nothing serious could ever be established between us again. Doug is not to be trusted."

"All right. Is it possibly true that Professor Greenleaf's program is superior to Professor Drake's?"

"I'll tell you what Doug tells me. He says that when Drake conducts a demonstration of his system, it is always a canned demonstration. There is never a really open test."

"Enterprise Bank is interested in Greenleaf. It's interested in a voice-recognition system. If Greenleaf's is better than Drake's, there will be interested investors. We might think in terms of having him incorporate and underwriting a stock issue."

"So what do I have to do with all this?"

"If you can put us in contact with Doug and through him with Greenleaf, we would show our appreciation."

"A bribe?"

"Not at all. Compensation for services rendered."

"You want me to open talks between you and Doug Livermore."

"If we approach him directly . . . Who knows? Maybe you could tell him you are dating a lawyer from Enterprise Bank, who has expressed an interest in what Doug and Livermore are doing. Maybe we could arrange for him to see us together somewhere."

Sydney grinned. "Businessmen are as devious as academics," she said.

II

Ben Haye spoke to Dave on the telephone.

"So far, so good," he said. "The girl will put Giannini in touch with Livermore, and Livermore will put him in touch with Greenleaf."

"Then it goes beyond Giannini," said Dave. "Who's going to make the proposition to Greenleaf?"

"You want me to do it?"

"I don't think so. You are linked to me. I'd rather it be somebody independent of us."

"Giannini is a good boy."

"Yes, but he's with Enterprise Bank."

"True."

"Uh . . . Suppose Enterprise Bank terminated him and sent him out to Hong Kong. I think you told me he's not married. He's free to move. I can have Janelle call Chen and see if he would be willing to establish a smart young American banker as a Far East banker. Then, if the shit hits the fan he's out of sight and hard to find."

"They could trace him."

"Not if he's carrying a Hong Kong passport, which Chen can arrange, I am certain. He won't even have to get it forged. I'm sure he can arrange a Hong Kong passport for Giannini."

"Maybe he won't be willing to go."

"I leave it to you to convince him."

III

"Here's the deal, Professor," Joe Giannini said to Greenleaf a few days later. "We can put you in touch with investors who will be interested in putting up money to fund your research and development. But first we will have to put a crimp in Drake."

"Drake is a fraud," said Greenleaf.

Under the dinner table, Livermore squeezed Greenleaf's hand.

"His reputation is high," said Giannini. "His stock sells well."

"He's a fraud."

"If that word got out, it would slow him down at least."

Greenleaf shrugged. "I can say it, but who will pay attention?"

"Maybe you could recruit a few who will join you in your statement. We know how to get word out to the media. With Drake slowed down, your program can move quickly to the forefront—provided you have the money."

IV

A week later, a story appeared in newspapers all across the country:

PROFESSORS CHALLENGE VALIDITY OF DRAKE
VOICE-RECOGNITION PROGRAM

A group of university professors is challenging the validity of the famous Drake voice-recognition program.

Several professors of computer science, including Stanford University Professor John Greenleaf, suggest that the Drake program is deficient, inadequately tested, and unready for business use.

A number of professors, from various universities, have viewed demonstrations of the Drake system and

---

pronounced it "marvelous." Professor Greenleaf and the others suggest that the tests are staged demonstrations at which witnesses see only "canned" illustrations of the system in use and are not afforded opportunities to run independent tests.

"If anyone were allowed to sit at the terminal and run his own tests, the system's deficiencies would become apparent," said Professor Greenleaf. "I, for example, have never been allowed to get closer than to stand behind Professor Drake and watch him run a demonstration. I have challenged him on it, but he does not wish to be challenged. He does not wish to be subjected to the usual standards of scientific investigation."

V

On the day the news story appeared, a courier knocked on the door of Joe Giannini's apartment and handed him a package. He sat down on the couch and opened the package.

"Mine and yours," he said to Sydney Toller, handing her a Hong Kong passport in the name of Cynthia Kent.

"I'm nervous about this," she said.

"They are not forgeries. We had our photographs flown out to Hong Kong, and these are valid Hong Kong passports. The application says that we have lived in Hong Kong for ten years, before which we were British nationals."

The package also contained two first-class tickets on Cathay Pacific Airline. They were to go to Vancouver, using their new passports, and board a flight for Hong Kong.

"It will be a great adventure," she said. "I hope to God we don't come to regret it."

"We could struggle all our lives here and never realize what we are going to realize immediately in Hong Kong."

"We will have to learn to speak Chinese," she said. "I understand it is not easy."

"Our lessons begin immediately. I will go to work at the China Overseas Bank, and you will begin to teach at a Catholic school where the students speak English. You are right. It is going to be a great adventure."

VI

DECEMBER, 1997

On November 26, stock in Drake Research Services, traded on NASDAQ, opened at 27¾. By the end of the day it was trading at 15⅝. The following day it fell to 8½.

Reinhard Brüning in Zurich bought thousands of shares. So did Friederich Burger in Vienna. Axel Schnyder bought a bloc for his own account. Most of the money used by Brüning and Burger had been deposited to those accounts by Chen Peng. A trust account in China Overseas Bank bought some more.

Dave exulted. "Among us we own forty-two percent of it! Drake's investors bailed out as the stock dropped. They were speculators. They had no loyalty to him."

"That's the way it is with high-tech stocks," she said.

"How would you like to make another little run out to Hong Kong?"

"To do what?"

"Two things. The chief one is to coordinate strategy with Chen as to how we're going to squeeze Drake. Secondly, though, I want you to make sure all the loose ends are neatly tied with Giannini."

"I assume," she said dryly, "that Greenleaf is not right. I mean, I assume Drake is on the right track."

"Both Chen and I, and Ben Haye, have had that looked into. Greenleaf is a jealous nut. He's an obsessive academic. He'll work on something—and work on it and work on it and work on it— but he'll never come up with anything. He's like an artist that won't give up his painting, though someone is willing to pay a price, until he adjusts one final brush stroke."

"He served his purpose."

"He sure as hell did."

"But Drake still owns the controlling interest," she said.

"We'll have to find a way to squeeze him. I have one or two ideas. I imagine Chen has as well."

VII

Drake and his wife sat at the dinner table after they had finished and the children had gone off to play Nintendo until their bedtime.

"It's a goddamned catastrophe," he complained. "Greenleaf . . . That *son of a bitch!*"

"I don't think it *was* Greenleaf," said Julie. "I think somebody is behind Greenleaf: a raider, trying to take over."

"Who?"

"Look at the stock register. *Foreigners* moved in. Zurich, Vienna, Hong Kong."

"I still have controlling interest."

"Yes. But the big drop in the stock is drying up financing."

"It will recover."

"In time."

"We can look at it this way—If we have raiders coming after us, that means somebody has confidence in the system. Otherwise, why bother to try to steal it?"

"A valid point."

"Well . . . the system is worthless without *me*. And I'm not about to be run over."

"Well . . ." she said. "We can think about this and talk about it all evening. But we're going to watch Letterman in bed, like always; and when that's over, I don't want to think or hear about it. This business has spoiled nights we can never recover."

Drake nodded. "Can't let it spoil our lives," he said.

VIII

Professor John Greenleaf sat down in Ben Haye's office.

"I understand that Mr. Giannini is no longer with Enterprise Bank."

"That is true," said Haye. "He resigned."

"Well . . . he made certain commitments to me, on behalf of Enterprise Bank. He made certain financial commitments—that is, to make certain financial assistance available."

Haye nodded and smiled faintly. "Well . . . You understand that the bank cannot be bound by any commitments made by a former employee, whatever they were."

"He promised me."

"Even so—"

"Where is Mr. Giannini now?"

"I really don't know. He seems to have left the city."

"I . . . have been counting on the commitments he made."

"If you want a loan, Professor Greenleaf, apply for it. We will look into the possibility and reach a decision."

IX

JANUARY, 1998

Janelle did not leave for Hong Kong until after Christmas and New Year's. They celebrated the holidays at home. Once again, they drove out to Wyckoff, taking Alicia Griffith, Janelle's mother, with them. Dave's family liked Janelle, and they liked Alicia. They never guessed that Alicia still turned tricks.

With Janelle away, Dave returned his attention to Tabatha Morgan. He had been able to see her a few times in the past six months, but with Janelle at home it had been difficult, as he had warned it would be.

As soon as Janelle was aboard her plane, Dave called Tabatha at her office and asked her to meet him for dinner. He took her to the Four Seasons.

She was impressed. He ordered a single-malt Scotch for her.

"Well . . ." he said. "Are you still looking for something I'm doing that is against the law?"

Her gaze fell from his face to the table. She smiled faintly and shook her head. "I'm focusing on other things right now."

"You haven't given up on me?" he asked, half teasing.

"Maybe," she murmured.

"I sent you a gift," he said.

"I used it," she said with a faint blush.

He had sent her a two-hundred-dollar gift certificate to one of the Coopers' Cheeks stores. Having no idea what would fit her, he had sent the certificate rather than try to buy.

"Something pretty?"

"Something for *you* to see," she said, lifting her chin and speaking more boldly. "I assume you gave it to me so I could buy something for you to see."

"Yes."

"You flatter me."

Two hours later, in her apartment, she showed him what she had bought. He had been right in guessing that not everything sold in a Cheeks store or in Victoria's Secret would fit her. She had chosen what would.

She came out of her bedroom wearing a loose, sheer black shorty nightgown, open in front, happily flaunting her heavy breasts. Over her crotch she wore a small black triangle of fabric, held in place by elastic strings that circled her waist and ran down and between her cheeks and up to join the waist string behind: a G-string. It did not cover her thick bush of pubic hair. She wore thigh-high black mesh stockings and black patent-leather shoes with stiletto heels.

This big, husky woman was more than a bit absurd in this erotic outfit. On the other hand, her innocent effort to please him was completely appealing to Dave, and he felt moved to embrace her and kiss her.

There was more. In her left hand she carried a pair of steel handcuffs.

"You complained that I made Janelle sit and talk to me in handcuffs," she said. "So handcuff *me*. Take the key and put it in your pocket and handcuff me. To be honest with you, I've always wondered what it feels like."

He slipped the cuffs onto her wrists and closed them. As he brought his hands around he began to massage her nipples.

"*Dave . . .*" she whispered hoarsely and pressed her face to his and kissed him.

He held her arms and kissed her hard on the mouth.

She moaned and said she wanted him to take her to bed. "Only the beginning of the evening," she muttered.

On her bed, he pushed the G-string aside and mounted her.

Back in the living room, he poured them drinks and asked her if she wanted the handcuffs taken off.

"No!"

She sat with her head on his chest, raising her face only to take a sip from her drink or to kiss him.

She sighed. "We've got no future, have we, Dave?"

"There is no such thing as a prophet, Tabby."

"Tabby . . . Tabby, the cat, is going to give her kitten a bath."

In the next twenty minutes she licked every inch of him, from his ears to the soles of his feet.

Later, she brought out her Polaroid camera and invited him to take pictures of her naked and wearing handcuffs. She posed playfully, flattered that he would want such pictures. That was more serious. He took the pictures home and locked them away. They might become useful sometime.

TWENTY-EIGHT

I

FEBRUARY, 1998

Janelle accepted Chen Peng's offer of his suite in the Mandarin Oriental Hotel. One of her reasons was his sophisticated communications facility there.

"This telephone line is scrambled," he explained to her. "E-mail from here is encrypted. So are faxes. My agents in New York have already called on Mr. Shea and installed the necessary correlating equipment on his computer and lines."

They began to talk with Dave.

"Drake inherited money," Dave told them. "That's what keeps him afloat. His grandfather was one of the founders of Intercontinental Petroleum, and Drake inherited a bloc of it. He's held it. He hasn't sold it off and diversified. One of the bluest of blue chips. He feels secure in it. Now . . ."

"If Intercontinental fell on the market . . ." said Chen.

"Right. It will take money."

"More than that," said Chen.

"Well . . . Our specialty," said Dave. "I'm looking into it. Intercontinental has got to be vulnerable some way."

Chen invited Joseph Giannini and Sydney Toller—now Bradford Smith and Cynthia Kent, according to their Hong Kong passports—to dinner at his magnificent mansion on The Peak. Janelle was there, pushed by Chen into the temporary role of hostess in the household. Chen's wife and his daughter and son-in-law dined separately in a dining room on the second floor and were not invited down to be introduced.

This was how a Hong Kong patriarch could act. Janelle was not the first young woman introduced into his home as though she were the mistress of the household.

Chen had given her still another cheongsam, this one white with gold-thread embroidery, with ankle-length skirt slit to her hip.

They ate the kind of dinner Chen had served to Janelle that night in the Mandarin Oriental—the birds' nest and shark fin soup, the goose webs, all served elaborately with champagne.

"I hear that you are well settled in at the bank," Chen said to Giannini.

"I have a lot to learn."

"If we had another special assignment for you, I assume you would undertake it."

"Of course," said Giannini. He and Sydney talked this over. They were happy with their adventure, but they realized that they were completely captive to Chen Peng.

"Well . . . we will watch for opportunities."

"If I may ask, what happened to Professor Greenleaf?"

Chen smiled. "The bank simply explained to him that a commitment made by you was no longer valid, since you had left. They invited him to apply for a loan if he wanted one, but he hasn't done it."

After dinner, the four went out to the swimming pool and sat at a table where assorted fruits were served, with more champagne.

"Perhaps the young ladies will favor us by going in swimming," said Chen casually.

"I didn't bring a swimsuit," said Sydney Toller.

"It won't be necessary, dear," Janelle said with a grin as she pulled down her cheongsam.

Sydney was visibly, painfully reluctant, but she stripped down and went in the water.

II

MARCH, 1998

Intercontinental fell into Dave's hands. It operated a number of tankers, but on Sunday, March 8, its newest and biggest super-tanker, the *IntPet Oman*, rammed a pier of the Verrazano Bridge. The huge tanker had been moving very slowly, almost not moving at all. The bridge shuddered but was not severely damaged. The tanker was hardly damaged at all.

An editorial on Monday morning said:

> Sunday's accident, the *IntPet Oman* hitting the Verrazano Bridge, sent a shudder through the bridge but should have sent a far greater shudder through all New Yorkers, indeed through everyone living on the East Coast of the United States.
>
> Suppose the tanker had been moving a little faster, which ordinarily it would have been, except apparently for want of confidence of its captain. Suppose the collision had knocked down the bridge. That could have been repaired in time, at huge cost. But suppose the tanker had ruptured and spilled its millions of tons of crude oil. The economic and environmental consequences to the metropolitan area would have been incalculable. The incoming tide would have spread the oil throughout the harbor and up the Hudson. New Yorkers might have wakened this morning to find the harbor closed and the waters covered with a thick coating of heavy oil.
>
> The risk to this area is inexcusable. The ship could have picked up a harbor pilot just after passing the Narrows, but Intercontinental Petroleum chose to have its own crew guide the ship through the Narrows.
>
> Thought should be given to banning Intercontinental ships from New York Harbor, indeed from every harbor

in the United States, until the company abandons its arrogant, public-be-damned attitude and adopts proper safety procedures.

Dave telephoned Tabatha Morgan. He invited her to see a demonstration of the Reitsch program, at the Manhattan offices of Navigation Simulation, Incorporated.

"Sit down, and we'll let *you* navigate a supertanker through the Verrazano Narrows."

She couldn't do it, of course. Neither could he. Then a representative of the company sat down and took a simulated supertanker under the bridge and into the harbor.

"You can bring any type of ship into New York or New Jersey, into San Francisco, into Rotterdam, into Hong Kong, and so forth. The system can simulate weather conditions, tide conditions, traffic conditions . . . Pilots learn and practice on the system, without risking anything more than their egos, until they become proficient. If Intercontinental tries to navigate into harbors this company simulates, without this training, it is egregious negligence."

"Why don't they?" she asked.

"I thought you might want to look into that. They damned near caused a major disaster for New York."

A day later a news story appeared:

The Coast Guard reports that *Intpet Oman*, the ship that nearly caused a disaster for this city, discharged the contents of its bilge into the Atlantic, some fifty miles off New Jersey.

The office of the United States District Attorney announced that it is conducting an investigation into possible negligence amounting to violation of maritime law.

At the same time, a committee of the United States Senate will open hearings on the safety of tankers in general and intercontinental tankers in particular.

Dave had done a little to orchestrate the investigations. Tabatha hadn't thought of it until he took her to see the simulator. Three calls to political friends had contributed to promoting the Senate investigation.

Intercontinental stock began to fall.

III

Alexandra was in disciplinary lockup once more, for three days, for "smarting off." She hung on the bars of her cell and sobbed. This meant certain forfeiture of whatever small chance she'd had to be paroled on her first hearing.

She might have had a parole hearing in 2000. Now the first possible hearing would come in 2002, and they would flop her. She couldn't control her mouth. She controlled herself, but she couldn't control her mouth. God, she might have to serve her max! That would keep her in until 2012, when she would be sixty years old!

The best years of her life. What should have been the best years of her life.

What she could not guess was that Dave was seriously trying to get her a commutation. He had a politically connected lawyer working on it. The argument was that she had acted in a fit of anger, after a whole life in which she had never committed another crime. She had spent six years in prison for a few minutes' hysteria. She was a capable, intelligent woman, extremely unlikely to commit another crime.

"What am I to tell them about what she will do when she comes out?" the lawyer asked.

"Tell them I'll give her a job. Emphasize that I forgive her."

He did not tell the lawyer that Alexandra's trust fund, in Zurich, was worth more than ten million dollars, with accumulated interest. Also, he had transferred some of it to Hong Kong. He figured that out there he would place her beyond any inquiry into anything she might know about his early business. He had discussed it with Chen Peng on their secure line, and Chen had agreed he would get her a Hong Kong passport. Released from prison, Alexandra would disappear. She would, in fact, be unable to return to the States, since conditions of any commutation would undoubtedly be that she remain in New York State and report periodically to a parole officer. She would be a fugitive. She would be under Dave's control, and Chen's.

"Tell them I will give her a responsible position. She will be entirely self-supporting. Tell them it's a waste of a human life to keep her in prison, especially when the man who was her victim forgives her and is willing to help her."

"It is not impossible, Mr. Shea," said the lawyer. "Do not in any way suggest a bribe, which would not work. On the other hand, it would not hurt if you laid some money around, politically."

"Arrange it," said Dave. "Tell me where it should go, and you can be my agent for distributing it."

IV

APRIL, 1998

Dave's father died. He was just sixty-eight years old. Janelle was in Hong Kong, and he asked her mother, Alicia, to go with him to Wyckoff. His mother and brother knew Alicia and liked her. It was acceptable for her to accompany Dave as Janelle's surrogate.

Dave paid for the funeral, so it could be more elaborate than the family could afford. He sat and stood through the uncomfortable rituals: not just those at the church and graveside but also the horror of receiving guests at the funeral home during two sessions of "viewing." Nothing was done in the simple and abbreviated way he would have done it. Everything had to be done "properly," lest people should talk. That included exposing the body to public view.

"He was a hard worker," one woman said. "I guess it just wore him out."

"The town will never be the same without him."

"I'll never forget the last time I saw him—"

Dave nodded solemnly and thanked each guest.

Dave reviewed his mother's financial situation. The house was paid for. She would receive a monthly check from Social Security. Dave called on Cole Jennings and handed him a check for $250,000. He instructed him to establish a trust fund for her, receive the income, and deliver the monthly checks to her himself.

"Tell her it's from a savings account he kept on the side and didn't talk about. Tell her he'd been quietly slipping money into it for years, just in case. Tell him he'd made you trustee for it. If it needs more, let me know."

"I'll take care of it."

"I don't see you much anymore. When Janelle comes back, you must come over and have dinner with us. Somewhere. You can stay in our guest room."

Through all of this Alicia was at his side, and many people assumed she was his wife.

"You certainly did marry well, Dave. This time."

"Alicia is my mother-in-law. Janelle is in Hong Kong, on business."

"Oh . . ."

"I'd be lucky to have a wife like Alicia, if I weren't married to her daughter."

Alicia overheard, of course, and squeezed his hand.

They had intended to drive back to Manhattan after the funeral, but the funeral had to be followed by a reception at the house and that had to be followed by a family dinner. It was almost ten when they could get away, and they still had to check out of a Holiday Inn.

"What the hell," Alicia said as Dave drove her toward the motel. "One more night won't hurt us."

They sat down in the bar before going to their rooms. Neither of them had had a drink all day. Dave had supposed there would be drinks at the reception, but there hadn't been.

"I can't tell you how grateful I am to you, Alicia," he said.

"It was the least I could do for you, Dave. You held up very nicely, but I could tell you were under a hell of a strain. Your father was a fine man."

"What's the old phrase? 'A life of quiet frustration.' "

"Which inspired you to—"

"Never live that way."

"Well, you sure as hell don't."

"Alicia . . . I said back there that I'd be lucky to have you as my wife. I meant that. You have been a tremendous comfort to me. Could I in any way encourage you to be one more comfort?"

"For Christ's sake!"

He put his hand on hers. "I know . . . There are reasons why not. But—"

"Goddamnit Janelle—"

"Must never know, of course."

"Am I to understand you want to establish a now-and-then thing when she's out of town?"

"No. Here's what let's do. I'll give you a thousand dollars. That way it's the other kind of relationship. A night's satisfaction and no obligations on either side. Clean. No emotions. No regrets. Once. Never again."

"Bluntly stated, you want to buy me as a hooker."

"Let's think of a euphemism for that. What word do you use, really?"

"I don't use any word. I try not to think about it."

"But guys don't fall in love with you and come slobbering around afterward, do they?"

"No . . ."

"Well, neither will I. A quick, clean relationship. Starting now and over when we check out in the morning."

Alicia shook her head, but a small smile came to her face. "You're a real bastard," she said. "Janelle has told me you are. I'm damned glad she knows it. If she didn't, I'd manage some way to do what your second wife failed to do."

V

Dave and Chen were not interested in acquiring control of Intercontinental Petroleum, only in driving its stock down.

Chen, through confidential agents in Washington, supplied counsel to the Senate committee with information and misinformation. Executives of the company were grilled before the committee, some of the hearings being televised. As always in congressional hearings, information and misinformation became inextricably mixed, and all of it went out as information.

Chen had agents in the Middle East. They supplied oil suppliers with newspaper clippings and suggested that loading oil onto Intercontinental tankers risked very bad public relations, not just in the States but in Europe as well. A few of the suppliers continued willingly to sell oil to Intercontinental but insisted it be shipped in other companies' tankers.

The stock continued to fall.

Willard Drake had notes out: the mortgage on his home and one on his laboratory property. Enterprise Bank bought that paper. For the moment, all it did was notify Drake that his payments were to be made to Enterprise from then on.

"What the hell is going on here?" Drake asked his wife over breakfast, as soon as the children had left the table.

"We are in deep, deep shit," said Julie. "Somebody has decided to have us. And whoever it is, it's no small deal."

"They think they're going to take my system away from me? No goddamned way!"

"We have to think this through," she said. "They'll offer you big money. *Big money.* To work for them. Like I said before, think of it as a compliment. If they're willing to go to these lengths to acquire your work, they must have confidence in it."

"I'm an *independent* man!"

Julie shook her head. "No man is."

VI

Most nights Janelle and Chen slept together in the suite in the Mandarin Oriental. Not every night. Twice he had dinner brought. Usually, though, he took her out to introduce her to restaurants. One evening they ate on a terrace on The Peak, enjoying a view of all Hong Kong. Another evening they went on his yacht to a small island where they had their dinner in a distinguished fish restaurant, where Chen chose their entrée from among the fish swimming in huge tanks near the entrance.

That was a Chinese custom. To middle- and upper-class Chinese, fresh fish meant alive when the diner selected it. The same was true of chickens. When a diner ordered chicken, the chicken was beheaded and prepared while the diners were having their hors d'oeuvres.

On these occasions she always dressed in one of her growing collection of cheongsams. Tonight on the island, this one was yellow.

Janelle was acutely conscious of the bodyguards that hovered near, wherever they went. Gurkhas. Chen's Rolls-Royce limousine was armored, and always there was at least one other car preceding or following, carrying the fierce-looking little men. A short, ugly automatic rifle lay on the seat beside the chauffeur. Chen was determined not to be kidnapped.

On the evening when they went to the island for the fish dinner, Chen asked, "Would you like to try another of the Glorious Postures tonight?"

"Yes . . . Lord Yang," she said simply.

He spoke to the captain of his yacht when they went back aboard. The captain used a cell phone to make a call—the purpose of which would become apparent to her when they reached the hotel suite.

He had told her he had the special furniture some of the Glorious Postures required, and while they were on their way there servants had set up a piece of it.

It was a frame, consisting of sturdy vertical posts at either end, plus two horizontal bars. The top bar was an ordinary round rod, of polished black wood. Below that some eighteen inches was a thickly padded, silk-upholstered board, about four inches wide.

"You see?" he asked. "You climb on a chair, grip the upper bar with both hands, and I will help you lift your knees over the lower bar. You hang there. You see what the posture does? It offers you deliciously. And I promise you it will not only be I, but you, who will find the experience delicious."

Janelle was skeptical but she slipped out of her cheongsam and shoes and climbed on the chair as Chen instructed. She gripped the upper bar tightly with both hands. She thrust her chin forward over the bar, between her hands. He helped her lift her knees over the lower bar and let her weight settle. He gently pushed her knees apart. She hung there, spread open. The posture was not as comfortable as the first posture had been, but it was not entirely uncomfortable either. She was aroused by it.

"My Lord Yang will do the thing quickly," she suggested. "I could not wish to remain this way very long."

He undressed quickly and stood in front of her.

"Fragrant Lady Yin," he murmured as he put his face down to her and sniffed at her parts. "I would not think of doing it to you, but the woman's wrists are usually bound to the bar."

"Making her helpless."

"Yes. But I would not even think of doing that to you."

He stood erect and shoved himself into her. He did not prolong the set as he had with the other Glorious Posture, but proceeded quickly. This posture produced an angle of penetration that gave Janelle two shuddering orgasms.

TWENTY-NINE

I

JULY, 1998

Cole Jennings came to see Dave in his office at Banque Suisse. He sat down across the desk from Dave and suddenly covered his face with his hands and began to sob.

"Cole! For God's sake, what's the matter?"

For a minute Cole could not speak. Then he lifted his red, tear-streaked face and said, "Emily is dying . . ."

"*Oh, my God, Cole!* How? Why?"

"Cancer. It's terminal. She's on chemotherapy. She's wasting away. She's lost her hair. She has two months, maybe three."

Dave turned and stared at the big saltwater aquarium that stood not far from his desk. It had been installed and was maintained by an aquarium service. The colorful fish glided around placidly and were a relaxing sight to him. He sometimes wondered if they knew anything or understood anything. Tears filled his eyes.

"Is there *anything* I can do?"

"There is nothing anyone can do."

"Jenn is at home, right?"

Cole nodded. "It's having a horrible impact on her. Not to mention what it's doing to Cole. Fifteen years old . . ."

"Would you like to send the kids out to Hong Kong until it's over? It would be a hell of an experience for them. I'll go with them, or Janelle will. It might distract them from—"

"I'll mention it to them. I don't think they'll go."

"To be away during an ordeal . . ."

"No. I don't think they'll go."

II

SEPTEMBER, 1998

Emily died on September 18. Dave and Janelle were there for the final days, then for the ceremonial anguish that followed until she was cremated and the urn of ashes buried. Cole did not allow a "viewing." People talked, but that was the way it was.

Jenn did not return to Ann Arbor for that semester. She accepted Dave's invitation to go with him and Janelle to Hong Kong, where they stayed ten days in the Mandarin Oriental and Janelle saw to it that she saw as much as possible of the fascinating city while Dave met with Chen and they planned their strategy for taking over Willard Drake's company and system.

When they came home, Dave and Janelle invited her to spend evenings with them in Manhattan. She was a fully developed, beautiful girl. Janelle took her shopping for clothes. When she returned to Ann Arbor after the holidays she was a more sophisticated young woman than she had been. And marked as she always would be with the agony of her mother's death.

III

DECEMBER, 1998

"Ho, Shea."

Alexandra had lost her office job and was mopping, wearing blue dungarees. She looked up into the face of the officer who had written her up for "smarting off."

"Ma'am?"

"Going to the super's office," the officer said.

An hour later, after a long wait in the superintendent's waiting room, Alexandra was allowed into the office.

"Shea, hmm?"

"Yes, ma'am."

"Every year at Christmas the governor issues a very limited number of pardons and commutations. I can't imagine why, but you got one. Your sentence is commuted to time served, subject to certain conditions. You'll be on probation, so to speak. Meet the conditions and you won't have to come back here."

The release process was not easy, and it took a week. The probation department found her a modest room and a job as a waitress in a coffee shop. She left the prison in what she might have called slops, a dress the prison provided since she had gained so much weight in the past six years that the clothes she came in with would not fit her.

She moved into her room. The shared bathroom was down the hall. She went to work. In point of fact, she was not sure she was any better off. Somewhere she had millions of dollars, but it was not apparent what good that was going to do her.

Then—

Janelle appeared outside the coffee shop when Alexandra left work.

"*You . . . ?*"

Janelle went into the street and hailed a cab. "C'mon," she said. "We've got places to go and things to do."

In her uniform as a coffee-shop waitress, Alexandra felt conspicuous as she entered the apartment building and rode up in the elevator. She entered the apartment, wonderingly. It overlooked the East River and was more spacious and luxurious than anything she and Dave had ever shared.

She felt shabby. She *was* shabby, and slovenly.

"Here," said Janelle. She handed Alexandra a silk dressing gown. "Change into that. You want to take a shower first? What do you drink?"

"I haven't had a drink for so long I hardly remember. Scotch."

"Well . . . relax. The shit's over. As from now, you're a probation violator. But don't worry about that. Dave and I are going to take care of things. You'll sleep here tonight. In the morning a woman from Saks will be here to outfit you. She'll bring a hairdresser and cosmetologist. Then—"

"If I don't show up at that job tomorrow—"

"It's all worked out, Alexandra. You know Dave. When he decides to work something out, it's worked out. I mean, after all, a woman with your money is not going to live in a room and work as a waitress, no matter what the State of New York says. Trust us."

"*He* got me out?"

"Well, you didn't think it was Santa Claus, did you?"

Alexandra did take a shower. She washed her hair with shampoo and not bar soap for the first time since she was arrested. She studied herself in the mirror and decided, tentatively, that the damage could be repaired, in time.

When she came out into the living room again, Dave was there. He took her in his arms and kissed her on the cheek.

"What have you got worked out, Dave?" she asked.

"I've got to have a picture of you," he said. He had a Nikon camera and took several shots. A young man was waiting in the foyer and took the film cartridge away to be developed.

"Why?" Alexandra asked.

"Your passport has expired. The photo has to be laminated in your new passport."

"I haven't applied for one."

"Taken care of. Did you ever hear of Lucinda Harker?"

Alexandra shook her head.

"Get used to the name. She's you. She was born in London, educated at Cambridge. You can fake that. I know you can. She went out to Hong Kong in 1979, to work for Barclays Bank. Seeing the approach of the Handover, she applied for Hong Kong citizenship. It was granted. She carries a Hong Kong passport. She doesn't need a work permit for Hong Kong; she's a citizen. If you stay here in New York, the millions you have in trust will do you little good, because you'll have to work at a menial job and live in squalor. If the district attorney figures out you have major money, you'll be in deep shit—because you emphatically denied to Tabatha Morgan that you had any such thing. Maybe that will put me in deep shit, too. So . . . you go out to Hong Kong as Lucinda Harker. I've transferred part of your money there. You can live damned well. In an exotic place. All you have to do is stay out of the States, where somebody might see you and recognize you. Alexandra Shea is dead. Welcome, Lucinda Harker."

"How much money have I got?"

"More than you can ever spend. I'll give you a detailed accounting—where it is and how much."

"Lady of leisure . . ." Alexandra murmured skeptically.

"We'll find something for you to take part in at one of our enterprises. You won't be bored."

"I'll do what you say, it can never be worse than where I've been."

"Where you've been will never be again. As soon as you've got a wardrobe, we'll drive you to Boston, where Lucinda Harker will board a flight for Vancouver, where she will transfer to a flight on Cathay Pacific. Some young American friends will meet you at the airport in Hong Kong, settle you in a hotel until you find an apartment, and show you around the city. You'll love the place. You have a facility for languages and will learn Chinese. A whole new life . . . Lucinda."

IV

JANUARY, 1999

Janelle knew Dave occasionally visited Tabatha Morgan. She accepted that. She accepted his judgment that it was an expedient thing to do. He had shown her the pictures of the naked Tabatha, clad only in handcuffs. She remembered resentfully how the woman had made her sit in handcuffs in her office, and she took satisfaction in knowing that Dave was making a complete fool of her.

In preparation for Dave's visit, Tabatha had donned a new G-string, consisting of nothing but a cluster of beaded cords that hung to her knees and swung when she walked, alternatively exposing

and covering her crotch. She wore thigh-high black fishnet stockings and her black patent-leather shoes with stiletto heels.

Tabatha poured drinks. From the kitchen she said, "I suppose
you know Alexandra has disappeared."

"You had to expect that," he said casually.

He stared at her through the kitchen door. At the counter pouring drinks, her back was to him. Nothing covered her ample buns.

"You wouldn't know anything about it?"

"She never contacted me. I wouldn't have known she was out
except that I read it in the paper."

"You worked on her release."

"I did try to help her get out. I thought she had done enough
time and that keeping her in prison was a waste."

"I have something for you," she said.

After she put their drinks down on the coffee table, she went
in her bedroom and returned with a file folder. She handed it
to him.

"What are these?" he asked as he ruffled through some twenty
or twenty-five sheets of paper.

"My God! You rifled the file? Can't that get you in trouble?"

"No one but me knew what I had. It was my case. If someone
inherits my files, they won't get that."

"Why did you do that, Tabby?"

"Do I have to tell you I'm in love with you? I have never been
in love before, except for puppy love for boys who abused me when
I was in high school. I have never been treated like a woman. I
know it's hopeless. You're married to a glamorous genius. But if
you'll see me now and then and let me kiss your feet—"

Dave looked at her. "You never have to kiss my feet, lady. You're
all woman, those others didn't know what to do with that."

V

FEBRUARY, 1999

Willard and Julie Drake sat across a desk from Ben Haye, CEO of Enterprise Bank.

"It's a relatively simple matter," said Haye. "I'm afraid you owe two overdue payments on your mortgages, Mr. and Mrs. Drake. This is a *bank*. I have to know when we may expect payment."

Drake slumped. "My Intercontinental stock, my inheritance, has gone to hell . . ."

"I am aware of that. A few months ago we would have been willing to let you hypothecate that stock as additional security on your mortgages. Now . . . Intercontinental seems to have too many problems. And without the dividends on that stock, we don't see any income for you, Mr. Drake. We don't want to foreclose, but—"

Julie spoke. "My husband developed and owns the finest computer program in the world."

"At the moment generating no income that I can see."

"It *will*. It will."

"When?"

Drake sighed. "I can't say."

Haye shook his head. "Then what security have we, against your notes?"

"I know," said Julie. "I know what you'd *like* to have."

"And what is that?"

"Our stock in Drake Research Services, which owns all the rights in my husband's system."

"Which is worth . . . ?"

"Billions, potentially," she said. "Billions."

"Potentially."

"Yes," she said.

Haye drew a deep breath. "Would you be willing to place this stock in a trust?"

"A trust doing what?" Drake asked.

"It occurs to me, Mr. and Mrs. Drake, that you are not businesspeople. The trust, controlled by the bank, would try to market your idea on a sound basis. Your potential billions might then become real billions."

"Who votes the stock?" Julie asked.

"The trust," said Haye.

VI

MARCH, 1999

Not yet quite eighteen, Jenna had the experience she had long wanted: to be a nude dancer in a club. In Detroit, in a club called Blue Magic.

"Something has got to be understood, kid. My girls do not turn tricks. I run a dance club, not a whorehouse. You do it once and I find out about it, it's bye-bye."

"I wouldn't have it any other way," said Jenna. "And what's more, I won't do lap dancing. Look, no touch."

"A girl after my own heart," the man said.

Thereafter, she caught a bus into Detroit early each evening and returned on the last bus, at one in the morning.

She had sat in the club and watched several shows, to learn the moves. She came on the stage wearing a pleated, plaid microskirt and a tight sweater. She was billed as "Sweet Terry Coed." No such thing as striptease existed anymore. Within her first half minute on the stage, she took off the sweater, exposing a sheer bra, then the skirt, exposing sheer bikini panties. Within another two minutes, they were gone, and she performed nude.

A polished steel pole held the center of the stage. Performers climbed it and hung on it. Clinging to the pole, they could spread their legs and show their shiny pink parts. They would lie on the floor and spread again, showing even more, using their fingers to open themselves wider.

Some performers gripped thick candles, burning, and poured the hot candle wax over their breasts. One poured cream over herself and licked it off her nipples. Between performances the stage had to be mopped.

Jenna resorted to no such gimmicks. She did not pretend that she danced. The blaring music was incidental and had nothing to do with her performance. All she did was show herself off, completely naked and completely unashamed. Immediately she was one of the favorites of the Blue Magic. She was conspicuously young. She was beautiful. And she conspicuously enjoyed herself. She conveyed to the men who watched her that she enjoyed showing herself to them.

Newspaper ads for the Blue Magic featured her name and photographs of her. Oddly perhaps, no one at Ann Arbor identified the Sweet Terry of the ads as Jenna Jennings.

She received fifty dollars for each performance. Usually she appeared twice a night and went back to Ann Arbor with a hundred dollars cash in her handbag. She established a bank account, hired an accountant to see to her taxes, and accumulated money.

Within a few weeks Jenna's motive for dancing nude changed completely. She had wanted the experience, but boredom set in. Now it was the money that counted. She was depositing five or six hundred dollars a week. She decided to talk to "Uncle" Dave about investing. When she went home for the spring break, she transferred most of her money from her Michigan bank to Banque Suisse.

Her father knew nothing of this.

VII

APRIL, 1999

Gaining control of Drake's corporation and his voice-recognition program was a coup for Dave Shea and Chen Peng. The Drake software was the most valuable property in the high-tech industry—or potentially so, if properly exploited. It could make DRS a competitor for Microsoft. Suddenly the two partners were major players in the computer field.

They kept low profiles, but who controlled was unmistakably clear.

They named Willard Drake as CEO of DRS and set him up with

a large salary and a golden parachute. They named Julie Drake vice president and set her up with the same.

Drake gave up his notions of being an independent man and turned all his attention to continuing development of his system.

VIII

"My *mother! My mother, for Christ's sake!* Is there no goddamned limit to you?" Janelle screamed.

"She told you?" Dave said calmly.

"No. Your brother told me."

"Why . . . ? A whole year later."

"Don't go blaming him. He didn't mean to tell me. I just found out, that's all."

"How?"

"Mother has a friend. She was taking care of Mother's apartment and her dog while mother went to New Jersey with you. Well . . . the goddamned dog died. He'd been sick. That's why Mother asked this friend to take care of him, rather than put him in a kennel. This friend tried to call. Mother had told her she'd be in the Holiday Inn. They rang her room repeatedly, but she didn't answer. She didn't mention this to me for a long time. But she's a gossip. And she told me. So I called your brother. I asked him where you and my mother were the night after the funeral. He said you two came to the reception and then went back to New York. I called the Holiday Inn. He lied for you. He knew perfectly well you had not gone back to the city. You didn't check out until the next morning."

"We were out to dinner."

"At two A.M.? Anyway, I called him again. I told him I knew you had not left the motel that night. So . . . your brother thought you should have a photo of your father, which he had forgotten to give you. He came to your room about midnight and knocked on the door. You wouldn't let him in. You accepted the picture through the door and said thanks. It was obvious there was a woman in your room. He went to my mother's room and knocked. She did not answer. Dave . . . *You were fuckin' my mother!*"

"What does *she* say about this?"

"Faced with it, she admits it. She says it was just once and just a hooker-John relationship. *But she's my goddamned mother! You son of a bitch!*"

"Are you saying you haven't done something with Chen Peng?"

"He's not *your father!*"

"Janelle . . ."

"You're doing it with Tabatha Morgan. That's business. Chen Peng is business. But not *my mother!*"

"I—"

"You haven't got a goddamned grain of decency in you. This marriage is over."

"We've got an awful lot tied up together."

"And I want my share. We'll go on having a business relationship. But the marriage is over!"

IX

She called Chen Peng from a pay phone. A private line where she would not be asked to identify herself. A receptionist with a soft oriental voice answered, "CP Enterprise, may I help you?" It didn't matter whether she gave her name or not, the receptionist knew her voice.

"Chen Peng," Janelle said, trying to stop her tears. She didn't know whether she was crying from anger or sadness.

Peng's voice came through the phone. "What a nice surprise to hear from you, Janelle."

She minced no words. "I'm leaving my husband."

Peng sat thoughtfully for a moment. "You sound very upset."

"Oh, yes, I am very upset, Peng . . ."

"You are a smart woman, Janelle. It's sometimes better to let your anger run its course, then make decisions."

She couldn't control herself any longer. "He slept with my mother."

"I see," he replied.

"I want to destroy him," she said. "Can you help me?"

"If that's what you would like," he answered. "But it will take some time."

After he hung up the phone he sat quietly and thought, Americans have very peculiar ways.